BAD MEN
AND WICKED
WOMEN

ERIC JEROME DICKEY

BAD MEN and WICKED WOMEN

DUTTON

DUTTON

An imprint of Penguin Random House LLC
375 Hudson Street
New York, New York 10014

Copyright © 2018 by Eric Jerome Dickey
Penguin supports copyright. Copyright fuels creativity, encourages diverse voices,
promotes free speech, and creates a vibrant culture. Thank you for buying an authorized
edition of this book and for complying with copyright laws by not reproducing, scanning,
or distributing any part of it in any form without permission. You are supporting writers
and allowing Penguin to continue to publish books for every reader.

DUTTON and the D colophon are registered trademarks of
Penguin Random House LLC.

LIBRARY OF CONGRESS CATALOGING-IN-PUBLICATION DATA
has been applied for.

ISBN 9781524742195 (hardcover)
ISBN 9781524742201 (ebook)

Printed in the United States of America
1   3   5   7   9   10   8   6   4   2

Set in Janson Text LT Std
Designed by George Towne

This book is a work of fiction. Names, characters, places, and incidents either are the
product of the author's imagination or are used fictitiously, and any resemblance to actual
persons, living or dead, business establishments, events, or locales is entirely coincidental.

For Carolyn. For Virginia. For Lila. For Vardaman.

I believe that there's another man inside every man.

1922

Color is not a human or a personal reality; it is a political reality.

James Baldwin

BAD MEN AND WICKED WOMEN

CHAPTER 1

MARGAUX HAD CHANGED races.

When I rushed into TGI Fridays and left the summer's oppressive triple-digit heat at my back, I searched for a twenty-something woman with melanin-filled skin, was hunting from booth to booth, when someone eased up behind me, touched my shoulder. When I turned around I saw a pale woman covered in tats and body piercings, a shapely number as Goth as Melrose Boulevard.

"Ken Swift?"

"Yeah? Do I know you?"

"It's me."

"Me who?"

"Margaux."

Last time I saw her she was a beautiful shade of brown and had dark, wavy hair. But she'd scrubbed away her melanin, her skin now that of an untanned white woman.

Broke my fuckin' heart and left me speechless at the same time.

Nervous, she said, "You got here just in time. I think our table is ready."

Her cell phone rang as soon as she said that. She looked at the number, frowned, didn't answer. I imagined my ex-wife had done that a million times to my calls after she left me.

TGI Fridays Ladera was crowded like microwaved chicken wings were the best meal ever created. I had asked Margaux if she wanted to meet me in Inglewood at Zula Ethiopian and Eritrean Restaurant in Hyde Park Plaza, a place I'd eaten at least once a month since they opened, but she had turned down that offer. Now I understood why. This shouldn't have surprised me. But it did.

After we were seated, awkwardness and silence covered us. Other Afrocentric sisters in the room gave me the side-eye, looked at me like I was a traitor, a sellout. Black men grinned, checked out Margaux. She had the skin of a white woman, but her shape remained African.

Margaux sucked the metal in her tongue, then asked, "You okay?"

"I'm fine. You okay?"

"The way you keep looking at me. I don't like people staring at me like that."

I relaxed my gaze. Regrouped. "How much money did you say you needed from me?"

"I think you heard me loud and clear when I said I wanted fifty thousand."

"That's a lot of money."

"How soon can you get it?"

I rat-a-tat-tatted my fingers on the table, exhaled. "Let's break bread and talk about it."

Her knuckles were still dark. I'd bet her elbows and knees and the tops of her toes were still of the Negro hue too. Those areas couldn't be bleached and she'd never be as white as the photos Rachel Dolezal's parents probably keep on a dresser. I felt their pain in my bone marrow.

We read the menus, gave our orders, then were stuck facing each other.

Margaux wore gloomy makeup, dusky lipstick, and many tattoos.

She took in my trendy wardrobe, shook her head like she didn't approve of my wearing straight-leg jeans and a gray suit coat over a T-shirt with Muhammad Ali on the front.

I asked, "How many body piercings do you have?"

"Why, Ken Swift?"

"I see four in each ear. Your lip. One in your nostrils."

"I have one in my clit and one in each nipple. Is that what you want to know?"

"Was just asking."

"Should I tell you what the one in my tongue is all about?"

"Maybe we should talk about the weather."

"No, we can continue chatting about the things you see wrong with me."

"I never said anything was wrong with you."

"The one in my tongue, do you want to know why I have this one?"

"No need to take the talk any further."

After the waiter brought our meals and left, I picked up my spoon and took a mouthful of clam chowder. My taste buds were too refined for fast food. I was particular about what I ate away from home. Very biased. Margaux cleared her throat and I raised my eyes, looked at her. Palms down on the table, she shook her head and stared at me like I was a sacrilegious heathen.

Margaux said, "Did you lose your religion too?"

"I read the Bible. I grew up being forced to read the Bible. I was an usher before anybody knew Usher was Usher. Was in church every Sunday. I know all about the Good Book."

"Really? So what's your favorite part?"

"When Jesus is alone talking to God by himself, and someone who wasn't there is writing about it firsthand. That always amazed me. In court, they'd call that hearsay and throw it out."

She tsked, ran her hand over her blond-and-red Mohawk, bowed her head.

"In the name of Allah, the beneficent, the merciful—"

I said, "You're Muslim now?"

Her hands became fists. "Would that offend you?"

"Not at all. I mean, I know most of your relatives are Christians, and I heard that some of your relatives are—"

"Let me give thanks to our creator for the food so we can get down to business."

"What's your favorite *ayah* or *surah* in the Quran?"

"It depends on my mood. Many *ayah*s send trembles down my spine contingent on the message they convey." She gave her serious answer, held eye contact. "Yours?"

"My favorite is Maryam 19:41–57."

"You know the Quran?"

"I read. Bible. Quran. I read *Final Call, Watchtower,* and Jewish newspapers. I read what everyone offers. I dated an Afro-Mexican when I was in high school and learned her Spanish, and when I was twenty-one I married an Ethiopian who spoke Amharic and learned her language."

"May I pray now?"

I nodded. "Pray."

When Margaux was done blessing the food, she crossed her arms. She said, "I'm expecting."

I paused. "You're pregnant?"

"Two months."

"You're not showing."

"I'm pregnant."

Without transition, I blurted out, "Why the bleaching?"

"Only took you five minutes to ask."

"Why are you doing this to yourself?"

"I want to be beautiful."

"Black is beautiful. White is a'ight. You're downgrading."

"Everything is a joke to you."

"Not everything. Definitely not this. Explain this to me."

"Light-skinned girls get picked more on all the dating sites. Look around the room. See how black men respond to light-skinned women. You don't even have to be pretty and light-skinned, just light-skinned, and men think you're gorgeous. But if you're light-skinned and built like Beyoncé, you're treated like you're a goddess. They let you across the velvet rope. Light-skinned girls get proposed to quicker and more often. Light-skinned girls get to be wives and dark-skinned girls get to be baby mommas. Colorism is real. Drop *beautiful* into Google. See who shows up."

"In the movies. That's the only place dark-skinned women don't win."

"Are you blind? All men, regardless of race, prefer exotic women over black women."

"Black women are exotic."

"Well, the rest of the world didn't get the memo. And don't be overweight and dark."

I nodded. "Is bleaching skin haram in Islam?"

"I guess you haven't heard of the Indian skin-lightening cream's billion-dollar industry. The Asians are obsessed with fair skin. Asian husbands want their wives to be more beautiful. They make their wives bleach their skin. And being light-skinned, it's safer. Much safer."

"Black models are sitting in tanning booths darkening their skin to get more work."

"And those same models would be cast as hood rats in a trap video."

I took a breath, nodded. "When did this . . . this new you . . . when did this start?"

"I wanted to when I was a tween. I had to wait until I was an adult."

"How long has this been going on?"

"A year." She tapped her nails as her leg bounced; she was upset. "Maybe two at this point."

"What did your mother say?"

"We don't talk that much."

"But she knows."

"She knows."

I had no words, but spoke what was on my mind. "This is about self-esteem."

"Why not change what we can change?"

"'No one can make you feel inferior without your consent.' Some people say that Eleanor Roosevelt said that."

"A rich and influential white woman, right? If she did say that, then that FLOTUS was telling other white women how to feel, white Christian women, not black women. And definitely not Muslim women."

I let that go. My eyes went to the basketball game on the big screen.

So did hers. Until her cell phone rang again. Again she looked at the number and didn't answer.

I asked, "What's wrong?"

Margaux frowned at the television. "The team I need to win isn't winning."

"I meant the phone."

"It's an ex."

"He keeps calling like a bill collector on payday."

She turned her phone off.

I said, "Didn't know you were a sports fan."

"I hate USC. I need them to lose this game."

"They're killing it this season. USC doesn't lose at home."

"I don't really give a shit about them."

"If you don't give a shit, why do you care if they win or lose?"

"None of your business."

There was a man sitting at the bar, mixed in the thick of the crowd. He was my age, five foot eleven, the build of middleweight. Jake Ellis. He held a Corona in his hand as he eye-fucked every woman he rated as being a ten.

My attention went back to the woman seated in front of me. A whiter shade of pale, tall, all curves, the body and shape of her mother, and her mother's mother. She wore black jeans and a black blouse that showed a little too much cleavage. The other men in the room noticed her blessings. A lot of the men were attracted to her Goth style.

I knew men. I was one. Women who looked like her made men think anything goes.

I said, "Your baby daddy—"

"The *father* of my child. Don't insult me and don't you dare denigrate him."

"As you denigrate me."

"Deservedly so."

I rat-a-tat-tatted the table. She clicked her tongue ring against her teeth.

I asked, "Still with him?"

"Yes. We're engaged. He would be here now, but he had a meeting."

"What does the *father* of your child do?"

"He's a writer. He's working on this sci-fi horror thing, like the movie *Get Out*."

"Every third person in Los Angeles has a script. Has he sold anything?"

"Not in a while. Pitched a few ideas. Had an option. Got ripped off on a different deal."

"Hollywood is Hollywood."

"Some people owe him some money, but he's going to have to sue to get his money, and he doesn't have the money to get an attorney so he can sue, so he's getting fucked over."

I echoed, "Fucked over."

She looked at me like she didn't care if cursing like that offended me.

"You live with him?"

She nodded. "In Hollywood. We rent a three-bedroom house."

"How much that set you back a month?"

She hesitated. "Six thousand."

"Damn. That's . . . seventy grand plus two thousand for every trip around the sun."

"It's a nice house. Very progressive area. Hollywood people. He can network."

"But it's not your house. You're keeping your landlord rich while you network."

"I pay a third of that."

"Two grand."

"My fiancé pays a third."

"Twenty-four thousand a year."

"Then there is another roommate."

"Man or woman?"

"Depends on the day of the week. One day in Tims, the next in a pink skirt."

"Your man should be taking care of two-thirds of the rent."

"Based on?"

"The baby in your belly and the fact that you're about to get married."

"He's not balling like that."

I sat back, smiled, nodded. "Young lady, what you're telling me doesn't jibe."

"What doesn't jibe?"

I laughed a little. "Your momma was a good liar, and I think you picked up her habits."

She knocked that tongue ring against her teeth, unamused. "I have no reason to lie to you, and don't disrespect my mother."

"You said it's a three-bedroom house. You and your man are in one bedroom, already living like man and wife, and someone else is in the second bedroom. Who is in the third bedroom? You and your man should be paying *one-third* of the rent at most, not two-thirds."

"We met as roommates. He was there first; then I moved in."

"I know how it goes. Few drinks. Few laughs. Space and opportunity."

"We all paid a third in the beginning. One thing led to another."

"Who makes more money?"

"Why?"

"Just asking. You're out of college now."

"I'm going back to grad school soon. My mother expects that of me. And I made that promise to her. So I have to go back to please her. Eventually. After the baby, I guess."

"Babies change everything."

"It won't for me."

"Babies become the masters and you become the servants."

"Everything will be fine."

I didn't challenge her. "You're working now?"

"Jet Propulsion Laboratory in Pasadena. JPL."

"That's a long way from Hollywood in traffic."

"I catch the train. He keeps the car during the week."

"You're paying for him to be able to sit up and write and not work?"

"We're a team. His scripts are good, especially the one about slaves coming back."

"Coming back from where?"

"All the slaves killed in the Middle Passage come back to life."

"That was over two million Africans."

"Plus the slaves who died and were lynched come back to life all over the world."

"That's over twenty million. Lot of extras."

"CGI."

"Then what?"

"Revenge meets karma. They converge on America, France, Portugal, and London."

"Like *The Walking Dead*, only with a mission statement?"

"No, they are alive again. Allah brings them back for retribution."

"How do they know who's their enemy?"

"It's based on melanin. They can sense it or smell it. Haven't worked that out."

"They kill white people?"

"Yeah."

"You think anyone in Hollywood is going to allow you to make a film like that? They will write about white people killing white people wholesale, or can imagine aliens coming here from other planets doing the same, but you know they won't ever let a movie about blacks killing whites the way whites have killed blacks and Native Americans make it to the big screen. Hell, in the last *Birth of a Nation*, they didn't let Nat Turner kill much before he was lynched."

"We're going to get it made."

"Sure. Can't wait to see that at the AMC."

"Don't be condescending."

"So no matter how much cocoa butter she wears, Rachel Dolezal gets killed."

"A lot of people who have been passing are exposed."

"You'd be safe."

"Don't insult me."

"Interesting concept."

"He's trying to get a meeting with Hazel Bijou."

"Have no idea who that is."

"She's black."

"Black people in Hollywood are working for whites and Jews. Just saying that factually."

"So, until this pops off, no, he's not in a good place financially. And he's stressed-out."

"Still, if he's your baby dad—"

"Don't call him my baby daddy."

"I stand corrected."

"Regardless of who pays for what, all of our money goes to the rent. Sometimes we have fifty dollars left over to get us through two weeks, and sometimes we skip paying a bill."

"You work and only have fifty dollars? Where are your investments? Your 401(k)?"

"Car insurance. Gas prices are high. And health insurance is a monster. Renter's insurance. Cell phone. Internet. Food. We eat gluten-free. We don't do canned foods. We don't do McDonald's or Popeyes. Eating healthy costs a lot of money. Taxes, both state and federal. Money goes out faster than it comes in. Feels like we get paid to pay bills. And I'm a girl. It costs a lot more to be a girl than it does to be a boy. We have other needs."

"You're an adult now."

She rubbed her nose, tense, stressed-out. "Being an adult is so damn expensive."

"Welcome to the club."

"I was forced to join."

"We all are."

"Eventually membership to a carefree childhood expires."

"Having a baby will drive disposable income down and the cost of living through the roof."

"I wanted to talk about that."

"Okay."

"We want to get married before I start showing. Same as you and my mother did."

"Times have changed. People don't care about a black woman being pregnant and unmarried. Actually, they laud it now. It's a choice, a sign of empowerment, of getting what you want and making men disposable until the bill comes; then it's on his side of the table."

"Thanks for that helping of misogyny with a dash of bitter mansplaining."

"You're asking for a lot. I didn't ask anyone for anything. Not one dime."

"Well, I want to get married."

"Yeah, being pregnant will make a lot of women suddenly feel that way."

"And I don't want a wedding like you had. I don't want a sad shotgun wedding."

"There was no shotgun wedding. No one was forced to get married."

She shrugged. "I've never asked you for anything. Never. Not once."

"And now you're asking for it like there is an acceleration clause."

"Fifty thousand isn't that much to ask for."

"That's more than most people make in a year. Some don't make that in two years."

My brown-turned-white daughter said, "You going to be able to do it?"

"This is sudden. Why didn't you talk to me, have a conversation about anything, even the weather, before now? You don't just call somebody up, not even your estranged daddy, asking for that kind of money and expect him to have that kinda wad warming up his pants pockets."

"You owe me."

I sat back, head tilted. "I owe you? How in the hell you figure I owe you anything?"

She took a breath, her nostrils flared, and the fissured dam that held back her issues broke; the animosity she felt for me all came out in four flaming words. "*You were never here.*"

"Talk to your mother about that. Talk to her parents. Ask for the truth."

"She said she didn't know where you were."

"She lied. My address hasn't changed. I haven't moved in . . . over two decades. I still live where I lived when we were married, same place you lived from birth until you were about five."

"She told me you never really sent her much money."

"That's a lie. A big lie. I paid for your private schools and I sent her plenty of money to make sure you had a roof over your head. I handed her twenty grand at a time, and she got used to living the high life. I gave her so much she lived off of money that was meant to take care of you."

"Liar."

"Child, don't you ever call me a liar."

"Then don't lie. And I'm not a child."

"I had hoped she would save some of your money. Yeah, when I had big money I sent big money. I always put you first when it came to that. Then things went south, money dried up, and after I sent her my last dime, I had nothing to send for a while. I almost lost everything."

Again her nostrils flared with resentment. "You never called me."

"I called. She didn't let me talk to you. She took you from me. The East African side of your family kept you from me. Told me to keep away. So, I waited for a call. That was like waiting on Godot. Your mother knew where I was. After we divorced and she ran back to Diamond Bar and got remarried to someone her parents approved of, she came to see me more than a few times. She came once a week, on Wednesday afternoons, until her second husband found out."

"Momma came to see you for what?"

"We were only good at doing one thing."

"Don't lie on my momma."

"You say you don't know me. Well, you don't know your momma either."

"Liar."

"Don't keep pushing that button. Disrespectful child, don't think I won't get ugly in public."

"Then stop lying."

"She doesn't tell you the truth, and I'm the liar? Get your momma on the phone. We can all talk right now. I wasn't hiding. I've never hid from the government, a man, or a woman. I took care of you each month and never missed a payment. Without fail or court order."

"I still had to eat."

"I paid without fail for eighteen years. Until you were an adult."

"College wasn't cheap."

"I know. I had student loans. Had my own debt to pay because of dropping out of UCLA."

"Things a father should do, you didn't do."

"What should a daughter do? Just walk up to her dad with her hands like cups and ask for fifty grand like she thinks I own a chain of five-star hotels that have my name on the door?"

"Don't turn this around. Don't be selfish."

I clicked my teeth and said, *"K'ebet'i."*

"Did you just try to call me a brat in Amharic?"

I snapped, "I called you a spoiled brat, Tsigereda."

"Don't call me that name. Not you. Never you. You get to call me what you named me."

"You remind me of your mother, Tsigereda. Tsigereda is what she called you."

"Don't ever fucking call me by my Ethiopian name. You are not worthy."

"Watch your fucking tone. When I was growing up, my daddy would have slapped me across Greenwood for saying some bullshit like that, *Tsigereda.* Then my momma would have found me and slapped me back across town to my daddy. And he would have slapped me back to my momma. That slapping match would have gone on until I had some sense in my head."

"Times have changed, Ken Swift."

"I guess they have. I bet you've never had a spanking in your life, never have been given the extension cord, a house shoe, or had to get switches from a tree. Keep it up. Keep calling me by my first name like I'm your first cousin and talking to me like I'm less than a bill collector."

She didn't give a fuck. I had no power when it came to her, no influence.

I said, "You came here to try and tear me down. Is that what this is about?"

"You left. Like a coward."

"I never left. Your mother left and refused to bring you back for me to see you."

"You know my first strong memory of you? I remember crying when you left."

"I remember. But you have it wrong. That was when your mother left me."

"It doesn't matter who left who. You have to be present to have a relationship."

"She took you from me and kept you away from me."

"No, she didn't. You left her and turned your back on us."

"I didn't."

She paused. "What happened with my mother and Auntie Lila?"

"Have you seen your godmother?"

"Not since I went to live in Ethiopia."

"You lived in Ethiopia, or went to visit?"

"I lived there. With my mother and my daddy."

"I'm your daddy."

"You're my father. He's my daddy. I call him Dad."

"You call Yohanes your dad."

"He's the only man I've known as my daddy."

"Wait. Hold on." I shifted, blinked a few times. "When did you move to Africa?"

"I was ten." Again she clacked her tongue ring against her teeth. "Maybe nine."

"After your mom's family and I had the big falling-out."

"We stayed in Ethiopia four years and ten months."

"Now I get it. I had called for about three years before I gave up. You were in Africa."

She nodded. "We moved all of a sudden. My mother and my stepfather were arguing, and the next thing I knew we were packing and on a plane to Addis Ababa. They pulled me out of a private school in Diamond Bar and put me and my American accent in Bingham Academy."

Stunned, realizing that's what had happened after her stepfather had caught Jimi Lee in my bed, knowing that was what had happened after her grandfather and stepfather had attacked me in front of my building and beaten me on a cold, rainy day, I asked, "How was it over there?"

"We were in the heart of Oromia regional state. It was crowded. People were sociable, everywhere chatting. I remember being bored a lot. It took forever to get anything done. Felt like everyone moved in slow motion, especially the government. My stepfather complained about that all the time, that and went on and on about how he hated you as much as he hated Mulugeta Asrate Kassa. Traffic was worse than here. Buses were overpacked. People were hit by cars and no one cared. Shopping, you had to negotiate for everything. Horrible Internet connection. But I enjoyed Asmara, in the Eritrean Highlands. We drove to Massawa, on the Red Sea coast."

"I heard it was pretty over there."

"It is. Modern, clean, and friendly, but not everywhere is sparkling. Places like Lalibela, where I had some relatives, I didn't like it there. A pickpocket stole things from us in Bole. Same thing happened again at Merkato. That market was large and crowded. I had food poisoning at least five times. When we took a taxi, we had to ride with a dozen strangers. My American accent earned me the side-eye. I couldn't relate, and neither could my mother. But I loved the coffeehouses. My mother and I would go to Tomoca, then go shop at Eliana Mall. Sometimes we went to Mokarar and had coffee. She also dragged me to Alem Bunna, Kaldi's Coffee, and Yeshi Buna. That was our thing. All of those places make Starbucks seem like an overpriced joke."

"Was it safe there?"

"Inside the city."

"Outside the city?"

"There were lots of fights, lots of skirmishes."

"So, Ethiopians do more than battle with words over philosophies."

"Violence is everywhere. Some people are paid to make violence for a living."

She said that last sentence as she looked in my eyes, clacking that metal against her teeth. It felt like we'd almost connected, but my heart was beating fast, and I felt the resentment driving the next question. "Who gave them permission to take you out of the country?"

"Why would they need your permission?"

"Because I'm your father and taking you without my permission is a criminal act."

She rolled her eyes, made a face like she could taste something disgusting, and said something nasty in Amharic. Just like that, bonding was over, and the moment of calm that felt like we could connect was gone. I was about to break it down, tell her a long story, was going to tell her about her mother, about her East African relatives, but instead I took a deep breath.

I said, "You don't know me, but I know you."

"What's my favorite color? What's my favorite food? What music do I listen to?"

"Even if I don't know those things, we're family."

"We are not family. You donated sperm and left the scene of the accident."

"You can bleach your ass until you make Casper the Friendly Ghost look darker than Wesley Snipes at midnight, but *we're family*. Love me or hate me, be Muslim, Christian, or atheist, fascist, or antifa, I'm still your goddamn father. Nothing can change that. *Nothing*."

She huffed, arms folded, closed off, superior. "Do you still hurt people for a living?"

Our eyes met. She sucked her teeth, then gave me the evil eye. She held her malevolent glare as I gave her the hard look many bad men had been given before I'd broken them in two.

A few people watched us like we were the best reality television show going.

Margaux looked at a girl. "Dafuq you look at, fugly dark-skinned black-ass bish?"

Margaux issued that insult like she was repeating what other fools had said to her.

I said, "Margaux. Unless that's a quote from the Quran, that's not very Muslim of you."

"I don't like people staring at me like I'm an animal in a zoo."

"Lower your voice, Margaux."

"Lower yours, Ken Swift. Lower yours."

The pretty girl muttered something and turned away, but not before I saw pain in her eyes. Black women of all hues have had to endure so much, could never just be seen as human beings. Darker skin staring at lighter skin had triggered a war, had been the first shot fired. Margaux's words had cut her deep and strong, but now Margaux redirected her venom at me. My daughter. She was an adult, more disrespect than blood, angry, coming at me like she was my enemy. So I had to talk to my rebellious seed like she was an adult. Because she was my enemy.

CHAPTER 2

I TIGHTENED MY jaw. "Stay in your lane, Margaux."

"Momma told me. I know what you did in Florida. You killed a man."

I sat up straight. "Are you wired?"

She saw my instant paranoia, read my angst, grinned, then laughed.

I took a slow breath. "Never been to Florida, Margaux."

She said, "Balthazar Walkowiak."

My hands became fists. She said that name and I saw flashes, saw that foreign man come out of a bathroom in his home with a gun he'd had hidden in a plastic Ziploc bag in a toilet's water tank. He had exited the bathroom running at us, yelling and shooting, almost killed Jake Ellis. Balthazar Walkowiak was a cunning man, a rough man in this business. Before he could shoot us dead, when his gun had jammed, I had rushed him, thrown a dozen hard blows, then gotten him in an LAPD chokehold, the dangerous chokehold that put the bone in the forearm hard across a man's windpipe, the infamous chokehold that had killed many black men back in the eighties. Walkowiak was as strong as a man on PCP, probably because his system was in overdrive. I choked him while Jake Ellis used his one good arm to throw knock-out blows. Nothing made Balthazar ease up. He bled all over me, Jake was bleeding, and even with Balthazar Walkowiak in a chokehold, he rag-dolled me around the room, smashed me into walls, broke mirrors, then threw his head back into my face and bloodied my nose. He almost knocked me out. I had to choke him until I killed him. Jake Ellis came to us while we struggled. By then Jake had a kitchen knife in his hand. I wasn't going to let Balthazar Walkowiak go until his soul left his body. If he had gotten free and gotten to another gun he had stashed in his crib, Jake Ellis and I would have been the ones in the back of a van going to the Everglades to be fed to the alligators. Jake Ellis went into a stabbing rage. I remember the sounds of that blade plunging into that man's flesh. Time to time, in my dreams, I heard Balthazar Walkowiak's neck pop while he was being gutted, then felt his spirit leave his body as he finally went limp. And Jake Ellis kept on stabbing the dead man. Our blood was all over the place: Jake Ellis's from being shot and mine from being thrown into the mirrors. My cuts were minor, but they had set free my DNA and the same for his. After that, it was a blur, but I remembered how the gators rushed to feed on Balthazar Walkowiak's bloody corpse. By then San Bernardino was there, showing us what to do. My daughter had said that name from twenty years ago and widened my eyes with bad dreams. Couldn't play it off. My reaction told her that those two words were a bull's-eye.

It took me a moment to speak, my tone softer. "You're shaking me down for money?"

"You abandoned me. Will you give the fifty thousand to me or not?"

I had to sit back, take a breath. My head wanted to explode. "If this is how you feel, if this is the way you see me, if you think I'm this horrible deadbeat dad who does horrible things to people, since you're so righteous, why do you say you want me to stand in your wedding?"

"Who said that? I never said that. I don't want you to stand with me."

Being facetious, I said, "Oh, so I'm not invited?"

"You can come. As a guest. Come see the wedding you didn't give my mother."

"And you need me to help come up with fifty grand to make this fairy tale, the one where I show up and watch my bohemian daughter get married, where I show up persona non grata and stand on the sidelines; you want me to dig deep into my bank account and make that happen."

"So is that a no?"

"It's not a yes."

Margaux put her fork down, wiped her hands over her jeans, actually played patty-cake on her toned legs. She shook her head three times before she slid her chair back. She rose from the table, picked up her purse, pulled out several tissues, then began nodding.

I told the colorless, grungy, rebellious child, "You have dewdrops in your nose."

She took out her wallet and let two twenties fall to the table, and they fell like leaves from a tree when the seasons had changed for the worse.

I stood up. "Sit back down."

"You don't tell me what to do."

"I read people. I read body language, so I know when someone is lying, and I read between the lines. You call me for fifty grand, saying you're pregnant and now you're going to get married, saying your boyfriend has people who owe him money. That and the forty-eleven stories you've told me in the last five minutes make no sense. First, you're pregnant."

Hand over her stomach, she nodded. "I am."

"Then you want to get married."

"I do."

"Then you want to penalize me because you think I was a deadbeat dad."

"You were."

"That didn't work, you pulled your trump card, pulled a name out of your hat, and made the last threat. Don't end up going down a steep road with no brakes. Watch yourself."

"For whatever reason I want it, or need it, get me fifty thousand."

"And you say your momma told you about Florida."

My daughter shifted but gave no answer.

I leaned toward her. "I think you or your boyfriend are in some sort of trouble."

"Think whatever you want."

"I think that's why you need fifty large. People need that much money all of a sudden when their backs are up against the wall. And that would be the only reason you would call me. Your back must be against the wall, and coming at me was your last resort. I don't know if someone is shaking you down and now you're shaking me down, but that's the feeling I get."

"You're smart as a kakapo."

"Insulting me won't make my wallet open."

"But it could make a jail cell close."

"Or it could seal the lid on a coffin of someone who don't know who they're messing with."

"Is that a threat? And this is why you will never win Father of the Year."

"I think you're after me because someone is after you."

"Why would anyone want to shake me down?"

"Cheating. Gambling. Paternity. Embezzling. A long list of white-collar crimes. Sex with a minor. Compromising photos. Murder. Drugs. Pornography. Incest. Passing. I've heard it all."

"You've had an interesting life. The life of a liar and a man who instigates violence."

"I don't instigate anything."

"Violence and murder."

"You insult me, and you came from between the legs of a cheat and a liar."

She repeated, "Balthazar Walkowiak."

"Saying that name will dig a grave big enough for you and anyone putting you up to this."

"That's a threat?"

"That's a father trying to protect a daughter who doesn't know what she's fucking with."

"You're no father. My grandfather and grandmother assured me of that. My mother told me how both your mother and father disrespected her when she met them for the first time."

"And your East African relatives were less kind to me the day I took them to dinner."

"You've never been much of a father. I have no evidence of you ever being present. I have seen pictures of me and my mother from the day of my birth, but there are none of you."

I bit my bottom lip, inhaled emotions. "I'm as much a father as you are a daughter."

She stared me down, made her tongue ring clack. "Fifty thousand, Ken Swift."

I surrendered an irritated smile. "Fifty thousand or what?"

We held it right there. Her eyes filled with tears.

I asked, "What are you afraid of?"

"Balthazar Walkowiak."

"You think this is a joke?"

"Look at that expression."

"Don't ever say that name again."

"That is what you're afraid of."

"Ever."

"That's all I need to know."

She wiped her eyes, blew her nose, then threw her snot-rag into my clam chowder. She sashayed away like she had thrown water in my face. Mohawk bouncing, heels click-clopping across the tile, her quick and heavy steps took her through the bustle, chatter, and cheers of the crowd at the packed sports bar. It sounded like the world was cheering for her. I should've known this would be the worst day of my life when I saw the coldhearted way she looked at me.

Anger rose and I felt like slamming someone's head into a wall until it exploded.

Jake Ellis saw her leave, finished his drink, then left the energetic bar, made his way through the rambunctious crowd, smiling at attractive women along the way. Women noticed him too. He glanced in the direction Margaux had gone. Jake Ellis had on off-white jeans, a tan fitted T-shirt paired with 1000 Mile boots and a cream hoodie, sleeves pulled up to his elbows, all his gear high-end and trendy. Jake Ellis loved clothes and loved to be fashion-forward. He had great posture and confidence, a Denzelesque walk, strong arms, and a V-shaped torso, just like me.

When he got to me, he did the African-finger-snap thing. "That was really Margaux?"

"Yeah. Talk about a surprise."

Jake Ellis glanced toward the bar. Three sisters grinned at Jake Ellis, their nonverbal communication a lustful love song. They had moved from looking at his face to staring at his body, that thing that women couldn't help doing when they were sexually attracted to a man.

I told Jake Ellis, "I'm forgetting something. My gut is telling me I'm forgetting something."

"Bruv, you've said that three times since I picked you up."

"You sure we didn't have a second job?"

"Today? Just Pasadena. You okay, bruv?"

"Get me out of this place. Before I hurt somebody."

We stepped outside into the heat wave, stood on the sidewalk facing Starbucks. I didn't see any bad news. No cops. No league of East Africans had come with Margaux to attack me in the heat of the sun as they had once done in the rain because of Jimi Lee. No slave catchers came after me. Margaux had my body temperature up. I was sweating. LA was in a drought and the hottest days since the dinosaurs were upon us. It was still over one hundred, arid heat that felt like a convection oven.

My mind was on one direction, and my road dawg Jake Ellis had his mind on another. A couple of sisters with amazing natural hair parked and came our way, sashayed from the searing heat rising from the blacktop lot toward the urban chain restaurant, hair lightened in the color of summer. Loved the way a black woman moved. The rhythm in her hips, the bounce in the backside, the eyes that said look but don't touch. Both were dressed summer sexy and Afrocentric, like they had bought their amazing Kente-patterned outfits from either Congo Square or the shop Lagos over in Leimert Park. Or maybe they had been to Nigeria or East Africa.

Jake Ellis said, "Bruv, hold on a second."

The Ghanaian went to the ladies, flashed his smile, said a few words. They laughed, and then he kissed the prettiest one right there on the spot. When that moment was over, Jake Ellis smiled, waved good-bye to the woman, and peacocked away like it was no big deal. She fanned herself, grinned so hard I could count all of her teeth, and went inside the restaurant.

I asked Jake Ellis, "Who was she?"

"Never seen that pretty woman before in my life."

"How do you get women to do that?"

"Sometimes all you have to do is ask."

We did a fist bump, dabbed, then headed toward Ellis's convertible Mustang.

He glanced at his watch. "Hot as hell. Are you sure you want to go to Pasadena before dark? Gonna be a lot hotter up that way, and you know how I feel about this dry desert heat."

Mind ablaze, I ignored the question and cleared my throat. "We need to roll by Home Depot and get anything?"

"I have gear left over from the Arizona job in the car. I'm prepared. Saw and hammers."

"Pasadena is a Princeton graduate, a supposed hard-ass from Boston."

He nodded. "So was the man in Arizona. Hard-ass was talking shit, until we arrived. How much does this man in Pasadena owe San Bernardino?"

"More than two hundred thousand."

"Since when?"

"Six months or so ago. He stopped taking San Bernardino's phone calls last month."

When I opened the passenger-side door, that new-car smell rose. Last month Jake Ellis had rocked a Range Rover. Now he leased a convertible for the summer. Jake Ellis changed vehicles every six months so he never had to register the car with the state and have tags. License plates were easy to trace. People could do that online nowadays.

I moved the book *Them* by Nathan McCall from the passenger seat and tossed it in the back, where it landed on a library. *Crossing the Color Line: Race, Sex, and the Contested Politics of Colonialism in Ghana* was next to *Voices from Leimert Park Redux* and five other hardbacks. Jake Ellis had just as many relevant books in his spot as I did.

While he was struggling to get out of the crowded parking lot, we passed Margaux. She was sitting in her ride. An old Nissan covered in bird shit. That told me wherever she lived, she parked outside on the streets, and under a tree. We made eye contact. She was broken down. My daughter was crying. A fist squeezed my heart. I told Jake Ellis to fight traffic and loop back. By the time we made that journey, my daughter was gone.

Jake Ellis asked, "You have Margaux's number?"

"On my other phone."

"Where is it?"

"Only brought my San Bernardino phone. Left my personal one on the charger."

The parking lot was a disaster, its ingress and egress horrible, making it difficult to exit. Cars pulled in and out of parking spaces and made it too damn hard to turn around. That was when I saw three helicopters flying over the area. Heard sirens coming from all directions. Police cars in the lot. The Bank of America had been robbed again and the slave catchers were a day late and a dollar short. I didn't care about the bank robbery or the po-po, only Margaux.

I said, "She's gone."

Jake Ellis looked up at the sky, frowned at the ghetto birds. While we were stuck trying to get out, a dilapidated brother came up to Jake's window. Jake had a .22, held it down low.

He talked fast: "Hey, bro, Imma be honest and look I need twenny to buy some crystal meth and I don't want to rob nobody and so you can give me twenny so I don't end up in jail."

Jake Ellis said, "Nah, bruv. Can't help you, not with that."

I said, "Brother, you're in bad shape. You need to be in rehab."

"I did rehab. Chicago in 2012. I'm from Stone Mountain, Georgia. Out here by myself."

I reached in my pocket, handed the man two dollars.

"That's it? Muh'fucker, I asked you for twenny. What two dollars gonna get me?"

He threw my money back in the car window, cursed me like I was the devil.

Jake Ellis drove on, fought to get by the police, the flashing lights, then passed a group of Mexicans who were on the corner, holding up signs, trying to collect money to pay for a funeral.

"Something is wrong, bruv. I know you. What went down between you and Margaux?"

While he drove, I gave him the play-by-play of my lunch date with my daughter.

Jake Ellis said, "Bruv, Margaux cursed you? Your daughter cursed you?"

"If I had had a son and he addressed me the way Margaux just did, I would've beat his black ass from one end of Sepulveda Boulevard to the other. Then I would've taken him to In-N-Out Burger, and we would have sat and eaten Double-Doubles and had fries and milkshakes, ate like father and son while we had a hard talk like a father and son should."

"I just would have kicked his ass."

With the sun shining down on us, Jake Ellis fought his way over to La Brea and struggled north toward I-10, downtown LA rising in the distance.

"Bruv, I see Margaux's mother wasn't with her."

"My daughter was riding alone. I can't imagine her mother putting her up to this."

"You haven't seen Jimi Lee since when?"

"Since that night her second husband caught her in my bed."

"Yohanes?"

"Yeah. That motherfucker."

"She cheated on you with Yohanes too. Cheated on you first. Then left you, married Yohanes and cheated on him with you. You put up with it for years."

"I was in love with a woman who never learned how to love me back."

"Young, dumb, and full of come."

"That too. Not young and not dumb anymore."

"That's debatable."

"Rachel Redman?"

"The Eskimo. The singing Eskimo with roots that go back to Eritrea."

Someone else was in my life, a nice, beautiful woman, a singer named Rachel Redman. But Margaux's mom had snared my heart. I'd never loved another woman as much as I had Jimi Lee. Not for lack of trying. I thought I was free from what had happened two decades ago.

In my mind I saw her, eighteen, with warm brown skin, hair wavy, cascading down her back. I tried to blink her beauty away, but I was pulled in deeper. Again I was twenty-one, in bed with Jimi Lee, making love to the girl I thought was the most beautiful woman in the world, rocking the bed and making so much turbulence I expected oxygen masks to drop. I met her on Sunset Boulevard at a place called Club Fetish. Three hours after we met, she was in my bed, in heaven. I was the second lover she'd had, and the first boy hadn't put enough loving on her to make a difference. Her first orgasm was with me. We fucked all night and she came back the next day for more. I took Jimi Lee from her boyfriend that night. Literally pulled her out of another man's arms and she fell into mine. It was at the beginning of a wild summer. I was going to be her boyfriend for half that summer. But a few orgasms later, she was pregnant, and by the end of summer we were married, living together in Leimert Park. Pregnancy changed everything for both of us. She had given up Harvard. I dropped out of UCLA. Mississippi married Ethiopia and had a child.

Five years of lying, cheating, and unhappiness followed. She cried all the time. I found fault in everything she said or did. Because of the pregnancy, her father had kicked her out of their home, sent her away penniless. We had conflict and I broke away from my family. We went from fucking like rabbits to no sex. After she lost her chance at

Harvard, she withdrew from the world. Years later I found out she had been on antidepressants. Those had numbed her moods and probably taken away her sex drive. Her moods were up and down, uneven: one day smiles, the next day screams. Her best friend, Lila, had told me about the antidepressants.

Then I was angry because my wife had kept that a secret.

I had been rejected sexually and emotionally and it didn't feel like much was left spiritually. I had been shut out of every part of her life. Like I was a stranger. I was hurting inside, depressed too, secretly crying my own dry tears, but I never stopped loving her.

After she left me, after she ripped Margaux from my life, Jimi Lee came back to my bed. I don't know, but maybe she was off the medication by then. There were a few years of us hooking up a couple of times a month, rocking the headboard and cheating on other people. That ended when Jimi Lee's second husband came banging on my front door like a madman. Yohanes banged on my door while I banged his wife. He sent the Horn of Africa after me.

Jimi Lee was his wife, but she still felt like she was my wife.

I thought I'd gotten away from that marriage from hell, but now the old feelings were back, so I guess I was just on parole. Like a prisoner, I sat in my mental cell, eyes closed, surrounded by a wall of old memories. Jake Ellis killed my unwanted trip down memory lane when he jammed hip-hop on KDAY. He cranked it up, rapped, blew the whistle, and got hyphy.

"You okay over there, Ken Swift?"

"Bro."

"Talk to me, bruv."

I clacked my teeth twice, exhaled. "Margaux mentioned that job in Miami."

His face went serious and he turned the music down. "What does she know?"

"She said the name Balthazar Walkowiak. She threatened me."

Jake Ellis's jaw tightened. "Bruv, that changes every fucking thing."

"That's what that lunch was all about. She demanded fifty thousand."

"Tell me every word my black-turned-white goddaughter said."

"Bro."

"Bruv, talk."

We passed encampments for the homeless, passed a tattered man facing the streets, taking a piss. We passed women living in tents situated in the shade, the screens open so they could breathe the exhaust from cars and buses. Tent cities were the new normal in most parts of Los Angeles. Dozens at every turn. Gentrification in Downtown had pushed out the unwanted and created mini skid rows all over. That displacement had become so common we didn't notice.

My concern remained with Margaux.

I told Jake Ellis all my daughter had said.

It didn't show, but I was scared.

I couldn't remember the last time I'd been scared.

CHAPTER 3

I TOLD JAKE Ellis all Margaux had said about Florida, and his temper flared.

Jaw tight, my partner in crime said, "Florida is San Bernardino business."

"We killed Balthazar Walkowiak. And fed his body to the alligators."

"Does she know that part?"

"She didn't say. She was pissed and walked away."

"There is no statute of limitations on murder. And she knows what we did?"

"She knows who; not sure about all the what. I guess Jimi Lee told Margaux."

"And she brought that to you? San Bernardino won't care that your daughter is pregnant."

"I'm her target. Only me."

"You are not the only one involved. I'm involved. So is San Bernardino."

"Bro, she's after me."

"What if she talks and the law comes after you?"

"I won't talk. I'm no stool pigeon."

"And she wasn't wired?"

"I don't think she was."

"Fifty grand as hush money?"

"Came at me like I was Bill Gates and had fifty thousand in walking-around money."

"Wouldn't put it past Margaux and Jimi Lee to team up and come at you hard."

"I think this is just my daughter. A daughter who has been brainwashed into hating me."

"What's your plan to get fifty grand in your hands, Ken Swift?"

"Does your landlord have a rich older sister half as fine as she is?"

Jake Ellis said, "If she did, you know my car note would be getting taken care of too."

He changed the music, played "Iskaba," a song by Ghanaian Wande Coal. I straightened out my Muhammad Ali tee, then reached inside my suit pocket. There was a flyer for a three-bedroom, three-bath home on Eleventh Avenue in Inglewood. House was going for $649,000.

I tossed the flyer out the window, let it go wherever deferred dreams went.

"Bruv, littering is a thousand-dollar fine and a week of picking up litter on the side of the freeway."

"Well, back up and I'll find my trash in the middle of all the other trash and pick it up."

He checked the rearview, didn't see the hashtag makers' flashing lights behind us.

I barked, "Was dealing with Rachel last week, now Margaux's bullshit this week."

"That fling Rachel Redman had with the rich Russian a few weeks ago, that's over?"

"Said it was a reactionary fuck. Whatever that means."

"Should I pay the Russian a visit on your behalf?"

"My days of fighting a man, of fighting *men*, over a woman are behind me."

"I don't need you to go with me to put the Russian on a stretcher."

"It's starting to feel like being with my ex-wife all over."

"Well, you know your type."

"And they know theirs."

"You've been real quiet about it all day. Don't get an ulcer over a wicked woman."

"I'm stressed. And hungry."

"Hot and hangry."

"Headache kicking in."

"I'm starving too. We'll get us some food."

"Just don't get me any more pissed than I already am."

"You get pissed, get to work, lose control, and try and beat folks through a wall. We got to Arizona and all of a sudden you were violent and beating up Asians like Mark Wahlberg in 1988."

"Rachel Redman got under my skin and I lost the plot in Arizona."

"Rachel and that Russian shit had you going Mike Tyson up in there."

"Anger has to go somewhere. Anger, orgasms, and a sneeze; those are three things, once they get started, I can't stop. And when I'm hungry, my anger only gets magnified."

"We better get you some real food. Being this hot and hungry, bad combination."

"You see that ungrateful . . . you see her stand up and throw her snot-rag in my chowder?"

"Everyone saw."

"Well, I was going to reintroduce you. But, bro, you saw shit went south from the start."

"Bruv, her skin shocked me more than her hair and tattoos and nose rings and all that confusion she had going on. But that skin. People in Africa do that mess day and night. Over half the women in Ghana bleach. And Nigeria is worse. I see the Ethiopians are in the same line."

"Hurt to see that confusion on my own child."

"From where I was, her body language was strong. She was on a rampage."

"She hates me like no other. Hurts when your own child hates you. Hurts a lot."

"Glad you didn't reintroduce her to me. If she is making threats, I don't want to meet her."

"Let me see your phone."

He handed it to me. I went to Facebook, put in Margaux's name. Nothing came up.

I said, "I'll find Margaux. She has to be on social media. Everyone her age is."

Jake Ellis reached for his phone. "After Pasadena. We're off to work. Need you focused."

"You're right. Being worried about her mother was what went wrong in Florida."

I gave him his phone, let music from Africa try to take me to the motherland. I imagined sundry warm brown skin tones passing me on the streets, imagined men and women with a similar hue anchoring the news, on the billboards, seated in all political offices. I wanted to know what it felt like to be where they cared about and looked for missing black girls. I wanted to be in a place where I felt the way white people felt in America, like they controlled and owned everything.

I tried to distract myself by thinking of Rachel Redman, imagined her kissing me. That woman could kiss like no other. Rachel Redman was the only good thing I had going in my life.

But the distraction didn't last. What had arrived was more powerful than any kiss.

Margaux on my mind, my ex-wife back in my heart, we headed to Pasadena.

CHAPTER 4

I COOKED THE wild rice and steamed the veggies, everything perfectly seasoned, then opened the cabinets, stood impressed by the round adobe melamine dinner plates. It was a contemporary kitchen, very modern, and had design elements I'd seen only in high-end magazines. Extensive marble throughout. Stainless fixtures against dark wood. There were two islands, one a workstation, the other a breakfast bar.

At least seventy-five palm trees framed the mansion. Each was twenty feet high. All palm trees were imported, but the ones that made this property into a beautiful jungle cost at least forty-five hundred dollars each.

I said, "That Olympic pool is the bomb. Deep end is fifteen feet deep."

"He spent a few hundred thousand on that. That's how you launder your money too."

"Pool that deep in earthquake country is probably built outside of code."

"Just like the walls around the property. They are higher than the norm."

"Special permits?"

"Rules never apply to the rich. They grease palms and get whatever they want."

"Look at the pictures of his wife on the wall."

"Looks like a movie star."

"Look at the sculptures all over."

"Rich men get it all. They get the castle. The woman. The life."

"Yeah. And everyone else has to hustle and settle for what they leave behind."

Giant Ziploc storage bags were on the counter next to giant Hefty bags and Saran Wrap. They had all been put to use.

Jake Ellis looked toward the palm trees and high walls, the privacy that framed a large backyard and the magnificent swimming pool and asked, "Those bags are waterproof?"

"The Ziploc? Oh yeah. Wrapping everything in Saran Wrap first will keep 'em dry."

"Don't want complaints from San Bernardino."

I whistled. "Glocks. AKs. Heckler & Koch G36s."

"He kept one in almost every room."

"Proud member of the NRA."

Jake Ellis said, "You know that means Negros, Return to Africa, right?"

"Funny. You're a regular Michael Blackson."

"Michael Blackson is one funny motherfucker. Crass, curses too much, but funny."

Jake Ellis stopped staring at African art. Statues and art from the motherland were mixed with the European, Asian, and East Indian art, all of that mixed with family portraits, wedding pictures, and art by Kimberly Chavers, David Lawrence, and Jacob Lawrence.

Nervous, I asked, "We got all the weapons, right?"

"Bruv, don't get worried."

"What worries me is that you don't get worried about shit that should worry you."

"You get worried, then you make me get worried, and I don't like being worried."

"Don't be so damn cocksure."

Margaux wasn't off my mind, but she had become a low hum. I was focused on this job. This would be over in an hour, no more than two. Then that hum would become a roar.

Jake Ellis asked, "How much you think a kitchen like this cost?"

"Shit. Over one hundred thousand. Easy."

I motioned toward the living room and den. "As much as those Samsung hundred-and-five-inch curved 4K TVs all over the place. I'd bet he's spent a million on televisions."

"He has an Olympic-size pool but didn't turn the heat on."

"As hot as it is up here, leave the heat off."

Jake Ellis nodded. "How many pieces of this salmon you want?"

"Just one. But I want a big salad."

Jake Ellis checked on the salmon at the same moment the gates opened to the mansion.

Jake Ellis said, "Showtime. The Bentley is joining the Ferrari, Jaguar, and Benzes."

The Garretts had passed through the high walls and pulled onto their property. They parked in the five-car garage and entered the house through the heavy wooden door that led from the garage into a mudroom, and from there into the well-appointed gourmet kitchen, where we waited.

CHAPTER 5

MR. GARRETT WALKED in carrying a dozen shopping bags. He had on top-shelf golf attire and a Boston Red Sox baseball cap. Looked like they had played nine holes, then gone on a Rodeo Drive shopping spree. Each bag probably had at least two grand worth of goods.

His wife entered snapping, "Then tell me why two are missing."

He barked, "How would I know?"

"Why would you even need them if you don't use them?"

"For the last time, woman, they aren't mine."

"Who opened the box, Dickie Bird, if not you?"

"Don't raise your voice at me, Elaine. *Woman*, don't ever raise your voice at me."

She could stunt double for Jennifer Lawrence. Mr. Garrett was a fat Ben Affleck. He weighed at least three fifty. Pictures around the house showed him thinner, stronger, younger.

She persisted. "Did the box open itself and two just get up and walk away? Or were they stolen? You should know what's in your Ferrari. It's your goddamn favorite car."

"I will check with the Koreans who detail my cars."

"Yeah, let's blame the Asians."

"They are the ones responsible."

"You have a quick answer for everything. Everything is always some-one else's fault. Nothing is ever your fault. *Nothing.* Not even this. No matter what, you have the perfect—"

"Woman, what did I—"

They stopped their heated conversation when she shrieked and dropped her bags. We were right there, not hidden, but they had been too busy arguing to notice us across the room.

The man of the hour jumped when he saw me setting the formal table. He reached to his empty waistband in a way that told me if he had a gun, he would have come in shooting, killed us both, earned a key to the city, then went out to dinner for steak and lobster.

But I gave him a peek at the .38 I carried under my coat. He tightened his jaw, squared up, then spread his fingers to show he was unarmed. Trouble wasn't new to him, the man born and raised in Boston, son of a bank robber who ran his business in Arkansas, Tennessee, Texas, and Alabama in the sixties and seventies. Bad news and trouble were in Mr. Garrett's blood.

Tense, knowing how bad this could get, I said, "Welcome home."

Mrs. Garrett scurried behind Mr. Garrett, and even though she didn't say a word, it was in her frantic body language: Let Fatso die first. I'm the graceful blond European woman of good stock; I'm sup-posed to live to see the credits role at the end of any horror film.

She stepped on dropped bags, trembled. "Sweet baby Jesus. We're being robbed."

Mr. Garrett snapped, "Who the fuck are you niggers?"

His powerful Boston accent carried across twelve thousand square feet like an overseer's alarm.

Jake Ellis tilted his head sideways. "Did he call us *niggers?*"

"Fucking moolies. Why are you niggers in my goddamn home?"

Jake Ellis frowned. "Lower your voice and show some respect, mayo sandwich."

"You don't give orders, nigger. Not in my house."

Garrett's wife pulled his shoulder. "You called him the n-word,

Dickie Bird, which is very offensive, unless it's in a song, but even then, well, people like us shouldn't sing it, not in public, but you called him that bad word, and he's unhappy about that, so he insulted you back, that's all."

I stepped toward Garrett. "San Bernardino paid us to stop by."

"You broke in my fucking house under the orders of San Bernardino?"

I nodded and pointed. "How this dinner goes is up to you, Mr. Garrett."

Mr. Garrett looked to his left and saw what was on the floor. Ten feet of plastic had been laid out. Along with tools from Home Depot that could build a house or cut a body to pieces.

"Nigger, is that supposed to scare me?"

Jake Ellis did African finger snaps. "If you had sense, you'd be pissing your pants."

"If you had common sense, you wouldn't be in my home. You wouldn't even be in Pasadena. Back in the day we had laws; we had ordinances to keep your kind out." Garrett smiled as his eyes went from Jake Ellis to me. "San Bernardino sent two nigger derricks to break in my home, to cross this line, over this fucking financial disagreement?"

Confused, the terrified wife asked, "Derricks? Their names are Derrick? Both of them?"

Jake Ellis said, "No, pretty woman. A derrick is someone sent to execute someone."

"Nigger, don't talk to my wife."

Her voice shook. "Execute?"

Jake Ellis said, "Your husband is in big trouble. He might end up on the gallows."

"Gallows? You mean like hanging? You're going to hang him? And me?"

Jake Ellis snapped his fingers the African way. "Your boo is in debt and refusing to pay."

Mr. Garrett frowned at Jake Ellis, glared at him like he wanted to rip his head off, then again at me, shot me the same vile look. It had no impact. He'd end up dancing on air if he made one false move right now. Garrett glanced toward the living room, toward two spots where he had hidden guns. A man like him, even now, was contemplating his next move.

I said, "We put the Glocks in a safe place. Same for the rifle you had in the kitchen. Matter of fact, we moved all of your guns and automatic weapons. Same for the sharp knives."

"You niggers stole my guns?"

"We're not thieves."

Jake Ellis added, "I took out all the house phones too. And your Wi-Fi is down."

Mr. Garrett yielded a soulless smile. Danger lived behind his eyes. He inhaled, looked toward the kitchen, offended. "You niggers cooked my salmon?"

Jake Ellis said, "I sure in the fuck did."

"Why?"

"Because I don't eat fried chicken."

"Moolie. That's Copper River king salmon. Cost fifty dollars per pound."

The wife said, "But he paid a lot more than that because he had it flown in by private jet."

"You had the nerve to break in my home and touch my things? You cooked my food?"

Jake Ellis said, "We can let the food finish cooking and eat, or I can take you into the living room and have you stand on the plastic. I don't give a fuck which way this goes, honky."

I said, "Enough. Let's sit, be professional. I understand your point of view, Mr. Garrett. But you know San Bernardino. So let's try and push refresh on this before it goes off the rails."

I pulled a chair back and politely asked Mr. Garrett to cop a squat. He took a breath, nodded at his wife as if to say everything would be all right, then put his butt in the chair.

I reached into his pocket and he snapped, "Don't fucking touch me."

"I need your phone."

He took his cell out, slammed it on the marble floor. Jake Ellis took the wife's cell, rested it on the counter. Mrs. Garrett was confused. I pulled out a chair for her. She sat and then I scooted the chair up. Hands folded in her lap, pristine and proper, she looked at me.

Programmed with good manners, she automatically said, "Thank you."

My southern programming kicked in and I said, "You're welcome."

Garrett commanded, "Don't talk to my wife. Not one word."

Jake Ellis sat next to the woman, did that to piss Garrett off. "You're pretty enough to be the queen of Belgium. You're Becky with the good hair."

"Don't call me that. I hate when people call me that."

"You're a model?"

"Thank you. Not a model."

"Such pulchritude."

She scrunched her face. "What does that mean?"

"Means you're beautiful."

"That word sounds ugly. It sounds like a bad attitude."

"You're rocking a sybaritic lifestyle."

"You know a lot of ten-dollar words, huh?"

"How old are you, about nineteen?"

"Nineteen? No way. Almost thirty-four."

Mr. Garrett said, "Leave her out of this, and let's deal with the issue at hand."

Jake Ellis snapped, "Was I talking to you? When me and my partner are ready to deal with the issue at hand, we will deal with said issue. You ain't running a damn thang up in here."

Jake Ellis went back to Mrs. Garrett. He spoke to her in the kindest voice, gave her the Jake Ellis smile as he told her, "Your man is filthy rich. He makes a lot of money, but a woman needs more than capital. I bet he doesn't give it to you like you want it. I bet you been craving a man who can dip real deep and hit the bottom and all four sides at once. You like a good fucking."

Mr. Garrett erupted. "Stop talking to my wife like that!"

She shuddered, put her hand to her chest. "Oh my. Oh my sweet Jesus."

"I bet you hate it because you want to get it the way a real man gives it to a delicate thing like you. Even a little thing like you wants a rough rider, wants to feel like you are more woman than a big woman. I bet he goes limp and dies in the furrow. And I bet you my last dollar you ain't had good loving since God knows when."

Mr. Garrett stood and exploded. "Nigger, one more word to my wife and—"

Jake Ellis stood. "Who the hell you talking to in that tone? I know it ain't me."

Mr. Garrett's wife begged him to sit back down, grabbed his arm, pulled him.

Only took a few hot words to set a man like Garrett off.

Jake Ellis said, "Come this way and see how fast you fall down."

Mr. Garrett barked, "Tough talk doesn't scare me."

Mrs. Garrett shivered, made a mousy sound, didn't blink as she looked at her husband, checked to see if he would stand up like a warrior and be emperor of his stronghold.

I stepped in, said, "Mr. Garrett, have you heard of the Boys of Bukom in Africa?"

"Bukom? Never heard of it."

"It's a small slum village on the coast of Ghana."

"He's an African. I knew that. He reeks of Ebola. Smells like poverty. Now my house smells like famine and disease."

"Bukom has produced more champion boxers than anywhere else in the world, per capita, that is. That man you're disrespecting is a world-class pugilist. My friend trained without headgear, on concrete, not in a ring with a mat that forgives you if you get knocked down, or catches you and lets you bounce if you get knocked out. He trained on unforgiving concrete. He trained to never lose, to never be knocked down, because you fall there, you hit the concrete and get knocked out twice. He trained outside. In Ghana's heat. No ropes, so they learn to not back down. You're facing a warrior who has never gone down, not even on one knee, but he's put many out for the count. He doesn't know how to lose. He won't quit until you're expired or the earth has fallen into the sun."

Garrett pointed at Jake Ellis and ordered, "African, leave my wife alone."

Garrett sat back down. When he was seated, Jake Ellis took his seat again.

Jake Ellis winked, yielded a playboy grin. "I think this PYT likes me a little bit."

"San Bernardino's issue is with me, not with her."

Jake Ellis didn't back off. "I'm being saluted by fat, hard nipples."

She lowered her head. "Cold. I'm just a little cold."

"I bet your nipples are as pink as this salmon."

Mr. Garrett opened and closed his hand. "Don't talk to her like that."

Jake Ellis said, "Look at me. Pretty young thang, give me your eyes for a moment."

She slowly, reluctantly raised her head, then gradually turned her eyes to Jake Ellis.

He smiled at her. She shuddered, then exhaled, and closed her eyes for a moment.

He asked, "You love your husband like Belle loved Kunta Kinte? Or are you his Kizzy? He thinks that money he has and that wedding ring make you property. I think he cares about you the way slave master Tom cared about Kizzy. He'll turn on you one day. They always do."

"I'm offended. You don't know anything about me or my husband."

"Pretty woman, I know people. I can look in his eyes and see what kind of man he is. He's old, fat, rich, and white. White men have been horrible to white women all of your lives and you have failed to recognize that, you know that? You were his chattel back in the day."

"Chattel?"

"You were his chattel and the black man was his slave."

"I don't know what chattel means."

"You were his property. He owned you and didn't allow you to own nothing, and you still don't get fair pay. He's your enemy. Not just mine and the Mexicans' and the Muslims', if he's that kind of colonialist. You think you're special, because you're a pretty white woman, but he's tricked you. White man wants you so he can have white babies, that's all."

"We don't have children."

"Well, still, I bet he doesn't respect you."

"Please, stop talking to me."

"He respects nobody but other white men. Your man is cut from the same cloth. You're a trophy that'll stop looking brand-new after a while, if you haven't already lost your shine."

"That's not nice."

"You're a midnight chew toy in high heels and thong. I know what I'm talking about. Man like this, once you reach a certain age, he'll leave you curbside and bring in the new model."

"He wouldn't put me on the streets. Why would you say something as mean as that?"

"He would."

"He can't. At least I don't think he can. I'd have to review our prenuptial agreement."

Jake Ellis laughed at her, shook his head. "A prenuptial? Bet he got you good."

She clenched her jaw. "Why is that funny?"

Jake Ellis shrugged. "Real love doesn't need no prenup. You have a business arrangement. The contract he made with you supersedes the agreement you have with God. And white men don't believe in God. They claim they do, they wave Bibles, but their actions are more powerful than their hypocritical words. They believe in some image of a white supreme being. He is worried more about his assets than taking care of where your ass sits. You've been played."

Her nostrils flared, and her lips wanted to move, but no words came out.

Mr. Garrett said, "Not a word, Elaine. Not one more word, woman."

She shifted, looking angry at Jake Ellis and resentful of her husband for silencing her.

Garrett said, "I want both of you the fuck out of my home. This is not called for."

I said, "In time. We eat, then chat, and we decide how this goes."

"I'm not eating. This food could be poisoned for all I know."

Jake Ellis kept chatting with Mrs. Garrett. "I bet if you leave him before ten years, or if that snowflake decides to file for a divorce behind your back, you don't get nothing but the clothes on your back and thong in your ass crack. And he can do like Tom Cruise did his Australian wife—"

She said, "Nicole Kidman?"

"Yeah, her. She was blindsided."

"Is that what happened?"

"They were at the ten-year mark and Tom Cruise dumped her."

"For no reason?"

"Pussy got old, man went cold."

"That's not nice."

"This fool will probably do the same, dump you before ten years hit, cut his losses, get a younger version of you, and jump up and down on that leather sofa in the living room while you're somewhere broke, crying your eyes out. You'll end up on a sofa, in therapy, all broken down."

Mr. Garrett slapped his hands on the table. *"Enough."*

Jake Ellis grinned. "Your husband is a smart man. Plans ahead. He has his hands in the opioid trade, but no one can touch him. Same for fentanyl. It comes in from China with a layover in Mexico before hitting his people in the US, and he's never involved. But he runs it. Sells poison fifty times stronger than heroin. Drugs that no wall will stop. They come through points of entry, and on planes, trains, and automobiles. You think you matter that much? You are here to make a criminal look respectable. You're chattel wearing diamonds. When he cuts you loose and time comes to divide the house, he'll throw you out on the streets and give you what's outside, while he keeps all of what's inside to himself. I bet that's how that contract reads, right?"

"Stop talking to my wife."

"You ain't the boss, not while I'm here."

Mrs. Garrett bounced her leg, terrified.

Jake Ellis said, "Hey, PYT. Look at me for a second."

Mr. Garrett told her, "Don't look at him. Ignore him."

Jake Ellis whispered, "It's okay. Look at me, PYT."

Garrett's wife opened her eyes and regarded Jake Ellis again. She looked at Jake Ellis, and Garrett lost that struggle to control her. She had leaned away from Jake Ellis when she sat, as far away as she could from both of us, the men who had broken into their home and commandeered their kitchen. Now she leaned in his direction, the way you did a confidant.

Jake Ellis said, "Sorry. I got upset, kind of went off the rails a bit. I scare you?"

"I'm okay."

"You're staring. Trying to memorize my face for the police or something?"

"Just never seen skin so smooth." She shrugged. "I bet you have a good dermatologist."

"Not used to a white woman looking at me like that. I'm used to y'all clutching your purse and dialing 911 just because I'm walking down the street minding my own business."

She said, "I've always thought black men were handsome. One of my good friends is black, and her brother was always trying to get me to let him take me out to the movies and stuff."

"You had some black man in your bedroom before?"

"No. Never dated anyone black. Or anyone at all. I was an ugly duckling."

"You don't have to date a black man or be pretty to have sex with a black man."

"I never slept with black guys."

"That's your rite of passage."

"Never did. My friends did when they were high or drunk, for fun."

"Where you from? Vermont? Idaho? Montana?"

"I'm from Compton. Grew up about twenty miles away from here."

"No, you're not from the 90220 where they have that sexy-ass mayor."

"Aja Brown?"

"She's smart as hell and got sexy on lock."

"I was born there. Used to live there. Just like Kevin Costner."

Garrett grunted, shifted, incensed, his finger moving like he had an invisible gun in his hand, and each time he was shooting Jake Ellis, and sometimes he was shooting his wife.

"You're from Compton and you never dated a black man?"

"I told you I didn't."

"You have a nice body. Nice bottom. Sure you're not black and passing for white?"

"Two white parents. Four white grandparents."

"White as far as you know. Lot of folks were passing and took that secret to the grave."

"My husband jokes and says that when he saw me at work, he thought I was a black girl until I turned around. That happened a lot; still does, especially if I had my hair in French braids and had been to the beach and had been out in the sun for a long time. I can get a real nice tan. My nickname at work was Apple Booty. I used to play beach volleyball. Loved it. Working out in the sand makes your core strong and booty tight. Black girl at my job gave me that nickname."

"The nickname fits."

"I'm not racist. I have black friends. And Dickie Bird can't be racist. He has slept with black women. You can't kick it with, or sleep with, black people and be racist."

"Heart can be racist, the message never makes it south to the dick."

"For a burglar, you sure love to insult people."

"I'm not a burglar. Nothing has been stolen."

"You talk more than I do. But go ahead."

"PYT, my point is you and I have more in common than we both realize. The way I see it, we live underneath a global power structure that has an imbalance and creates perpetual injustice and daily stress for anyone who is not white, male, Christian, and heterosexual."

"In English, please."

"Colonialists have power on a global level. They are perpetual liars. Ask the Native Americans. Again, I do not have to cite numerous cases and offenses on the continent of Africa."

She paused, like she had to comprehend what was said, then nodded as if it suddenly made sense to her, then nodded again and asked, "So what's the solution as you see it?"

"For whom?"

"Africa. Black people."

"We have to earn the respect of the rest of the world."

"How does that happen? You seem to be the smart one at the table. How?"

"Colonialists respect nothing, not as a collective. United, they are the locusts of the world."

"I don't know what that means, but it sounds horrible."

"The US and Britain both control by fear. The Middle East used to be stunning, but look at it now. *Locusts.* What they have done to India, Parliament should all be lined up and shot. The European has imposed his values and bombed all that he couldn't control. Colonialists have to control or destroy that which they fear, or the colonialists know the chickens will come home to roost."

"Well, I pray for peace."

"Praying fixes nothing."

"Blasphemy."

Jake Ellis said, "Until America's blacks, British blacks, Africans, East Indians, and the West Indians organize, until we can drop bombs at will and do it without apology, until we do like the colonizers, those men who look in the mirrors and think they see angels, until we create our own manifest destiny and are willing to fight and kill and ruin the world to have it, we will stay at the bottom. We could organize, run them all out of Africa, and make them pay for all they stole."

Mrs. Garrett was rattled. "That sounds crazy. What you said is insanity."

"And African slavery wasn't insanity?"

"You're talking about killing people . . . based on the color of their skin."

"What a concept. Google 'lynching in America' and see who's the strange fruit."

"Don't talk to me like I'm an idiot."

"I am only flipping what colonialists have done, using their playbook, their rules."

"I don't believe in all that killing. I'm a Christian. We don't kill people."

"You must have a version of the Bible in which Jesus dies of old age."

"We don't talk that way. We don't go around killing people."

"What were the Christian Crusades if not a murdering spree?"

She was flustered. "You make me feel . . . stupid. I don't like feeling stupid."

"That is not my intent. I enjoy spirited conversations with beautiful women."

Mrs. Garrett fell silent. Looked at her nails, bounced her leg.

Mr. Garrett said, "Woman."

"Don't call me that, Dickie Bird."

He said it harder. "Woman."

She gritted her teeth. "I'm fine. This *woman* is fine."

Jake Ellis said, "This sort of non-Kardashian conversation too heavy for you?"

"I'm not your enemy. I don't owe anyone any money. I know nothing about drugs."

"Relax. This is only a conversation. I'm only offering you an intellectual conversation."

"Well, I'm not intellectual. I'm a pacifist and, yes, I watch the Kardashians."

Jake motioned at the art. "You benefit from all my enemy has stolen from Africa."

"Why do you keep talking to me? You are here for Dickie Bird, not me."

"I'm putting you on the auction block. Evaluating your worthiness."

"What does that mean?"

"You're the only trophy in the house that can talk."

"I'm not a trophy."

"Winning you represents success. Educated or not, intellectual or not, talented or not, you are the ultimate American trophy. Society says you're worth more than a black man or woman."

"More bullshit."

"Each time I meet a woman I like, I try to understand why she is worth her weight in gold."

"I'm just a girl from Compton who has moved twenty miles away to Pasadena."

"But in America, are the smartest, better-educated black women worth as much as you?"

"What do you mean?"

"A pretty woman like you was recorded at a hotel. Peephole lawsuit. They awarded her fifty-five million. Black man was killed by a cop in front of his girlfriend and child, killed while complying with the colonialist's commands, and his family was given only three million. Three million will make you rich for a few years, but fifty-five million makes you wealthy. The white woman was not dead. A white woman being insulted was worth more than a young black man's life."

"I'm being attacked based on the color of my skin."

"Imagine how Michelle Obama has felt for eight years and counting."

"I happened to be *born* what they call white. Same as I *happened* to be born a woman. I have no control over any benefits or detriments that came with my preexisting conditions."

Jake Ellis chuckled. "See? You do know a few ten-dollar words."

Head lowered, eyes wild, she frowned at him. "I don't like people laughing at me."

"Then laugh with me."

"Shit ain't funny. Not a goddamn thing."

"Now I hear the Compton inside you."

"Whatever."

"You seem to have a good soul. But a woman with your preexisting conditions still has the power to point and lie about a black man and have a mob of Garretts come running with a rope. Woman like you told a lie and a city in Oklahoma ended up burned to the ground."

"You're a bigot. But you're not the first bigot I've met. Can't say this conversation is new either. I've been tiptoeing around racism all my life. Living in 90220 wasn't like being in Malibu."

"Really?"

"Wasn't easy being white and almost everybody else was black or Mexican."

"Bet the brown and black OJs were all over you."

She paused, then surprised me. She chuckled.

"Look at that smile. Don't lie. I bet you have a few *Jungle Fever* stories to tell."

"I was a mud duck to the bone."

"Body like a black woman and the advantages of being white."

Mrs. Garrett smiled.

Jake Ellis. The intellectual enforcer with the golden tongue.

Garrett stared, nodded. Quiet. A quiet man was a calculating man.

A quiet man who smiled like a monkey baring its teeth was a dangerous man.

Monkeys smiled that way when they wanted to kill their prey.

A timer went off and everybody jumped.

Jake Ellis said, "The food is done."

Mrs. Garrett said, "Smells real good. Smells like we're in a five-star restaurant."

"Well, pretty woman, I hope you are hungry."

"I'm starving."

Mr. Garrett said, "Woman, don't touch the food. It could be poisoned."

"Dickie Bird, let's not be mean."

Jake Ellis said, "Be ready for the best meal you've ever had."

"You cooked?"

"I went to culinary school in Ghana before I went back for another degree in Nigeria."

She paused, shocked, surprised. "Oh. Jesus. They have a school in Africa for that?"

Jake Ellis looked confused, then understood the mix-up. "Culinary means cooking."

"Oh. Oh. I thought it was that other funny word that means . . . Jesus . . . never mind."

"I have to ask." Jake Ellis laughed. "Were you thinking of the word *cunnilingus*?"

"I am so embarrassed." She laughed, turned red. "I went to junior college one semester. Then I met Dickie Bird, and everything changed. You went to a real university and learned all sorts of things. No wonder you talk that way. You're the king of big words. You're smart."

"People are surprised when a black man is intelligent, shocked when a white man is not."

Mrs. Garrett smiled like the woman Jake had just kissed outside of TGI Fridays.

CHAPTER 6

THE ENERGY BETWEEN Jake Ellis and Mrs. Garrett had changed. Mr. Garrett growled, frowned at me, saw I was just along for the ride. His wife moved two inches closer to Jake Ellis, continued chatting. I placed a meal in front of everyone, the food hot from the oven and stove.

Mrs. Garrett told Jake Ellis, "Maybe God placed you in my life at this moment."

"For what purpose did your negligent God send me to be in your presence?"

She shook her head. "Outside of talking about killing everybody because you want to show them that you can be as evil as they can be, you have my mind on the awful prenup."

"Break it down. Tell me about your prenup."

Mr. Garrett spoke up. "Don't. Woman . . . *don't*. It's not their business."

She stared at her husband. Nostrils flared, she considered, then turned to Jake Ellis.

"If he divorces this *woman*, I get twenty thousand for each full year of marriage."

"For each full year?"

"No prorating. I didn't understand *prorating* at the time. I never used big words. I mean, *pro* usually means good, positive things, but in this case *pro* was like being conned."

"Just twenty thou a year? That's below the poverty line."

"Poverty line is at twelve thousand dollars. Somewhere around that much. I have relatives so poor that two thousand a month to them would be like winning the California State Lottery."

"Well, that's not much better than poverty in California. You know twenty thousand here is like eight thousand in Mississippi or Arkansas. If you divorce, you'll still need at least a part-time job."

Mr. Garrett said, "That's enough, Elaine. Time to shut your trap."

Jake Ellis said, "Shut the fuck up before I become a *nigger* and shut you the fuck up."

Mrs. Garrett shivered and her eyes watered; then she shook her head.

Jake Ellis asked, "Who was your lawyer? He needs his ass slapped until he's disbarred."

She sniffled. "Well, the lawyer is a woman."

"She needs to be slapped twice for not looking out for your best interests."

She looked at her husband. "I used his lawyer."

Jake Ellis chuckled. "Using his attorney. That was smart."

She shot her eyes back to Jake Ellis, nostrils flaring. "I know he rail-roaded me."

Mr. Garrett reached for his woman's hand. "This is done. Don't upset my wife."

She snatched her hand away. "My whole life I've been getting screwed over."

Jake Ellis asked, "Why you use his lawyer? That was his army. That was the enemy."

"She seemed nice. Until the two-faced bitch brought the papers when we were about to get married. I was in my wedding dress, and his lawyer marched in. Everyone was already at the church, and it was almost time for me to walk out, so I felt like I didn't have much of a choice."

"He fucked you over. You're in your prime. These are your best years."

"I'm almost thirty-four with no kids. My prime is in my rearview."

"These are still your baby-making years, if you want a baby."

"Almost last call." She sniffled. "So, how much do you think I should get?"

"I'd say he should pay at least a million for each year."

"That's a lot."

"Look at your yard. I bet he pays at least one hundred thousand a year to keep it nice."

"Yeah."

"You're sleeping in his bed and don't think you should get more than the gardener?"

"He'd never agree to that much. Not for me."

"I bet that snowflake can afford it. He pulled a fast one."

Mr. Garrett sat calm, jaw tight, left hand opening and closing.

Mrs. Garrett returned her attention and aggravated body language to Jake Ellis, said, "Well, Dickie Bird said the money part was not important because we'd be together forever."

"If it wasn't important, then he should've said you could have it all if he ever filed."

"Well, I didn't think about that either. There was a lot of fast talk, double-talk, that made no sense, and again, I was in my expensive wedding dress, and people were waiting for me to appear. And the contract had big words, complicated phrases, and I felt stupid trying to stand there in front of people and pretend I understood what it all meant, so I just signed the bullshit."

"He got you to sign and now you're trapped because he's holding all the cards. You know it's true. I bet you're scared to say something or do something because you're afraid you'll lose this lifestyle. You're just another piece of furniture. Get old, start to look outdated, next thing you know a Salvation Army truck will pull up and drag you away like you're a tax write-off."

Her eyes watered. Her bottom lip quivered. She struggled to keep it together.

Mr. Garrett commanded, "Don't listen to this troublemaker. He knows nothing about us."

Mrs. Garrett wiped her eyes, voice shaking. "Why did I have to sign the prenuptial?"

Mr. Garrett cleared his throat. "It was standard. Everyone has one."

"Did you have to put that in my damn face while I was in my wedding dress?"

"It had slipped my mind, and my attorney brought it to my attention at the wedding."

"But it couldn't have slipped your mind for four more hours?"

"I had forgotten. How many times do I have to say that I had forgotten?"

"Really? But you remembered it *right before we married*? That has haunted me ever since that day. I ain't said nothing about it, but it haunted me. I felt like a fool standing in front of your attorney, and the bitch had papers for me to sign, and said if I didn't sign them right then and there, there would be no damn wedding. *I was in my wedding dress.* I had my makeup on, so I couldn't even cry. A woman can't cry after she puts her makeup on. The lawyer wouldn't let me leave the room. She told me that if I left, the wedding was off, so I had less than a minute to decide. My momma was right there next to me. So were my sisters. I felt like a goddamn fool. We were in church. It happened to me in church. Under God's eye. I didn't want to sleep with your lying ass that night, but I had to, because it was my wedding night. That's why I was crying when I walked down the aisle. God had abandoned me. That's why it was so hard for me to say my vows. I'd been railroaded in church. I wasn't crying because I was happy. I lied. It was the saddest day of my life. To make it worse, the sex wasn't that damn good. I know I was almost a virgin, didn't have experience, but I know what feels good. First time we had sex, it was horrible."

"We're past that."

"You're past that, so we're past it, right? Is that how everything works?"

Garrett told her, "Your life is *much* better than it was when I met you. You were a waitress at Coco's in Compton. *In Compton.* Do you think you would have managed this on your own?"

She snapped, "I'm thirty-four goddamn years old and I don't have not one goddamn baby. You know what the age thirty-five is? When a woman is getting too old to have a baby. At my last appointment, my doctor told me I needed to consider freezing my eggs. That made me cry. Even if I have a baby now, I'll be old and the kid will be young. I'm technically . . . literally . . . some word . . . old enough to be a *grandmother*. I didn't want to be an old woman with a newborn baby. You've had me here, in this mansion, a castle built to have a big family, and . . . and . . . and . . ."

"Freeze your damn eggs. Don't make it an issue. We can always hire a surrogate."

"I don't need no stranger having my baby for me. That's ludicrous. If she carries the baby, then it's *her* fucking baby, not mine. I want my own goddamn baby—labor, stretch marks, and all."

Mr. Garrett slapped his hands down on the table with enough force to make the food dance. She recoiled. I jumped too, was about to jump up and throw a few blows. Garrett huffed and puffed. Jake Ellis was amused. So was I, at Jake Ellis's skills. He was a master instigator. He could make your left hand get into a death match with your right hand just to entertain himself.

Jake Ellis pressed on. "How much does he give you? C'mon. It's just us talking."

Her voice trembled. "He gives me almost two thousand dollars allowance a month."

"About five hundred a week. Month with five Fridays, you're getting shortchanged by five hundred bucks. Twenty-four thousand a year. Gives you as much as you'll get in a prenup."

She sniffled. "And I have to buy toilet paper and whatever with my damn money."

Jake Ellis chuckled. "So, you're using your money to buy tissue so he can clean his ass."

She looked down, anger rising. "Wish you had been there on my wedding day."

"His lawyer gave you an ultimatum, and that ultimatum was on his behalf."

"Bitch walked in and *bam*. Papers thrown in my face like she was making it rain at a strip club. Ten damn pages of shit in legal talk, with big words and double-talk, *bam*, in my face."

"Right before you married. But you know that was on his behalf.

An attorney ain't just going to show up at a wedding and find you at the last moment, not without his direction."

"On the day that was supposed to be the most special day in my life. I was livid."

"How did that make you feel as a human being?"

"No one has ever asked me that. About anything."

"I'm asking. Men like Garrett dehumanize every nonwhite man and every woman. I care."

"Everybody who said I was ugly and dumb and I'd never amount to anything was there. People who thought I'd never marry were there. I didn't want to be embarrassed."

"But you were humiliated."

She glowered at her husband. He had no empathy for her plight. It was business. She stabbed her fork into her salmon, stabbed it like she imagined she was stabbing her husband.

He said, "Don't eat that food."

She said, "I hope it is poisoned. I hope to God it's marinated in garlic and cyanide."

"Don't eat it."

She took an angry bite; then her eyes lit up.

She inhaled; then her eyelids fluttered as she exhaled, "Ahhhhh-hhhhh."

Mr. Garrett jumped up. "You piece of shit. *You poisoned my wife.*"

She died a thousand times, each time a little death.

CHAPTER 7

MRS. GARRETT CLOSED her eyes. "Oooh. My. Gawd. Help me, Jesus. Help me, Jesus."

She stomped her feet three times, like she was summoning the Father, Son, and Holy Ghost. Then she opened her eyes. Mr. Garrett touched her, but she moved his hand away.

She licked her lips, took another big bite. "This salmon is orgasmic. *This is really good.*"

I sat back down. Mentally I had floated in and out of their conversation, but my mind was here now, no longer on Margaux and Jimi Lee, my angst no longer on Rachel Redman.

Mr. Garrett's lips turned down. He was disappointed we hadn't killed his wife.

The Bostonian from Princeton said, "So the food is not poisoned?"

Starvin' like Marvin, I took a bite of my salmon, then took another, and another.

His wife said, "If you don't eat your piece of salmon, Dickie Bird, I sure will. It's delish."

Then Jake Ellis took a small bite of his, washed it down with sparkling water.

I ate. Jake Ellis ate. Mrs. Garrett ate the fastest.

Garrett scowled. Lips moving, no words leaving his aggravated face.

His wife had another religious moment. "Dickie Bird, it's so good. It's better than sex."

Jake Ellis said, "That depends on who you're having sex with."

Mrs. Garrett laughed, her breasts bouncing, as happy as they'd ever been.

Jake Ellis laughed along with her. "See, PYT, you do know how to smile."

Mrs. Garrett took another fast bite. "My salmon *never* comes out this good."

"Not everybody's good with seasoning. This is what I call my magically moist salmon."

Like a record on repeat, Mr. Garrett barked, "*Stop talking to her.*"

Jake Ellis stood up, picked up the magically moist salmon on his plate, and slapped the Boston gangster with Princeton credentials across the face. Jake Ellis did African finger snaps, went and got another piece of salmon, then sat back down, put a napkin across his lap, picked up his knife and fork, cut a small piece of fish, then eased it into his mouth. The wife stared at her husband, salmon slithering across his face. She slapped her leg and laughed at her husband.

"Dickie Bird, you look so silly. Like a cartoon. You look real stupid right now. You look the way I felt when your bitch of an attorney came in and, *bam*, hit me with that prenuptial agreement."

Jake Ellis complimented Mrs. Garrett. "This is a real nice spread you have here."

She blinked. "Thank you, friend. It used to be owned by some silent film star, then by some action movie star, then by some rapper, then by some big-time director, now by us."

"Never seen this much art in one place, except the British Museum. They stole art, statues, and sculptures from Africa. If they gave back all they stole, museum would be empty."

"You are so political. Do you ever turn it off and have a normal conversation?"

"For me this is normal. I analyze what I see in the world. My place in the world. Even if you are not political, even if you choose to remain naïve, everything around you remains political."

"I just live here. Art shows up in boxes and I put it up on an empty wall."

Jake Ellis whistled. "You hired a professional decorator to hook your joint up like this?"

"Did it myself and saved us a lot of money."

"The whole house?"

"All twelve thousand square feet. I think we have twelve thousand square feet. I forgot."

"I'd bet you ten dollars you've never lifted a finger to do labor."

"Architecture was my favorite subject at Compton High. Love it. That and interior decorating. I drew the initial layout for the pool, gym, and the basketball-slash-tennis-slash-volleyball court too. I don't swim, but Dickie Bird does, so I designed a pool for him. Well, the shape of the pool. I have no problem knocking down walls and putting down tile. It's relaxing. I knocked down two walls and opened up the space in here. Did it and helped the workers carry all the trash out. I'm a blue-collar Compton girl. I came out of the womb working hard. White skin and all. White didn't mean we had it made. I went three days with no food once. And I used to look forward to school because I knew I'd get to eat lunch. We had it rough. Not all of us get to sit in an ivory tower from birth. And also, for the record, something is always broken when you have a house, especially one this size. A toilet seat needs to be replaced or the commode he uses needs to be retightened, and I always try and fix it myself before I call the First American Home Warranty people to send someone out. Most things can be fixed in twenty minutes."

"Handywoman, if you are ever in West Africa, come and make my home look this nice."

"It's just a hobby. I like to make things prettier and spaces more functional."

"With the rich folks you know, your hobby could make a lot more than twenty G a year."

"Never thought about that. I guess I could do that for others. And get paid. And stay busy. Again, not like I have kids. We have room for at least five kids. And those rooms stay empty."

"How many bedrooms does a palace like this have?"

"Nine. Twelve if you count the two extra offices. His and mine are on separate floors."

"Nine and two are eleven. You said twelve. The other bedroom?"

She laughed. "It was converted into my private closet. Fucking cool, huh?"

"Are you serious?" He laughed. "So your closet is so big it could have its own bathroom."

"It does. I have a king-size bedroom that I use as a walk-in closet. It has a beautiful Murphy bed. And a television. I can sleep or nap in there. I have a keypad and the only way it opens is if it recognizes my fingerprints. I have to protect my shoes. The money he gives me, I buy two pairs of shoes a month. It's like retail therapy. I lock them up because relatives steal. His relatives, not mine. He bought me sixty pairs of shoes after we married. He used to buy me things all the time, most of it before we married. Now I buy my own stuff. I have close to four hundred pair."

"You should give me a tour."

Mr. Garrett told his wife, "You won't show that miscreant a damn thing."

Mrs. Garrett jerked, slowly turned her head, and scowled at her husband like she had forgotten he existed in the universe, like he had walked in on her giving Jake Ellis fellatio.

Jake Ellis stood up from the table, hands in fists.

Mr. Garrett slapped his hands down. "There will be no tour."

Mrs. Garrett slammed her own hands down on the table. "Will you tear up that prenup?"

Her voice carried, echoed from wall to wall. Jake Ellis smiled. I did the opposite.

Mr. Garrett commanded his wife, "You will not take him upstairs."

She snapped, "Yes or no: Will you call your attorney now and have the prenup revoked?"

"Woman."

"Dickie Bird."

He sucked his teeth. "Let's let them leave; then you and I can talk business in private."

"What you did was cold-blooded. And it wasn't done in private. *You did it in front of my goddamn mother,* asshole. You didn't give me time to *think* on it. *Not one damn second.* It was an ultimatum. *And this is my goddamn ultimatum.* Make that call, or I take my friend upstairs."

He said, "I can't do that. Not now. Not before we talk."

"Then I guess there will be a tour."

Jake Ellis slid Mrs. Garrett's chair out like a gentleman. She rose, smoothed out her clothing, then stood like a lady, bowed her head a bit. She thanked Jake Ellis with the softest smile. He nodded and reciprocated the grin. It was so formal I thought they were about to bow and curtsy. I expected parlor music to come on and then they would dance up the walls like Fred and Ginger. Jake Ellis followed her out of the dining area. She pointed out art on the walls.

"So, you're actually from Africa?"

"Ghana. But I spend a lot of time in Nigeria."

"I have friends who go to Africa for vacation. They go once or twice a year."

"Couples?"

"Just women. Neighbors. They're older and never invite me."

"Maybe because they go there to have sex with African men. Rich women love to go to Africa to have sex with African men because they want sexual satisfaction like never before."

"Is that what they're doing?"

"They want a generous lover with substantial offerings."

She laughed. "Substantial offerings. Can't say I've ever had that before."

"So, tell me about all of this art. Some is African. Some is definitely stolen."

They took to the wide and circular staircase, chatted like buddies moving through a museum. Last view I had of them, Jake Ellis was shoulder to shoulder with Mrs. Garrett. I think they were holding hands. Then I couldn't hear her talking anymore.

Mr. Garrett sat in rage. His wife had defied him. An African had insulted him.

I handed him a napkin. "Salmon. A chunk is slithering down the side of your face."

He yanked the napkin from my hand, wiped the intense anger from his reddening eyes.

I said, "Eat your dinner. I might get another piece of that salmon."

"You don't fucking tell me what to do. Not in my own house."

Jimi Lee was on my mind again, then Rachel Redman, then Margaux. Out of habit, I checked my pocket for my personal phone, then remembered I didn't have it with me. On the charger at home. Felt anxious. Still couldn't remember what else I was supposed to do today. I just knew Margaux had brought me the name of a dead man and threatened to tell what she knew. If it had been anyone else, they'd've ended up at the closest alligator farm.

Margaux was my daughter. She had me in check, maybe even in checkmate.

I spoke out loud. "I need to get up on fifty thousand dollars."

Mr. Garrett thought I was talking to him. "Is this some sort of a shakedown?"

"Nah. Someone is having issues and came to me, is shaking *me* down. But right now my pockets are like rabbit ears. They are shaking me down thinking I'm living large like you."

"And you expect me to pay an extra fifty to alleviate your plight?"

"Nah, man. Just thinking out loud." I glanced at the expensive art, wondered how much it was worth on the black market. "The devil is dancing in my empty pockets and I'm talking out loud."

Garrett had the monkey grin again. "He better not put a finger on her."

"I'd worry about another preposition."

"You think everything is a joke."

"No man can control what a woman does. You might as well try and catch a river with your bare hands. I was married. *Was.* My wife touched as many men as she wanted."

"You should have killed your wife."

"Thought about that more times than I can count. Loved her too much."

"She was a whore."

"Don't call my ex-wife a whore."

"She was a whore. All women are whores. You know that, and I know that."

"I never called her out of name. You won't either."

"But you don't get pissed when I said you should have killed her."

"Chris Rock said that if you haven't contemplated murder, you ain't been in love."

"If not a whore, what did you call her?"

"I called her my wife. Then I called her my ex-wife. Eventually I stopped calling her."

Mr. Garrett evaluated me. "You have a better-than-average education, for a black man."

"Backhanded compliments make my day."

"Come work for me."

"And do what? Build a house? Or pass out prenups?"

"I need some muscle. New muscle. Last crew I had, I sent them packing. You caught me in between guards, you could say."

"San Bernardino knows. That's why we came today."

"That explains a lot. A former guard probably snitched. That's the only way you would know where all of my guns were. Same for the code to the gate and to my house."

"Most men have a price."

"San Bernardino is a thorn in my side. I usually have men at my side. But I've gotten relaxed."

"How relaxed can a man be if he lives with a loaded gun in almost every room?"

"All are legal. All are registered."

"Most guys who stockpile have a legal stash."

"I've had situations before. Not unlike this. And will again. A man with money is always a target. San Bernardino isn't my only problem. That's why I need strong men, smart men like you."

"Would be a conflict of interest at this point. First thing you'd want me to do would be go upstairs and handle my coworker. Then you'd give me a gun and send me after San Bernardino."

"I'd give you a modified AR-15."

"Of course. What was I thinking?"

"I'll start you at one hundred and fifty thousand. Think of it as a signing bonus."

"One fifty to sign, and then what?"

"A salary. Mid six figures. You'd get a paycheck every two weeks. You'd get medical and dental. It would be legit, so far as the money goes. Would come with a title and a permit to carry."

"You are making a tempting offer."

"Cash to sign. We can negotiate the rest. Just shake my hand. Gentleman's agreement."

"You're serious."

"As a motherfuckin' heart attack."

I sat back and looked at his extended hand. I was one handshake away from big money.

Margaux could get her fifty. I could get a house. That was a life-changing amount of money. I thought about it, considered that capitalistic offer for as long as a commercial break on the *Love Connection*, then shook my head, but felt like a fool for turning down that offer.

Mr. Garrett said, "You're levelheaded. Not simple. Saying *nigger* didn't rattle you."

"Don't call me a nigger."

"I'm just saying you hear the word *nigger* and don't lose it."

"Now would be a good time for you to stop talking."

"In Nazi Germany, the few coloreds that were there, they were easy to identify and didn't have to wear a yellow star, and they were of no consequence. You know why? Hitler could take blacks away and no one would care. The Jews, they had to be marked. The gays had to wear pink triangles. Can't just look at a man and tell that he's gay. Or Jewish. Blacks, your skin marks you. Your skin is your triangle. Germany never had a Negro problem, not like here in America. They kept black Germans in their place. The black German men knew better. They would never touch or say a word to a European woman. They would've been sterilized. They would've been charged with racial defilement. They knew not to get close to white women. There was a price."

"What's your point?"

"Lessons have to be learned."

"San Bernardino has the same philosophy."

"Some people still don't know their places."

"Some people."

"San Bernardino knows me. This was done to piss me off."

"Like my buddy said, I guess your people are used to doing the invading."

"This has nothing to do with skin. You broke into my home. If I had walked in and saw two albino midgets, I would've asked why the fuck two albino midgets were in my goddamn house."

"Quit while you are ahead."

"A lesson will be learned. And know this: I will always be ahead of men like you."

"Men like me?"

"Men of a lesser god."

He said that like he was in control, like he was as powerful as Ozymandias from the Watchmen. He picked up his fork, stabbed his salmon, ate slowly, nodded, waited impatiently.

He said, "And you say you and your friend have stolen my guns."

"No one said we stole anything."

"You have my guns."

"You could say that."

"A disgruntled employee sold San Bernardino inside information."

"One can assume."

"Smart move."

"Question?"

"What?"

"Why would one man need twenty-seven guns?"

"In case he runs into a pack of niggers and they have twenty-six."

CHAPTER 8

JAKE ELLIS AND Mrs. Garrett appeared at the top of the dramatic staircase.

Jake Ellis was pontificating. "Accra is amazing. On Valentine's Day, everyone wears red."

"So, Ghana and Nigeria are different places."

"Nigerians think they are the best, but they have stolen from Ghana."

"Can Africans steal from Africans?"

"We are different nations. Right now there is literally a music war going on."

Mrs. Garrett said, "And that music you said I should listen to? Tell me the names again."

"I love Asa. Best thing out of Nigeria. Sarkodie is the king of Afrobeats in Ghana. Navy Kenzo, Ali Kiba. Diamond Platnumz. Yemi Alade. Tiwa Savage. I could name at least fifty more artists."

"Do most of the men look like you?"

"Not to me."

"I mean, do the people have nice skin like yours?"

He laughed. "There is no one type of African, just like there is no one type of African American. You'll walk and see an albino, or a light-skinned African, and run across many Africans who can pass for white or are of European descent. There are pale Africans. You'll see people who remind you of your friends from Compton, and will see Africans who bleach their skin. Just like here, the more famous many Africans become, their skin lightens to reflect their status."

"And how do you snap your fingers like that?"

Jake Ellis laughed, amused, as he did that African finger snap a dozen times.

She laughed. "I can't do that. Feels like I'm going to sprain my wrist."

"Your index finger must collide with your middle finger when you twist your wrist."

"What does it mean when you do that?"

"It means many things. It means to hurry up, be quicker. It means my car won't start. It means a woman is pretty. It's punctuation, it's frustration, it's how you feel at the time."

Jake Ellis snapped while she failed miserably.

She had on a different dress. Barefoot, she walked like she was dizzy, lightheaded, and ecstatic. Jake Ellis sat down, looked across the expensive table at Mr. Garrett. Mr. Garrett snarled, frowned at his wife, jaw tight, shook his head, not a word spoken.

Done eating, I said, "Now, about your issue with San Bernardino."

Garrett cleared his throat. "This insult wasn't necessary. My people in Boston will wire the money as soon as I give the go-ahead. Now, get out of my house so I can wash away the Ebola."

Jake Ellis said, "Sucks to not be in control, don't it? Don't you hate that somebody can just walk up and hit you just because they feel like it? Can walk away with your woman and you can't do shit about it? Now, piss me off again and end up with a bad foot like Kunta Kinte."

Mr. Garrett regarded his wife, pissed off. "And you? You come back downstairs, different clothes on. What happened up there? What just happened in my house while I sat here?"

"Nothing happened, Dickie Bird. I just showed our guest parts of our beautiful home."

"He watched you change?"

"He waited in the hallway like a gentleman."

"That uppity nigger is not a gentleman. He's filth, if anything."

In a cheery voice Mrs. Garrett asked Jake Ellis, "Room for dessert? I have some gelato."

Mr. Garrett's hands became fists again. "The gelato is mine."

She said, "Dickie Bird had it imported from Gelateria Dondoli in Italy."

"Don't give them my gelato."

"Was that prohibited in the damn prenup? Let me think. Nope. Nope, it wasn't."

"Woman, sit your ass down. Let them leave and go buy a watermelon from a Mexican."

Silence covered the room.

Mrs. Garrett said, "Oh, they are definitely getting gelato. As an apology. Gentlemen, we have chocolate, vanilla, and fruit flavors, champagne, lavender, and gorgonzola cheese flavors."

Jake Ellis said, "I'll have some of each."

She beamed. "I prefer the pistachio flavor at Gelateria Crispini in Umbria, Italy."

"Bet you enjoy eating this by the pool."

"Oh, I don't sit by the pool much. I have a fear of water that's deep like that. I mean, sometimes I will sit in the shallow end and put my toes in, but not for more than a minute."

"Really?"

"It's called aquaphobia. I still have dreams about drowning and wake up screaming. Always have since I was a little girl. My momma said that in my past life I must have drowned."

Jake Ellis followed her into the kitchen, again laughing and whispering.

I used Jake Ellis's phone, took photos of Mr. Garrett, sent those to San Bernardino, let the boss know we had done what we had been sent to do, and no shovel needed. It occurred to me to search for my daughter on social media not using the name I called her, but using her true first name, her Ethiopian name, Tsigereda. I was about to do that, but my work phone rang.

It was the boss. I handed the phone to Garrett.

He snapped, "You fuck! You gaffled me and now you dare send two niggers to my home? Fucking Shylock, I told the niggers I'll pay. I will have my people send you the money by midnight. Yeah, every dime by midnight. But I won't forget this. You set me up; you weren't going to—you fucker! You are the most arrogant motherfucker I have ever met. No, you look in a mirror, you piece of shit. You sent niggers to my house. You know the difference between niggers and black people? Well, neither do I. You're a piece of shit, your entire operation is a piece of shit, no one cares about your threats, and after this transaction is done, our business is over and I can launder elsewhere, and know that if we ever cross paths again, day or night, you better run the other fucking way because if I get my hands on you, I will knock all of your fucking teeth out."

In a slobbering rage, Garrett hung up on my boss and threw my phone back at me.

I said, "I didn't see that coming. San Bernardino won't like that."

"San Bernardino ain't shit without me. You salmon-stealing niggers aren't going to be satisfied until you encroach upon and steal everything real Americans have worked for."

Jake Ellis had come back to the doorway when that outburst had sucked all the oxygen out of the house. Garrett scowled at Jake Ellis, then at me, then gave it all to Jake Ellis. Jake Ellis did those wicked finger snaps. Mr. Garrett gave Jake Ellis that cruel monkey smile. The wife of a jealous man stood back, nervous, and watched it all, breasts high, nipples hard like diamonds.

WHILE JAKE ELLIS taste-tested every flavor of gelato imported from Italy, I packed up our gear. Mr. Garrett couldn't get us through the foyer fast enough. But Jake Ellis wasn't done.

Jake Ellis went to Mrs. Garrett, and like he'd done with that winsome sister in the TGI Fridays parking lot, he pulled her into his arms like he had claimed her, and he kissed her. Softly. He held her ass and kissed her in front of her husband, gave her a deep kiss, made her swoon.

Mr. Garrett focused on Jake Ellis. That Boston gangster stare. That harsh monkey smile.

Jake Ellis reciprocated the expression, said, "I'll give you the first shot."

"Where are my guns? Just give me one and one bullet."

"I'm talking going toe-to-toe. That's how real men fight, not with guns."

"San Bernardino should have told you who I am."

"I know who you are. You're *nobody*. Without guns, men like you are nobody."

"You have a lesson to learn, and I'm going to teach you that lesson."

"Come on. Teach me. Learn me a lesson."

"I knew cocky niggers like you. Niggers from Dorchester. Knew niggers from Roxbury and South End. They learned about me. They know me like other gangsters knew Whitey Bulger. When I walk the street, when I walk in their ghetto, it becomes my ghetto. They see me coming and cross the road. And if it's raining, they will throw their bodies on puddles so I can walk and not get my shoes wet. I show up and the craziest of the niggers act like they have some sense, and one nigger brings me a cup of Dunkies while another nigger gets me an ice cream coated with jimmies. Same respect when I go to the North End. Niggers bring me Georgetown cupcakes, niggers bring me Sweet cupcakes. Niggers'll bring me beers from Coogan's and a Fenway frank. Go to Dorchester and ask the Irish, the niggers who are more nigger than you niggers will ever be niggers, the *half-ricans* who wish they weren't niggers, and the *habla español* niggers who I am."

"You can show me who you are right now."

Jake Ellis waited for Garrett to make a move. A war was about to start, and this was the epicenter of another Elaine race riot akin to the one that had happened in the Arkansas delta.

Jake Ellis said, "This Boston bum is just another coward with Twitter courage."

Mr. Garrett ended his monkey smile and the hard man casually walked away.

"Ebola-scented African, this is done. Off my property. I won't ask again."

Jake Ellis shouted, "I can't hear you. Want to man up and say that to my face?"

Garrett turned around, came back. Not afraid. Again smiling like everything was okay in his world. "You know why niggers are like Mondays? Nobody likes Mondays. So, last time, both of you Mondays get the fuck off my property or I'll have you arrested."

"You're about to run out of your nigger allotment."

"My allotment? Oh, I have an allotment? So I can't tell you that my favorite Dick Gregory book is the one entitled *Nigger*? Not the book *Nigger* by Randall Kennedy, but the book *Nigger* by Gregory. I don't want you to get confused because there are so many *Nigger* books out there. I have an allotment? So, it would offend you if I say that my favorite Richard Pryor album is *That Nigger's Crazy*? My favorite Denzel movie is *Training Day*. My favorite line in the whole movie? When he says, 'Nigger, please.' No wait. 'My nigger.' That's the line. 'My nigger.' How can you have a well-appointed and powerful word to yourself, a word that you claim you hate but regurgitate all the time, yet no one else but a nigger can use so freely? Do niggers have nigger allotments, or just men like me? I mean, some of you moolies call each other niggers like it's the only noun, verb, and adjective you know how to spell. And most of the time you spell it wrong. Just like with Pryor and Gregory, I'm old-school, so the original spelling, the way they spelled nigger on their albums and books for the world to see, that is the only correct spelling as far as I'm concerned. When I say 'nigger' it offends you, but when you call each other a nigger, you give each other a high-five and a hug like you're part of NWA. I'm confused. You call each other niggers in America, Kanye and Jay were niggers in Paris, and those niggers have stolen a word invented by a white man and made themselves billionaires, and I bet they never sent a thank-you card. Your rappers have infected music with the word *nigger* and now it's all over the world. I hear that African niggers are calling themselves niggers like American niggers. I know a little about African niggers. I travel. I'm not dumb. I can turn on satellite radio right now and niggers are calling each other nigger like it's their first name, middle name, and surname. The niggers on Jamie Foxx's radio station called each other niggers all day and night. So, do this, nigger, take it as a compliment that out of respect, like Mark Twain, I have learned to do the same. I mean, let's be real. Don't expect me to listen to Tupac and skip the best parts of the goddamn song. He says 'nigger' like it's poetry and I can feel his pain and loathing and resentment. And love. He loved niggers. Don't expect me to do the same with a Biggie record. Don't expect me to hear a Richard Pryor joke or a Tiffany Haddish joke or a D.L. Hughley joke and leave out the best parts when I retell it. That nigger comedy on Netflix is another level of poetry. And don't expect me to think more of niggers than niggers think of themselves. You call yourselves niggers. I'm going to follow your lead and do the same. Besides, I like saying it, to be honest. Nigger, nigger, nigger. It elevates your blood pressure, messes you up, and that sensitivity makes me laugh, considering all the bullshit niggers have to say about everybody else. Everybody is riding the nigger wave. Whites call themselves niggers for kicks. But the wetbacks. Have you heard them? Wetbacks call each other niggers more than niggers call each other niggers, so I guess they want to be the next set of niggers America has to keep in their place. Nigger, nigger, nigger. That pisses you off a lot more than if I called you a tar baby or a jungle bunny. Only have to say one word for niggers to lose their minds. And that is the word they call the most offensive in the world. Yet you have that shit on repeat. Nigger, upsetting an uppity nigger like you, that's hilarious. It's the funniest shit, nigger. The funniest shit since niggers were set free. What say you, nigger?"

Each time Garrett said *nigger*, it was like a knife being twisted in Jake Ellis's gut, and that double-edged blade went from his gut into mine. Jaw tight, I told myself that it was just a word. Couldn't let Garrett see me sweat. But Jake Ellis was African, and where he came from, men like Garrett were the minority. Jake Ellis hadn't been brainwashed to be passive, hadn't been programmed to turn the other cheek, to let white men and white women spit on him. He never stepped out of the way of a white man or woman, never backed down to a man based on his color.

Garrett said, "You act like you're the first bad man. Nigger, I was a bad man before you were born. And, nigger, I'll be a bad man long after maggots are eating away at your dead body."

Jake Ellis stood, riled, hands in fists. "After San Bernardino is settled, we will meet again."

"I look forward to it. Nigger, I look forward to seeing you again. Just know this. 'All I got beef with is those that violate me; I shall annihilate thee.' That's some Biggie Smalls for you. Now, while I'm nice, African nigger, leave before I force you to get down on one knee and bow to Zod."

Jake Ellis told him, "I bow to no man. Only to my god, and he's not yours."

Garrett marched on: "And stay off that nigger Twitter. Living on the Internet will keep you worked up. I can tell by your bigoted conversation you're on leftist social media way too much. Niggers like you find something to be offended by every day. Or you wake up and invent something to be offended by, and I find that as offensive as fake news. You wake up and shit on America before your first cup of coffee. If niggers hate America so fuckin' much, there's always Africa."

"And if you hate niggers, there is always Europe."

"Not for Europeans, you'd still be a baboon-fucking spear chucker."

"Go back where you came from. Go back into the caves of Caucasia."

Garrett grinned. "Uppity nigger got a lesson to learn."

The man from Boston moved through giant double doors. Pushed them open wide.

Jake Ellis exhaled like a bull ready to charge. My blood pressure was way up.

Garrett called out, "Alexa. Play John Lennon."

Without hesitation, Alexa answered like a loyal servant. "Which song?"

"That song from 1972. 'Woman Is the Nigger of the World.'"

"Playing 'Woman Is the Nigger of the World' by John Lennon and Yoko Ono."

The former Beatle began to sing. And Garrett conducted and sang it louder, sang about women being seen as subhumans, slaves, property, seldom educated, no gust, no confidence, scorned for trying to be a man. Once upon a time, some women were burned alive when their spouses died. For a white woman to believe she was oppressed, she had to be compared to the race of women dehumanized the most. Even then, many didn't believe it. White women couldn't fathom they were chattel. It meant one thing when Lennon sang it, but when Garrett played it, it felt ominous, deadly. Garrett was threatening his wife. Jake Ellis's eyes told her she didn't have to go back. Mine told her that she didn't have to go back, but she sure as hell couldn't go with us.

Garrett called back, voice calm yet strong, "Elaine. *Woman.* Come inside. Find me a deck of cards so we can play a game of spades."

Mrs. Garrett looked at the mansion as if she couldn't imagine another life, and she reacted as if her peniaphobia was about to start acting up. She didn't want to fall back to her side of Compton. Compton had a beautiful side. I could tell she wasn't from that part of a good city with a bad reputation. I didn't have to be a gumshoe to see she was a wife and a moll combined. She lowered her head and left without saying good-bye, moved like an agile and apologetic puma. From the front, there was a lot of glass. The house was made to showcase the luxuries and art inside. We saw Mrs. Garrett rush up the staircase. Lennon sang, but Mr. Garrett roared louder than the instruments, and off-key. The man of the hour had done his best to be cool, calm, and collected in front of us, but once his front doors closed, he had let loose. Sounded like he was screaming, throwing plates, turning over chairs. I was glad we had hidden all of Garrett's guns, left them wrapped in Saran Wrap and tucked in Ziploc bags, all of that stuffed into Hefty bags, drowning in the deep end of his Olympic-size pool.

Jake Ellis spat and scowled like a fighter who had lost for the first time in his career, his anger, his disappointment, powerful like Tyson after being downed by underdog Buster Douglas. Just like with Tyson and Douglas, there would be no rematch. Jake Ellis had to take this L and go home. If San Bernardino had seen this level of unprofessionalism, hell would have broken loose.

John Lennon sang us off the property. As Jake Ellis pulled into the dry heat, I tried to remember how many times Garrett had called his wife *woman*. If a white woman was the nigger of the world, it made me wonder what a black woman was in this world, if not the universe.

CHAPTER 9

THEN WE WERE in the Mustang on the way back, top down, hella hot evening air blowing on our heads, air conditioner cooling our feet as dry air sucked moisture from my flesh.

Jake Ellis fumed, "He went to Princeton? This is an American top-shelf education?"

"I grew up around men like him. Mississippi. Oklahoma. They are in California, Oregon, and riding the trains in New York too. Men like him will call a black man a racial slur over and over like it's his Viagra, and when a man like Garrett gets hit in the eye, he'll sue claiming assault."

"What's an uppity nigger?"

"A black man who thinks he's better than the lowest of the low white men."

"Well, he's an uppity honky."

"That knife won't cut hot butter."

"That peckerwood. He acts all big-man, like the colo from Babylon."

"Peckerwood. Sounds funny when you say it. Like Woody Woodpecker–wood."

"I heard a comedian use that word a few times."

"Black comic?"

"White comic. He said it was an insult. But I ain't never called a white man that. Everything you call them sounds stupid and is ineffective. Honky sounds more stupid."

"I forgot. Besides colonialists, what y'all call them in Africa?"

"*Obroni* or *oyibo* or *oyinbo*. Depends on where you are."

"Peckerwood sounds better. Especially the way you make the letter *p* pop."

"Bruv, I need your black people to create better insults for white people."

"There are no better insults. Nothing you say carries the same history. No white man was called a honky or redneck before he was lynched, because they weren't lynched. There are no pictures of hundreds of black folks smiling as white men were hanged from trees by their necks. They were odd people, but never strange fruit. Black people didn't take pictures of whites hanging from trees, then make those into postcards to send their relatives. No white organization had to wave a flag from its window announcing a white man was lynched that day. Black people had to send that message to other black folks. Whites never stepped off the sidewalks to let blacks pass. Whites have always had the right to look a black man in his eyes. There was no Caucasian version of *The Negro Motorist Green Book* telling white people where and when it was safe to travel, no book needed to tell them where they could eat or find a bathroom so they didn't have to go on the side of the road or in the bushes. White man has always felt powerful, if not safe. He's always been more comfortable. He has never been the black man's chattel. His folks weren't crammed in the bottom of a ship. When they call us niggers, they're doing more than insulting. They're pouring salt on unhealed wounds, throwing four hundred years of history in our faces. They're reminding black men and black women that we were enslaved, that we're free because men like him begrudgingly decided to free the poor niggers, that in this system the poorest and worst of them are still better than us, that in their eyes, and that by law, by his law, we can still be beaten, lynched, or gunned down. They're reminding you what they can still do to you."

Jake Ellis did that finger snap. "They can do that to the black American with one word."

"Bro, we're called that out of the womb. By the time you're in kindergarten, you know there is a difference. You sense the danger. You see how your folks react when called a nigger by white folk. They react like the whip hitting Denzel's back in *Glory*. You see big black men get scared of little white women because they know the destruction one white woman can cause. You learn how to survive that shit on the daily. You get called that playing sports. If you're alone, white boys band together and come up behind you, call you nigger to scare you, and that's white-boy fun to them. Men like Garrett call you that in the boxing ring. Playing football, the other team yells it in your face to get you off-balance. They know how to rile you, just like Garrett knew how to pour gas and throw a match on your soul. Our worthiness, humanness, has been defined by this melanin-blessed epidermis. It's their definition of us, but it doesn't have to be our definition of ourselves. Still, I feel you, bro. Every black man or black woman will be called nigger one time too many. Some will cry and walk away mad, and some will snap and beat the fuck out of a fool."

"Black people are the abused housewives of America. Make the Beatles sing that."

My mood took over the music. Put on Jay-Z. "The Story of OJ." Bumped that shit.

Jake Ellis said, "Thought you weren't bothered."

"Never said I wasn't. It's a struggle, but I just didn't let the situation control me."

"This time. I've seen you beat that word out of many men's vocabulary."

"When I was younger."

Maybe I felt older today. A man's daughter telling him he was going to be a grandfather had that effect. Jake Ellis sped down Colorado Boulevard, then got on the Glendale Freeway.

As we came up on unforgivable traffic I reached for his phone.

He said, "Bruv, you know I don't like people using my phone."

"Give me the damn phone. I need your Twitter, Instagram, and Facebook so I can do a search."

"You want to invade my social media. You're pushing it."

"Put in your password."

While traffic was at a crawl, he hit his password, one that had uppercase letters, numbers, and a haiku using Ghanaian words, then handed it over, the page to Firefox and his last search opened.

I asked, "Who is this naked woman on this website?"

"What naked woman? Oh, her. She's a Ghanaian-Nigerian actress. Christabel Ekeh. Someone tried to blackmail her with nudes, so she jumped the gun and released them herself."

"These naked pictures are mild."

"Not in Ghana. Not for a woman who is a celebrity there."

That made me wonder if my daughter had the same issue.

I closed that, then tapped the app for Facebook, went to his account, searched for Margaux. This time I used her Ethiopian name. I searched for Tsigereda. Her name was a common name. I scrolled down the page. Her new complexion stood out from the rest. She had used her first name and her mother's maiden name. Again I was insulted.

I said, "I found Margaux on Facebook."

I CREPT HER page. Saw her relationship status was listed as IT'S COMPLICATED. She had pictures of her as a little girl in Ethiopia. A brown-skinned child in a sea of brown-skinned East African women and girls. That was the daughter I remembered, only she had dressed American when she was under my roof. Other pictures were post-bleaching, images of her standing in the lot at Griffith Park, Hollywood sign in the background. No one would know the little brown girl and the adult were the same. It was a safe page, the kind you had when you worked a real job and didn't want to have your employer creep it, then have a reason to fire you for some political comment that was a bit too honest. She was in groups, with men of many cultures, but I didn't see any pictures of her and anyone who looked like a boyfriend. Didn't see what I was really looking for, pictures of her mother. I had no idea what my ex-wife looked like now. The last image I had of her was when her husband banged on my door, of how her pretty brown eyes widened and she panicked, of her nakedness as she rushed to get dressed. My last image of her was sheer terror, fear of Yohanes.

Jake Ellis asked, "Anything good?"

"Still checking."

"What you got?"

"She checked in at the Grove."

"Where?"

"Starbucks."

"When?"

"Two minutes ago. Head that way and maybe we can be there in thirty minutes."

"We have to meet someone from San Bernardino."

"We can swoop by and still make the meet."

"If your daughter checked in, she wants someone to know she's there."

"I was thinking the same thing."

"Somebody she didn't want to message."

"She didn't check in at TGIF."

"She didn't want anyone to know where she was."

"She didn't want them to know she was with me."

"What else you got, Sherlock?"

I went down Margaux's page, saw other places she had checked in. Crept her friends list. She had fewer than one hundred. Tried to see who she was, understand her life. She frequented other mom-and-pop coffee shops in Hollywood: Javista Organic, Groundwork, Verve. She checked in late evenings at spots hopping with hipsters until the wee hours. She went to one over and over, 101 Coffee Shop on Franklin, and didn't check in there until after midnight, so I assumed she was restless and that spot was near her six-thousand-a-month rental house. She checked in at the studio called the Lot yesterday morning around ten, then at Grauman's Chinese Theatre yesterday afternoon around three. She was either on vacation or taking sick days from her job. She checked in at JPL in Pasadena a lot, but not in more than a week; she had checked in a few times at Kaiser on Sunset. All of those announced check-ins added up to nothing in my brain. I wanted to see my daughter, but not with Jake Ellis at my side. Enemy or not, she was still my daughter, and if Lite Brite was in trouble, love me or not, it was my job to fix it.

THE STARBUCKS WAS at the Third Street / Fairfax section of the Grove, connected to the historical Farmers Market. A lot of exotic mom-and-pop eateries were side by side with fruit and vegetable vendors in that section. It was at the far western end of the six-hundred-thousand-square-foot outdoor shopping plaza, the opposite end from Nordstrom, Banana Republic, the movie theater, and a large fountain with Las Vegas flair. It was acres of shopping for the moneyed, but it was a diverse crowd. Having pale skin covered in tats wouldn't make Margaux stand out, not this close to Melrose. We hopped on the trolley, Jake Ellis on the left, me seated on the right, and we searched for Margaux. Was impossible to see inside the stores. East Indians. Pakistanis. Jews. Whites. Asians. Blacks. Latinos. It was like that old Coke commercial from the seventies, where they wanted to teach the world to sing in perfect harmony, except in this reality every tenth person was a celebrity and every second person thought they were more important than a celebrity.

I said, "Could be a waste of time. Would be different if she had checked in at Macy's or the Apple Store. If she was just getting a cup of coffee, she would be gone before we got here."

"We are here. This is important. We will look for her a moment."

"How are we on time?"

"Short."

I nodded. "They have at least fifty shops and just as many kiosks, most for women."

"You used to bring Margaux here when she was a little girl."

"Yeah. I used to bring her here when she was a little girl. Brought her here and bought her expensive American Girl dolls, the ones with the brown skin." That memory flashed as we passed that store, and that recollection lasted as long as a curt exhale and a frustrated grunt. Then I went on, saw the bookstore coming up on our right. "Took her to Barnes and Noble once or twice. She was four or five when we did that. She would ride on my back the whole time."

Jake Ellis searched the crowd. "She could be anywhere."

"My child might see me first and hide. Or get spooked and call for the cops. Everyone has to pay to park in the lot, so I'd bet she would be in and out before the parking fee kicks in."

"First hour free. Next hour two bucks, but free if you get it validated at the movies."

"Lite Brite made it sound like every dollar mattered."

"Lite Brite?"

"Don't tell her I called her that."

"I'm sure she's called you worse."

"No doubt. She called me worse a few hours ago. When she demanded that money."

"What if she's meeting with someone and it has to do with that fifty thousand?"

"I don't want to cause a scene, not like we did at TGIF."

"I do. If someone else knows about Florida, I want to meet them, and meet them good."

"I know you do. And that meeting will end with a shallow grave being filled."

"We'll ride the trolley to Nordstrom and walk back and look in the shops."

"And we could still miss her." I motioned at the crowd filing into the high-priced Pacific Theatres. "Especially if she went to a movie."

He hit his complicated password, handed me his phone before I could ask for it again.

I said, "Good idea. Let me see if she checked in anyplace else."

"What else you see on her social media? Look for her momma. See if she checked in at the same place. If she did, then they might be in this blackmail on a black male together."

I searched to see if Jimi Lee had a Facebook page, searched for her birth name, then tried her nickname, searched for East African women named Jimi Lee, found nothing.

The trolley left without us and I moved into the heat, head down, trying to not bump into other people while I stalked Margaux's Twitter. Her page was private. I searched for her on Instagram. Another private page. That was a dead end.

I gave Jake Ellis back his phone. He wiped it off, got rid of my germs.

He said, "You're sweating."

"It's fucking hot and I'm carrying heat."

Walking back, I saw her. I saw Margaux. She was outside, near a restaurant, in a section that led to five or six levels of parking on this end of the Grove, feet away from the large fountain.

She was with a guy, a well-built young man who was about six feet tall, had to be in his midthirties, definitely older than Margaux, and she was arguing with him the same way Mrs. Garrett had been arguing with Mr. Garrett when they had entered their mansion, only this was a lovers' spat being performed in public, around many people. The confrontation was intense, but contained. The guy had on shorts, sandals, tank top, dark shades. He rocked a three-hundred-dollar haircut. He had a movie star look, but a lot of losers down here had the same barber.

Jake Ellis said, "What's the move, bruv?"

"Give it a second."

"Looks like he's about to hit her."

"I wish a motherfucker would."

Jake Ellis fell back and I moved forward, went toward Margaux, easy steps, like I was approaching a wild horse, didn't want to scare her and make her go wild. Her argument was frustrated whispers. I couldn't tell if the guy she was in conflict with was black or white. It had to be her boyfriend, the baby daddy, maybe not too happy to hear she was having his baby. The closer I got, as I moved by women dressed in Lululemon yoga pants, as I moved by women walking with their nannies as their nannies pushed their employers' baby strollers, as I passed by hipster and yuppie fathers carrying their newborn babies, as I stepped by families who didn't mind the heat as they moved from air-conditioned business to air-conditioned business, the boy with my daughter looked more Arab, the kind from the Horn of Africa, mixed with the African nations in that region. I counted up from zero, and by the time I was at twenty, Margaux turned, felt my energy invading her space, shifted like she knew someone was staring at her, turned to curse the intruder out the way she had cursed out that girl at TGIF, but saw it was me, blinked, and shock covered her face. She said something to the guy, and he looked at me, saw my hard expression, and he turned around, mixed with the mainstream crowd, headed for the escalators. I went to where Margaux was. She was wide-eyed, expression incredulous.

"You followed me?"

"Who was that guy?"

She shivered, wiped away more tears. "I don't believe this."

"Believe it."

"How did you know where I was?"

"We have the same DNA."

Jake Ellis passed by us. Margaux didn't notice him. I don't think she had had a good look at him back at TGI Fridays, not when he was in the bar, not when he was driving. Her mind was too focused on me to see that my partner in crime was following the boy she was arguing with.

"Who was that guy?"

"My ex."

"What do you mean your ex? Not your boyfriend? You broke up with him?"

"Why are you following me?"

"Answer me."

"He's my ex. Not my boyfriend. I used to date him . . . not long ago."

"You're seeing two men?"

"Not your business."

"Don't cheat on your present with your past and expect it to last."

"How long have you been stalking me?"

"What does he have to do with you calling me all of a sudden?"

"Do you have the money?"

"I'm here to see what's going on."

"Don't follow me. Not unless you have the money."

"I'm your dad."

"You're my father, not my dad."

"You have to trust me."

"Ken Swift, I don't know you."

"You were worried about USC winning."

"So what?"

"Gambling debt? Is that what this is all about?"

She walked away from me.

I followed her. "Where are you going?"

"Leave me alone, Ken Swift."

"You have to trust me."

"I have to meet my boyfriend. He's the one I trust. He's the one I'm hurting."

"How are you hurting him?"

"Not your business."

"Are you juggling two guys?"

"Fuck off."

"*K'ebet'i.*"

"Call me a spoiled brat. At least I'm not a murderer."

I snapped, "Tsigereda."

"Don't call me that name."

"Tsigereda."

She shouted, "Balthazar Walkowiak, Balthazar Walkowiak, Balthazar Walkowiak!"

People stared at us. Security looked our way, concerned, hands on guns. They didn't see a father arguing with a daughter. They saw a hip black man bothering a white Goth woman.

Margaux said, "The price is now seventy thousand."

"If I don't have fifty, how the hell you think I have seventy?"

"Follow me again, and I swear . . . I'll mention that name to the police."

"Sure."

"And I'll need that money in two days."

"What happens in two days?"

"You heard me. I need that money in forty-eight hours."

"And if I don't have it in forty-eight hours?"

Desperation lines rose and aged her before my eyes. "I need that money."

"Margaux."

"Balthazar Walkowiak, Balthazar Walkowiak, Balthazar Walkowiak."

My daughter walked away, headed back toward the Farmers Market part of the Grove. I waited where I was. Jake Ellis was back in five minutes. By then Margaux had vanished.

I asked, "What you get on that pretty boy with the Hollywood muscles?"

"Got the plates from his whip. He's driving a two-seater BMW."

"Balling."

"Cherry red. Last year's model. That's the guy who knocked her up?"

"She said that's her ex-boyfriend. Not the sperm donor."

"He left in a hurry. Like a sperm donor."

"He got spooked."

"That was guilt."

"Guilt like a motherfucker."

"Well, he had a hot number waiting in the car for him to get back."

"Player."

"Big-time."

I took a breath, mind on Margaux. "If there are two guys, maybe she's in a situation."

"He saw you, then left like he was scared too."

"Like he thought I was a hit man."

"Or worse. An undercover cop."

"He make you?"

"Nah. He was busy looking back like he was checking for you. I followed him up the escalators until he got to his level, then let him move on before I walked behind him."

I looked at my hand, at my complexion. "He wouldn't know I was her dad."

"Depends on how long he's been around. Pre-white or post-white."

"Right now Jesus wouldn't know I was her dad."

"No fault of yours."

"Maybe she is seeing two guys and don't know who knocked her up."

"I watch *Lauren Lake's Paternity Court*. Lot of that don't-know-who-the-daddy-is going around. It's an epidemic. Don't think your extorting daughter would be immune to such treachery."

"And maybe this is tied to her needing the fifty large."

"How would fifty thousand fix that? I could see it if the guy wanted that much to pay her, to coax the girl to get rid of it. Spend fifty grand now, save a few million in the long run. But this is the other way around. That's if she is pregnant. Is this a con? Something else could be popping."

"Something else. Regardless. She sees me as the cash cow."

"What did she say to you?"

"Was furious I had found her. I shook her. She mentioned Florida."

"Again."

"She raised the amount to seventy."

"She penalized you for tracking her."

"Said she needed it in forty-eight hours."

"She's in a fix."

"She is." I nodded. "Dared me to follow her again. Told me to fuck off."

"Yeah, you should have had a son. We would've beat his ass real good."

Jake Ellis's San Bernardino phone rang, stopped that conversation. He answered.

He looked up at the sky as if he saw the satellite that gave our coordinates, said, "We stopped at Barnes and Noble in the Grove to get a book on Ethiopia Ken Swift wanted. I know you don't care about Ethiopia. Yes, I'm sure he knows too. We won't be late. About that. Well, we had no idea what Garrett was going to say. Well, he was nicer to you than he was to us. I'm sorry. No, I wasn't trying to be funny. I didn't mean that in a disrespectful way. Apologies."

He talked for a moment, rubbed the bridge of his nose the whole time, then killed the call.

I said, "San Bernardino has us on a tight leash. Been that way all week."

"We need to get to the next meeting spot so we can wrap this day up."

"Sounded like I heard some screaming. The boss never screams."

"Garrett got everybody in a fucked-up mood."

"Think he'll pay by midnight?"

"If not, there will be a war by 12:01."

I walked side by side with Jake Ellis, the weight of my .38 on my right side.

I said, "Get those plates on that boy's German hoopty run. See what you can find out."

Jake Ellis took out his personal phone, sent a text message to one of his contacts.

He said, "Will be done by morning. No later than tomorrow afternoon."

"Why so long?"

"Not everybody is working today."

"We are."

"Not everybody jumps for us like they do San Bernardino."

"Must be nice."

"San Bernardino scares you."

"San Bernardino scares everyone."

"I know. Scares the hell out of me. Makes me want to go back to Africa."

CHAPTER 10

WE LEFT THE Grove like Batman and Robin, hit Third Street, mixed with the pandemonium in the Fairfax District, fought to get to La Brea, then mixed with slow-moving madness, went south. Jake Ellis put on something by Nigerian singer and songwriter Mr Eazi. "Leg Over."

I said, "West African artists are killing the game right now."

He wasn't ready to let go of whatever was brewing inside.

We let that sweet vibe try to alleviate a sour mood. The song ended and a nasty look returned to his face, and with residual anger, his hands strangling his steering wheel, he barked out his thoughts, said, "Garrett's colorless people crawled out of ice caves in Europe."

Garrett was no longer on my radar. My concentration remained on Margaux.

I wanted to know whom she had been arguing with.

My mind tuned Jake out, and I went back to my issues, my life, my new trouble. Not that I wanted to talk about it over and over, but Jake Ellis was driving like a maniac, in a foul mood.

I diverted him from Garrett and pulled him into my world.

I said, "I failed as a husband and now I see I failed as a father. I won't get over that shit."

He made an exasperated sound. "Bruv, you were twenty-one. Marriage is for grown folks, not children with raging hormones. Both of you needed time to grow up. Jimi Lee was nineteen."

"She was nineteen, a child gone wild, using fake ID, drinking and dancing on Sunset."

"Most marriages are henna."

"I wanted mine to be a tattoo."

"Lot of money being made in tattoo removal."

"That severe depression some women get after they have a baby. She had that."

"Might have been part of it, but it was more than that with Jimi Lee, and you know that. She had scholarships to Ivy League schools and gave it all up when she got knocked up."

I nodded. "Man, when we were twenty-one."

"Before you met Jimi Lee, bruv, we was on Sunset three-peating every weekend. We probably made the stock in Trojans double."

"Magnum should have at least sent us a thank-you card."

"Or we should have sent them one."

"You ain't never lied."

"The eighties started off nice. Lakers were killing it. We had the Rams and the Raiders. Pretty women were everywhere. Westwood was the place to hang out, until the Rolling 60s shot at that Mansfield Hustlers Crip, missed, and killed that girl. After that, your police chief Daryl Gates had the LAPD down there by UCLA busting as many black and brown heads as they could. They did all they could to run blacks out of Westwood and keep them corralled on the dark side of town."

I nodded. "One life in Westwood had more value than all the black lives in South Central."

"If I remember it right, they called 1988 'The Year of the Gang.'"

"Should have been called the decade of the gang. Crack sales were at an all-time high. White man brought the drugs into the community and everyone fought to sell dope to get rich."

"Bruv, the nineties were rough. That teenage girl Latasha Harlins was gunned down by that Korean lady, and the white-lady judge didn't give a damn about that fifteen-year-old black girl, let the Korean walk. People think the Rodney King verdict caused the LA riots, but it was the one-two punch of Harlins and King. City on fire for days. Koreans were on roofs with guns shooting at black folks. The riots did a billion dollars in damage to LA. Surprised we made it out alive."

"I think that was when I first decided I wanted to escape America. That shit was too much. As soon as a black man turned off La Cienega and hit Wilshire toward Rodeo Drive, Beverly Hills cops were pulling you over and had you on the curb until they made up a reason to charge you."

"Dirty cops were planting drugs left and right. Clean cops said nothing. So all were dirty."

"Imagine if we had had social media back then. Twitter would have been on fire."

"Bruv, you have it now and they still doing the same thing as they did back then."

"In the nineties, I wanted to get on a plane and get away from this madness. Away from gangs. I was scared of the cops, and the Crips and Bloods had me scared to wear blue or red. Gangs were insane and people were getting killed over the color of their shoestrings."

"All you had to do was get a one-way ticket and follow me across the ocean."

I nodded. "You have a house in Ghana. You have your degrees. You're a culinary king."

"You spent your money on Jimi Lee. I used my stash to go to uni, to build a home, and vacation in Brazil. I chilled in Belgium. France. Smoked weed with models in Amsterdam."

"I was twenty-two, married to a nineteen-year-old, and we had a newborn to feed."

"That lasted how long?"

"Five years."

"Once you were divorced, you could've traveled around the world with me."

"Time flies. Margaux was nine or ten the last time I saw her."

"You could've been gone ten years ago. I told you about the Senegalese girl."

"Yeah, you did."

"I had her waiting on you. Girl was beautiful as beautiful gets. Like you like them. 'As dark as the tents of Kedar.'"

"You went to Song of Solomon and got biblical on me."

"She would've been biblical and taken you to heaven every night."

"I missed out on a religious experience."

"She was nineteen then. Had been in university since she was fifteen. Smart and sexy. If you'd gone over, you'd have had a loyal inamorata the moment you stepped off the plane. She was ready for you. She was excited. I thought you'd eventually come over, and I talked you up to her big-time, almost every day. She got her degree in nursing but was a singer and dancer too."

"I didn't want to miss my daughter growing up. I stood next to Jimi Lee while she was in labor for those fourteen hours, then saw Margaux being born. I saw my daughter move from being inside Jimi Lee's belly and welcomed her to the world. I held her first. Best day of my life."

"How'd that work out? Tell me, remind me, how did that work out?"

"Compatriot, kick me while I'm down."

"It's easier on the knees that way."

"Shut up."

"Did you ever take a DNA test? Are you sure Sammy Sosa isn't her real daddy?"

"Shut up."

"Michael Jackson? Put on 'Billie Jean' and see if she yells 'he, he, he' and moonwalks."

I laughed at my friend as he ranked on me. "Stop it, bro."

"You better laugh at all of my jokes."

"She went to those private schools. Black schools weren't good enough for her mother. Margaux is Mississippi and Ethiopia. And now I have lived to see identity was sold to my daughter through a lens of people who don't understand her. I mean, you don't see a lot of white people shipping their kids to black charter schools to get educated. But my people here in LA are not happy unless their kids are at an expensive private school. Then they can put that bumper sticker on their cars as a message to others that they are the right kind of black. My daughter has bleached her identity, bro. I wasn't there to stop that shit. My job would have been to shut it down. Not everybody can take being teased or have someone insulting your natural hair day and night."

"Bruv, it is not your fault. Jimi Lee kept her from you."

I snapped, "Bro, I fucking know that. I didn't fight hard enough to keep my daughter."

Jake Ellis was unmoved by my outburst. He smiled because he knew my buttons. "All you did was fight. Lot more to it than just that. You had to deal with her family. With her father. With her mother. The way they treated you, how they came at you, bruv, that was war."

"I know that. I was there. I had to live . . . suffer through that day and night."

"Bruv. I'm trying to keep it light. But I get you. Assimilation is strong here. But your daughter is right. Higher value is placed upon being light-skinned here, and it is the same way in Africa. They still raise the colonialist there. They say if you are going to church and you see a white man on the way, you better go back home because you've just seen God."

"Is that a joke?"

"Not a joke. They say on church day, if you see a white person, you've seen God."

"That's ridiculous."

"Walking on water. Men living in whales. Most beliefs are ridiculous."

"So some Africans think their god is a white man walking down the road on Sunday."

"Some believe that being white, or as white as you can get, means you're highly favored."

"Jesus. Always considered Africans black and proud."

"The white man influences all. Will pick apart a culture until nothing is left but the bones."

I took a breath. Redid my past in my mind, imagined different choices, found a better life than this one. "You're right. Staying here after my divorce was a waste of time. All I did was work and pay alimony and child support. I worked on taking care of others and did nothing for myself."

"You could've been crying on the soft, nurturing breasts of a Senegalese woman."

"And you say she was real pretty?"

"Gorgeous. Like the French actress Aïssa Maïga."

"I was on the rebound and didn't need to be under another woman's spell."

"Women make you weak."

"Never weak, bro. Just wasn't raised to be a player."

"Why didn't you go to the islands and meet one of those soca queens?"

"Bro, the way they can do isolations and only move their asses is some voodoo shit."

"Nothing moving but that booty whining and popping. They make God cry tears."

"That African blood still runs hot in those island girls."

He asked, "Ever?"

I shook my head. "Never."

"Bruv, you ain't lived until you've ridden the waves an island girl makes at midnight."

"All those Sandals commercials show dark-skinned black people skinning and grinning and serving drinks to way too many smiling white Brits. They just show dark skin entertaining and smiling and massaging suntanned pink skin. Euros are having fun while dark-skinned people tend to their every concern with a smile. Nah, bro. Slavery is over down there, right?"

"You know when they advertise California, they show Beverly Hills, not Leimert Park."

"Black people not allowed at those hotels?"

"Same black people that are allowed in Beverly Hills. Blacks with money."

"Black people like massages too. We like to have fun. We like food. We like dark-skinned black people to oil us up and rub us down. We love black people. We have some in our families."

"Why not just get a gorgeous American girl?"

"Was burned out on America and trying to get back home to Africa any way I could."

"Africans from most nations are trying to get to Atlanta, New York, LA, and Miami."

"Wanted to be where I saw billboards with black faces. Magazine covers with black faces. African movies. A nation with a black ruler. That's where my head was back then."

"You could've traveled the world with me and met all kinds of pretty girls. I could have taken you places where the moment they see black men, they treat you like royalty. Or you could've finished university abroad, had five degrees, three masters, and four PhDs by now."

"Five degrees?"

"I know Africans who speak ten languages and have more degrees than that."

"And still broke."

"Education is about more than profit. A man should never leave from learning."

"You're right. I never should have dropped out of UCLA. I was so fucking close to my dream I could taste it. One year away. But that summer. I met her. That summer was so hot, was so hot it scorched all my dreams." I paused. "My life was better before I met Margaux's mom."

"You'd drop that Eskimo Rachel Redman if Jimi Lee showed up and flashed a nipple."

"Not even if she showed a whole titty. They should be sagging by now anyway."

"That long black wavy hair down her back. Petite with a nice shape. Perfect skin."

"Shut up."

Jake Ellis laughed. "Sagging or not, you'd fall for her and be glad you did."

That truth silenced me, sent me back to old memories and bad thoughts. The way I felt with Jimi Lee at the start, how I would get inside of her and she made me want to weep and moan, how we would rock and roll until there was no jazz left for the jazzing, I remembered. She was a small woman but that little red rooster rocked me in slow motion like she was a big woman, got on top and worked me and made my orgasm feel like it weighed three hundred pounds. I remembered the melody; I remembered the harmony. I remembered being in a bad love.

Jake Ellis asked, "You ever hear from Margaux's godmother out in Malibu?"

I shifted, broke away from my erotic daydream. "What?"

"Gelila. Lila. Margaux's godmother. What happened to her?"

A guilt-laced memory from a heated night came to me in flashes. Jake Ellis knew all of my crimes, but not all of my sins. "I have no idea. After the fight, everyone broke contact with me."

"Lila was a Jessica Rabbit. Rich girl was a hot number. Living in Malibu and rocking that little red Corvette. Bet that sex was good. I should've tried to get that just to say I got that."

I cleared my throat, glad that the walls in my apartment couldn't talk. "She was the only woman I ever saw you shy away from."

"Bruv, I didn't shy away. She's Ethiopian. I'm Ghanaian. I'm superior by a long shot."

"She said the same about you."

"She lied. Ethiopia has a smaller GDP. They are landlocked. Our literacy rate is higher."

That made me chuckle. "East Africa and West Africa can be like Crips and Bloods."

"More like USC against UCLA. Nigeria and Ghana are like Crips and Bloods."

"I've never understood the rivalry between African nations. Most of it seems childish."

"Some folks in her country look down on the rest of Africa."

"Because they were never colonized. None are the descendants of African slaves. But, hell, everybody in the world looks down on everybody. Mississippi looks down on New York as much as New Yorkers look down on Mississippi. Stuff like that never mattered to me."

"Lila was beautiful. Sharply bridged nose, eyes that make you think she had some Chinese in her background, high cheekbones, long face, narrow, high forehead, broad brows, long legs, sweet bottom, always well dressed, always smelled good, articulate, brilliant, and everything about her went together, made her look amazing. She was Jimi Lee's best friend, and your daughter's godmother, so I never tried to dig her out. She would've wanted to get serious. Lila would look at Jimi Lee, see her married with a kid, then try and achieve the same status."

"If you can pass on a woman like Lila, then you'll never get married."

"Not without a sharp blade threatening my nuts."

"What if she makes the best Jollof rice ever?"

"Ethiopians don't make Jollof. If they did, I wouldn't touch it."

"But what if she learned and made Jollof twice as good as yours?"

"She can do that, we could marry, but we have to live in separate houses."

"That's not a marriage."

"Neither is living with a nagging wife who refuses to have sex with you."

"Been there, done that."

"But as pretty as Lila was, if she made good Jollof, she could make a man give up polygamy. But that Jollof would have to be so good that God himself would give up his powers."

"Africans are passionate about their Jollof rice."

Jake Ellis told me, "West African women have had fights in the streets about who makes the best Jollof. Ghanaians, Nigerians, Senegalese, people from Sierra Leone and Liberia, have fought and had Jollof cook-offs, have had contests over Jollof that way your country cousins in the 901 argue over who has made the best barbecue ribs during Memphis in May."

"My cousins are your cousins. They talk funny to you and you talk funny to them."

We laughed and moved on to new subjects—the Lakers, the Rams, USC, the upcoming concerts at Hollywood Bowl, wondered how much decent tickets for Maxwell's or Janet's concert tour would cost, but I knew Garrett was off Jake Ellis's mind as much as Jimi Lee was off mine.

My daughter was a liar, just like her mother. And with a few words she had demanded money, broken my heart, then sashayed away, never looked back, just like her goddamn mother.

When we were mid-Wilshire and passing the taco shop owned by Danny Trejo, the dude from the movie *Machete*, I said, "I think Margaux has a gambling problem."

"How so?"

I told him about how she said she needed USC to lose a home game.

He asked, "You think she's fifty thou deep because of gambling?"

"Could be. She wouldn't be the first on my side of the family with that habit."

"Who bets against USC at home? They might as well have lit their money on fire."

I nodded. "Someone desperate. And my daughter sounds like she's desperate."

"How that guy fit in?"

"Bookie? He's here to collect the fifty large she owes."

"He left like he was running from slave catchers. She said he's her ex-boyfriend, right?"

"Could be a lie. She's a liar. You said he had a woman waiting in the car."

Anxious, Jake Ellis nodded. "We need to get back to San Bernardino business."

Something profound was on Jake Ellis's mind. I knew him. I knew that stern expression.

The Ghanaian knew me. He knew I was stressed.

And with all that stress on my mind, a soft hum reminded me I had forgotten something.

CHAPTER 11

JAKE ELLIS STAYED on La Brea, then hooked a left on Washington, zoomed toward LA's heart. The area was mostly Spanish-speaking with enough signage to feel like we were in Tijuana. Colorful murals and graffiti. Barbed wire around businesses. Wrought-iron bars on the windows of the homes, making most look like diminutive prisons. I thought we were rolling up on a dozen pictures of Hitler, but it was the president's orange face on the Führer's body.

Jake Ellis pulled over. Two minutes later, a Mini Cooper pulled up behind us. The driver of the Mini was Latina. Purple cowboy boots. I SUPPORT DACA T-shirt on. Hair brown, pink, red, and purple, tied back in a ponytail. Colorful tats spilled out of all sides of her Daisy Dukes. Sun-kissed legs. Keen brows. Face frustrated. One of San Bernardino's overworked employees.

In accent-free English she said, "Whaddup, homies. Long time no see."

Jake Ellis said, "Whaddup, Esmerelda."

I motioned at her attire. "Aren't you scared to wear that T-shirt nowadays?"

"We're safe in Los Angeles. Sanctuary city."

"Well, keep out of Arizona."

She countered, "And you should keep out of Saint Louis."

"It's the sixties down there. All they need is German shepherds and water hoses."

"Neo-Nazis are up this way too, in Torrance, Redondo Beach, and Hermosa Beach. I was just alerted on my phone. They call themselves the Rise Above Movement. Or RAM. Don't confuse it with the football team. They have videos telling each other to say the fourteen words."

I asked, "What are those?"

"'We must secure the existence of our people and a future for white children.'"

"Sounds like paranoia to me. Impossible to maintain their definition of white."

"That purity crap is bullshit. They're mutts acting like best dog in show. Most of those racists need to publicly take DNA ancestry tests, then sit the fuck down with the other losers."

I said, "The junkyard dogs are barking the loudest."

"This is why we should unite. Blacks and browns should've always been united. You know we used to be united. We were the Los Angeles Pobladores. Forty-four brave settlers and four warriors from Mexico founded Los Angeles. Over half of the group was of African descent."

"I know. People have forgotten, but I know."

"We've been led to believe we are each other's enemy, and instead of being as strong as the Amazon River, we're separated like the Black River and the White River in Brazil. Too bad we only unite on Cinco de Mayo. Or when a riot is in progress, but even then, we're competing."

"Everyone competes for everything. It's called capitalism."

She grinned. "Or dating."

"That too."

"We need to unite the other three hundred sixty-four days too. And not just on special occasions to break out a window in a

Korean-owned business to snatch a flat-screen or take a new sofa as reparation."

"Tell your people and I'll tell mine. But I don't think it'll help."

"I know. They like sofas and TVs."

"Oh yeah. Those riot sales are better than being on *The Price Is Right*."

"But on the real. We need to come together. We are the majority. Together we are the mainstream. We must go in one direction and be powerful like the Amazon River. Especially the way things are now. We're back in the fifties. They want us to either disappear or shut the fuck up."

I nodded. "Divided we just watch each other fall like we each have cultural dyspraxia."

"Cultural dyspraxia." She tendered a small smile. "If you have time, march with us."

"San Bernardino got us on the clock. But I hear you're at protests every day."

"If they come for us, they'll come for you. The KKK will march down Crenshaw."

"And the Nation of Islam will be there to greet them, along with Crips and Bloods, and some old-school Black Panthers. Fools know where to go, and know where to not go."

"They know to picket down by Disneyland, or in Simi Valley."

"Exactly. In this box, our box between the 10, 405, 110, and 105, they can get a permit to march, but if your people and my people show up, there will be a lot of blood on the dance floor."

She slid Jake Ellis an envelope. "DACA rally is in front of the Wilshire Federal Building."

My partner took the envelope, felt its weight. "Was starting to wonder if that was for us."

She was more comfortable with me than she was with my African friend.

She went on talking to me. "It pisses me off that so many Mexicans who were lucky to be born here are not siding with the Dreamers.

Since they are citizens, those anchor babies think that they will be accepted more by America by shunning Mexico and acting as white as possible."

"Part of the conditioning."

"They think that since they can speak English with no accent, the ones who can't speak perfect English are below them."

"It was that way with former slaves, with freed men, and men who had never been enslaved. Freed people didn't want their daughters and sons to be married to former slaves. They were adamant about that piece of status, almost as bad as the people against race mixing."

"With us, the ones here don't want their children marrying wetbacks."

"The invisible class system that runs through my community, just like with yours."

"Speaking Spanish or the Queen's English, we're all the same to them. Our own will turn on us and push us up front so the violent racists can beat us, will help the racists, and then they will be beaten as well. We have too many traitors. Way too many deserters and spies."

"We all have spies. Africans captured Africans and sold them to the slavers for guns. The FBI had Uncle Toms inside the Black Panther Party and used their lies to bring the group down."

"I saw a movie where Jews betrayed Jews and turned them in to Germans. They sided with Hitler. That blew my mind. Jews pretended to be German, like my people pass for white."

"There will always be sellouts. Judas wasn't the first, but he raised the bar."

"I have to get back down on Wilshire so I can stand in this heat and be heard."

"Aren't you afraid ICE will just round up everyone down there?"

"We can't keep living in the shadows. Hiding and being afraid takes too much energy."

"Never a dull moment."

"All of this fighting reminds me of one of my favorite quotes. 'To be led by a liar is to ask to be told lies. To be led by a tyrant is to sell yourself and those you love into slavery.'"

I asked, "Malcolm X?"

She grinned. "Octavia Butler. *Parable of the Talents.* One of my favorite books."

I grinned. "Hey, wonder if you can do me a favor?"

"What's that?"

"We have tags to a car. I'm having issues with this dude. Personal thing, if you know what I mean. Can you get the DMV on it? We have a contact, but they seem to be on vacation today."

"Day like this, everybody not socially aware is at a beach."

"The city is a baking parking lot."

"You know how LA gets every Friday. How soon you need this DMV thing?"

"It's sort of urgent."

"Sure. I have a hookup at the DMV in Inglewood."

Jake Ellis showed me the info he'd put in his phone. I showed it to Esmerelda.

She said, "Well, Ken Swift, I'll need your number so I can call you."

I gave her my private number, then asked, "How much will this set me back?"

"You scratch my back, I scratch yours."

"Quid pro quo."

"Something for something."

"Favor for a favor."

"Cool."

"Cool."

She hurried back into her Mini Cooper and drove away. The bold message on the back of her DACA T-shirt read WE WANT TO BE HUMANIZED, NOT DEMONIZED. Jake Ellis handed me the envelope as he pulled from the curb, then followed the Mini Cooper east. The Mini Cooper didn't have any license plates, nothing that could be traced back to the DMV, same as this Mustang.

"That cutie was bending your ear and flirting hard."

"No, she wasn't. She's recruiting people to fight in this ongoing civil and cultural war."

"She likes you. Had her suntanned breasts all in the window for you to look at."

"I maintained eye contact. Kept it professional."

"She was happy to get your number."

"It's a business situation. All about Margaux and whatever she has going on."

"See how Esmerelda made her booty do that happy twitch when she went to her car?"

"That's just how she walks. She used to dance. Rachel Redman has that same walk."

"Third time she's talked to you that way. You always passing it up."

"If only I were more like you, then I'd break protocol and investigate."

"Go investigate Esmerelda, like Rachel investigated the Russian when you left town."

"Thanks for always bringing that up."

"Nice tanned legs. Tight little body. Fit. Solid. Bet she can salsa her ass off."

"She's barely older than my daughter."

"And she wants you to make her call you daddy."

"Bro."

"Bruv. Should I follow her for investigation?"

"If I was still twenty-one, I'd be up there in the car with her, investigating my ass off."

Traffic remained bumper-to-bumper on every freeway and on every main street.

"Ken Swift, what do you think it would be like if black Americans had been freed, then given their own state to live in? What if you had been segregated and given land that way?"

"Like those internment camps they call reservations?"

"No, I mean a real state. Like North or South Dakota. Like the many white people who wanted an all-white state, what if they had given black Americans an all-black state of their own?"

"If they had us all corralled in one spot, you know they'd've tested the A-bomb on us."

"Think so?"

"They injected black men with syphilis. Operated on black women with no anesthesia. Used black babies as alligator bait in Florida. Burned down Black Wall Street and kept it out of the news. They would've dropped an A-bomb on us and nobody would have ever known we'd existed. The government has done a lot. Now slave catchers are shooting us in the back."

Esmerelda turned left at Crenshaw, and I assumed she was headed toward DACA rallies and heated protests near UCLA. Jake Ellis tooted his horn and turned right, headed south toward our side of LA, where Muslim brothers were at every intersection selling *Final Call* newspapers and bean pies. I looked at the money, mostly fifties, a few twenties, knew it was our standard fee, then handed Jake Ellis half. He put his part in his pocket without counting it. I folded my bills, wished I had earned fifty thousand, then stuffed my part of the payday in my suit pocket.

I looked in the side mirror, saw what was behind us, then said, "Slave catchers."

Six police cars zoomed our way. Came up behind us like a raging storm.

Jake Ellis said, "Drop your .38 in the stash spot while I trafficate."

I was already stashing my gat before he told me. Jake Ellis turned on his right blinker, pulled over to the right. The fleet of squad cars took to both lanes, passed doing over sixty, the Rodney King brigade wailing and hot on the scent of someone else on the *se habla español* side of town. When One Time was a half mile away, Jake Ellis signaled, then pulled from the curb.

Jake Ellis said, "*Koti* been on the move all day."

I nodded. "Always on the move on this side of town."

Jake Ellis shook his head. "I don't know about that Dreamer shit Esmerelda is selling."

"What you mean?"

"If people are here illegally, they are not supposed to be here. Her argument is emotional. Makes no sense. They are illegal and want to go march to protest. That's ridiculous."

"It's the intersection where political and emotional meets culture and entitlement."

"I don't like your new president. He reminds me of Nigerian conmen. But why everybody on the left mad at Adolf Twitler? Bomb-Dropping Obama deported illegals both day and night."

"Don't diss my boy."

"He split up a lot of families, in between dropping bombs like a Gap Band record."

"Tread lightly."

"Illegal means illegal. They are breaking the law and are mad because they're getting called on breaking the law. She's right about the dissension. I went to a board of directors meeting. Legals hate illegals because the illegals want to skip the long line because they have jumped a wall and picked a few berries. And that anchor-baby thing makes no sense."

"We've never talked about that. Same immigration problem in Africa?"

"At least three million are in Ghana alone. Most of the beggars on the streets. Illegals have no jobs and poverty brings crime. That is a fact. The same as here, but different. But here, the illegals coming here to have babies, American babies, and demanding rights, is ludicrous."

I said, "Like she said, this was their land."

"Was. Like this car used to belong to Ford, then the car dealer. Now it's mine."

"You were antsy when she was talking. You wanted to debate all she said."

"If some country was giving out checks for breaking the law, I'd rush there too. They are not having that madness in Mexico or Central America, yet they feel entitled to it up here."

"Closet conservative."

"Ghanaians, Kenyans, Tanzanians, and Nigerians love your arrogant president."

"You and Garrett could have been friends."

"Oh, that racist coward blew a chance at an intellectual debate from his first sentence."

We talked more, but something remained off. I'd been his friend most of my life. I knew when Jake Ellis was pissed off. I was pissed too, that sit-down with Garrett heavy on my mind.

Jake Ellis said, "We have to talk about Margaux before we go home."

I nodded. "I know."

CHAPTER 12

WE CRUISED AND five minutes later we were in Culver City, in the zip code named after a real estate developer from Nebraska, back when only a certain race of people could buy property and the Jews were locked out, Italians were treated like shit, and the black man wasn't allowed to own anything but his own misery. Jake Ellis parked on Washington Boulevard right under the Expo train line, the route that stretched from downtown LA to Santa Monica. Everything west of here was majority white. If you drove east, within ten minutes, you'd swear you were in Mexico.

As we got out of the car, I asked, "What's this new spot called?"

He motioned at a sign. "Platform shopping mall."

We walked side by side. "Bro, anything here black-owned?"

He laughed. "Bruv, c'mon, now. Popeyes chicken ain't gluten-free."

"I see SoulCycle. That's not a black business?"

He laughed harder. "Black people lost the right to *soul* when the *train* went off the air."

"Yeah. The top soul singers are Adele and Sam Smith."

This part of Culver City was filled with shops that sold shirts and dresses that cost more than a Walmart worker's paycheck. Cost seven dollars for a small ice cream. Simple folding chairs sold for 1,250 dollars. Cost eight dollars for juices. Area was clean. It was crowded and quiet at the same time.

A little nervous, I asked, "I left my .38 stashed in your car. We have a job here?"

"You don't need it. Stuff on my mind."

My nostrils flared. "What's going on, bro?"

"Bruv, I'll get to that."

"Well, you know I don't like being in the heat and sun like you do."

"Won't be but a minute. I need to decompress, get Pasadena out of my blood."

As we eased into the area, families looked at us. They looked at us, but no alarms went off. If I was still in my twenties, this same crowd would be uneasy. A black man in his twenties was always seen as a threat. We were all Trayvon or Mike Brown. I'd lived long enough and aged out of that group, but a black man never aged out of being seen as trouble from sea to shining sea.

Jake Ellis got an ice cream cone, smiled like a two-year-old kid, and I copped a single-origin espresso. We copped a squat on a bench outside of Blue Bottle Coffee, watched the heat-loving young Europeans and their spouses and seeds living in the absence of too many brown- and black-skinned minorities. They were as at peace without us as we were without them.

Jake Ellis said, "This is my secret chill-out spot. Calmer than the Grove. I used to chill at the Villas at Playa Vista. Real nice down there too, especially if I take a date to happy hour or to the movie theater; real impressive down that way. Actors and Clippers and Lakers live down there."

"Sounds like gold-digger central."

"You know it."

"Why are we here?"

"Because being around you is stressful."

I asked, "How long you been peeping this spot?"

"I've been coming here a month or so."

"Lot closer to the house. Small. Few shops. No crowd. Perfect."

"Cool to have a couple of chill-out spots to choose from."

"It's quaint and sterile. All the businesses face inward, so from the streets you can't tell what's up. My bet is that they don't want everybody knowing this spot is here."

"It's like leaving the world I know and sneaking into the basement heaven."

"The basement?"

"In my heaven, Ghanaians are on the top level. In the penthouse eating Jollof."

I asked, "How much rent over this way?"

"Same as the Villas at Playa Vista."

"Which is?"

"Between three and five thousand a month to rent a cracker box."

"Makes sense. We're in a saltine bubble."

"But it's a nice bubble. So nice people should talk with French accents."

"Birkenstocks and fat wedding rings."

Jake Ellis said, "Don't hate. They dated smart, married money."

"Bet they married without a prenup."

"You know what I see when I look at these people?"

"Success?"

"Felons. Criminals. People don't look at this crowd and think criminals, but they are. We assume they are clean, but they have DUIs and felonies on their records, and they get second, third, and fourth chances. Even with a prison record they can get a better job than a black man with no record and a college degree. These men file for bankruptcy every chance they get, shake off debt, and I bet they have more than one baby momma and are behind on child support."

"The neo-Nazis have taken over Twitter."

"Most of those hooligans are violent criminals, but the police let the thugs wear masks and gloves and do their thing from Berkeley to Charlottesville. If you use or sell Silly String on Halloween you can get a thousand-dollar fine and/or six months in jail, but these goons can wear masks and attack you and nothing happens. You get rounded up for small things. For anything. They are stupid criminals, unemployed, selling meth, selling opioids, selling cocaine, drinking and getting high, on probation for robbery and theft, DUIs up the ying-yang, lost their licenses for failure to pay child support, and are inbred, herpes-spreading, HIV-ridden lunatics who have turned racism into a cult fueled on their low self-esteem and unwarranted anger directed against my people."

That assessment got a slow clap from me.

I said, "Jake Ellis, you are the most interesting man in the world."

"*Bruv*, you know I look at them the same way they look at us. They know nothing about me, yet judge me. I know their history, have read of their global massacres. Their religious leaders are pedophiles, or pedophile-adjacent. They've never scared me. I can look in their eyes and they know I have seen their souls and know their truth. They've learned nothing about us and expect us to know everything about them. They cheat their way to the top and use nepotism as a crutch. They are put in charge of Africans much smarter and get to take the credit for African American excellence. I speak eight languages, and they talk to me like I'm the stupid one."

"And they still call you nigger."

"Bruv, that is the only bullet they have in their gun."

"Silver bullet."

"And the silver was stolen from the mines of Africa."

I nodded. "And they manage to hit us in the heart every time."

"What do you see when you look at them, bruv?"

"I see people who used to hang out on the Sunset Strip, drinking, popping pills, waking up with strangers, people who loved to have three-ways and orgies, then grew up."

"They still have three-ways. They still cheat on their spouses. They are unhappy."

I said, "And they have low credit scores."

"That part. Bet most of them have credit scores below six hundred. They are struggling."

I asked, "Your conclusion?"

"Told you. They are no different from us, yet they think they are superior."

"No different. But in reality, they have police departments and a military, and one percent of them have more financial power than all the blacks in this country will ever have."

"If they have power, it is only because you give them power."

"We didn't give them shit. They had guns and kept them away from us."

"Guns. Take away their guns, the tables turn, and the colonialists run. You heard Esmerelda talking about RAM. They are organizing, buying up guns, have training camps, and are planning a war. The way black people have been treated, I'd think you'd be doing that."

"Yeah. Well. We live in the mouth of madness, but we're not the ones gone crazy."

Jake Ellis sucked his teeth. "Weak men need guns in every room."

"Weak men and gangsters. With guns in their hands, both are grave makers."

"Bruv, if all black people ran out and bought twenty guns, laws would change."

I nodded. "Well, yeah. From jaywalking to voting rights, they make the laws. They banned Chinese in 1882. Banned Indians in 1917. Banned Africans in 1924. Japanese internment in '42. Now the Muslims. That's not including Jim Crow and Black Codes."

Jake Ellis said, "You know what a law is?"

"Educate me before your ice cream melts all over your hand, African."

"Just some bullshit a rich, powerful colonialist writes down. He can write down any kind of immorality, and doesn't have to be fair to nobody but the man writing it down, and if it's unfair, that bullshit law doesn't apply to him or his people. Whatever he wants, he can make legal. Whatever he is afraid of, he can make illegal. Whoever he despises, he makes laws that say they have to leave *his* country. His law said he could rape black women and it wasn't a crime. I have read his laws, both new and old. He brought those same laws, writing on paper by his own hand, to Africa. The white man is his own god. He can use ink and paper, and people act like it's just as good as the commandments your Moses allegedly brought from the top of some mountain in the Middle East. White man wrote down that everybody in Africa could be kidnapped and enslaved. He wrote down that the largest continent was a slave field, said that all the dark-hued human beings there were no better than cows, and men like him, men who could not bear the heat of his own god's sun, men like him looked at what he had written down, and because it was in the white man's book, in the white man's language, that was the law of the world. No one polled Africans. They stole people from West Africa. My people. The Dutch. The Spanish. The British. Your America. Like it was a contest. They stole your ancestors. My people. Because even though they knew it was immoral, they wrote down that it was legal. And wypipo from all over joined in."

"Wypipo?"

"White people. That's what they call them on Black Twitter. Wypipo."

"I read that some pope went to Cameroon and stood up in front of everybody and apologized to black Africa for the participation of white Christians in the slave trade."

"What does an apology from one man do? The systemic damage was done. What action came after the apology? What came with that apology? Did the pope go down into the basement at the Vatican and sell some of that African art they stole over the centuries and offer money to *revitalize* what they destroyed? Were diamonds and gold returned? Was a check sent from Europe to any part of Africa? Nah, bruv. Didn't no butter come on that toast. That toast was dry and didn't have no jelly or jam to make it sweet. It was a political apology, meaningless and never acted on, used to keep Africans in a white religion paying monetary tribute to a god who will never accept them. It was no better than the man who beats his wife, buys her flowers the next day, then beats her again the day after. White man's apologies are as good as his treaties have been with the Native Americans. With Africans. With Haitians. With black Americans. The pattern is hidden in plain sight. When you apologize for your wrongs, after that comes *actions*. Where was the goddamn *action*? Who here got forty acres and a mule? I know slave owners were reimbursed for losing their slaves to morality. Slave owners were reimbursed. That is like paying the rapist, the burglar, the thief, because you made him stop his crime. Slaves received nothing for their free labor. Who did America value? And don't get me started with the church. The church reinforced the establishment of colonial governments, especially through the destruction of societal, ethnic, and religious systems in Africa. One man apologized? Must be nice to be able to destroy other cultures, say you're sorry, and walk away with reparations in your hand."

"Jake Ellis, you should give a seminar at Eso Won. Or do a TED Talk."

"Who would listen? Truth only works with those holding empty cups. White people, *wypipo*, *why people*, whatever you want to call them, have done the damage. They try and make themselves out to be the *normal* ones. They write the laws for others based on their point of view that everyone else is less human. Muslim, Native American, African, African American, all seen by them as less human. That's why a man like Garrett can stand in my face and call me a nigger forty-eleven times. That word was his slave master's whip today, and I felt every lash."

"Motherfucker had the nerve to tell us what should insult us, and what should not."

"White privilege mixed with deep-seated hate and ignorance and lack of a soul."

I nodded. "Maybe President Abraham Lincoln was right."

Jake Ellis licked his cone. "How so?"

"Racist Abe argued that blacks and whites should've been separated. Everybody's favorite Republican said that the black man was inferior, would always be inferior, think he said we were incapable of learning, and stressed that blacks and whites should be separated."

"*We were separated.* We were in Africa and they were over here raping, pillaging, and spreading diseases. We were apart until Mr. European decided he didn't want to pay other white men a fair price to raise cotton, sugar, and tobacco. He partnered with Britain, crossed the Atlantic in ships named after their god and his son, kidnapped, killed, bribed with guns, and brought back slave labor to keep from paying his own people. *We were separated.* The good Christians stole Africans and made America great."

"Outside of a race war, like you told Mrs. Garrett, how do we fix it?"

"Just like Nigeria, America needs purging. And the purging has to start first with the educational system and the religious establishments. You can't depend on the oppressor's god."

I sipped my coffee and nodded. "My people have done a lot of marching and praying."

"Your people are wearing out good shoes and begging an earless god."

I took a breath, thought about my life, remembered all the black people like Baldwin who had left, found a place black people were treated better, and almost never came back. Josephine Baker. Nina Simone. Langston Hughes. Charlie Parker. Richard Wright. Paul Robeson. Wherever they went, it wasn't ideal, but it was a different breed of white people, not that crowd that grew up and were brainwashed by *Birth of a Nation*. There was no Klan mentality. They were given respect.

"You're right. I should have left here at least fifteen years ago."

"You say that over and over and over and over. You are a scratched record."

"I could have lived in Liberia, Switzerland, England, and Barbados awhile."

"You could have gone to Ghana and met that beautiful Senegalese woman."

"Just keep rubbing it in."

"Am I lying?"

"I should have. She could have helped me forget an Ethiopian."

"No woman could do that."

"Well, she could have had fun trying."

"You would have had African babies."

"Yeah. Wanted more kids. But not by different women."

"And now Margaux is pregnant and wants her father to give her fifty grand."

"Seventy."

"That's criminal."

"That bothers you."

"It seems to bother me more than it bothers you, and that bothers me. And now with the trip to the Grove, we see someone else, another boy may be involved."

"Yeah. That was why he ran away so fast."

"If he knows you killed a man, that we killed a man, but he doesn't know who I am as of yet, then our reputation was here before we were."

"We killed one man. One accidental murder."

"And no matter how it happened, that enhanced our status with San Bernardino. We moved up in pay grade. A man only has to kill one person to be seen as a killer the rest of his life. That is our reputation. Jimi Lee knew that. In the end, maybe she saw you as a killer, bruv."

"I was her husband. I was her protector. Her provider."

"You may have been her husband, but she saw you as a killer."

"It was more than that. I was African American and she was African."

"She told her family things. They thought you were a dangerous man. That was why a village came to ambush you. Forty men ambushed you, and I bet each one of them was afraid of you. You were a lion battling a pack of hyenas. Your daughter knows about Florida. We cleaned up the scene, but you never know about DNA. We didn't leave a bloody glove, but you never know. Never know if a drop of blood was left behind. The dead man went missing and I know they searched his apartment. I know they looked for traces of blood. If Margaux says that man's name, put it with yours, or ours, even if there is no dead body to be found, just based on circumstantial evidence, on the word from your child, a child who has no reason to lie other than the hate in her heart, we could be dead men walking. I need to know how many she has told about Florida."

"She's not after you. She's been raised to hate me. I'm not human to her."

"If she comes after you for fifty, she'll come this way too, if she knows I'm in America."

I said, "I want to convince myself that she wants that money to go away and have a big African wedding in Addis Ababa."

"Don't lie to yourself. That will keep you from lying to me."

"I know. Pregnant or not, I know there's more to it than that."

"Your daughter is pregnant."

"I think that part is true."

"Why so certain?"

"Before she said it, she put her hand on her belly."

"Before or after, as an afterthought?"

"Before."

"A mother's instinctive move to protect her unborn child."

"From me."

"From the world."

"I wanted to hug her and she rejected me, was protecting her child from me."

Jake Ellis was almost amused. "You're about to become a grandfather."

"Grandkid will dislike me as much as its mother and her mother."

He paused, thinking. "How many people we done hurt?"

I shrugged. "Hundreds."

"One job got out of control."

"San Bernardino will never let us forget that."

"One. That was a turd in the strawberry Kool-Aid of life."

"And Margaux knows about that."

Jake Ellis did an African finger snap, gruffed. "She knows the dead man's name."

I inhaled, rubbed my temples as I exhaled. "Never wanted her to know about this life."

"Bruv, she has to keep her mouth shut."

"I know."

"If Margaux causes a problem, we both know San Bernardino has ice water for blood and won't care if she's your child."

"I know."

"San Bernardino won't care if she's pregnant. San Bernardino won't give a fuck about whoever was in that red BMW, and won't care about the pretty woman he had at his side."

"I know. San Bernardino will protect the interests and reputation of San Bernardino."

"You'd have to handle your own kid, bruv."

"I know. Esmerelda will hit me back. Tomorrow we can make a house call."

"If Margaux talks, if she gets mad because we tracked her to the Grove and the cops come for you, I will have to tell the boss what's been popping today. San Bernardino will handle her. And while you are locked up, San Bernardino will pay people to get to you from the inside."

We stopped talking, let the dry heat and smog sit on us for a moment. Overhead there was a rumble. A metro train passed by going west toward Santa Monica and the beaches; then another sped by going east toward downtown LA. I wished I hadn't gone to meet my daughter.

I said, "I'll look for Margaux tomorrow. I'll stalk her Facebook, see where she checks in, then get in my car and surprise her. Same for the boy in the red car."

"I can go with you. Or we can split the tasks. You go after one. I go after the other."

"I'll do it on my own. Let me try and find my daughter before it goes off the rails."

"You don't have a choice. You go see your daughter. I go visit the boy in the car."

"We still have plastic and a shovel in the trunk of your car."

"I stay ready. Put a man in a four-foot-deep hole, and soon as the cold dirt hits his face, he starts to talk. And if he doesn't talk, then I keep tossing dirt until I fill up the hole."

It was easier talking about slavery, the three-fifths compromise, the Confederacy, the Klan, Black Codes, Jim Crow, eugenics, lynching, the war on drugs, and mass incarceration than this.

I said, "With all you said, this history lesson, I should have been madder at Garrett."

"Bruv, nah. I should've been unaffected like you."

"The way my life is, sometimes I wonder if I'm living in a comedy or a drama."

"Ain't no laugh track. This shit is real. I have a bullet wound to remind me."

"Just because we don't hear laughter, don't mean nobody's laughing."

"Nothing funny about catching lead. Not a damn thing."

With every political conversation, we not only pointed the finger at the rest of the world but we also pointed our fingers at ourselves. We debated or agreed on right and wrong, real and perceived, as an exercise more or less, and sometimes, like now, when we were at a swank spot, I liked to think we were Du Bois and Baldwin at a café on the Champs-Élysées, Josephine Baker and Nina Simone at our sides, talking about the struggle while we were being intellectual and prophetic. Then I felt the weight of an imaginary .38 in my pocket.

I knew who I was. I had been trying to not be this man since I was eighteen.

One job for San Bernardino had led to another and then another.

This had become my prison.

We got up to leave and I glanced at a twenty-something who had been checking out Jake Ellis. East Indian. Mane long and wavy. I'd seen her spying this way, biting her bottom lip, twirling her hair. She had watched Jake Ellis lick his ice cream cone, had eyed him while he pontificated. Jake was the Beyoncé of African men. The cute millennial was with her oblivious husband and precocious child. Jake Ellis winked. She smiled, bounced her foot faster, and again bit the corner of her lip, touched her tresses. I'd never met a married person who didn't regret matrimony, at least for a moment. She had love; it was next to her. Sometimes a baby made love-crazy, fuck-happy couples pull apart. Babies changed the topography of marriage. Marriage became a business; it was no longer fun. Girls wanted to have fun. Most girls. The woman I married had had much fun. Men like Jake Ellis had winked at her, and she had taken them to her bosom.

I said, "Don't look back at that man's wife."

"She's looking at me."

"Let this one turn to stone."

"I think her husband just caught her."

"You make white men want to act out on rage like Michael Douglas in *Falling Down*."

"I wish a motherfucker would."

I shifted, uneasy. "One more thing."

"What, bruv?"

"When you were upstairs getting your tour, Garrett tried to bribe me."

"How much?"

"One hundred and fifty grand. Said he'd pay me in cash."

"That's about . . . six hundred sixty thousand in Ghanaian cedi. Over fifty-three million Nigerian naira."

"He's not the first one with deep pockets to try and bribe one of us."

"Make sure you tell San Bernardino."

"Tomorrow. Again, let Garrett pay up first. Don't want any more complications."

Jake Ellis turned. "Let me go over there and get me a kiss from that sexy MILF."

I grabbed his arm, and we both laughed as we left the white man's overpriced bubble.

Jake Ellis said, "I have to get you home."

"For what?"

"You left your phone home. In case Esmerelda rings and has that info."

"I still can't remember what else I had to do today. But right now, it doesn't matter."

CHAPTER 13

A **MIDDLE-AGED CHRISTIAN** brother dressed in black jeans, gray T, and an LA baseball cap was in the heat, on the corner of Vernon and Crenshaw, holding a large white sign that read JESUS SAVES GANGSTERS TOO! The top half of the word *Jesus* was colored red, the bottom blue. The reverse for the word *gangsters*. People who passed thought it was red, white, and blue, but it was only red and blue. Blue signified the Crips. Red stood for Bloods. On the opposite corner was a Muslim sister selling copies of *Turning the Tide*, the newspaper for the New Black Panther Party. This wasn't Culver City. We waved at the brother and sister like they were family, then cruised back into the heart of Leimert Park, where black scholars preached that African Americans and descendants of black or Negro slaves in other countries were the true descendants of the ancient Hebrew Israelites. We cut through the business district, passed by theaters, hair salons, coffee shops, Eso Won bookstore, bicycle repair shops, and Jamaican restaurants. The area had been designed to be self-contained. Anything anyone needed was no more than ten minutes away. That was the new selling point. Jake Ellis did an easy drive down Degnan, another well-kept street lined with palm and evergreen trees. Air warm, minds troubled, we found our way past dozens of two-story apartment buildings and turned east on Stocker.

We were back off the Crenshaw strip, where too many used the sidewalks as garbage cans. My daddy told me that the way the streets in a neighborhood looked was the way people saw themselves. We were back a few blocks from where people were always popping off and the music was always loud. Our section was pretty quiet, four blocks or so from the main drag, a lot cleaner than the Shaw. The only noise came when the middle school let out. They were the ones who littered. Our box of pride was bounded by Exposition Boulevard on the north, West Vernon on the south, Crenshaw on the west, and South Van Ness and Arlington Avenue on the east. There were maybe thirteen thousand people living in this small box. Most were black, had been a black neighborhood since white flight, but now the demographics were changing. Posters reading RESIST GENTRIFICATION or WE SHALL NOT BE MOVED, WE WILL IMPROVE were in almost every yard and on every light pole.

A war was going on. Between blacks and America, it was a never-ending war.

It had been a long day. I didn't need another fight. But one was coming.

An Asian man in a van was parked, hustling T-shirts with Afrocentric sayings. HARRIET TUBMAN MOURNS FOR FREDDIE GRAY. MY PRESIDENT WAS BLACK. I CAN'T BREATHE. Sisters were yelling at him for having the nerve to co-opt black culture and black pain to make a dime on black blood.

On this side of town, people rocked Obama T-shirts. Hardly a USA flag, but there were plenty of flags from the islands and Africa. The American flags most owned were folded, in drawers, given to families after a relative was killed serving a country that never served them in return.

Someone was pulling out of a parking spot and Jake Ellis waited, music down low; then he parallel parked in front of his classic edifice. His one-bedroom spot was east of Degnan, a block from Audubon Middle School. Leimert Park was a pre–World War II neighborhood made of modest Spanish-style homes, charming bungalows. Compared to

Culver City and Pasadena, everything looked dull, worn. But it was our zip code. A group of white teens wearing black slacks, white shirts, and black ties passed. There were ten of them. Young Mormons. They were probably going up into the hills to go door-to-door in Baldwin Hills, tasked with selling their faith, one that didn't include black people until not that long ago. If ten blacks tried to walk through those boys' neighborhood selling blackness, they'd all be on a curb, handcuffed while cops made up charges.

While we sat there another group of sisters sporting dreadlocks, braids, perms, and Afros came down the street, passing out flyers, talking to the community. An orchestra of soul sisters, mothers of the earth. I always kept eye contact, let the breasts live in the periphery, had learned to notice and not ogle. The sisters made their way to us, came to the window to hand us flyers.

Afro said, "Investors from overseas want to buy buildings and turn them into Airbnbs."

"Serious?"

"It's getting out of hand. Come to the meeting."

"Will do."

Jake Ellis said, "I heard they want to make our apartments expensive condos."

She said, "That's one way to legally force the people to move, no matter how long you've been living there. They'd have to pay us about ten grand each to relocate. Which is nothing."

I said, "That would be the ultimate gentrification."

She said, "Would push most of the people living here out. Older folks have been here renting thirty and forty years. People on fixed incomes, where will they go? No one will be able to buy where we live now. People worked too hard to get out of the projects to have to go back."

I nodded. "The train line has accelerated a change."

She huffed. "I call that train what it really is."

"Which is?"

"An overground railroad for them to come and Columbus new places."

"People on Crenshaw wanted that train too. We're landlocked and need that train. We need to be able to get to the beaches and put our toes in the dirty sand and cold ocean too."

She rolled her eyes, wasn't about to hear anything I was saying. "They've changed the name of the area from South Central to South LA. Now we're like SoHo and NoHo. We went to bed in South Central and woke up in SOLA. First they claim it; then they rename it."

I said, "I'll be at the meeting."

"Black lives matter."

"Black lives matter."

We agreed on that; then they moved on. I read the flyer. Local activists and national leaders were fighting gentrification and promoting wealth building, demanding development without displacement. I wondered how many wars a black man had to fight in his lifetime.

I wondered if I had gone to Africa ten years ago whether I would care about any of this bullshit.

But everywhere a black man went, there were more problems.

Jake Ellis said, "Wonder why they never use the word *gentrification* in any brochures."

"Who?"

"Wypipo. They never use that word in their brochures."

"What word do they use to make it sound nonpolitical and palatable to the naïve?"

"*Revitalized.* Sounds like those vagina-rejuvenation ads."

"Overground railroad."

"Hidden in plain sight."

Our world was restless. Since that first boat trip, it had always been restless.

Jake Ellis's phone rang. He frowned at the number. Didn't answer. Phone rang again.

He answered, "Hey, sweetheart. Not tonight. Can meet you tomorrow. After I hit the boxing gym. Santa Monica. I will meet you. Call the W Hollywood. Get a suite. By lunchtime."

His car was on and his phone connected to the Mustang's speakers via Bluetooth. Without asking, the system put the call on speaker. He did a finger snap that echoed like a curse.

Mrs. Garrett said, "I've had enough of this life. Money laundering. Drug dealing. God knows what else. He has taken control over my life. Since we've been married he's told me where I can go, where I can't go, has restricted my movements. I'm supposed to be a feminist."

"For some, marriage is ownership. It just depends on who owns who."

"He says he does it to protect me."

"A dog on a long chain is still a chained dog."

"I'm going to call Gloria Allred. She doesn't play. She's a real feminist. I can win this."

"Elaine, I'm driving right now. And I'm still on the clock for my employer."

"Didn't mean to babble."

"You're safe?"

"I'm in my closet. I locked the door, put my red-bottom shoes on, eased into something a little more comfortable and a lot sexy so I could sip wine and eat the last piece of your magically moist salmon in peace. I can tell you went to *culinary* school. This food is truly an aphrodisiac."

"Your husband?"

"He's gone, I think. Not sure. House is huge. Can't hear him screaming right now."

"Tell me everything tomorrow. We can order a big lunch and mimosas and chat."

"You stood up to my husband. I've never seen anyone stand up to him."

"Had to show him who was the real man."

"That scared me and felt good at the same time."

"I could tell."

"He doesn't love me like Kunta Kinte loved Belle."

"It shows. Your bruises told me a lot."

"I don't want to talk about those. I don't want to feel like a fool and cry again."

"Okay."

"Can I tell you a secret?"

"Tell me."

"I want to be with you."

"Do you?"

"I should have left with you."

"You know you couldn't do that."

"I'm so wet right now I could drown."

"Tomorrow."

"A generous lover with substantial offerings that won't die in the furrow."

"I will massage your wounds and then take you to Africa."

"Substantial offering. I've never had that before. Those words are stuck in my mind."

"Good-bye for now."

As she eased her phone down, she said, "Alexa, play my love songs."

Massaging the bridge of my nose, biting my tongue, and shaking my head for that entire exchange, I shifted where I sat, knew I had heard more than Jake Ellis wanted me to hear.

I said, "Be careful."

"Bruv, when she undressed, she had bruises. Her clothes had covered them. New and old bruises. She is a woman living in a cage like an animal at the zoo. I told her that."

"Let her get her revenge somewhere else."

"Can't put the toothpaste back in the tube once it's been squirted out."

"If she wants to be a remora feeding off a great white shark, not your business."

"I know. But the things I do are to get at Garrett."

"You pimp-slap a man with his own salmon, eat his gelato, then make plans to screw his wife. You're a bad motherfucker. Can't say I like it, but I admire a man who can pull that shit off."

"Ken Swift, you're the *bad* motherfucker. I'm the *baddest* of the *bad* motherfuckers."

We eased out of his Mustang as four Asian women jogged by. They all waved.

Jake Ellis asked, "Ever remember what else you had to do?"

I shook my head. "I'll check my phone when I get home."

"Let me know the moment you hear from Esmerelda. Or Margaux."

"Will do."

A horn blew, a soft, friendly beep. Creeping underneath imported palm and evergreen trees, it was a black Tesla Model S. That car snuck up on us. Made both of us jump. A breeze made more noise than that electric car. The driver parked and came our way, hips moving sweetly.

Jake Ellis looked at the time on his phone. "Guess she finished teaching early tonight."

"Business classes at USC, right?"

"Engineering. Civil. We're going to watch a movie called *Charlie Steel*."

"*Charlie Steel*. Never heard of that one. It any good?"

"It was banned in South Africa during apartheid. I'll put it and a few more movies in Dropbox and send you a link; then you can download them whenever you feel like it."

Cars slowed as the MILF strolled. That rich West Indian woman was as beautiful as Miss Haiti, Cassandra Chéry, only she was more mature and still had a natural, smoldering, confident, sexy walk. The world rarely showed the beauty of Haiti. Jake Ellis smiled at her and she smiled at him. Her hair was in a curly, kinky Afro, about twenty inches of powerful ethnic pride. Silver earrings matched her mane. Her full lips were a shade of deep violet. She was a powerful woman of Haitian descent. Daughter of a politician and a professor, former member of the Black Panther Party, astute businesswoman, gym rat, and novelist. If not for the silver hair, in those skinny jeans, with her traffic-stopping shape, I would have thought she was a collegiate woman. Her perfume was soft and sweet, dabbed on just for Jake Ellis to make her sweat it away during an act of congress. And congress was but a moment away from being in session.

Without pretense Jake Ellis said, "Catch you later, Ken Swift."

"She's married. Be careful. Don't need a Haitian-Ghanaian war in Leimert Park."

"If her husband knows where she is, then he knows not to come to my door. He can give her that fistful of tears when she gets back home. He knows that when she's with me, she's mine."

"I'll find Margaux."

"Since you put her info in my phone, I will monitor her Facebook too. Will see where she checks in. I will see if she and Jimi Lee are in this thing together. I will help you fix this."

I regretted I had used his phone. But that toothpaste couldn't be put back in the tube.

The lovely Haitian paused five steps away. She grinned. I nodded at her, then walked away from Jake Ellis and Dr. Maeva Fouche, let Jake Ellis reach for her hand, kiss her on the lips twice, then escort the sensual property owner up to his rent-free one-bedroom palace.

She was carrying an overnight bag. She wasn't planning on leaving before sunrise. If she was staying, Jake Ellis would have to make her a big breakfast in the morning. Women never let Jake Ellis go until he had loved them thrice, ate them twice, and made them two good meals.

I walked away, paused just long enough to watch teenagers doing McTwists on their skateboards. Reminded me of me twenty years ago. I was a skateboard king back then.

A block later I came up on my fading yellow two-level apartment building, one just as old as Jake Ellis's structure, but not as nice on the outside. I had lived there for eighty seasons. Most of the buildings on what we called apartment row were two levels, a few had between four and twelve units, and most had been constructed between the thirties and the sixties.

My random thoughts vanished when I saw someone standing under my window.

The aggravated stranger paced the uneven sidewalk in front of my building. His body language screamed he was pit-bull angry. He saw me and stopped marching, called out my name, and as soon as I paused and gave that gaze of confirmation, he clenched his teeth.

He charged at me, became a raging bull with his hands in fists. Whoever he was, he had been waiting for me to bring my black ass back home. Same as others had done years ago.

My hand went for the .38 I carried, but I had left it sleeping in Jake Ellis's Mustang.

My backup .38 was upstairs chilling out in my apartment, probably watching Netflix.

I didn't know if my aggressor was armed, if he had come to break bones, or if he was here to kill. I didn't know if he was alone, or if car doors would open and forty men would attack me. My gut told me Mr. Garrett had sent someone after me and Jake Ellis, only he had found me first. The madman yelled and charged at me like a wounded bull intent on killing a matador.

In my mind, I heard Garrett rapping lyrics by Biggie Smalls.

Not only did this motherfucker have a beef with me, he'd come to annihilate me.

CHAPTER 14

MY ENEMY WORE unbridled anger, paired with black jeans and a gray hoodie. He was six-three, about 190 pounds between toes and 'fro. Light-brown skin with reddish hair that was more wavy than kinky. The killer swung hard, clipped my ear, and that sting woke me up, told me this shit was real. I bobbed and weaved, and before he could come at me again, I became the next Brown Bomber, threw six fast blows, ate his ribs and stomach up the way termites eat wood, gave him some spots of pain to think about, and with the wind knocked out of him, it was all but over. He dropped like a rock, mouth bloodied, redness spreading across his face and tongue, collapsed holding his ribs and his nuts. That low blow to his family jewels was intentional. I ain't got no problem clocking a man in the sacs in a street fight, because it's a damn street fight. I checked to see if he had backup. No one else came running my way. I yanked his hoodie up, made sure he didn't have a gun or a tool to shank me; then I kicked him twice, put two solid roundhouse kicks into his gut. Again, he dropped to his knees. Fear had replaced his rage.

My voice dressed in fury, I asked, "Who sent you after me?"

"I came to whoop . . . your bitch ass."

"Who sent you?"

"Margaux. She told me what you did to her when she took you to lunch."

"You're her pit bull?"

"I'm her fiancé."

"She wasn't wearing an engagement ring. Boy, don't come here lying."

"We're having a baby."

"She's having a baby. Man can't do nothing but get a woman pregnant."

"Let me go."

I shoved the fool away from me. This was the boyfriend. Another goddamn pretty boy. A light-skinned number covered in tattoos, just like my child. Not until I pushed him away did I see his ears. He was into lobe gauging, had a green circular symbol of Buddhism in each ear. His mouth was bloodied because I had hit him so hard his nose ring had been set free.

I snapped, "You came to where I live to confront me? Boy, messing with me, *especially today*, will get your young ass dragged down ten miles of bad road on your ugly face."

"You made her cry today."

"Boy, *I am her father*. We have the same blood. Understand that, boy? *We are family*. What went on between us ain't your business. And you came after me? What's this? Nobody puts Baby in a corner, and you're Patrick Swayze and you came to put her old man in his place?"

"Motherfucker."

"Were you with her at the Grove?"

"You were at the Grove?"

"You didn't know?"

"I was in the car when she came back. You made her cry twice in one day?"

"She tell you why she was there?"

"It was none of your business."

"Who was the guy in the red car?"

"What guy?"

"Do you have any idea what the fuck is going on?"

"I love Margaux. That's all that matters."

"You're the writer, or the other guy is the writer?"

"What other guy?"

"Are you the writer?"

"I'm the writer."

"Why does she need fifty thousand?"

"Get away from me."

"Oh, you're not surprised about that part. Who needs the money, you or her?"

His face was contorted in anguish. He struggled to breathe. I looked at him and saw myself. Ethiopian loving had gotten the best of him too. I sighed at the dumb-as-fuck, lovesick, pathetic mutt; wanted to strangle him until his eyes popped out of his head, but I held his shoulder and said, "Lean forward and let the blood drain so you don't choke to death."

He snatched away from my helping hand and cried out, "You bwoke my nose."

"I didn't *bweak* your nose. The concrete *bwoke* your nose when you *fwell* on your face."

"You *bwoke* my *fwiggin'* nose. I'm going to sue you."

I feigned like I was going to clock him again. He took off running. He galloped to the next building and dove into a dirty Nissan, same bucket Margaux had been driving earlier, and left screeching. Too many cars and too many eyes were out for me to hog-tie him and drag him around back to the garages. He ran the red light a block up, almost crashed. My daughter had sent her street-dumb Romeo clown to beat me up.

I said, "I should've snatched those ugly-ass earrings out your damn ears."

He was with her at the Grove, but she had left him in her car when she went to meet with her ex-boyfriend. And her ex had left his woman in his whip. That told me nothing, not right away.

As life moved on for the denizens and traffic sped by, my concentration, my attempt to make all of this bullshit make sense, was interrupted when someone applauded.

Across the street, in the two-level that was dull green and white, some of the stucco chipping away, one of my neighbors stood in her window. She waved at me. She always looked conservative, wore frameless glasses that made her look innocent, a contradiction to her smile.

It was Bernice Nesbitt. My African-British neighbor. Long brown hair parted on the side. Skin the hue of café au lait and she was just as hot. Tall, with curves. She was gorgeous, had North Africa, maybe Algeria, in her British blood, wavy hair. Bernice had lived there at least ten years, since she was about twenty-one. She was more fit, sexier now than she was when she was twenty-one. California living and the weather had done her good. She'd come to this side of the pond to attend university and rarely went back to the land of beans and toast.

This was a déjà vu moment from another ugly familial moment a decade ago. Today wasn't my first time being jumped right at my front door. Last time I had been attacked, it was a rainy day, and that was the day I had met Bernice. She had seen it all. As she had seen this bullshit.

She asked, "Should I call the bobbies? Or y'all sticking to the stupid code of the streets?"

"Just some business between two fools."

"Same thing you said a few years ago when those East Africans came after you."

"Rule's the same. Don't involve the slave catchers. Don't want to get shot in the back."

She nodded. "That thirty-second row about a woman, money, or a parking space?"

"Every fight a man has, on some level, is about a woman."

"Because men like to park inside of other men's women."

"Some spaces don't like staying unoccupied too long, especially overnight."

"Yeah, right, whatever. You're good at not answering simple yes-or-no questions."

"Haven't seen you standing in your window watching the neighborhood in a minute."

"Still not answering; cool. Anyway. I thought you knew. Went back home for a month."

"Did you go back to break into the royal family's crib and steal the Koh-i-Noor diamond they stole, snatch it from the Queen's crown, and take it back to its rightful owner in India?"

She laughed. "No, silly."

"You disappoint me. They say whoever holds that diamond rules the world."

"Next time I'll meet the Queen for tea and let her get ganked for her riches."

"Get that diamond and take it back to your people in Africa."

"You know I hate politics and that Afrocentric babbling."

"So you vacated the US for a while."

"Went back home for Carnival."

"Never been to a Carnival."

"Then you're not living. I almost got to whine this soft booty up on John Boyega."

"Bet you had him ready to pull out his light saber."

"For real, though." She laughed. "You should go across the pond."

"What does London have that we don't already have here?"

"Roundabouts."

"We have one in Long Beach. It's called a traffic circle."

"London has over ten thousand."

"You mean it's so boring over there you had to count them?"

"The one you have here is a dull monstrosity. Ours are the most beautiful in the world. Ours go around windmills, Chinese pagodas, and all sorts of amazing structures. Some even have homes in the middle. I've seen yours, so it's only fair you see what mine have to offer."

"Added to bucket list. Way down at the bottom, but above getting married again."

"Follow me on Instagram if you want to see more of the things I did whilst in London with my family and friends. I posted hundreds of pictures. My costume was provocative and sexy."

"Might check it out." I nodded. "How are things at LMU?"

"Almost done."

"You're doing the most. Traveling, getting educated, working that black-girl magic."

"Living my best life. Hey, there was another coyote attack last night."

"We're seeing more coyotes around here every night. Raccoons too."

"Oh. Did you hear about the dead guy they found in the house on MLK?"

"What went down? We have another hashtag?"

"Bro had been dead in his bed for over a month and they just found him."

"What happened?"

"No idea. The guy was about forty. Pretty much our age. Died in his sleep. Had dry rot before anybody noticed. Bloody sad to check out and nobody misses you for over thirty days."

"You have your guy to make sure that doesn't happen. I see him there most nights."

"I'm a free agent." Her voice smiled. "Just dumped the randy bloke I was seeing."

"What happened with you and the fireman? Thought I sensed wedding bells."

"Ain't no bitch hotter than me, but the wanker kept putting out fires all over the city."

"No shit? Sounds like you had some drama."

"Bitch found me on social media. Sent me all the e-mails they had exchanged. Sent me all the text messages. Long story. Probably why my head hurts. Need to work it out after I study."

"Even when you look like Bey, they go Eric Benét."

"Come closer so I don't have to yell. I'll make sure no one is sneaking up on you."

A car passed; then I sprinted across the street, ran across the island of evergreen trees in the middle of Stocker. Bernice and I had had a couple of moments. Late nights, sometimes loneliness and a man's needs got the best of him. Same for a woman. Women were as curious and as deceptive as men. They were just better at the game. Few years ago, I had gone over there to put together a dresser she'd bought at Ikea. Drank while I assembled her goods, then drank and played bones after, drank some more, ended up touching hands, then kissing, feeling each other up, and when the heat was too hot, we ended up half-naked and boning like boning was going out of style. Between the sheets, she was wicked. We never talked about it. We talked like it never happened. I'd been living in this zip code for twenty years, the last ten single. This area was apartment row, hundreds of single women and single moms, so it was a hot spot for a man, be he single or married. Lots of women, new ones moving in every month, the supply always replenished.

Neighbors walked by. I stood next to a palm tree on the dried grass underneath her window.

My British neighbor lowered her voice. "Jesus, now I feel like I have stage fright."

"Why so?"

"I'm feeling anxious all of a sudden."

"What's going on?"

"So I'm single again."

"Pretty women never stay single long, unless it's by choice."

"That was a hint."

"Was it? I'm too direct to pick up on a lot of hints."

"I'm flirting."

"Oh. Thanks for the heads-up."

"Still kicking it with that chocolate Eskimo?"

"When she's in town."

"When she's at your place, I can hear her doing vocal warms-ups all the way over here."

"Why you ask?"

Bernice winked. "Been a long time since you came over to visit. Like three years or so."

"More like four. Knowing what I know, can't see why a man would cheat on you."

"Knowing what I know, I see why your ex-wife used to sneak back every Wednesday."

"She didn't come every Wednesday."

"I bet she did come every Wednesday."

"That was years ago."

"Do you remember the things I liked to do?"

"Oh yeah. Especially with your breasts. Not many sisters can do that."

She whispered, "Oh, what you have is very nice too. You surprised me. And it was indeed a pleasant surprise. Was like meeting a man from the Caramoja tribe in northern Uganda."

"You know I'm seeing the Eskimo."

"Last time *you knew* I had a man."

"Yeah, I knew. I had met him once, so I broke the code."

"You owe me one. You made me a cheater. Fair is fair."

"You're serious."

She laughed. "You look surprised."

"It's been years. I've been available most of that time. You could've stood in your window and used a light and flashed an SOS signal. Or you could've showed up at my door at midnight wearing a trench coat and holding a bottle of wine from 7-Eleven. We could've checked this out."

"I don't want to date you. Would be odd to date a man who lived across the street."

"But having a sleepover every now and then?"

"Wouldn't be out of the question. As long as we had an understanding."

"Last time you stopped talking to me after."

"Back then I was scared the guy I was seeing would look at you and be able to tell something happened. I really liked that guy. Actually, thought I was in love and he was the one. But you gave me that strong bone and I liked it. To feel this way about one man, and to feel another way about another. Scared me. Didn't want drama. But you were chill about that night we had, didn't get all into your feelings and make it complicated. You went on about your biz and you didn't trip and try to come between me and my man. Most guys keep coming at me once they have been in between. Maybe that feeling of rejection was new for me. I think it turned me on."

"It wasn't rejection."

"Maybe you should cross the pond for a sleepover every once in a while."

"Why are you coming at me like this today?"

"Ken Swift, you look good in that jacket and jeans. Saw you leave this morning. Damn. Yeah, you are looking pretty hot. So now you know. I've put that in your ear. So what's going on?"

"The Eskimo."

"You don't scream, I won't holler."

"From what I remember, you do both."

"What happens on this side of the pond stays on this side of the pond."

"Really?"

"Really. I see you with her. She looks all happy and shit. Makes me kinda jealous, and makes me want you again at the same time. Makes me want to pray naked with your penis inside me. Jesus. That penis. Hard to explain, you know? And the way you fight. Very arousing."

"Well, last time I was in a fight out here in the streets, you saw me get my ass kicked."

"But not before you had beat up about five of them."

She had seen Jimi Lee's family bring me a big African-size can of whoop ass. She saw them attack me. That was the only time someone bested me and I didn't go after my revenge.

My smiling neighbor looked down like a queen in a castle and said, "I've been turned on since back then. You have this balance of being street and being a smart brother. You fit into two worlds. I think I've been hot for you about ten years now."

"Never knew that."

"I know, it sounds very opportunistic. But you don't like hints. So I'm being as direct as I can while I still have the nerve. That strong bone. We could be the perfect fuck buddies."

"You're pranking me, right?"

"This look like a prank?" She flashed her breasts. "Remember this playground?"

I whispered, "Damn."

She whispered, "I remember how you made me feel. Not many men can make me come, but you did. That thing you did when you were on top of me and straddled me, good Lord."

"I remember the things you did to me as well."

"Do you?"

"You were comprehensive."

"I'm over the last relationship. I need to have some fun. Don't crave anything intense. Not looking to have my heart broken again. Don't want to be broken like singer Adele had been, especially since I can't sing about it and become as rich as a queen. Don't want anything that will change my life. Just want to drink, play bones, and have sex. Or we can skip the bones."

"You're making my day. After a day like today, you're making my day."

"Come over later and I'll make your night. But you have to be gone before sunrise."

I nodded, knew the first rule from Booty Call 101. "I'll look for you in the window."

Then with a broad smile and a final wink, Bernice Nesbitt disappeared from her window.

I jogged back, crossed the street to my building. I checked the mailbox at the bottom of the stairs. I threw away the junk mail; then I opened bills from DirecTV, State Farm car insurance, car registration, State Farm renter's insurance, and my health insurance at Kaiser.

Not many women came at me like that. She was one of the light-skinned numbers, had that complexion that many admired and many despised, a half-and-half woman who was never seen as black enough when it came time to pump a fist and quote from Baldwin and Angelou.

If I had had a baby with her, if she had been Margaux's mom, then there would have been no bleaching. Maybe Margaux was right. Women like Bernice Nesbitt had it better. Bernice was categorically black, yet she was light enough to marry a prince and no one would see her as a hard-core black woman. I'd had her once. And she wanted me in between her thighs again.

When she came it was beautiful; with each orgasm, she sang like Angela Bofill. Last time I had tried to fuck her into oblivion. Reverse cowgirl, she'd tried to ride me to the same destination. The next evening, she was all lovey with her boyfriend, holding hands, walking to a book signing at Lucy Florence. I was at that same book signing. Standing almost next to her and her man. She didn't look my way, acted like my tongue hadn't opened that sweet crevice, like I hadn't eaten her pussy until she came crying, acted like she'd never had me down her throat. She was my secret. It did boost my ego. It turned me on. I needed that distraction.

But that heat went away. I wondered how many men I had stood next to, men who had had my wife when I was married. My face became a frown. I thought about Margaux, and the heat Bernice Nesbitt had generated became a glacier. I had to get my phone, search for my daughter while Jake Ellis was taking his beautiful Haitian lover to Africa. If Jake Ellis was looking for her, he might put his Haitian lover to sleep, then make a trip without me. I'd get my car out of the garage and spend the rest of the evening looking for Margaux. I'd look for her while I waited on Esmerelda to call me with info on Margaux's exboyfriend. When that was done, if the mood remained, if common sense was still on hiatus and I didn't end up once again covered in blood with dead bodies at my feet, I could cross the pond and relieve my monumental stress as I ascended to heaven.

I went up my stairs two at a time, reading mail. The last letter was an announcement that the building had been taken over by McBroom Property Management. They were black women, so the *gentrifiers* hadn't taken over everything. Didn't fucking matter. Black or white, a landlord was a landlord, and money was money. An opportunist was an opportunist. My rent was about to go up. I laughed. Not one fucking good thing had happened since I woke up this morning.

I leaned against the wall, inspected my ripped jacket, wanted this day to be over.

I wanted to drink dark liquor and wake up after tomorrow's tomorrow.

Bernice Nesbitt's illicit offer made me want to say fuck it all, run away, cross the pond, join the cheaters, and fall between some warm thighs, down stroke, and work off some stress too.

But this day wasn't over. Margaux was coming after me, was

desperate and was going to be relentless, and at the same time I had to save my child from Jake Ellis. I had to save her from crossing a line and waking up the rage inside of an already pissed-the-fuck-off San Bernardino. Against Jake Ellis or against San Bernardino, I might have to do what a father was supposed to do. I knew that was a battle I couldn't win. I had killed before. I knew I couldn't kill again.

Jake Ellis had no such problem. He'd buried many men in the soils of Africa.

A noise and anxious voices made me jump, and again I reached for the gun I had left in Jake Ellis's car. Hands in fists, tense, I checked behind me, was ready to pounce like I was a cornered black panther, made sure no one had trailed me so they could try to shank me or run me down at my front door. No one dangerous was there. Just people passing. The boy with the bloodied nose hadn't doubled back with a gun in his hand. Fifteen white people walked by. All looked like investors on a tour. They were their own kind of trouble, the kind that was legal, the kind that had laws written in their favor. But I should've considered what kind of trouble might be in front of me. Distracted, I didn't notice that the deadbolts were disengaged, not right away. I never left the apartment without putting those on. Mine had been masterfully undone. That was a sign.

As soon as I opened my door, I was attacked again. The same way Jake Ellis and I had burglarized our way in in Pasadena and waited on Mr. Garrett, someone had been waiting on me.

CHAPTER 15

THE CRIMINAL HAD bypassed two deadbolts to get inside. She was in my living room on the cream-colored sofa, resting on her back, eyes on the spackled ceiling. She didn't gaze at me, but I considered her silhouette. Her left foot was on the floor, her right leg over the arm of the plush sofa. She wore luxurious stockings and a garter, matching bra, and sexy high heels.

Looked like she had just gotten off work and decided to do a B and E to pass the time.

A .38 was on the floor next to her, within reach. That was my backup .38. It was loaded. It was always loaded. In South LA an unloaded gun was as useful as an oversize paperweight.

I looked behind me, saw no one else who had me on their list, then closed my door.

My intruder bounced her foot and calmly asked, "Where were you all day?"

"How'd you get in?"

"There ain't a door I can't open in less than a minute."

"One day you'll tell me why you really left Alaska."

"You know why I left. Every time I tell you that story, you get aroused."

"You stabbed a white man in Whittier, Alaska. That man was your husband. He used to take tourists for rides on his snow sled, sixteen lightweight dogs. He didn't come home for two days, and you went south to Whittier looking for him. Pissed him off. He attacked you. Beat you halfway to hell. That was a bad move on his part. He was outraged because you caught him with his mistress. You stabbed him as many times as you could stab a man, and got on a train, went back home to Talkeetna, up near Denali National Park, where the honorary mayor is a cat named Stubbs. Police came for you. They found you at the hospital, in bad shape, in bed, an IV in your arm, eyes swollen, body covered with the bruises your husband had left behind. They handcuffed you to the bed. Then decided that was unnecessary, took the handcuffs away. When the hospital released you, they took you to jail. Trial. It was big news in your small town. Black Eskimo kills her white husband. A reverse OJ situation in Alaska. You beat the rap. Left Alaska. Changed your name."

She hated me for bringing that up, her life when she had lived where three great Alaskan rivers kissed, the place where she used to do glacial tours with tourists, the place where she worked on the railroad, the place where it was harder to find blacks than it was to find Cinnamon Hitler's bone spurs, the place that held her shame. Once upon a time the beautiful Rachel Redman was a small-town girl who had lived in a hopping town in the land of the midnight sun.

She demanded to know, "Where were you all day, Ken Swift?"

"Stabbed your abusive ex-husband in Whittier, stabbed him while he was still in his mistress's bed, and now you've come to shoot me and maybe write a song and sing about it."

"And if I pull this trigger, I'll make it pop until it stops, long after you drop."

"Bet the Russian you mess around with would love that. He'd pay for your defense."

"Don't start with that shit. Don't keep throwing that one thing in my face, you hear me?"

"Don't waggle a gun at me while you talk. Don't point a fucking gun at me."

"You don't get to tell me where to point a gun, not today."

Chinese food rested on the end table, on top of old newspapers. Grubhub. Asti Spumante was at her side. An *L.A. Focus* newspaper was on the table, opened to HEADLINES FROM AFRICA. Shaken, I stormed through the living room. Rachel followed me, her sexy booty wagging in protest. Wicked woman followed her bad boy. She was queen with a sexy ass and a loaded .38. This was the woman I was seeing now. Her blood-line went back to Eritrea. She had taken a DNA ancestry test and that had been the result. Another East African woman was giving me grief.

I said, "Stop following me. Don't push up on me when you're angry like that."

"I go where you go. You go to the bathroom, I'll hold the toilet paper."

"Go watch television."

"Nothing on but bad news."

"You are bad news that makes all the other bad news seem like good news."

"Nucca. You don't deserve this love. Only so much of your bullshit I can take."

"What did I do?"

"Are you being serious right now, nucca? Are you serious? You are joking, right?"

She'd spent two years with the Russian, had been the cause of his divorce. Rachel was no saint. She did what she had to do. She was both an open book and a mystery. She had a lot of devil in her blood. She could break into a locked room and you'd never know she'd been there, and that came with years of practice. She had left Alaska and had left her reputation behind her.

Her burgundy dress was on one of my wooden hangers. The hanger hung from a hook on the bedroom door. It was a curve-hugging, above-the-knee showstopper, a dress that didn't require a bra and would show cleavage to the areolas. It was the kind made for a woman on stage singing her heart out under the spotlight. I could roll that dress up and put it in my back pocket and still have room for my wallet, cell phone, two condoms, and a pack of peanut M&M's.

I asked, "So, are you coming from work or on the way to a gig somewhere?"

"Are you fuckin' serious? What do you think I'm doing here looking for you?"

I faced her and met her undying fury. Her jaw was tight and tears were in her eyes, sitting there like lakes begging to become streams that led to an ocean to be created at her feet.

She picked up the .38 and stormed toward me. She handed it to me, butt first.

I put the gat away and asked, "What did I do wrong this time?"

Hands on her hips, her words came hard and fast. "You don't remember."

"Remember what?"

"*Today is my birthday.*"

I groaned. "Shit."

Her birthday. That was what I had been trying to remember all day long. Margaux's call, that slice of blackmail, then Garrett, had had my mind going in many directions. I stood like a statue, mouth open, no defense.

The lakes in her eyes finally became two streams. "You forgot, huh?"

"Shit, shit, shit, shit, shit."

"Hashtag, men are trash."

"Happy birthday, babe."

"Hashtag, unbelievable. Hashtag, men will always be trash."

"I am so sorry. I forgot. I've had too much other shit on my mind today."

"More important stuff?"

"Yeah."

"Could you at least lie? I mean, fuck. Couldn't you at least say some stupid shit like, 'Sweetheart, did you think I was a thoughtless narcissistic dumb-ass? I ordered the best present online, didn't even use a Groupon, and I wanted to surprise you, but the stupid delivery guys made an error, and I've been out all day trying to sort that out. But, hey, since they fucked it up, we can just run out and have a beautiful dinner, candles and red wine, Italian cuisine or whatever you want, and I'll buy you twelve dozen roses, get you a dozen pretty gifts, take you dancing, and when we're done, we can swoop by Beverly Hills and buy you that drop-top Lamborghini Huracán Performante you wanted.' But did you say any of that? Hell no. 'I forgot' is the best you got?"

"Rachel, dammit."

"Hashtag, wish I could unfuck you. Hashtag, I hate you so much right now."

"Stop acting crazy. The day has been hell and I forgot. I'm so sorry."

"I called you. Called you over and over. Was mad. Then got worried and came here. Broke in and hoped I would see a dead body on the floor that looked like you. Called you again."

"When you did your B and E and came into my apartment uninvited, you saw that I left my phone here on the charger. You've been here awhile, so I know you've snooped around."

"If you can't remember my birthday, then don't bother trying to remember me."

"One more chance, Red. It's been a hella day. Let me make it up to you."

"That *was* your one more chance. You vanished on me once, now this. Glad you weren't ghosting me. Or dead. I had no idea what was going on. I even left a note at Jake Ellis's place."

"Rachel . . . Red . . . let me talk. A brother can't get a word in when you're on a roll."

"I can't keep doing this. It's time for me to swipe left on this relationship."

"What does that mean?"

"I'm done waiting for you to fit me in. A man will make me a priority in his life. A man who cares about me will remember my birthday. This was important to me. This would have been our first time celebrating my birthday. And you forgot? I've wasted six months of my life here."

I stepped toward her, moved like my feet were stuck in dried concrete.

She raised her right palm. "Keep away from me, Swift. Don't touch me."

She got her dress zipped up, found her composure, walked out the door, eased it closed.

I said, "I got ninety-nine problems. And a woman is every one of them."

I went to the bathroom, washed my face, then told myself to try to catch Rachel Redman before she was gone for good. I changed pants, put on a fresh Ali T-shirt, another three-button jacket. When I stepped out the front door, Rachel was standing in the hallway, back against the wall. She didn't glance in my direction when the door whined open.

"Wow. Took you ten minutes to come after me. Ten fucking minutes. You didn't even try and stop me from leaving. Do you even want me in your life? Am I wasting my time?"

"I'm the one who should be asking you that question."

"Don't try and turn this around."

I paused, felt defensive, decided to deal from the bottom of the deck to try to get in a win, then said the name of my rival, "Vitaliy Zavadskyy."

"I told you, I ended that. When I'm done, I'm done."

"You saw the Russian again *after* you were done."

"You didn't call me for two weeks. I'd only been seeing you a month and it felt like you popped the panties like a boss and ghosted me. You know how y'all do it. Put in all the effort to get a taste, then mission accomplished. You vanished for fourteen days and fourteen nights."

"*I was working.* You knew I was working. You knew I was out of the state."

"If I don't hear from a man who is supposed to be my man for a week, all bets are off and I move on to the next episode. We had had a few good nights, but men get new pussy and get amnesia, so I figured you had found some newer pussy, then slipped and bumped your head. Look at this. Why would you not call this for two weeks? Why would you want to take that Mandingo stick and give the Shaka Zulu dick-down to some thot and you had all of this sexiness trying to hook up with you? Because that's what men do. You didn't call me for more than . . . six hundred thousand times two seconds, whatever that is. Over twenty thousand minutes. You left me lonely. As far as I knew, you had done like prison bae Jeremy Meeks did his wife and was off in Tur-key having sex with some millionaire thot like Chloe Green. Fuckboys ain't loyal. You might've turned starboy. You were gone and doing your own thing. So, I did mine."

"I ain't no motherfuckin' starboy. See? Now you have me cussin' for no reason."

"You were MIA for six hundred thousand times two seconds. One million two hundred seconds."

"I don't need to hear from you every eighty thousand seconds to know we're good."

"Well, I do. Learn the ways of a woman, or you'll never have one for long."

"Don't act like I walked out without a word. I told you I had to go work for San Bernardino. You knew I was going back east to do what I do to get what I got."

"They have these things called phones all around the world. No matter where you had to go, they had phones. Even if you were in Villa Las Estrellas in Antarctica, or working in La Rinconada in the Peruvian Andes, or beating up folks in the Scandinavian town of Longyearbyen, you could've found Internet and Skyped a sister. Or sent a text. You know my numbers, my social media, and my e-mail addresses. *Nothing.* I gave it a week. Seven whole days. You know what it feels like to wait to hear from a man you're crazy about for a hundred sixty-eight hours? I gave you over six hundred thousand seconds, and I didn't care how you reached out to me, even if you sent a postcard. Nothing."

"You broke down the seconds? Why would you do something insane like that?"

"Because I felt every second. Do you want to know how many milliseconds I waited?"

"If women are nuts, you are the leader of the pack."

"This woman is nuts because she loves you. But I know how to *unlove* a fool. I can *unlove* you as easy as I unfollow assholes on Twitter. I can mute and block you in real life."

"Don't do crazy shit and blame it on love. If you're flying over the cuckoo's nest, own it."

"I waited seven days. One-fourth of a month. Not one word from you. Not one emoji. Wherever you were, I assumed you were swimming in recycled pussy. That's why I moved on."

"You didn't move on. You reversed and went back to the Russian's bed."

"You were gone for fourteen days. This was your pussy. But after day seven, if it hasn't been touched, licked, stroked, or otherwise nurtured, due to neglect, this pussy reverts back to the original owner and she can distribute the goody to whoever she wants, however she wants."

"I didn't smash anybody. You couldn't wait to get the Russian back in your bed."

She stood in her red dress with her head held back, expression of a silent scream.

I chewed my bottom lip. "Your Russian lover hit you up today?"

"He's not my lover."

"You slept with him. That pissed his wife off."

"You slept with those pretty girls from South Africa and Namibia."

"A year, maybe two before I met you."

"They still message you."

"Once in a while."

"I wonder why."

"I don't see them. You read the messages. Your Russian is still in your life."

"The Russian is past tense."

"You fucked him a month ago."

"It wasn't a month ago, it was five months ago, and I'm tired of you bringing that up."

"A month ago, Rachel."

"You know what? You really need to forget about last month and worry about the future, as in if we have one."

"Did he call?"

"*Fuck.* Yes. The Russian called."

"When?"

"At six this morning."

"That was early."

"You should've called me at midnight. You should've been there whispering in my ear, kissing my neck, then had me facedown, ass up, singing Stevie Wonder's birthday song."

"The Russian told you happy birthday."

"I guess I'm important to somebody."

"I guess the Russian is important to you too. You said he tried to buy you a nine-hundred-thousand-dollar condo downtown, wanted to buy you that to get you to come back to him."

"It cost eight hundred and fifty thousand and I'm not trying to be no man's side chick. Too grown for that."

"But he's ringing your phone day and night. So what's really going on?"

"The jerk caught me when I was at the gym in my complex doing weights."

"Your ex asked to take you out on your born day?"

"You didn't."

"Did your ex buy you a born-day present?"

"Did you?"

"What did he buy you?"

"A Gibson guitar."

That hurt paused me. "Which? That Hummingbird?"

"The 1959 Les Paul."

"That cost three grand, right?"

"Twelve thousand."

I swallowed, felt my head throb. "Big Money Grip still trying to win you back."

"He'd buy me a drop-top Lamborghini if I asked him to."

"On your knees, talking to the mic."

"Baby, if I got on my knees, he'd buy me a Lambo dealership, and you know that. I ain't never talked to that mic. I will give it to you like that. I used to. And you still forgot my birthday."

"You going to keep the guitar?"

"I told my ex I can't accept his gifts anymore. I wasn't impressed. My face said it all."

"You saw the Russian?"

"FaceTime. You have heard of FaceTime? People do that with special people."

"The guitar? How did he get that to you?"

"Was shipped to my apartment yesterday so it would be there on time."

"You're keeping it?"

"You need to worry about if I'm keeping you."

"What did you talk about?"

"He rambled about the house in Hollywood Hills, the one he bought for about two million and now it's listed for three million. Then my ex sent me a picture of his hard-on."

"He did what?"

"Sent me a damn dick pic."

"Did you send him something?"

"Hell no. Why would I do something foolish like that?"

"Not like he hasn't seen it before."

"He's seen this ass, and I've seen his package before, but that didn't mean I wanted a pic. He's not my man and he knows he's not my man, and him sending me a dick pic, especially when he knew I was seeing someone else, that mess is fouler than the foulest of the foulest foul."

"What happened then?"

"Oh, is the nucca who forgot my birthday and did a disappearing act acting jealous?"

"What happened?"

"Then I called him, cursed him out in Russian, we argued, then I blocked him."

"You blocked him?"

"Happy? And, nucca, I blocked you about two hours ago too."

"That motherfucker sent you a dick pic and you blocked me?"

"Don't you dare come in here and flip the script. You can't remember my birthday?"

The intensity in her face, the firmness in her eyes, softened me up a bit. It looked like she was thinking about everything at the same time. I remained motionless in the open doorway for a moment, then got down on my haunches, my eyes everywhere but on her. She moved around, shifted. I did the same. We fought to not look at each other. We both lost at the same moment.

Rachel said, "I want to be happy. If not with you, then with someone else."

She turned and headed toward the stairs, high heels clicking, keys jingling, but she took only five heavy steps. She sat down on the concrete. I sat next to her, kissed her wet eyes.

I said, "I'm sorry, I'm sorry, I'm sorry. Can we move on now?"

Rachel stood up. Her legs juddered, threw her off-balance. I'd never seen her upset before. It scared me. I grabbed her shoulders and she eased her arms around my neck.

Her insides were shaking. I held her a couple of minutes, until she was in control. She took a step away from me. My phone rang. This had more weight, so that call was ignored.

She said, "Your friggin' phone has been buzzing nonstop since I broke in here."

"I figured it would be ringing all day today."

"Who is Jimi Lee?"

"Jimi Lee? You know that's my ex-wife."

"I thought she was Ethiopian."

"That's the American name she used."

"It's almost Ethiopian New Year."

"Is it? I lost track of their calendar years ago."

"You see your ex-wife today to celebrate?"

"We have no reason to talk."

"Why is she blowing up your phone?"

"No idea. Child support and alimony days ended years ago."

"Why was your ex-wife calling you back-to-back-to-back all day on my birthday?"

"About my daughter. Our daughter. I told you about Margaux."

Rachel backed down from Category 5 to a tropical storm. "Oh. She okay?"

"My kid called out of the blue."

"She's an adult now."

"Yeah. We met for an early lunch."

"How was that?"

"She's bleached her dark-brown skin. She's paler than Lady Gaga now."

"She's gone from being the dark Lil' Kim in the nineties to the beige Lil' Kim now?"

"That was the start." I nodded, wrestled with emotions. "She brought the drama."

"What kind of drama?"

"Long story short, she cursed me out, left mad, so I guess her mother is pissed off."

"Tell me everything."

I posted a fake smile. "We can talk tomorrow."

"And some asshole was banging on the door not too long ago."

"I saw him downstairs. We had a short meeting."

"What trouble have you gotten yourself into this time, Ken Swift?"

I redirected the conversation. "What can I do to fix this birthday faux pas?"

She took a hard breath. "You're the man. Figure it out."

"How about I take you to the Mark Taper Forum to see that new play *Head of Passes*."

"When?"

"Next week. I'll buy the best seats and see if I can get you to meet Phylicia Rashad."

"*My birthday is today.*"

I was too drained to have another fight.

She cried. "Wish you could look inside me and see how much I love you."

"You're right. I've been asleep at the wheel. I'm awake now."

"You forgot my birthday."

"I forgot this time, this one time, but you know what I didn't forget? You're Alaskan by way of East Africa. Your people are Eritrean, but you've never been to Africa and aren't really interested in going to Eritrea. You're five seven and a half, weigh one thirty, thirty-two–twenty-three–thirty-six, and you like it when I cook okra, you love my greens, you love my baked barbecue chicken, but when I break out the grill on the back porch you're going to eat until the last rib is gone; you like creamy peanut butter and hate that I only buy Jif crunchy, you make the best sweet potato pie for a woman not from down south, you'd rather bake food than fry because you hate cleaning the stovetop, you put honey in your coffee, you put honey in your grits but you prefer cheese grits, you put honey in your oatmeal, you like brown sugar in your spaghetti, you don't eat coleslaw unless you make it, you only eat the thick turkey bacon, you prefer pork bacon over turkey bacon, you think tofu is the devil, yet you pile pineapples on your pizza and think that makes it a food of the gods when pineapples on pizza should be a sin, and you hate Jake Ellis because he makes better Jollof rice than you can make. And you wear size seven shoes. I can go on and on."

"I weigh one twenty. You called me fat."

"Did you hear all the things I didn't forget?"

"That means I'm fat and I'm not a priority. It's time to swipe left."

"You're quitting me?"

"We're done."

"We can be done with each other after tonight."

"You're taking me out?"

"But not if you're going to look like a brokenhearted raccoon."

Rachel Redman smiled, new tears in her eyes, new rivers flowing, new lakes forming.

"You know all the things I like. Down to the grits."

"And I like you."

"Like? All I get is you like me? So, you love cheese grits, and like me?"

"You weigh one twenty now?"

"In my mind."

She came back inside, kissed me twice, then ran to the bathroom to fix her face.

She called back, "I'm still mad at you."

"Just get the ugly off your face so we can go and have some drinks."

I went to the window, frowned down, made sure no one else was waiting on me.

Across Stocker, on the other side of the pond, I saw Bernice Nesbitt. She waved at me. Rachel came and stood next to me, spied out the window. By then the Brit was gone.

Neighbors initiated call-and-response. Someone played Mic Stewart's "I'm Not from Brooklyn." Gyft's "Caskets" played hard. Wizkid. SZA. Lost Kings. DJ Quik. Team Gentrification introduced themselves, played No Doubt, Dave Matthews Band, Taylor Swift, and Nirvana. But then again that might not have been Team Gentrification. Black people liked the same music.

Rachel Redman danced up against me and yelled, "Oh my God. Someone is playing 'Confidently Lost' by Sabrina Claudio. This is why I *love* this part of the neighborhood."

"Nothing like this up in the land of penguins and dog sleds."

"Nothing like this at all. This is what I love about this part of Los Angeles. The black pride. Long-lost relatives have found each other here. Leimert Park has so much life. The drums jamming in the park on the weekend. So much fuckin' life with my melanin-ites. I love my people."

"Keep rolling that booty up on me like that and you better assume the position."

"Stop pulling at my dress. And get your hot hand off my breast."

"Get that Alaska ass off me before it gets baked. Keep it up. I'll tear that dress off you."

"Your stressing me out is why you don't deserve this pussy ever again."

"Pussy is an ugly word."

"Stop it. Don't start sucking on my neck trying to make me weak. And it's still too damn hot in this apartment. Don't get me all sweaty. Stop rubbing that bamboo up on me."

"Please baby please baby please baby please?"

"No baby no baby no baby no."

"Just the tip. You know you love it."

She smiled, rubbed her fingers along my erection, then moved away from me.

"And tell that basic bitch across the street to stop looking over here."

"She's just watching the neighborhood. She's our nosy-ass Mrs. Kravitz."

"If those old women hadn't been walking by, I was going to put her ass in check for looking over here. I was in the window, didn't have any clothes on, and she was watching me."

She walked away. I checked my phone to see if Esmerelda had called or sent a message. There was nothing. I knew the info wouldn't come that fast, not for me. I wasn't San Bernardino. A thousand thoughts came, and I exhaled, had to refocus. My erection waned. Sanity returned. I took out the money I had been sent by San Bernardino, put most of the loot away. On the dresser was a worn brochure and old application for UCLA. I threw that in the garbage.

Then I stood still a moment, wishing things would change on their own. But I'd always been a man of action. I took out my phone, dialed the number that had popped up this morning.

Margaux answered. "What do you want, Ken Swift?"

"Let's get one thing straight. Don't ever address me by my first name. I'm your daddy."

"You jumped Kevin."

"Now I know the idiot's name. I didn't jump him, but when I got home from the Grove, he was out here, waiting on me. He assaulted me. Said you sent him. He tried to draw first blood. I have a witness."

"You broke his nose and maybe his jaw. He doesn't have insurance. Had to give him my Vicodin. We're going to sue you. We're going to sue you and kick your old ass for what you did."

"Can I meet with you and that fool tomorrow?"

"This is too much for me. I can't take this."

"What's too much?"

"Life. Everything."

"Let's handle this like adults."

"You have the money? That's the only reason you need to call me."

"We got off on a bad foot. I just want to meet and talk, maybe try and do the day over."

"The seventy thousand I need? If you follow me again it will become one hundred thousand."

My daughter hung up. I remembered a quote by Martin Luther King Jr. It said everything we saw was a shadow cast by that which we did not see. Margaux had left me in the shadows, in the darkness. Hands dank, throat tight, unable to blink, I couldn't deal with Margaux's bull-shit.

Not tonight. This reminded me of dealing with her mother's bull-shit for years.

If Jake Ellis went after Margaux, so be it. I was her father, not her god.

Rachel came back, asked, "Are you driving your hoopty and letting the top down?"

"Not if we're drinking the way you drink when you start drinking."

"You okay?"

I took a slow exhale. "I need to drink the way you drink tonight."

"You never drive your car anymore. You barely have any miles on that thing."

"The boys in blue can't Rodney King with a bro on GP if he's not driving."

"Hashtag, passengers become hashtags too. Hashtag, they kill black women."

"Stop that childish hashtag bullshit."

"Stop acting like it's only the black *men* they kill. Sisters have a long roll call too."

"Can we talk about this on the way out the door?"

"Makeup on fleek, dress is hot, and these protuberant buttocks popping and ret ta go."

"Let me order a four-door stranger-driven chariot for my queen."

"No ride sharing. I don't share nothing, not even an Uber."

"Your stubborn, difficult, sassy ass better remember I'm the same way."

"Don't vanish seven days, won't happen. And take some supplements for your memory."

I left that right there, Margaux in my heart, the Russian on my mind, jealousy rising. I told God I didn't mean what I had said about hoping Jake Ellis found her. That was my biggest fear. If he touched her, best friend or not, that Ghanaian knew I would have to kill him. Or die trying.

CHAPTER 16

I SUMMONED AN Uber and we headed to where the young, millennial, and restless congregated, L.A. Live. Rachel Redman was on Periscope, letting her followers know it was her born day. I waved at the unseen crowd of nobodies who sent hearts and messages from all over the world. She posted a lot of pictures, never anything political, just pictures of her. She was beautiful, and some women used their appearance as a basis for self-worth and posted photo after photo online. She needed to be liked, noticed, and appreciated. I had a war in my mind and it felt good to leave the battlefield, to be able to leave my world and fall into hers, no matter how vain.

She said, "You better get your phone out and post a dozen pictures of us."

I took my phone out, checked to see if Esmerelda had hit me up, saw nothing, then did what Rachel Redman told me to do. Posted a few pics of us on my Facebook and Twitter. Did that to prove to her that I wasn't ashamed to be with her, that there was no other woman. She needed to feel secure, be in control too. She needed to own and wanted to be owned in the name of love. I was married five years and my ex-wife had barely taken pictures with me, so this was new.

Rachel said, "I'm tagging you in all my pictures. Retweet and share."

"Thought you didn't share."

"Don't piss me off. You are still in the doghouse."

"I don't have a lot of online friends. And only a few people follow me."

"I'll up your status. Let them know you're with your bae having a ball."

I took her to Rock'N Fish. She switched to Facebook Live and narrated her birthday evening from the door to the table. She had over one hundred thousand sheep following her, but followed only four or five people. She was a front-runner, not a hanger-on. From the door, the joint smelled delicious and my stomach rumbled, despite having had salmon not that long ago.

It was the Hollywood, late-night, shallow, trying-to-get-laid crowd, turning it up. We squeezed by people who were on their phones, looking at a report on Jamie Foxx and Katie Holmes, not surprised that the brother had been shazaming that MILF for the last five years or so. But most were talking about the Kevin Hart scandal, cheating on his wife and getting extorted.

Hollywood was all about gossip. Gossip, food, drugs, and hot sex with strangers. Twenty years ago, this was the type of place I was at every Friday and Saturday night until the lights came on. A few of the younger guys and dolls were probably the grown-up children of a couple of women I banged when I was a teenager. This was the type of place where Margaux would probably hang out, very few black people.

My hand ached from where I had hit Margaux's pit bull in his stupid face. That fuckboy was lucky he was able to leave there on his own two feet and not unconscious on a stretcher.

The eatery was packed. Accents, foreign languages everywhere. Hot women checked out Rachel Redman's dramatic dress. We were in the judgment zone. Some gave her a look asking her to sneak away from me. After hours, in Hollywood, women loved women more than they did men. Men looked at her ass too long. I didn't say anything. If

I fought men for admiring her, for lusting, I'd be fighting until the end of days. It wasn't about their reaction to her, but about her reaction to them. She was focused on me. I regarded Rachel's sassy body language to see if this spot was okay for an impromptu birthday dinner, or if she wanted to go get another Uber and go somewhere fancier. San Bernardino had paid us well. I could take her to a calmer spot in Beverly Hills. She took selfies, smiled so hard I thought her cheeks were going to explode.

Like Julia Roberts, Eva Mendes, and Issa Rae, Rachel Redman had a Hollywood smile that lit up the room and charged the universe. Men judged women by their smiles. Smiles made women desirable, likable, attainable. But asking a woman to smile was the one thing that made a woman want to frown. Women judged me by how they perceived Rachel Redman. Awesome, sculpted bod on an overjoyed woman. I was confident, well built, an alpha male with a strong heterosexual vibe that made Rachel Redman act girly in my presence. Rachel Redman had the appearance of being well fed, well loved, and well fucked. Women wanted what Rachel Redman had. Made some want to take it. My neighbor had seen me with Rachel Redman many times.

We had drinks and prawns, crab and artichoke dip, followed by raw mini scallops served in the pretty pink half shells with ponzu sauce, seaweed, sesame seeds, and fish roe, then juicy Kapalua rib eye steaks. We ate, laughed, danced. Soon she was two Baileys, two shots deep.

A guy with a mouth painted in firecracker-red lipstick came over. Hair long and blond, expansive and expensive wig parted on the side, cascading down his back. He was dressed in tight red pants, Timberlands, and a cream blouse folded at the elbows. Some men would stare at his ass, get aroused, then get mad when he turned and they saw his Adam's apple; he was that kind of guy. In Leimert Park, if she was walking away or standing at the mall, with my programming, I looked at ass first, no thought. In other parts of LA, when I was in certain areas, I looked at face and neck before I checked to see if baby had back. I'd been duped more than once over the years.

Blondie hurried to my girl. "Excuse me, but aren't you the amazing Rachel Redman?"

"You recognize me?"

"Are you mad? That face. You are real beauty. You are fire. Beautiful. Articulate. Intelligent. Graceful. Powerful. I have liked all your pictures on Instagram. I'm spooked to actually meet you. I knew that was you. I knew it. You are killing that dress. You are a chocolate soufflé. Damn. Be glad I'm not straight like the sides of a square. But you could change my religion."

"Oh, I think I like you. You are my new temporary best friend."

"You are radiant. I can see the god in you. And you have a body like Amara La Negra and an ass like Erica Ash. Embrace that shit."

"Girl, you're going to make me cry. Okay, you can be my permanent best friend."

As his butterfly lashes blinked under his severely arched brows, his glittery red lips curved upward, exposed a super-white gap-toothed smile. "Gorgeous, ain't today your born day?"

"You remembered my birthday?"

"Facebook reminded me."

"I love your brows. My first time seeing braided eyebrows up close."

"When is your next show? I follow you and love reading about you singing in Japan and London and Switzerland. And I loved the pictures you posted in Lagos, Abuja, Accra, and Uganda. You always looking good. Girl, you know I want to be like you when I grow up."

"Trying to get a new agent. They booked me to sing the national anthem at a Rams game, but after that performance, you know, I think I'm about to make a few changes in my life. Cat who books shows in London heard my music, saw my YouTube page, and wants to meet me. We talked. He said it's time for me to move to the Big Smoke and share my talents with the people living in the London fog. He's right. I need a big change right now. And London can be the new start."

"You going over there with gorgeous Estelle, sexy Adele, and fine-ass Corinne Bailey Rae? And don't get me started on Craig David and that Nigerian producer Lemar Obika."

"Did backup or some work for most of them. Lot of talent is over there."

"Listen, are they paying you to sing the anthem?"

"Same they paid Jennifer Hudson."

"Girl, please."

"It's all about the exposure."

"So, you're kneeling or not kneeling?"

"Hadn't thought about it."

"There is no Switzerland in this situation."

"I have options."

"Rocking a black glove and raising a black fist like Tommie Smith and John Carlos?"

"You will have to wait and see how I decide to flow. This scares me. I don't want to be involved. And I don't want to mess up the song."

"What if a gun-carrying lunatic is in the crowd? They love making hashtags."

"Never thought about someone getting that crazy. But they do flip out."

"Think twice about singing that anthem. I mean, with all that's going on, it could end your career. Unless you have that Kaepernick money and you're banked up, I'd think twice. That fine-ass man can't get a job and you'll get stuck singing hooks on trap songs. You know how they do."

"Yeah. Easy to attack a black woman."

"You know they love going after black women. They went after Janet over a nipple that a white man exposed. His hand made it happen and she was blamed. He showed the titty and walked away unscathed. I will never say that motherfucker's name again as long as I live. How did Janet get blamed for what he did? The randy white boy exposed the power of the black titty and the nipple owner took the L. The take-away? Whatever we do is wrong. No matter how we do it, wrong. And if they do it, if they shoot us in the back or hang us in a cell, we still wrong."

"You are so right."

"Everything they do is right. Even the names we give our kids is wrong, unless it's the same made-up names they give their kids. If we don't use the names they like . . . job application deleted. Ain't that some mess? So, yeah, whatever we do is wrong. When you dislike someone, they can do nothing right in your eyes. Even when they are wrong, we catch the blame."

"You are definitely giving me food for thought. Don't want to get shot over a song."

"Can't kneel. Ha. All the black groups are saying is stop killing us and we want to be equal. And white extremists who consider themselves the only Americans say, nah. You better have your paper stacked before you go down on a knee, and you're in the unemployment line if you stand. No matter what you do, prepare to be dragged across social media like you're chained to the back of a pickup speeding down a dark road in Jasper, Texas. You know how they do it."

"I'm so glad you put those words of wisdom in my ear."

"Miss Isaiah, when I'm not dressed up like this. That's my real name."

"I'm so glad I met you, Miss Isaiah. You are amazing."

"OMG. I'm having a conversation with the famous Rachel Redman."

"Not famous yet."

"You're famous to me."

"What's your name tonight with your crew?"

"Tonight I'm Beyoncé Celeste."

"That name is dope."

"My girlfriends are Beyoncé Georgette and Beyoncé Simone. There are four more of us around here somewhere. We even have a Bey*incé* and a Bey*outcé*. We had another Bey*uponcé*, but she was tripping so we put her ass Bey*outcé*. Anyway, my princess, we are the Bey*oncés*."

"You don't say?"

"Oh, we *cé*." She moved her hand from side to side like the dancers in the "Single Ladies" video. "We *cé* day and night and whenever they play the queen's music. Honey, if we're at the mall and Bey comes on, we take over like a flash mob. Good thing they don't play Bey at church."

"I always wanted to kick it with Bey on my birthday."

"We can make that dream come true. Honey, we have light Bey, dark Bey, faux Bey, real Bey, rich Bey, poor Bey, and ugly Bey, but I'm the Bey of all Beys, and I'm your Bey tonight."

Rachel Redman laughed so hard her eyes watered.

The ecstatic fan asked, "Are you rocking Fenty Beauty too?"

"Hashtag, support Rihanna."

"Bish, you know those are the rules."

"You see the other *white people* makeup brands are suddenly trying to fake being woke and pro-black, posting all of their brown-girl products on Instagram? They ain't never done no shit like that *ever.* Rihanna comes to save us and now all of a sudden you notice black girls exist?"

They laughed like best friends. My opinion didn't matter. Never would among women. I knew to never make a comment about a woman's hair, clothing, or makeup unless she asked my opinion, and even then, my opinion would be however she felt about it.

A Jhené Aiko number came on and they yelled, broke out singing that hell wasn't a place, hell was other people, as they danced like misunderstood strippers. Rachel Redman was not to be outdone by anyone. Birthday girl let loose like never before, her voice angelic and soothing, the kind that made you fall in love. She turned it up, showed she was bad like Syd, SZA, Daniel Caesar, Sy Smith, dvsn, and Brent Faiyaz. The world applauded her singing. Rachel was a vibe, passionate, sensitive, an R&B woman with an R&B soul, a bad girl gone good, an angel with the voice of a wife, made to be a queen, and she wasn't a sister made for silly simpletons. While they had everyone looking our way, coming our way, dancing our way, I moved away, left the spotlight. I had a bad feeling. Was looking around to see if I was being watched, and not in a friendly way. My instincts said a storm was coming. My instincts were rarely wrong.

While they put on a show, I called Jake Ellis. "Let that woman breathe."

"We just got out the shower. Drying off. I have a minute. Whassup?"

"I saw some suspicious white boys in the area. Five or six."

"Mormons."

"They're not down our way when it gets close to dark. We're still their sundown town."

"What are you thinking? Margaux?"

"Not Margaux. Garrett was pissed."

"You know good and well he's not going to send none of his relatives this way. That yahoo doesn't want a war. He's a fake. Boston better stick to singing that John Lennon song and abusing women."

"Calm down, bro. *Chale*, I don't want my favorite *boga* to have a stroke."

He laughed. *Chale* meant "friend." *Boga* was a Ghanaian living abroad.

"Bruv, I haven't been called a *boga* since I was back home in Ghana."

I was going to tell him about Rachel and the Russian, Rachel and London, but his lover got up under him—heard her say something soft and provocative in French, spoke so whoever he was talking to would know he was with a woman. He made a sound, the kind a man made when a woman took him in her mouth. He took a breath, then said, "Bruv, let me call you back later."

I let him go. Had called to make sure he wasn't on the road after my daughter.

Rachel Redman moved through the crowd, came back to me, not dancing, not smiling.

"What bitch are you calling and talking to behind my back on my birthday?"

"Jake Ellis. San Bernardino business."

She looked at my phone. "Code?"

I told her while I pulled her closer, cupped her butt, squeezed, and pressed my finger into the crack. She wasn't having it and pushed my hand away, eyes green, on a mission.

She said, "Stop trying to Ben Affleck me."

"You like it when I do it."

"You really need to change your code to my birthday. Month, year, and day."

"Should I?"

"The code to mine is your birth month, day, and year, so, yeah."

"Didn't know that."

"You never try and creep my phone?"

"No. Why would I violate your privacy and do that?"

"That's what people do. You're weird."

"Childish."

"You're still weird."

"Sometimes you find out too much, and then it's impossible to have a relationship."

"Sometimes you don't know enough and you end up living a lie."

"Touché."

"You know momma don't play."

She turned my phone on, verified what I'd said, and her smile returned.

She asked, "You hurt someone?"

"Not today."

"Don't lie to me."

"Not lying. Just had a sit-down dinner in Pasadena."

"How much they owe?"

"About two hundred thousand."

"People get killed for one hundred ninety-nine thousand nine hundred ninety-nine dollars and fifty cents less than that."

"I thought the lowest rate was for the price of cheese on a Big Mac."

"You're getting too old for that life, Ken Swift."

"You're too old to wear a dress that tight."

"With this body and breasts like this? As hard as I work out? Never."

"Men are looking at you like it's dick o'clock."

"Women look at me like it's clit thirty."

"Yeah. You have secrets."

She poked her tongue out at me and crossed her eyes, then laughed at herself.

After a few more social media fans came and went and a dozen selfies were posted, we hit the bar. Baileys, beers, shots. Rachel Redman could drink. Said that was the Eskimo in her blood. She sang as we stood at the bar, danced, then put her arms round my neck. I held her booty like it was a life preserver. She loved that public display of affection. Birthday girl kissed me over and over. Old-school music jammed.

Total sang "Kissing You," and we slow-danced, grinded on each other like we were the only people in the room, and French-kissed and hummed the whole song. Rachel Redman was a fun drunk. A hot, sexy, dancing, singing, fun drunk.

But what I had just heard had left me disturbed, and I couldn't let it rest.

I asked, "When were you going to tell me about moving to London?"

"You mad?"

"Depends on what you say next. When was this decided?"

"I decided that this morning. I woke up alone, crying, feeling depressed. That's why I went to the gym so early. I was at the gym by four in the morning. You weren't in my bed. All those strangers were messaging me and sending me gifs, and all I wanted was one message from you. I wanted to wake up to you, then hoped you'd wake up and come to me, take me to breakfast."

"Sounds like you want to push restart on everything."

She moved her braids from her face in a sexy motion. "I need a new start."

"You're singing the national anthem at a Rams game?"

"I think when they play Seattle. But my agent is working to get me on the books."

Amazed, I repeated, "The national anthem?"

"I'm not kneeling."

"Your fans will hate you on Twitter."

"Yeah. Well. It's in my contract, if I kneel I don't get that Jennifer Hudson paycheck."

"They wrote that shit down?"

"In black and white. Someone else sang and kneeled, so they have shut that down."

"We asked to not be killed by the cops, for the slave catchers to be held accountable, and the most powerful country came apart like a cheap suit made at a sweatshop in downtown LA."

"Soon kneeling at sports events will be outlawed. Every black road ends in a roadblock."

"White House have something to do with that?"

"If I kneel, they'll call me a Black Identity Extremist."

"That's a thing? I thought she was making up some shit."

"It's real. It's the latest insult from the FBI. They'll probably bug my home like they did MLK."

"What are they calling the boys carrying assault rifles and Confederate flags?"

"Activists. Cousins. Daddy. Momma. Nephew. Children of the Corn get better press."

"Black Identity Extremists."

"Now you are extreme for identifying as black. Basically, we're Muslim-adjacent."

We looked at each other; then we laughed at the idiocy and shook our heads.

I said, "Wow. Extreme for asking to not be killed in the streets like dogs."

"Or whatever they are trying to call *unruly* Negroes these days."

"And they have a moratorium on kneeling."

"If I went out there and did a Kaepernick, I'd probably end up on the FBI's list like Martin, Malcolm, and would get set up like Assata Shakur. They'd find that old research paper I did on Islam versus Judaism. Quote things I reported about Israel and the Zionist ten years ago. Or they will pull that one Bobby Fischer quote from all the chess champion quotes on my pages."

"They'll have the IRS auditing you before you drop the mic."

She sang, "And my little legal issue in Alaska would be brought up, they'd bring up my birth name, resurrect that shit, and since I have some domestic violence in my past, even though it was directed at me and I had to put a motherfucker in check, I'd be the poster for the black woman America loves to hate. I'm imperfect, more Claudette Colvin than Rosa Parks. They'll use that as a reason to not give me my coins. And then I'd have to send you to straighten that out."

"Your fans won't care about your contract. Twitter comes down on folks hard and Black Twitter has a long memory and is less forgiving than the IRS was with Al Capone."

"Bullshit. They'll get over it. If they can get over Chris Brown and R. Kelly, they can get over my not kneeling. Just booked that gig. Don't want no shit. I just want to sing and add that to my résumé, and now I'm about to be caught up in some damn politics. Nina Simone got caught up in politics and they stopped playing her songs, killed her income. I need the exposure, and exposure means more money. I could use that bump. I mean, it's not like I'm Beyoncé. I don't have a ten-million-member Beyhive to back me up if I step out there in a white coat, then pull it off and have on fishnets, heels, all black leather, and rock a beret like the Panthers, fist up high."

"Brothers did that in the Olympics and were ostracized. No Wheaties box for them."

"On the real, you know I play chess. You know I am the queen of chess."

"You play so good you run them out of chess tournaments crying."

"In chess, something is thematic when a pattern reoccurs, which will infer it's not new because it has happened before. Paradoxically, every position in a game of chess is new after a couple of initial moves. However, you can train the eyes to pick out these patterns. When they become automatic, you begin to recognize themes over and over again. They begin to jump out to you. Themes save time; they give you leverage, an advantage; they help with memory."

"Okay."

"This is not new. Rejecting all black concerns, this is not new."

"Recurring pattern."

"But on this chessboard, when you make advancements, they change the rules. No matter what we do, no matter how peaceful we do it, the rules will always say we are wrong."

I took a breath. "Sure you want to take this gig in the middle of all of this controversy?"

"When has there ever not been controversy in some form since 1492?"

"I'm more concerned with you moving to the UK."

"I was going to tell you."

"Were you going to send me a postcard of you waving from the London Eye?"

"After I had everything sorted out. And it was definite and I had lodging set up."

"How would you handle a transition to London?"

"Same way people from all over the world come here and figure it out."

"And do you know how to use a bidet?"

"I'll learn. I'll get a flat, start over, write more songs, sing background and do studio work there until I get established. You can come with me and we can both start life over together."

"Become expats? What would I do across the pond the rest of my life?"

"What's important is I'd get you away from San Bernardino. And Jake Ellis."

"I don't have that kind of cash to pick up and restart my life right now."

"I'd take care of you. For a year."

"That's generous."

"I have no problem supporting a man who loves me, especially when I love him."

"How would I live overseas? You speak four languages. I speak one."

"Weren't you going to go to Africa?"

"What does that have to do with London?"

"You don't speak Yoruba or Oromo or Hausa or Igbo or Zulu or Shona or French. And your Amharic is awful. That English you speak here, you'd speak that same English there as we walk along the Thames. All you have to do is learn British slang, not curse, and you'll be straight."

"Yeah. But this skin won't stand out in Africa."

"Bullshit. Africans will know. We have African bloodlines, but our swagger is American."

"Americans are the cousins of the Brits, same type of oppression, same type of racism, another all-white government, and knowing that, you'd move me from one racism to the next."

"You're afraid?"

"Cautious. Knowing the crimes of Britain, I am cautious."

"You've lived in the same spot so long you don't know how to leave."

"England is in a war with Afghanistan, Iraq, Libya, Somalia, Syria, and Yemen."

"You've been around the sun forty-three times from the same spot. Don't be one of those people who are born and die and never travel any farther than Las Vegas. Vegas is nothing compared to the rest of the world. Vegas looks like the world turned on its side and all the junk landed in one spot, and people flock there like they are going to see the real Pyramids."

"It's dangerous. They have a lot of terrorist bombings over there, more than over here."

"Trayvon. Sandra Bland. You know the list. We're being killed here. The cops over here make the ones over there seem like angels. You won't fear for your life if you're stopped."

"Yeah, but that's different."

"How? Cops over there killed like five people last year. And they were armed."

"I hear they have gangs and stabbings on the streets over there."

"All impoverished areas have gangs. Black, white, everyone. Poverty equals violence because poverty is violence imposed on the people. Starving people is an act of violence."

"We'd be the foreigners in another land run by the colonizers."

"You're scared and making up excuses. See? This is why you need me."

"I hear they drink their beer warm. I mean, who does that?"

"They have these things called refrigerators. And they have ice-makers."

"They call their potato chips 'crisps.' And they eat cold beans for breakfast."

"So what? Ken, just pack a bag and leave. That's what I did in Alaska. I knew nothing about the lower forty-eight, other than what I saw on television. I didn't know any black people. I did it, and I'm a woman. You know how hard it is for a woman to do that? We have other considerations, other fears, a level of fear you will never have, and I did it, by myself."

"British people have bad teeth and drive on the wrong side of the road."

"They drive on the *opposite* side of the street."

"Do they even watch American football over there?"

"*Opposite* does not mean *wrong*. Here they teach you anything different is wrong."

"They celebrate black history in October, Mother's Day in March, and that's just wrong."

"Read my lips, nucca. What's different is not wrong; it's just different."

"You're serious about quitting America. You're giving up LA smog for London fog?"

"I'm tired of this reality show. Nothing going on but hate, hate, hate, hate, hate."

"Hopefully it will end soon."

"Look, I feel like I've done my time here in the land of faux Christianity and extreme capitalism. If I were a white woman, with all the singing lessons, with the piano lessons, with the guitar lessons, with all the dance lessons, with all the modeling, with all my heavy-handed Eritrean mother did to mold me into the version of being the woman she failed to be, with this insecure body that works out every day, sometimes twice a day, with the way I hit five out of eight octaves, the way I can go toe-to-toe with Chanté Moore, the way I can sing Minnie Riperton with Sy Smith, with this sashay that brings down the house, and this sexy red dress, I'd be mega famous. I'd be outselling Céline Dion on the Vegas Strip. I've conquered anorexia and beaten bulimia, both a result of a *loving* mother who made sure her daughter would not be fat *and* black. She's why I hate hot combs and perms and will never go back to using heat or the creamy crack. It's natural hair from now until the grave. I had to learn that an eating disorder is not a diet, and that self-harm does not equate to attention seeking. I have my issues, and small, embarrassing cuts in places that no one will ever see but you. I grew up with a face filled with pimples, wearing nerdy glasses, around no one who looked like me. Skin too dark, hair never straight enough, sounded like a white girl, only knew white guys, and married the first one who looked at me like I was the prettiest thing on the planet. I survived that abuse and beat a murder charge. Left town with that shame heating my backside. I have my ways. I'm difficult. But at the end of the day, I'm a very talented woman, an amazing black woman, yet I am who they hire to sing backup for the less talented. Black women with mega talent rarely rise beyond BET status."

"You say you've done your time like you feel imprisoned here."

"The biggest prison is your mind. I was imprisoned in Alaska. My mother was my warden. I love her, I will pay her bills, I will send her flowers, but I can't be around her. I understand why my father left one day and never came back. Free yourself. I want you to come with me. Get out of America. Get away from this mentality. It's not going to change. Look at the makeup of the people running the country. They have this shit on lock. Let's move on and see what else the world has to offer. Let's see what the USA looks like from the outside. Let's find some place where they don't consider kneeling as more disrespectful than the murder of black lives."

"You just dropped this on me without a warning. It's a lot to think about."

"We're here pretending to be Americans, but we're not. We have no constitutional rights here. No real freedom of speech. The Declaration of Independence and other documents were written by and for white men, by and for rich landowners, and blacks and browns and everyone else, we're trying to revise commandments and force ourselves to be included in that manifesto."

"You've given this a lot of thought."

"I'm more than a sexy, sassy, loud, and fun-to-be-with singer with an incredible ass."

"No doubt."

"We wake up fighting every day and acting like when they say *Americans* they are talking about blacks too. We're not Americans, and we're not Africans. We're *in-betweeners*, if anything. We're not enough of that to be that, and not enough of this to be this. We wake up rushing to get online to see who was killed while we slept. Enough. Let's bail and find our place in the sun."

"We wake up to bad news. Just like our parents did by reading the newspaper."

"And just like their parents did, only it was probably by word of mouth, or by looking up at the NAACP offices in New York to see if they had the banner saying another man was lynched."

"And I had to find out you're jetting by overhearing you talk to a stranger?"

"Again, I will take care of you. For a year. Ironically, with some supremacists chilling like villains in the White House, I'm making bank on my aerospace stocks. He dropped a bomb and stocks damn near doubled. And if he starts a war with North Korea, my stocks will quadruple."

"We didn't win the first Korean War. We didn't win Vietnam. We haven't won in Afghanistan. And now they want to go nuclear bomb–to–nuclear bomb against North Korea."

"Win or lose, I'll be making money every time they fire a shot or drop a bomb."

"My secret Republican with Democratic sensibilities. What do I see in you?"

"I always vote for my money. If it don't make dollars, it don't make sense."

"Good thing you have your own health insurance and birth control."

"You call what we do birth control?"

"If you get pregnant that way, we're going to have a long talk."

"Freak."

"You like it. Can tell you grew up around them white boys."

"And I give head like a white girl."

"Like two white girls on E."

"I know how to pull the soul out of you. This black girl is different. I know how to make you weak." She laughed, ran her hands over her braids. "Buy me another shot or two or three."

I waved down the bartender, got shots, then asked, "The Russian know about London?"

"Ken."

"Does he?"

"I didn't invite him."

"That guitar he just bought you?"

Her nostrils flared as she exhaled. "Can we talk about that later?"

"Are you keeping it?"

"You want to make this an issue now?"

"It's a simple yes or no."

"Later?"

"Sure."

CHAPTER 17

THEN THE ECSTATIC fan she had just met came over with a dozen fierce friends, and they gathered around Rachel and sang an amazing "Happy Birthday" at the top of their lungs. Her life became a musical broadcast live on both Facebook and Periscope. She told me she would be right back, and left singing and dancing with her new friends. I found a spot that wasn't crowded and checked my phone. Jimi Lee had called again. Margaux had called too. Still nothing from Esmerelda. I sent her a reminder text; then I turned my phone off. Now wasn't the time to fall into my past with no safety net. And I needed to let Esmerelda do her thing. Plus, I had to deal with Rachel, had to remain present.

I went to Rachel and found her on her phone. When she saw me coming her way, she ended her call, ended it talking in Russian. Then she was all nervous smiles. I didn't call her on her bullshit, just let it ride. I stole her away from the clutches of her endearing fan club. Now she smelled like a cloud of freshly grown sativa.

She said, "Oh my God. We smoked some Charlie Sheen."

"Never heard of that."

"Charlie Sheen OG. They say it's the tiger blood of weed strains."

"Sounded like you were on the phone talking to Putin on behalf of the president."

"The ex just called."

"Oh?"

"He saw the pictures I posted. He's jealous."

"What's up?"

"Told him to fuck off. If he wanted it, he should have put a ring on it."

She had a cigar in her mouth, resting like a phallus. She was beyond blissful tonight, so I wouldn't complain, just let her party until she dropped. Her phone vibrated. I felt it. We were that close. She ignored it. It was the Russian calling back. That took the wind out of my sails.

I shouldn't be jealous. But I was. He'd bought her that Gibson. I knew she wasn't going to give it back. And I wasn't going to ask her to. She had to do that shit on her own. I didn't want to bring up the Russian over and over and become preoccupied with some other motherfucker.

When I was with Jimi Lee I had lost too much sleep. I told myself never again.

Rachel danced as we found two seats at the bar. She moved against me like she was trying to give me an erection. I inhaled her and wanted to be inside her as deep as I could go. She scooted closer, so close we could be mistaken for Siamese twins, then put her warm cheek next to mine, rubbed her hands on my inner thighs, massaged my rising bump, smiled, kissed my lips, put lipstick on my face, whispered, "Can I tell my sexy boyfriend something?"

My cheek against hers, feeling the warmth of her face and the sweetness of her spirits-tinted breath I said, "Have I ever been able to stop you from saying that which you want to say?"

"That which? What, you're auditioning for Shakespeare in the Park?"

"Let me sound as smart as you without you fucking with me."

She crooned, "I came over to your place, freshly shaved and moisturized, looking sexy, smelling good as hell, wanted you to see me when I walked in the door, wanted you to see me and become speechless, get an erection and lose your mind, wanted you to take me as soon as I walked in the door, wanted you to make me get on my knees and open my mouth, wanted to suck you, drive you crazy. I wanted to do some of the things Skin Diamond does in her videos. I can't freak like her, but I wanted to take it to my limit. Wanted to talk dirty. Real dirty. I wanted to go full Brazzers. I wanted you to rock this ass and make me jazz, then jazz wherever you like."

"Damn. Are you talking crazy, or the alcohol has taken over your soul?"

"Boo, I want some of that." She kissed me. "And I know you want some of this."

"You wanted to party, birthday girl, so let's party until the spot closes."

"Almost longer than my face when hard, almost wider than my mouth. This is mine." She rubbed my cock. "Let's go outside. I want to put my mouth on you until you scream hallelujah."

I hummed in her ear. "Stop playing."

She sang. "Sucking you is all that I've been thinking of. Sucking you is so goooood."

"Don't mess up a classic romantic song."

"Sucking will feel better than kissing. I want to show you how I feel about you. Want to show you my appreciation *and* forgiveness. Want to suck you and make your brain fill with happy chemicals, prove to you that I'm yours, all yours; then I want you to let me ride you like a boss."

"Act like a lady."

She sang, "Fucking you is all that I've been thinking of. You fuck me so *goooood*."

"Kill the remix."

"Let's go outside in the cool air and find a place. Take care of me."

"I'm nursing my drink. And we're celebrating from crotch of night to the crack of dawn."

She took my drink, finished it. "Why are fine men always so fucking dull and boring?"

"That reverse psychology is not going to work either."

Her phone vibrated again. Again she ignored the juddering.

My tipsy lover pressed against me, her soft breasts all up on me, her hands as busy as the devil. "So, now you're punishing me? Is this because I didn't give you some before we left?"

I moved her braids, bit her ear. "Hard to punish you without punishing myself."

She licked my lips. "Don't move my hand. I know you want this. You know I want that. Waited all day for that. I still want that. You think I won't take it right here and right now?"

"Don't start nothing in this spot; you don't want to get the Kevin Hart treatment."

"Let's go turn this dress into a Lewinsky."

"Your classy, educated ass has a few drinks and starts acting like a thoughtless thot."

"Call our UberXL. Be nice and I'll give you some road head until we get home."

"In Chicago, Uber drivers get road head, not passengers."

"Ubers are the new mobile Snooty Foxes. Everybody has quickies in Ubers."

"Will add that to my bucket list."

"Did you know that only thirty percent of women swallow? I'm a minority."

I rubbed her legs. "Talkative. Giggling. Singing. Drinking like a fish. Acting silly."

"Hashtag, I love your fat penis. Hashtag, that length. Hashtag, girth matters. Hashtag, wider than my mouth. Hashtag, made for a longtime partner. Hashtag, and I'm the longtime partner it's made for. Hashtag, take me outside, find a spot, 'n' gimme some balls deep."

"Hashtag, you must be ovulating. Faded and ovulating."

"Hashtag, and if you weren't around, masturbating."

"You do that while we're doing it anyway. When you're facedown, ass up, you have that right hand down there working it out while I long stroke. That shit is your favorite position."

"I hate you."

I sucked her tongue. "Ovulating. And you want daddy all up in that."

She laughed. "When a woman is ovulating, that's when she's the horniest."

I bit her ear again, kissed her cheek. "Stop. People can see what you're doing."

"Let me jack you off under the table. Let me see if you can keep a straight face while I help you lower your chance of heart disease, stroke, and diabetes. Sex does that, you know."

"Stop. Your social media fans are enjoying recording the show with their phones. Someone will end up trying to blackmail you when you blow up."

"I want to blow you."

"Stop it."

"Your dick is amaze-balls. And it's straight like a baseball bat. No curve."

"Stop it."

"I want some of this right here to end my birthday night."

"Stop rubbing and feeling me up before you make me get hard."

"Before you set free five million swimmers?"

"Alaska. Stop."

"I'm going to ride you and make your toes curl up like fists."

"Keep talking that talk."

"I'm going to make this a three-hole night for you."

"Three-hole night?"

"I'm wet."

"You're drunk."

"Touch me, touch me, touch me."

"Touch yourself."

"Put your trigger finger inside me and make that 'come here' motion."

"You are an aggressive drunk."

"We gonna role-play tonight. You will be Black Panther and I'm going to be Storm. You're going to pull my braids and choke me and long stroke the mutant out of this little bitch. I'll set my Fitbit and count calories while you slap this ass. Be ready. I want thirty minutes of hot sex to burn off two hundred alcoholic calories, and I want my headboard-banging workout to end with a skeet of nitrogen, fructose, lactic acid, ascorbic acid, and inositol. Hashtag, protein shot."

"Since you know so much, how many calories will be in that protein shot?"

She Googled. "Twenty-five. You know I have to monitor my caloric intake."

"Someone is definitely ovulating."

"I do get nasty every now and then, don't I?"

"You think?"

"But your nasty Mississippi ass? You love my groceries like a fat boy loves cake."

"You make me wonder about the rest of the women up in Alaska."

"And to burn off the alcohol, we can run a 10K tomorrow when we wake up."

I put my hands between her thighs. "We can burn another two hundred calories in bed."

She hummed. "That will work. But I'm still going to the gym. Can't let myself get fat."

I traced the outline of her vagina. "Happy birthday, boo."

She quivered, brought her lips to mine, butterfly kisses. "Best birthday ever."

I sucked her lips while my fingers did the walking. "Best girlfriend ever. Love you."

"Love you too." Arms around my neck, she hummed. "You gonna make me cry."

"Let me see if you can keep that straight face."

She leaned into me, did Kegels on my finger. "You're gonna make me come."

"Want me to stop?"

"You gonna make me come you gonna make me come you gonna make me come."

I stirred her, and she bit her bottom lip as she rubbed my cock, held on to it, stroked me through my clothes, kept it hot until our round of drinks and shots came.

She was near rapture, licking lips, rapping. "Not gonna hide from that d. Too big. Stroke strong. Make me moan for that dick."

"Yeah?"

She rapped on. "I'll skydive for that d. No parachute. Legs open. Trying to land on that d."

"Ouch."

"Wake up for that d. Cooking breakfast. Butt naked. Mouth ready for that dick."

I laughed at her inebriated, off-beat, improvised rapping.

She kept rubbing me, said, "Do one for me. Make up one for me."

"I'll fly for that p. First class, dick hard, feenin hard for that p."

"Not too bad. One more. Please, please, please. One more."

"Hmmm. I'll catch a case for that p. In jail. No bail. What? Now another d in that p?" I stopped and shook my finger like I was a Jay-Z meme come to life. "Hell naw! Oh, hell naw."

She laughed. I laughed. We kissed. We were tipsy and silly.

She said, "I've had a *Being Mary Jane* life, but I want a *This Is Us* kind of love."

"Yeah. Me too."

"We can do this, you know. We can do this."

This was what a good love felt like. She was with me. Not with the Russian.

She asked, "Why are you looking at me like that?"

"Like what?"

"All primal."

"That body."

"Not the dress?"

"The body in that dress is what makes the dress worth looking at."

"The dress is mine, but this body is your body if you want to get me bodied tonight."

"Oh, you're going to get bodied, then I'm going to be all up in that body."

A Cardi B song came on, and the room was once again set on fire. Every sophisticated woman went hood rat, and every Pussycat Doll rapped the lyrics to "Bodak Yellow" like it was their national anthem.

Rachel Redman was up in my face, pointing in my face, making antag-onistic faces, acting it out while I did the Milly Rock. Women all over the spot were trying to outdo each other. A few Barbra Streisand–loving men were in their hard-leg lovers' faces doing the same. Rachel made me feel twenty-one again. Reminded me of back in the day when I was in the club with Jimi Lee and Ice Cube's "No Vaseline" came on and we turned it out. I did the Humpty Hump with Jimi Lee, did the Running Man with her. I had to move beyond being the divorced man who couldn't get over his ex. I wished those nights with Jimi Lee had been spent with Rachel instead.

Everything here reminded me of Jimi Lee. That apartment. And now Margaux. Maybe I needed to leave and go to London. Just take a chance on a new life. Maybe I needed to swipe left on everything. Because every-thing I had loved had swiped left on me a long time ago.

I looked at Rachel and my heart was on fire. She glowed when she looked at me.

That aroused me. The way she loved me aroused me.

When we sat again, I put my finger inside Rachel, stirred her. Made her leg tremble.

Rachel's eyes tightened with desire and she moaned. "I want you down my throat."

"No."

"I'll swallow. Hell, I'll gargle if that makes my boo happy."

"Stop being nasty."

"You're fingering me like you're a pervert and I'm nasty?"

"Look at me. Keep a straight face."

"If you don't get too rough, when we get home you can double-cross my pussy."

"You're drunk and vulgar."

"I'm affectionate when I'm being finger fucked."

"Let the d go. Stop fluffing me."

"I will when you stop fingering me."

"No one can tell you're turned on."

"Shit. My fat nipples are hard; they look like baby dicks growing out of my boobs."

"Don't get me hard."

"I don't care if they see your dick print. I want them to know what I'm working with."

"You like this."

"I love this."

"Look at your face. The way you bite your lip is so sexy."

She moved my hand from between her legs, put my finger in my mouth, fed me, then leaned and kissed me, sucked the taste of her arousal from my tongue, then sucked my finger.

She sang. "You love putting me on my belly so you can invade Africa when you come."

"Can you be a little louder?"

She sang louder, "I'm horny and tonight I want to ride my man and make his toes curl."

People near us laughed and applauded. I laughed and shook my head. Rachel Redman laughed the hardest, moved her braids, and kissed me again. She was impossible not to love.

She said, "I'm ready for some leg shaking, cursing, nails in skin, booty being slapped, oh yeah, baby don't stop. I want three orgasms before you bust a nut, and you can nut all over me."

"Damn, boo."

"Or in my ass. You love to nut in my ass."

"No pregnancy scares that way."

"I ain't complaining. The way you eat mom's pie, I ain't complaining about nothing."

"Eat you so good I drive you crazy."

"And you body me so strong you had me breaking in your house and waiting for that d."

We laughed and she rubbed me, masturbated me through my pants. That was why the Russian was buying her presents and blowing up her phone. Men wanted a woman like this.

She sang, "When we get home, I want to master-blaster. Smoke while you stroke."

"What do you have now? Sativa or indica?"

"Hollands Hope. Indica-dominant hybrid. My fans hooked me up big-time."

"Don't get addicted on the shit that had black folks getting put on lock for decades."

"Boo, I'm addicted to your loving. Got me breaking your locks to get me some cock."

I gave her soft, gentle kisses, not too much tongue at first. Then it was as if we were famished, bit by bit losing control. Rachel Redman was the woman I should have been with two decades ago. I'd marry her tonight. Alcohol had me feeling that way. I kissed her eyes, worked down her cheeks and licked the edges of her lips. Made her chase my tongue, and when she finally caught it, she sucked it gently, and we lingered awhile, nibbling and playing. I sucked her tongue like I was sucking her clit, and that made her lose it. She sucked my tongue like she was talking to the mic. Blood rushed from my brain and it was all down south.

Rachel downed her alcohol, chugged mine, did our shots, grabbed my crotch, dragged me through the crowd, blew farewell smooches to her fans, and hurried me toward the exit.

A MOMENT LATER, we were outside, in the open air, hidden in the shadows, cars, buses, and metro trains zooming by in the distance, the glow from the dramatic lights at the Staples Center not far away. We kissed and kissed. She held my stiff cock, rubbed me, masturbated me through my clothes while I nibbled at her neck, sucked on that spot that made her croon. Her knees buckled and her inner thighs shook. She let my cock go, shivered, then exhaled in a way that told me she wanted more. I worked her breasts out of her dress, licked one, then sucked the other nipple. My hand moved between her thighs. I massaged her heat through that red dress. Her legs opened; then I pulled her dress up, moved her panties away, got a finger inside.

She was damp, heat rising like the morning sun over Acapulco.

I was harder than times in 1929.

She moved against my hand. I fingered her, suckled her breasts and massaged that pearl, then looked in her eyes as she wiggled on my digit. She took my finger from inside her, sucked it hard, sucked until the juice was gone, kissed me as she reached for my pants, undid my belt. I hiked up her red dress and we tried to have sex perpendicular. Doing it standing up, between buildings, fully dressed, wearing hard shoes, tipsy, with a drunk Afro-Alaskan, that shit wasn't as easy as it looked in the movies. I was almost back inside her, then paused when a dozen people walked by. They didn't see us. I lifted her up, and the horny drunk wrapped her legs around me. She pulled her panties to the side, then cooed when I broke the skin. She said my name like I was her greatest sin. She made sounds like she was drowning, then opened her eyes, looked in my face, smiled, swallowed. I held her, made her bounce up and down, made her jewelry sing, made the change in my pockets join the choir on the break. I looked into her eyes and sang the "Happy Birthday" song to her. Cool desert wind blew across our damp skin.

"Let me down, boo. Let me down."

She eased down, meandered in a circle, took a lighter out of her little clutch purse, flipped the Zippo open, lit her cigar, made the air smell like we were in Snoop D-o-double-g's home, put the Zippo back, then puffed. Rachel Redman laughed, happy, then staggered and put her left hand against a wall. She puffed, made smoke rise around her like she was the boss of all bosses.

Rachel came back to me, stroked my erection while she smoked, masturbated me, then got down on her haunches, squatted, inhaled her Kush, then took me in her mouth as she exhaled smoke.

"You like that?"

My vocabulary was reduced to indecipherable sounds and curt moans.

She whispered, "That's right, baby. I got your ass singing like Peabo Bryson."

She played me like Coltrane playing his horn. It was beautiful, like a love letter written by Shakespeare. She sang, "Sucking you is all I've been thinking of. Sucking you is so good." I moaned like I was her background singer. She made it sloppy, made my toes curl inside of my shoes. Her head bobbed, and she licked and sucked like it was National

Ice Cream Day. Then she moved her hands to my thighs for balance, her gag reflex getting the better of her.

She hummed. "I want some of this holy water."

"Yeah?"

"Quench this fire. Pour it all over me."

"You got the fever."

"And I got it bad. You know how I get every now and then."

"Nature takes control of you right before your period."

"Period?"

"You heard me."

She laughed. "They should call mine a *sentence.* Once a month, coochie on lockdown."

A group of intoxicated Korean tourists stumbled out of nowhere, caught Rachel on her haunches, my shaft down her throat as her braids swayed with her wicked rhythm. They yelled in their language, then cheered and applauded as they guffawed. Rachel looked at them, my cock in her hand, stroked me as she told them, "Fuck off. Go somewhere and do some calculus, or mechanics and special relativity."

She damned them all, told the voyeurs to get all the way the fuck outta our business, and when they didn't, she flipped them off, went back to playing the sax, double-timing until I reached for her, and got her to turn me loose and stand up. She cursed her audience, called them tight-eyed perverts, yanked her red dress down, stumbled, picked up her cigar, almost lost her balance again. Her breasts fell out, and she tried to get her C-cups covered up again. I was too dizzy to help. She struggled with the girls while I battled and limped and fought to fit my Valyrian steel back inside my pants. We left in a hurry, the happy birthday girl laughing too hard and unable to run drunk in heels. My dick was hard and I was lightheaded. Her high heels clacking through broken darkness. Rachel Redman zigzagged back into lights that made L.A. Live as bright as the obnoxious Las Vegas Strip. Rachel cackled, staggered, wiped her mouth, licked the corners of her lips, tossed her braids to the side, then pumped a fist and yelled, *"Best birthday ever. Happy birthday to me."* We hurried away with her yelling at Siri to open the goddamn Uber app.

She stood in front of me, faced me, hid my erection. "You have pussy breath."

"Your pussy. And you have dick breath."

"Your dick." She kissed me again, mixed our flavors. "Can't wait to get you home."

"My balls are so blue they're about to turn black."

"You didn't come. That's what it felt like while I was waiting on you all day. Like that." She moved against my erection.

"You're torturing me."

"I know. I wanted to make you come, but I don't want holy water all over my dress."

"I'll buy you a new dress."

Rachel grinded against me. "I'm going to love you so damn good."

"No freaky business in the Uber."

"*Nucca*, if you'd driven your BMW, I'd've given you the best road head *evah*."

"As thirsty as you're acting, I doubt if we would have made it inside the car."

"I'm thirsty for you. This fever is strong. So hot for your holy water to quench my thirst."

"I'm going to get you on your back, have your ankles at your neck."

"Then what?"

"Make you rock back and forth against my tongue in slow motion."

"You know I love that shit."

"I love it more than you do. Could do that all night."

"Tongue takes me to Jesus, but I want you inside me."

"I want to be inside you."

"After that ankle thing, I want you inside me."

"Balls deep."

"Your cock is huge."

"The better to fuck you with, my dear."

"The way you fuck me, makes me feel like I'm deep in prayer, like I've been taken to some holy place, transported to the Ganges River and your love washes away all of my sins. I come and I feel like I'm dying, like I am experiencing a holy liberation. No other man makes me feel that way. No one but you, Ken Swift. I'm yours. I am all yours, as long as you will have me."

"Damn."

"And that makes me want to suck you the way I do, makes me love you with my mouth, want to wake up your soul, to make you feel as weak for me as I fuckin' feel for you."

"Damn."

"That all you got?"

"Come here."

"Love it when you put your hands all over my ass like that in public."

"Do you?"

"I do. I want men to see me happy and let every bitch know you belong to me."

"I want to take you and find another spot and finish what we started."

"Uber is two minutes away. Get me home and I have a spot you can look for."

We stood on the side of the busy street, in a crowd, the promise of intense thrumming between us, in our breathing, in our eyes, in the way she squeezed her thighs to keep her desire from being unleashed, kissing like we owned the world, waiting on our Uber. Her nostrils flared with every breath, and mine did the same, lust and the need to come suffocating us both.

Birthday girl was ready for that d, and this d was ready for that p.

CHAPTER 18

LESS THAN TWENTY minutes later, we stumbled up the stairs at my building, loud as hell, kissing, feeling each other up. By the time we made it inside my spot, birthday breasts had been fondled and licked like candy. We closed the door hard. Her elegant outfit was bunched up around her waist. I bent her over, had her pretty face pressed against the front door, her panting deep, desperate, anticipatory, breathing that matched mine as I tried to get balls deep inside her.

"Put it in. Stop playing with me and put it in. Put it all the way in."

I pushed.

She was wet, but I couldn't get the head in. I staggered, pulled my pants down more, pushed again, and it was like I bounced back. Her expensive lace panties were in the goddamn way, cock blocking. I tried to pull them to the side, but I pulled so hard it hurt her.

"Take my panties off, Ken. Move Victoria so you can get inside my secret real good."

I growled, tugged her delicate panty until it ripped away, then slapped my cock on her dampness a dozen times, made her tremble and curse. Then I pushed. She was so wet I slid my sturdy baobab in to the root, made the birthday girl sing mournful songs about the goodness of wood. But the song she sang was an ugly off-key song. She gagged, burped, told me to stop, begged me to stop, then moved away from me, hand on belly, eyes tight, in excruciating pain.

"Oh no, oh no, oh no, oh no."

"What's wrong?"

"My stomach. Bubble gut, bubble gut. Oh God. Fuck. I got the doggone belly."

She tried to run, but she could barely stand. With those heels on, she wobbled like a deer that had been hit by a semi. Her ankle twisted, and I grabbed her before she fell down.

She gagged. "Take the wheel, Jesus. Take the wheel and get me to the toilet."

I helped her get up, and she staggered doubled over, like she was suddenly in labor. She panted, stumbled like she was running a country mile up a muddy hill. She made it as far as the carpeted hallway before she lost her dinner. I was on my feet, tried to pull my pants up above my knees by the time she got to the bathroom. She had on only one high heel, limped slowly, went up and down, taut ass exposed, firm breasts bouncing. She slammed the bathroom door.

Like a terrified child she called out, "Oh God. Please, God. Make it stop."

In the darkness, Rachel Redman plopped on the toilet. Her insides exploded like the Space Shuttle firing up its engines, the liftoff immediate. She declared she was dying; groaned as if an evil overseer with a whip was trying to convince her that her new name was Toby.

I turned the hall light on. The light flickered like a horror film, then settled.

She had created dramatic artwork in colors unique to my eyes.

Rachel Redman stopped chanting out her agony and cried out, "I need more toilet paper."

"I'm all out."

"Don't fucking fuck with me right now, Ken Swift."

"But I have a cardboard box I can tear up into small pieces."

"Then get me some damn paper towels from the kitchen."

"Gently, Bentley. I'm joking."

"Stop laughing at me."

"I'm not laughing."

She screeched, "Stop the cockamamie jokes and get the damn toilet paper."

I cracked the bathroom door wide enough to toss her a roll of Charmin two-ply, then stepped around the destruction in the hallway, took off my wrinkled pants and crinkled shirt, lobbed them onto the queen bed. Tired as hell, I dragged myself back to the kitchen, found a plastic bucket, filled it with hot water and soap, grabbed sponges and a mop, then hunted the cabinets, picked up the bleach, vinegar, and Fabuloso. Rachel sounded like she was in the middle of a terrorist attack. Bomb after bomb exploded. Prayers and pleas were sent up to a napping God. After each explosion, the toilet flushed twice. I pulled on yellow plastic gloves, went to the hall, and cleaned up a Rorschach of Chinese food, seafood, Baileys, and shots. When I was done she was still in the bathroom, in the middle of her war, suffering, moaning, cursing, crying out regrets.

"You okay in there?"

"The ride back in the Uber."

"You told the driver to drive fast as she could."

"She changed lanes a lot and hit too many potholes when we got off on Crenshaw."

"*You told the girl to drive fast.*"

"I think I got carsick or something. Oh, God. Hope I don't have a GI thing going on."

I cracked the windows, put the ceiling fans on low, then pulled down fresh sheets, changed the linen. A few minutes later she was in the shower. She gargled, brushed her teeth, and staggered out of the bathroom, used the walls to keep her balance, moved bent at the belly. She begged me not to go into the bathroom before next Christmas. She crawled into my bed, embarrassed, groaned like an old woman, and pulled herself into the fetal position, swore this was her worst birthday ever and that she'd never drink another goddamn Baileys again. I brought her some Pepto-Bismol to cement the contents of her belly. I made her take it, then propped pillows under her to keep her head elevated. When she was settled, I took a cold washcloth and draped it across her neck to hold the regurgitation at bay. Feeling aggravated, I grabbed the bucket and cleansers and went to the bathroom, double flushed before I lifted the lid on the commode, became Molly Maid, and cleaned up her mess.

When I was done, I showered, scrubbed my body like I'd been exposed to radiation.

I was in the bedroom drying off, listening to Rachel's deep breathing, making sure she didn't roll over on her back, start to regurgitate, and choke to death on my watch. Then her cell phone was on fire. I grabbed her electronic leash. The texts were in Russian. I turned the phone off. Had flashbacks. I'd been through this bullshit before. Wasn't going to travel that dark road again.

She was still on her back, sleeping the sleep of the ill. I didn't care. I was two seconds from waking her up, telling her to get out. I'd put her in an Uber and send her to her ex. Enraged, fighting bad memories, not wanting that era repeated with a new face, eyes wide, I cursed.

A lot of overlapping commotion erupted outside, aroused the streets. First I heard a car in the intersection, music loud enough to rattle windows from here to the freeway that was two miles away. Then tires screeched as some fool burned doughnuts in the asphalt. I went to the window, ready to scream out at the harbingers of rudeness, but they zoomed away, went to the next intersection and did the same, then moved on to the next block, then to the next corner.

I turned my phone back on, needed to check for Esmerelda. My phone rang. It wasn't my coworker. Didn't recognize the number. Had to be Jimi Lee or Margaux, back to blowing my phone up. I didn't answer, just turned the ringer down, left vibration mode on as backup.

A ghetto bird hovered over my postal code, and sirens were near. I went to the window. An ice cream truck was parking in front of the building to the east. I stopped looking at the truck when Bernice Nesbitt waved. My neighbor across the street was in her window.

I saw her. And I saw bare breasts. She squeezed them. She had magnificent breasts, the kind that would make a brother start praise dancing in the name of the Lord.

She was in a mood. And so was I. Alcohol had exasperated all I felt, good and bad.

The Brit had seen me come back home with Rachel Redman, and now she was challenging me, extending an invitation to keep her company. Without words, she asked me to cheat on my woman the way she had cheated her man.

Fair was fair.

Bernice Nesbitt didn't move away.

She was daring me to cross the pond, and to do it while my woman was feet away, as a thrill. The Brit's fullness was incredible. Tonight, the Brit wanted some Mississippi loving. Rachel Redman coughed. She coughed and broke the spell the Brit's Coke-bottle shape had cast. When one woman disliked another, she would destroy a man so she could become the victor in a catfight. I turned and Rachel Redman made a sound like she was dying, then Calamity Jane was calling hogs. I changed the cold towel I had on her neck. I shook her. She didn't move. I looked at the rise of her ass. That ass worked out twice a day, hiked, jogged, did squats, and took boxing classes. Solid ass. I traced my fingers along her beautiful skin, whispered her name, kissed her lips. Touched her nose. No response. Drunk. Dead to the world. She might as well have been on propofol. She couldn't see a hole in a forty-foot ladder and wouldn't be able to see me leave.

In two minutes, I could accept the baton of infidelity and be inside London.

Alcohol was in my blood, my moral compass offline, inebriated as I treaded in irony.

London was in front of me. A woman leaving me for London behind me.

Rachel Redman had gone back to the Russian. She said it had happened only once. That was the only way Rachel Redman had been like Jimi Lee. And that was one way too many.

Bernice Nesbit was flashing her SOS.

I owed her one.

She wouldn't scream.

I wouldn't holla.

I could say two tears in a bucket, sprint across the pond, be a moth-erfuckin' starboy like Jake Ellis, and feel a brand-new warmth. I yanked on a pair of green NinjApparel joggers and a Skywalker hoodie, slid on a pair of Timberlands; then I eased out of the front door.

As soon as I made it to the bottom of the stairs, an enemy was out on Stocker, waiting.

"Ken?"

The angered voice was familiar.

"Ken Swift?"

It was hard and intellectual and carried an accent that I'd never forget.

A car door closed and the enraged figure came toward me from a parked BMW. My enemy was dressed in reds and oranges, like fire, an ethnic outfit with amazing patterns, made of finer materials, like a beautiful number worn at a Bilen wedding. And with her colorful, fiery dress she wore a scarf in a way that could make one think it was a hijab. She always wore scarves that way, loved the stylishness. She was Chris-tian, not Muslim. At least she was Christian the last time I saw her. Here. Reminded me of the Somalian women, of the Oromo girls at the Horn of Africa and their bomb headpieces.

It was Jimi Lee. My ex-wife. The mother of my feral child.

My past had returned.

The chickens had come home to roost.

CHAPTER 19

JIMI LEE CREPT closer, her heels clicking as cars passed on the narrow street. She approached me like a woman who had stage fright, but the curtain was up and there was no going back. She was twenty steps away. I felt her anxiety. And I treaded in mine.

Rachel was in my bed. Bernice Nesbitt lingered in her window. Crossing the pond was no longer on my mind. I had almost done a Kevin Hart and gone Eric Benét. But fate had intruded.

I faced the woman I had married, the woman I used to want ten times a day. And just like that I was no longer forty-three. Once again, I was in my twenties. For a second, my face drifted into an unexpected smile, but I corrected that, became a hard forty-three again.

Jimi Lee let out a nervous breath and said, *"Indemin Alleh?"*

"De-hna ne-gn. I'm fine." I struggled to speak in her language. *"In-de-min Al-le-sh?"*

"How am I? I'm blessed."

"This is a surprise. *Rageme gize katayayen."*

"Yes, it has been a very long time. And you still speak and understand Amharic."

"But not enough to have a serious conversation with you."

"Can we talk?"

"We can talk. In English."

Jimi Lee was six steps away from me. She had returned to the scene of the crime. She was eighteen when I met her. Now she was forty. She had the birth date I'd never forget, because it was the same as mine. Her ethnic outfit was tailored, fitted to her curves. She pulled her scarf away. She let me see her face. Revealed beauty and let me see her traveling anger etched in a level of gorgeousness not many would achieve. Her hair was long, natural, wavy, amazing. I wanted her to be bald, fat, and unattractive and have stretch marks that looked like a map of the interstate system for the USA, but time had taken care of her the way servants took care of a queen. Time had been her friend. If she couldn't pass for eighteen, she could pass for twenty. I used to hold her ass and fill her with my desire.

And at the same time, I remembered the bad times, felt like I had last seen her as a child. Time had passed, and Pennywise the clown had returned to bring me brand-new horrors.

I said, "What are you doing here in Leimert Park parked in front of my building?"

"I tried to call you for hours. Since early afternoon. My daughter called me and told me she had a reunion. And that shocked me. So. Had wanted to try and have a conversation."

"Margaux told you about our lunch date."

"She was vague. Very upset and vague."

"And you decided to put on a stalker's shoes and come to investigate."

"Yes. I am concerned."

"What do you know?"

"She tells me nothing."

"She has a lot going on."

"What, exactly?"

"She won't tell me much more than that she needs money in a bad way."

"Why would she need money?"

"You have to ask your daughter. She needs money, and she needs a lot."

"She won't talk to me about whatever is going on."

I hesitated. "You see what she has done to her skin?"

My ex made a face like she was ashamed. "She has changed, suddenly cut me out of her life. I thought maybe she had come back to you, that maybe she hated me now for some reason."

"Welcome to Club Know Nothing. How did she know where I live?"

"My old journals. Old paperwork. She saw the address from old mail I received here."

"Then she looked me up. Found my number. Called me. Invited me to lunch."

"I had no idea."

"What does she know about Florida? About Balthazar Walkowiak?"

"Nothing. Why would you ask me that?"

"She knows."

"Not from me."

"Who else would she know that from? How else would she know about that?"

She took a nervous breath. "You still live here. Same building. Same apartment."

I nodded. "Same place I lived with you when I met you."

"This is a déjà vu."

"Same place, minus the furniture, pots and pans, and money you took when you moved."

"I didn't steal anything."

"No one said you stole anything. You just took everything not nailed down."

"My father's doing. It was no secret how he felt about you, about us as a couple."

"Sure. I bet it was. Him and whoever helped you move everything but the kitchen sink."

She laughed a little. I did too, then tried to remember the last time we laughed together.

She said, "I was nineteen when I moved here. Lived here until I was about twenty-five."

"We were married. Wasn't the best marriage. Wasn't much of a marriage."

"The brain develops back to front, with the frontal cortex, the part used for decision making, maturing later. Some say African children mature prematurely due to having African parents. My father said my siblings were normal, but I was the exception. I was his heartache. I don't think that part of my mind was fully developed. Nor yours."

"I think it was the weed you did. You smoked sticky green like Snoop Dogg."

"Could have been. Probably did have an impact on too many decisions."

"Yeah. I guess we both did some dumb shit disguised as fun shit. Still had bad times."

"We had good times too."

"We had a few laughs before the screams and the tears."

"Before I was pregnant."

"We had some fun."

She chuckled. "You were horrible at folding shirts."

"You were horrible at folding fitted sheets."

"No normal person can fold a fitted sheet."

"I can. It's so easy. Was funny watching you try, get mad, then throw it at me."

"Because you laughed at me. I don't like when people laugh at me."

"It was funny. As smart as you were, spoke four languages, conquered by a fitted sheet."

Her right hand drifted to her belly. "God, I was pregnant when I moved in this place."

"Knocked up. Up the duff. By a black American. A summertime booty call gone bad."

"That summer I was out of control."

"Your caterpillar days. When you hadn't become a butterfly."

"I flew too close to the sun."

"My wings melted too. Haven't been able to fly away since."

She shifted from foot to foot. "Lots of memories."

I nodded in concurrence, felt my own lot of memories. "Lots of arguments."

"We didn't always argue."

"We argued. I don't think we ever agreed on anything."

"Oh God. I remember the horrible things you said regarding OJ."

"I remember that uncolonized mind of yours taking the side of the wypipo."

"Hate can't fix hate. And living in the past does nothing for a better future. So, let's not revisit the past and let's see if we can move on. For the sake of our daughter."

"She's an adult."

"Yes."

"She grew up without me."

The winds made her royal dress move, made it dance closer to her maple-brown skin.

She looked at the building. "The last time I was here, the scariest night of my life."

"Your new husband was banging on my door, screaming your name."

"I remember that moment. Like no other. That moment is emblazoned in my mind."

"I could have killed him that night. He crossed a line."

"I was terrified."

"Yohanes came back here to fight and your father was with him."

"My father came here with Yohanes? What did he do?"

"I put my Mississippi Soul Stealer into his precious faux-virgin daughter's Ethiopian Queen of Sheba pussy and gave her a baby that he viewed as not Ethiopian and not black American, but some sort of a third race, and he couldn't stand that. He couldn't stand that a black American fucked his princess, nutted in her and put a baby in her belly. That drove him insane."

"Stop it. Please. That's uncalled for. I came here to be civil, not to stir up old hostilities."

"*What your father did to me was uncalled-for.* What your ex-husband did was what a coward would do. That punk ass didn't come at me man-to-man. I should've called in Jake Ellis. I should have called in other guys I know. I should've called in my family and started a tribal war."

My ex-wife couldn't hold eye contact. "What did my father do when he came here?"

"He hated that a black American had spoiled his princess."

"What did he do?"

"Ask your mother and the tribe. She probably orchestrated the entire deal."

"My mother would do harm to no one."

I laughed. "That's some bullshit."

She spoke in a nervous whisper. "Tell me what transpired."

"They ambushed me."

"Ambushed?"

"Right here. Where we are standing. They brought all of your relatives and friends."

"What happened?"

"I kicked their asses. I kicked forty men's asses, by myself, right here where we're standing, because I loved you like a fool."

"Forty?"

"That's how it will be written in my memoir."

"You're saying that many people came and attacked you?"

"And if I didn't love you then, if I didn't have a daughter that I didn't want to have a father on lockdown for perpetuity, you would've been buying forty pine boxes for your tribe of goons."

"I don't believe you."

"You don't have to."

"This was a mistake. Coming here thinking we could be civil was a mistake."

I took a deep breath. "How are you just going to just show up in my life like this?"

"I should have just sent you a long text message. Yes, this is a mistake."

"I've already realized that being happy that Margaux called me was a mistake too."

She turned to leave. "What transpires between you and my daughter, that is not my concern. She is an adult now. She makes her own choices, pays no attention to my advice."

"Like mother, like daughter."

She said things in Amharic, things I could tell weren't pretty.

I said, "Wait. Stop."

She stopped and turned to me. "I have pulled the scab away from an old wound."

"Yours or mine?"

"Ours. This wound connects you to me and me to you and us to our daughter."

Voices carried. I looked across the pond. Bernice was in her window enjoying the show.

Jimi Lee looked too, then frowned at apartment buildings that went on for miles.

I asked, "What's wrong?"

"Just amazed a lot of the people I used to see here when I was here, they are still here."

"People come and go. Some stay. Some do better and move away."

"Jake Ellis?"

"Two blocks that way. He was on Garthwaite awhile; now he's over here on Stocker."

"He came back from Ghana."

"Has been back a few years."

"San Bernardino?"

"Still working when there is work."

"You?"

"The same."

"UCLA?"

"Dream deferred."

"That's disappointing."

"More for me than for you."

She nodded. "Liquor Bank still there. And they have torn up Crenshaw for the new train."

"Progress. But rent's high and some people are struggling to pay off payday loans."

She said, "And congratulations on all the 420 shops paired with bar-ber shops."

"Bet you wished this was Sativa Row and Indica Lane when you lived here."

"Weed is probably why I ended up living here."

"Hormones."

"That too."

"Would you do it over?"

She said, "No."

"No?"

She stiffened. "No."

"Not even for Margaux?"

"Would you? Be honest. What we went through, would you do that again?"

"No. I wouldn't."

"I know what this is like. You have no idea what my life has been like. And I have a daughter who has been difficult. Very difficult. No, I won't lie and say I would do this over."

"Sounds like you were Bette Davis with her daughter. Or Joan Craw-ford with hers."

"My answer is no. Without hesitation. I wouldn't be standing here now. So, please, let's move on. Let's avoid another round of what-aboutery, or any form of mythomania. Serves no purpose. I'd rather suffer a bout of tenesmus than stand here and imagine what might've been."

"No problem. I'll keep it real. You were always the logical one."

"Not always. I only know that what we did was a lesson. And we both lost."

A group of teenage girls passed by, sexy clothes, hair whipped, talking, laughing, walking, texting, updating Twitter, Snapchat, Instagram, all smelling like the party room in a Kush factory, in search of a good time and cute boys, out to live out loud after midnight.

After they passed I asked Jimi Lee, "How long have you been out here?"

"I've been parked here awhile. Sitting and thinking. Tried to reach our daughter. Sent her a text. I didn't tell her where I was. She's nursing her boyfriend."

"Still have your key?"

"I'm sure you changed the locks several hundred times since then."

"Never changed the locks. Never thought about it." I paused. "When did you get here?"

"Couple hours ago." She hesitated. "I saw you when you came back from your date."

"And you've been sitting here since then?"

"Is she . . . the woman in the red dress you were kissing . . . is she your wife?"

I shook my head. "Only had one wife. Lost the taste for marriage after that."

"Where is the woman in red?"

"She's swimming in her European dreams right now. We can talk for a quick minute."

She paused. Looked at me the way she did when we first met. "You still look good."

I swallowed, batted away old feelings. "Thanks. You look nice yourself."

"I've gotten older."

I took in her figure, her face, her eyes. "You make forty look like the new twenty."

"You're still fit. You were always fit. Always boxing and running and doing weights."

"And here you are. Back at the scene of the crime."

She took another breath, her heart in her throat, shivered again. "I should go."

"You never should have come."

Jimi Lee didn't move. She said she was leaving but stood like a statue.

Then she nodded, then took a breath, shook her head, began speaking in Amharic. "*Ene betam nafike alehu. Hulu gize enafikalehu. Ketele yehm bohulu. Hulu gize ewed halhy.*"

"I don't understand a word you're saying. I've been drinking and my Amharic's offline."

"*Tesas cha lehu. Tesas cha lehu*, Kenneth Swift. *Ante turi sew neberk. Ante turu bale neberk. Ene hiwothn abelhsheu.* And most of all, *ene rasen ykr allm.* Never in this lifetime."

I said, "*Inae algeebanymi.* I don't understand. You're talking too fast."

She took a breath, regrouped. "My daughter said that you were very angry and bitter."

"She called me out of the blue. Talks to me like I'm some thot on Twitter."

"She has been taught to speak her mind. Too many women are silenced in this world."

"She threw a snot rag in my food. She flipped me off and cursed me in public."

"I don't believe that. She doesn't swear."

"I guess she knows you as good as you know her."

"She would never be that rude in public."

"Then had the nerve to send her sperm donor over here to jump on me. And I'm bitter?"

She wiped her eyes. "You hurt him. They messaged me that his nose is broken."

"Yeah, I *bwoke* his nose. Should've *bwoke* his neck."

She took a breath. "I'm about to become a grandmother."

"You're the mother of a black woman who's hiding inside the skin of a white woman."

"Yes, hiding."

"I was joking."

"I'm not. I feel as if she is hiding."

"Why?"

"I have no idea."

"She asked me for fifty thousand dollars."

"Are you for real?"

I nodded.

"Why?"

"You have to ask her."

We heard howls, animalistic screams. Jimi Lee jumped. I tensed for a second.

I said, "A dog is being attacked by a coyote."

"Oh my God."

Then a series of rapid pops, the report from what sounded like a .22.

"Oh my God. What was that?"

I said, "Coyote is being attacked by a dog owner."

Jimi Lee shook. "Can we not do this conversation out on the streets?"

"Did you come for a truce?"

"Don't be rude. Don't be inappropriate."

"Just checking."

Police sirens lit up Crenshaw, the sound carrying down Stocker.

Jimi Lee asked, "Can we go to the Denny's on Crenshaw?"

"And do what? Argue over a stack of overcooked pancakes?"

"Let's make this about our child."

"Jimi Lee, it's always been about Margaux."

"Please. *I'm not Jimi Lee.* That is not my name anymore."

"Jimi Lee is all you've ever been to me."

She made an angry face. "No one has called me that since the day I left here."

"My bad. How should I address the Queen of Sheba?"

"Dr. Feleke."

"Doctor?"

She nodded. "Dr. Feleke."

"You made it back to university. Where did you go?"

"First I went to AAU."

"What's that? Arizona? Arkansas? Alabama?"

"Addis Ababa University. I enrolled when I went back to Ethiopia. Then when I came back I finished undergrad at UC Riverside. Master's and doctorate at Cal Poly Pomona. Wasn't Harvard. But I made it back. Contemplating law school now that Margaux is gone from the nest."

I paused, inhaled the night air. "You got your doctorate?"

"It wasn't easy."

"I guess it was easier once your Wednesdays were free."

"It was wrong. It was. But after our Wednesdays ended . . . we went back to Ethiopia . . ."

"Your second husband took you back to Ethiopia to get you away from me."

She said, "They said I had mental issues. Which was a lie. But they all agreed to the same lie. The elders. They all said I had to be removed from this environment."

"They wanted to take you, reclaim you, and steal my child away from me."

"I had to confess that I had had an affair with you, that I had divorced you, then continued seeing you after I had remarried, and I had to tell them how many times I came here, and say sorry to my husband. I had to apologize for ruining my family's reputation in our circle. I had to admit I had lost touch with my roots, that I was no longer aligned with my parents' core values."

"Did you have to wear a scarlet letter too?"

"When everyone knows your secrets, you wear an invisible letter day and night."

Across the street, phone in hand, Bernice Nesbitt moved away from her window.

Jimi Lee said, "I used to have our baby in my arms, you'd be sleeping, or off to hurt people, maybe kill people, and I'd pace the floors, walk to and fro in that mousetrap, look out the window, and see people having fun, enjoying life. One night I was breastfeeding my daughter and saw a neighbor with a white man sucking her breasts. Will never forget that. I was in pain and she looked like she was on the highway to heaven."

"You envied that."

"She could come and go. She didn't have to deal with a crying baby."

She looked up at my window. I did the same, didn't see Rachel, took a deep breath.

The woman I had known as Jimi Lee said, "You never married again?"

"No, I didn't get caught up again, not like I did with you."

"More children?"

"No more children. You?"

"Yes. A son."

"Wow. Margaux didn't mention that."

"He's four. They're not close."

"With your second husband, I assume."

"Yeah. With Yohanes."

"You cheated on me with him, then on him with me."

"We're divorced now, but we had a son."

"Well, that son should have made the bloodline happy. Before that second divorce."

"But that only complicated my life and exacerbated the delicate situation between us."

"Not all men wear emasculation very well."

She paused. "Life became interesting. But my life has always been interesting."

I rubbed the bridge of my nose. "Did he abuse Margaux?"

"No. But. It was strained. He looked at her and all he saw was me with you."

"After you walked out, after our divorce, why did you come back to sleep with me?"

She took a breath, treaded in those memories. "Feelings. Confusion. I was young and I felt so much, I didn't know myself as a woman, didn't know how to handle the situation properly."

"Did you ever love me?"

"*Intin . . . Intin . . .* I had other ambitions."

"All you have to do is answer yes or no. Did you love me?"

"It's not easy to answer. Love was new to me. Love was like never having felt water on your skin, then you ease into a warm pool. It feels good, but you go deeper and deeper, never realizing you can become lost, you can lose yourself in its depths, in its current, become victim to its undertow, and drown. It's romantic, but all romantics eventually meet the same fate. Being in love requires you to give the rein that controls your heart to someone else. You lose control. Not everyone embraces losing control. Not everyone wants to drown."

I was sad, angry, and sick all at once. "But did you love me?"

"Not when we first married. We were still strangers. You were so different. I was in love with intrigue and mischief, with parental disobedience, with joining the fold and being bad."

"Were we in the same relationship?"

"Everyone is in an individual relationship, but perceives it as group effort. My relationship with you is not the same as your relationship with me. The eyes can never see their own face."

I paused, shook my head. "You hated being married to me."

"I married you. I tried. For five years, I tried. It was not easy for me, being part of a marriage society, an East African family structure that had no room . . . no room for . . . for . . ."

"*For a nigga like me.* A nigga who has been colonized rooter to tooter from day one."

Anger rose, intellectualism waned, she said something else in Amharic, took hard breaths as her sweet brown face reddened; tears suddenly fell from her eyes. She wiped them away.

I said, "Yeah. I am bitter and angry. I should've fucked your ass the night I met you and finished on your tits, then sent your enlarged sphincter back to Diamond Bar walking side to side."

"That's uncalled for. I won't allow you or any man to talk to me that way."

"We wouldn't even remember each other now if I had done that."

"Your lack of civility is reprehensible. You should seek counseling. You really should."

"That's all you got?"

"I see where you live. I see nothing has changed."

"Yeah, look down your little nose and shake your head that I still live here. Ever think that maybe I've been stuck here because of you? You know where my money went. You know I never missed a month paying for Margaux. *Never.* I could've bought a new car every year."

"It's impossible for you to stop blaming me for your failures and try and understand me."

I pulled on the reins. "How am I supposed to feel right now?"

She countered with, "How am *I* supposed to feel?"

"That was the problem." I laughed. "You never felt anything."

"Are you too self-centered to see the pain I have endured? I don't jump up and down and do the neck like the ghetto girls you are used to. You have to look at my silence to see my pain."

"You were a horrible wife."

"There is more to being a woman than being a wife. Men still think women are supposed to know their place, to be grateful when a man helps her in any way, let him lead, to be only with one man despite a man's natural shortcomings; perpetual misogyny and innumerable infidelities."

"Yeah, well, I sacrificed all I had for you back then."

"I abandoned my goals. I gave up Harvard." She ranted, "I was undereducated, no job, no money, no options, but I was still going to fight to be the best me and not be like the unmotivated women around here happy to be barefoot and pregnant and breed until their ovaries fell out."

"You were a pregnant teenager, but no one made you marry me."

"I did what I had to do to take care of my daughter. It was the logical choice, a legal thing I did to ensure we had a roof over our heads. When I said 'I do' to the justice of the peace, it felt like I would evaporate. Each day a part of me disappeared, and you never noticed that there was nothing left there, just a shell of a girl. And my needing freedom, not being able to fit into the man-created box reserved for being a wife, that was seen as nothing more than drapetomania."

"You're equating our marriage to slavery?"

"It was what it was, despite any good intentions on your part or mine."

"What, was I just your goddamn overseer for five years? What, did I go down on Auction Square in Memphis and buy you for a song?"

She snapped. "You bought me for twenty-five dollars. That's how much the marriage certificate cost, right? Yes, it's hyperbole, but that's how it felt. It felt like I sold my soul to the devil and my body to you. I'm sorry that I'm repeating a decades-old argument, but that's how I felt back then. My life was tied to yours. My soul was tied to yours. You wanted too much from me. You needed me to be someone I was not. Whatever I felt for you, what you felt for me was centuple. Attached to you, I felt lost. I had to let go of the rope that attached you to my soul."

"Margaux needed you too."

"Every second of every minute of every hour, and that overwhelmed me."

"I told you I would take care of you and Margaux."

"You did. That surprised me. You didn't walk away."

"If I had been Ethiopian would we be having this conversation?"

"You think that would change anything? That had nothing to do with what I felt."

"Or could we still be married? If I were from Addis Ababa, your parents would've accepted me. I had too much Mississippi mud in my blood for Africans born darker than me."

"You will never let that go. Like most men you are so petty, your views so myopic."

"Did you give your second husband a son and treat him the same way? Did you cheat him into the ground, then walk out and get a divorce? I hope he kept his son and not you."

"Eff you, you pathetic, uncouth donkey. You are no better than an animal in the wild."

"You didn't complain about that when you were facedown, ass up, legs shaking."

My ex-wife cursed me again, then turned around, her beautiful colors superhero-like, her ethnic pride as intense as the resurrected pain in my heart. She hurried to her car. She was as powerful as Makeda, and I had tried to be her King Solomon. Seeing her again hurt too much.

Hands in fists, I followed my daughter's mother, my philosophical ex-wife. Sneezes, orgasms, and my anger were three things that could not be stopped once they had started.

I said, "You always run away when it gets too tough. You haven't changed. I wish I could have insured our marriage so when what we had collapsed, at least I would have been paid, reimbursed for all I invested."

Hands flailing, she blistered me hard, fast, and unrelenting in Amharic.

I said, "African baby momma, your American baby daddy don't understand shit you said."

She seethed at my rudeness, then spat out the English equivalent of her insult. "Eff you."

She marched back, spitting more pent-up anger, faced me, eyes like tombs, cursed and insulted to the nth degree. A tsunami attacked an earthquake and on behalf of all baby mommas and baby daddies around the world, we stood on the sidewalk yelling at each other, my insults in English, hers in rapid Amharic; strong, powerful, hurtful; made me feel like I'd been gouged by the horns of a raging bull. It sounded like two countries on the verge of another tribal war.

My ex-wife jumped into her pristine BMW, put her eyeglasses on, started the engine, stared at me as the car purred, then screeched away from the scene of the crime. Blanketed in anger, I watched her tap her brake lights at Degnan, turn a hard right on red. She did a California roll; then she vanished, slipped into darkness that couldn't shadow my heart.

Only one thing was worse than a fool at forty. That would be two fools at forty.

Closure was for Julia Roberts and Hugh Grant movies, not for real life. Resentment was too good at taking root and could outlive the Great Basin bristlecone pine called Methuselah. The dark feelings between us, not even a soul-train line of hurricanes could uproot. I had had a falling-out with my daughter. That had been the first hurricane of the day. Had fought the father of my grandchild-to-be. Another hurricane. And now Jimi Lee had come here, a Category 5 following two Category 5s. She engaged me in the ring and worked me for twelve rounds.

She had caught me off guard. Showing up without warning hadn't given me time to deal with old feelings. I had lost it, argued with her like she was still my wife, my enemy, my betrayer.

I felt bad. I felt guilty. She was right about a lot of things, and those things were hard to face. I was wired a certain way, wired to be responsible. Yet she made me feel like shit. And that made me say rude things just to piss her off and try to break her intellectual ass down.

They said if a man was a fool at forty, he would be a fool the rest of his life.

I glanced over at Bernice's window. A soft moan came from her hole-in-the-wall, the sound a woman made when a man eased inside her. Somebody was deep inside London.

"Oh . . . God yes . . . Don't stop . . . Don't stop . . . Ooo-ooo . . . harder . . . harder."

A Rubicon passed, trap music loud. *"The ting go skrrrrrrrra pa pa ka ka ka!"*

That Rubicon's trap music covered other deadly sounds. Beasts charged from the east. Shadows stormed my way. Like rabid coyotes in the night, they had been in the cut, waiting to attack. They came at me hard, came at me fast, the same way Jake Ellis and I had gone after ruffians for San Bernardino the last two decades. I hit one in the face and he went down like Cassini crashing into Saturn. A second one was dropped like a bad habit and a third and fourth were coming at me, but a blow to the back of the head wobbled me. I saw more stars than at a Hollywood movie premiere. Acute pain registered and sobered me up and I started swinging, trading blows like I was fighting Tyson, Holyfield, Mayweather, and at least two others all at once, threw punches until my jaw caught a blow. The ground stopped me from falling through the center of the earth and coming out in the middle of the Indian Ocean, stopped my descent abruptly. Faraway sirens sang in the distance, the wail of a fire truck, and that triggered the barking of every dog within two miles. Fists rained down on me in between the kicks. They held me down, but I was strong enough to get two of the monsters off my neck. We wrestled until I had enough room to breathe. Strong motherfuckers piled on me like I had the football and was trying to get into the end zone. Bastards used their combined weight to weaken and suffocate me. For a few agonizing seconds, my heart beat so hard, beat so strong, I was unable to hear what they were yelling.

"Stay down," one of the tattooed shadows demanded. "Stay down or die, black man."

Unafraid of any man, I barked, "You motherfuckers got the right one on the wrong day."

Their leader said, "Be glad you and the kaffir stole all of my guns. All but this one. Otherwise I would have given each man a gun and they would've been trigger-happy and you might have had a Bonnie-and-Clyde moment. Be glad you stole my guns. Be very glad."

Garrett walked up, expensive hard shoes on urban concrete. His knees popped as he grunted, lowered his weight, and got down on his haunches. He reeked of anger, revenge, and some cologne that made him smell nicer and friendlier than he had been to his own wife.

The rich man made brief eye contact, and the madman expected to see a frightened dog. He saw anger, not fear. He saw that if I got loose, I would drop him screaming into a mulcher.

"You're a good fighter. Jesus, you can fight. You would've been worth it. I would've put you in a few underground cage matches, let you set free that Mandingo, Shaka Zulu rage, and won some real money. You knocked out two of the best cage fighters. You could've been rich."

"Back up off me. *Get off me.* I'm the wrong field *nigger* to fuck with."

"No, I'm the wrong man for a nigger to fuck with. San Bernardino should've warned you."

I fought, struggled, got a couple of blows in, hurt them good, but was outnumbered.

Amused and impressed, Garrett said, "Nigger, you should've taken the money. I would have thrown in Rams tickets, Lakers tickets, Dodgers tickets, and Kings tickets as a bonus."

I struggled to breathe, grappled with pain, sweated and choked out, "Fuck you."

"You left and my wife called a divorce attorney. She packed to leave. To beat some sense into her, I would have thrown in tickets to Disneyland. For three days. Hotel included. We can still work something out. Just whisper in my ear where I need to go to find the African."

Garrett waited a moment, wanted to see if Jake Ellis lived by me, waited to see if the Don Juan of Ghana bolted out to rescue me from a beatdown that would make LAPD proud.

Dogs barking in the distance, another modern-day Uncle Tom ran to where we were.

"We found six Mustangs within two blocks."

Garrett said, "The African was driving a convertible Mustang that had no plates."

"It's parked that way. Engine is cool. Lights are off in all the apartments. I checked as many mailboxes as I could to see who had an African-sounding name. Too fucking many."

"People around here street-park close to where they live."

"They try to. People like their ride outside their window in case the alarm goes off."

"Find a brick. Bust the windows. Sound the alarm and draw him out. Niggers love their cars more than women. He'll come out running. We'll wake up the neighborhood if we have to."

"I have a cinder block in back of the ice cream truck."

Mr. Garrett spoke to me. "Looks like I'm about to find the disrespectful African."

As I struggled, I warned my subjugator. "San Bernardino won't like this. Not at all."

"After this uncalled-for impoliteness, *you think I give a fuck about San Bernardino*?"

One of his goons said, "You want to shut this one up, Mr. Garrett, or should I?"

"Not before I talk to him. He can help me and make it easier on himself."

Another henchman asked, "Should I get the gas cans out of the ice cream truck?"

"No, it's hot as fuck, so get me scoops of ice cream in a waffle cone."

"What flavor you want, boss man?"

"*Of course I want the gas.* Stupid ass. Do what you're paid to do, nigger. All you niggers. Do what you've been paid to do. Get this nigger off the ground and into the truck." Then Garrett turned his attention to me and said, "Just tell me where the African lives. Which building. Up or down. He won't know you gave him up. He won't be around to come back at you for doing what's right."

A thug grunted. "This motherfucker must be on some flakka, Molly, MDA, and Ecstasy."

Garrett firmed his tone. "Give me the African and I'll let you go. You were professional. Give him up and I'll put five thousand in your pocket. This isn't personal with you."

I cursed. "You're dead, Garrett. All of you are dead. You are so fucking dead."

Garrett spit on the ground. "The Muslim you were arguing with. Was she another one of San Bernardino's workers? San Bernardino uses pretty women to do drop-offs and pickups."

"One of your guys is following her."

Garrett told me, "Give me the African. Last time. Or the woman will get what you're getting. Plus only God knows what else. Men get around a pretty woman and men will be men. Just like the African was with my wife, these ex-cons will be the same with the one you talked to."

They were shadowing Jimi Lee.

They held me down, I could hardly breathe, was sweating, but I growled, tried to fight them up off me, became Atlas lifting the world one breath at a time.

"This strange fruit won't give up, and he's stronger than Luke motherfuckin' Cage."

Garrett instructed, "Do what I paid you to do. Be ready to bury the African."

Above me, in my apartment, Rachel Redman was drunk, unconscious. They didn't know which apartment I had come out of, upper or lower, and I was glad they didn't care. My girl was in bed naked. My country had been invaded, and all invaders were killers and rapists. Across the street, Bernice was getting dirty after dark, not in her window. If anyone else saw, they were following the code of the streets. Wasn't their business. As far as they knew, it was ICE agents taking down a brother from Cuba or the Dominican Republic. Or they knew me, knew I was a bad man, and chickens had come home to roost. I had to fight. No surrender, no retreat. Garrett's thugs were following Jimi Lee. The rest wanted to put Jake Ellis in a pine box. I grunted, flexed, lifted them all, got those motherfuckers up off me, and we fell into a no-holds-barred life-or-death fight. They threw more blows, and I reciprocated with punches, elbows, and knees, thought I could turn this around until I took a blow to my chin that made my neck twist like an owl's. That blow was followed by another that shattered my soul. I felt the spirit of every dead man and woman murdered during the Middle Passage. I felt the anger and pain of every Congolese murdered by King Leopold II. I felt all of them rising like Margaux had said she wanted them to do in that movie her boyfriend was writing. All of a sudden that bad idea made sense to me. I heard them all telling me to win. I cursed Rachel Redman for getting me drunk. I cursed Bernice Nesbitt for drawing me out into the night, and I cursed Jimi Lee for accidentally setting up the bear trap that had snared me. They had created the perfect storm. If I had seen Garrett and his bushwhackers from my window, I could have crept out the back and come up behind them, .38 in hand, Jake Ellis at my side, and left bodies ready to be outlined in fresh chalk. But they had me. I knew they had me. A hoodlum caught me in a headlock, choked me while I tried to get loose, choked me the same way I had choked Balthazar Walkowiak in Florida, held me while the other kicked my black ass. Still I rejected death, and I lifted the one choking me, then we fell backward, and I dropped him on his head. I made it back to my feet, went up against three wounded warriors until a blow from the butt of Garrett's gun came down on my head, wobbled me. Garrett hit me in the face. He hit me hard enough to know the offer to work for him and for the tickets to the games was null and void. I tried to stagger toward my apartment, wanted to get upstairs, wanted to get my hands on my .38. His bushwhackers came after me. They were hurt, bleeding, but they persisted. Woozy, winded, captured; the next uppercut forced the sun to set inside my brain.

CHAPTER 20

GARRETT'S BUSHWHACKERS THREW a cinder block into the front window of Jake Ellis's leased Mustang, and as the Ford screamed, another henchman tossed a Molotov cocktail inside. Gun in his hand, standing off to the side like a hunter, knowing he could never beat Jake Ellis in a fight, Garrett waited for the African to appear. Jake Ellis did appear, came out fast, jeans and no shirt, had heard his car yelling for help, and the moment he was near the sidewalk, Garrett whistled, pointed, and, Pavlovian, three muscled hoodlums ran full speed, bum-rushed Jake Ellis. Those three palookas charged at a man who was stronger than Jack Dempsey and hit harder than Jack Johnson. They got the shit beat out of them. It was like watching Tyson in his prime beating up anyone who dared challenge him, only there was no ref to stop the fight. Jake Ellis was every bit the boxer I said he was. If I hadn't been attacked from the back, I'd have been beating heads into the ground with him, but Jake Ellis handled it. Those three contenders were on the ground with broken faces within thirty seconds. His hands were like bricks and his blows were like being hit with a sledgehammer. While those bloodied men inhaled and regretted fucking with Jake Ellis, Jake Ellis broke into a run, charged toward Garrett, but Garrett began shooting, shooting, shooting. Jake Ellis dropped and rolled, then ran toward the back of his building. The hoodlums Jake Ellis hadn't beaten down chased him. Jake Ellis didn't know I was their hostage, and he didn't know if they were strapped. The three he had bested limped and wobbled back to the ice cream truck, and under Garrett's direction, one of the hoodlums threw more Molotov cocktails toward the place Jake Ellis had appeared. Darkness was interrupted by the beauty of fire. Then the other pissed-off thugs I'd knocked out joined in, angry at their defeat, and yelled, tried to set Leimert Park on fire the way a city of infuriated racists had burned down my ancestors' home on Oklahoma's Black Wall Street.

One of the thugs accidentally dropped his cocktail and it fell at his feet.

The bottle broke; gasoline splattered and, *poof,* set him on fire.

He screamed.

Fire made bad men scream.

It also made bad men run.

Garrett and his boys hopped into the ice cream truck, pulled away, left the bushwhacker frying like bacon and running down Stocker toward Leimert Boulevard. The flaming bushwhacker ran like comedian Richard Pryor had run when freebasing had gone bad.

That bushwhacker tried to outrun the flames, tried to outrun the agony.

I was trapped in my own fist-induced agony, groaning, swimming in grayness and mumbles, almost unconscious. Then everything turned warm. Peaceful. I surrendered and the pain slid away from my soul. I didn't have to breathe. I didn't know if I was dead or alive.

CHAPTER 21

I FELL INTO another world. In that other world, it was seconds after my falling-out with Jimi Lee. I watched her speed away. But as soon as she vanished, Jimi Lee made a U-turn a block after Degnan. She zoomed down the wrong side of the street, speeding like the fool who had done doughnuts. My ex-wife came to a hard, dramatic stop in front of my building, in the middle of Stocker. She sat in her idling car, in her luxury BMW, lips trembling, lakes draining from her eyes.

She said, "I'm sorry for everything. I love you. Always will. Leave with me."

Feeling as I had when I was twenty-one, all I could say was, "Jimi Lee."

Then she said part of what she had said to me in Amharic, only this time in English: "I've missed you. Every day I have missed you. I realized how much I loved you when it was too late."

As she sat there waiting for me, I looked up and saw Rachel Redman in my window.

I looked back toward Jimi Lee, and she stood three feet from me, Margaux in her arms, our daughter no older than two years old. Jimi Lee was younger, twenty-one years old again. I looked back toward the window, and Rachel wasn't there. Now she stood three feet on the other side of me. She wore her red dress, had suitcases at her side, tickets to London in her hand.

Rachel said, "She doesn't love you. I love you, Ken Swift. Let's start over."

"Will you give the guitar back to the Russian?"

She paused. "I can't. He remembered my birthday. You should have remembered."

Bags in hand, she walked by me, tears in her eyes, walked until she vanished.

I left with Jimi Lee. And we did start over. Margaux was no longer in her arms. Not on our minds. Together we saw the Great Pyramids near Cairo. Fish River Canyon in Namibia. Mount Kilimanjaro. Went to Zambia and saw Victoria Falls. Valley of the Kings. Okavango Delta in Botswana. Ngorongoro Crater in Tanzania. We saw the wildebeest and zebra travel across the sprawling grasslands of Maasai Mara in Kenya to the Serengeti. Held hands and watched gorillas in the Virunga Mountains and traveled to meet the fifty tribes that live along the Omo River in Ethiopia. Then we were in Addis Ababa, in bed, done making love, resting.

The door to our hotel room opened and in came a white waitress pushing a serving tray.

"Daddy, you and Mommy want something to eat, or y'all making another baby?"

The white woman was our daughter. It was Margaux. It was my only child. My one true love. I opened my mouth to speak, but without warning I was flying, then cold, wet, drowning.

CHAPTER 22

Freezing water was in all directions. It felt like I had been body-dumped and come to in the middle of the Pacific Ocean. I was cold, drowning, couldn't tell up from down, swam the wrong way, panicked, then reversed my course, fought to get to the surface while my lungs burned like the bushwhacker hit with the Molotov cocktail. I was weighed down by my clothes, by my shoes, by my hoodie, restricted by pain. I got enough air, but I choked, coughed, vomited up the dinner I'd had with Rachel. Was hard to throw up and swim at the same time. I made it to the edge of the pool and held on for dear life. The moment I grabbed the edge, someone stomped on my hand. I let go, yelled in pain, then swam away, went to the other side of the pool. My audience followed me, forced me to go back to the middle of the pool. I bobbed a few times, then stayed afloat.

"A nigger that can swim like a fish. That disappoints me."

Water made my eyes sting, and I couldn't see for a moment. I had to get the coughing under control, still was in pain, still felt like death was closing in. Was spitting out water that had too much chlorine in the mix. I spat out that poison and other additives, including bodily products. I doubt if Garrett left the pool to go potty. I didn't see him, but I knew his fucking voice. I recognized the backyard, the mansion. There was an American flag hanging on a pole between palm trees. I was back in Pasadena. I'd been thrown unconscious into Garrett's pool. The deep end. He had done that either to shock me awake or to watch me drown. A league of bushwhackers stood next to a man in tan slacks and a Banana Republic hoodie, Garrett, the man with the golden gun.

The one Jake Ellis and I had missed when we had searched his crib.

But San Bernardino had told us where each gun would be. I didn't think San Bernardino came up short. My guess was Garrett had kept a loaded gun in his car as his driving companion.

He'd come home and we'd never searched his car.

I gagged again, threw up some more, struggled to stay above water. I kicked my shoes off, then struggled, managed to get my hoodie off. I looked like an idiot trying not to drown.

There was laughter. When massa told jokes, good slaves knew to slap their legs and laugh. When massa stopped laughing, good slaves did the same, at the same moment.

Garrett said, "I want the African. I'm not done. I want the African."

I said, "And after tonight, I'm sure the African will want you. Same goes for your wife."

"He ran away. He talked a lot of shit, then ran away."

"The gun probably had something to do with that. Not many run toward bullets."

"My wife won't want him. Well, he won't want her. Not after tonight."

Garrett whistled like he was calling a pack of dogs. And that rattled me. I hated dogs. And right now, a league of pit bulls could eat me alive. Seconds later the patio door opened. Two more hoodlums and a woman came from inside. She was in front. I didn't recognize her at first. Had no idea who the tall bald woman was. Her face was misshapen. She could barely open her left eye. She had a monstrous limp. She was naked. Stood with a hand covering her vagina, the other covering her breasts. He made her limp around the pool in front of a herd of strange men. It was Mrs. Garrett. She had demeaned him and he had taken it out on her after Jake Ellis and I had split the scene. She stopped near him. Her face was fucked. Her body was covered in bruises. Garrett grabbed her forearm, then shoved her hard, threw her screaming into the deep end of the pool. Mr. told Mrs. she'd stay in the pool until he said she could get out, same as he had been forced to sit at a table and watch her flirt and take sides with an African.

She panicked, fought with the water, slapped it with her hands, went under, managed to break the surface, was losing the plot. "I can't swim! Jesus, you know I can't swim."

"Learn, *woman*. Learn or drown," Garrett shouted. "And you booked a goddamn suite at the W? You used the credit card I gave you to have a date with the African? Don't you know I have access to every call and charge you make? *Do you think I'm a fuckin' dotard?*"

"The water . . . all the chlorine . . . stings my cuts. It's burning my head."

"Call the African to come help you. Call him. I want to see him as bad as you do."

"I'm drowning . . . please . . . please."

"Drowning ain't drowned. And you seemed to not mind drowning when you told the African he made you wet enough to drown." Garrett spat at her and exploded, "I bet our prenup looks pretty good now. I bet the life you had this morning, I bet you want that life back. I took you out of Compton. You were nothing. Just a waitress. I gave you a good life. *You weren't loyal.*"

His wife didn't hear him screaming because she went under, fought to get her wounded head above water, once, twice, then stayed under. She was fighting the water, unable to break the surface again, falling like a rock, drowning. I hurried, swam to her, dove under while Garrett told me to keep away, and despite the names he called me, I took a chance, pulled her up. She clung to me, sharp nails in my flesh like a terrified cat, and I had to fight to get her to calm down.

Every part of my body hurt, but I said, "Just relax. I got you. Just keep your head up."

She gurgled, spat, coughed, trembled. "I'm afraid of this much water. I don't do the deep end of pools. I don't even come out here to do more than put my toes in the water."

"I need you to pay attention." I spat out water. "I can hold you, but I need help."

"I'm going to make you sink."

"I need you to stop moving. Don't grab me. Let me float you."

She panted, got a mouthful of air. "How long can you do this?"

"Not sure."

"My right arm. It's hurt bad."

"What happened over here?"

"He threw me down the stairs. I had packed to leave and that mule kicked me down the goddamn stairs. He kicked me like a dog. And while I was on the floor, he cut off all of my hair."

"You're going into shock. I need you to relax."

"I can't fucking relax. I'm in pain. Excruciating pain."

"I know. I can see you're fucked up."

"You're fucked up too."

"I could use a gallon of Jack and a crate of Vicodin."

"Hurting bad. Jesus, Jesus. We're gonna die."

Her head was back, mouth barely above water, eyes wide and on the sky, choppy breathing. I moved us toward the shallow end. Garrett fired two shots into the water as a warning.

Garrett said, "She's a liar. I sat at my dinner table and let her talk to see what she would say. And she bonded with the African, told lie after lie. Let me tell you who she is. Let me tell you the truth. She's just another gold digger. A week before the wedding she was here on the phone, dancing, twirling, telling her Compton friends that this house was going to be her house. She went on and on about the house. Went on and on about how she had come up. That was unsettling. It was eye-opening. She told her friends that all of this would be hers."

His wife gagged on water. "It was just girls talking. We talk like that. It's fantasy talk."

Garrett asked me, "That sound like love to you?"

She coughed, shivered. "You've been upset about that and holding it in?"

"So, yeah, I had to stop thinking with my dick and protect my assets. I talked to my attorney, expressed my concerns, and was about to call off the wedding. But I didn't want to overreact. My attorney didn't want me to *under*react, and I trusted her. She was the voice of reason, so I told her to do what she had to do. My wife is deceitful. Most wives are. They cheat more than they are willing to admit. They cheat more than men, I'd be willing to bet. This one only tells half the story. She made it sound like I kept her destitute since we married. The bitch lied her heart out. First month we were married, she burned through sixty grand. That doesn't include two new cars and all the upgrades to the house to make her feel at home. Second month she spent one hundred and forty. I had to put an end to that before she burned through all of my money."

"It was cash you had lying around the house. Money from your laundering business."

"When you're given everything, you appreciate nothing."

"You had plenty of money. You could've wiped your ass with hundred-dollar bills."

"It was cash I earned. Cash I risked going to jail for. When you're not working, and spending someone else's money, it's like free money. It's easy to spend someone else's money. It's real easy to spend another man's money. So, yeah, she was put on a tight budget. She had this house, five cars to choose from, a thousand pairs of shoes, and she's still not happy."

"You gave me chlamydia."

"So what? Not like I gave you AIDS. Pop antibiotics and keep it moving."

"Cheating bastard."

"You broke my heart. Today you broke my heart. And I don't like the way that feels. But you're not worth it. You and your white-trash family, people I have supported since I married you, are not worth it. What was I thinking? Your gene pool? Why would I want to propagate that?"

"Please, don't do this. I'm sorry; I'm sorry. Please, don't do this."

"Today made it easy for both of us to stop pretending. A lot of people live on the edge of happiness, and it doesn't take much to push them and make them fall over the edge."

"Baby, please. I'm your wife. I'm your wife. Don't do this to your wife."

"I don't want to turn this moment with the lady in the lake into a long good-bye, and I won't spend too much time saying farewell my lovely, but I do want to watch you drown and slip into that big sleep. I could shoot you, but I want to keep the simple art of murder as simple as I can."

Again, she begged, asked me to swim her to the side of the pool. I started to move and Garrett aimed his gun at me. I kept us where we were. Garrett looked at his sentinels.

"If my wife gets out of the pool, since she's hotter on niggers than America is on that so-called nigger history month in February, all of you gentlemen can have a go. I'm sure she can take three of you at the same time. So have your fun. This one's on me. You have my permission. Then throw the slut back in the pool. If the nigger gets out, kill him. She likes niggers so much, let her drown hanging on to one. Let's let her have the romance she thinks she deserves."

He stood and looked at me holding her up, both of us struggling to stay above water.

Garrett yelled, "Get your hands off my wife. Let her drown."

I looked at him. He had his gun pointed at us, his audience waiting to see what he'd do.

Garrett commanded, "Let her go. I will not ask you again. Four . . . three . . . two . . ."

Garrett fired three more shots into the pool, the shots so close the energy from each shocked my system. His wife freaked out. Now Garrett was god. She fought me and the water, then went under. Death's nearness terrified her, made it hard to keep her wounded head above water. It took another minute without gunfire to calm her, to get her to float while I treaded water.

It was like trying to tread while holding an anchor. She made it hard for me to keep my body upright with my head above the surface. She forced me to use energy and swim. Without her I could have used my arms and legs to keep afloat, but even that would have been temporary.

Garrett laughed, angered and amused, more the former than the latter.

She swallowed water, crying. "I'm so embarrassed. Jesus, I think I boo-booed myself."

Garrett heard her. He laughed out his anger and his workers laughed with him.

I said, "It's okay."

"I defecated. I'm sorry I defecated. I'm potty-trained, I promise I am."

While Garrett laughed, I moved us closer to where I needed to be in the pool.

I said, "You're hurt bad."

She sobbed. "He kicked me down the stairs. Bastard raised his foot, kicked me down a flight of wooden stairs to the hard marble floor. *He kicked me.* I thought I'd broken my neck. Then I passed out from pain. People don't do that to dogs. He kicked me like I was less than a dog."

"I need you to stop talking. Don't fight me. Breathe normal, save your energy."

"Motherfucker kicked me down the goddamn stairs. Cut my hair off. He shaved all my hair. Told me he would make sure no other man ever wanted me. Laughed while he did that shit."

"Shhh. You're going to keep pulling us both underwater."

"Then he put his dick in me. *He was inside me.* My head was bleeding. He grabbed me and slammed me on my stomach and raped me while I was dazed, in and out of consciousness, unable to fight. But I tried. Scratched his face. Scratched that bastard good. I put my nails in him and he banged my forehead on the marble. I have a big knot. He hit me like he was fighting a man."

"Shhh."

"Mr. Big Shot has never fought a real man a day in his life. But he attacked me."

"Calm down."

"Fucker grabbed my arm, dragged me back up the stairs. *Up the stairs.* I couldn't stand and he dragged me, almost pulled my arm out of its socket. Then he locked me in my closet."

"Shhh."

"Never should have signed that prenup. Never should have kissed him. When his attorney came in, that was a sign. I should have run away. This is worse than Scientology."

"Okay, shut up. I need you to shut up. I'm going to show you how to tread water."

"I can't swim. I don't even put my feet in the water at the beach."

"Treading isn't like swimming. You just move a little to keep your head—"

"*Don't let me go.* Please, don't let me go."

"You're going to pull us under. Sweep your arms back and forth. Then do a flutter kick."

"I can't. My arms are hurt. I can only use one leg."

"Try." I kept her from going under. "Keep your body upright, and keep your head—"

Garrett fired into the pool six times, each bullet flying close to us. That stopped the lesson and silenced his wife's frantic words, but she cried. It was uncontrollable. Inconsolable. Hopeless.

"Jesus, no. No." She winced with pain. "My left leg, it's cramping. It's cramping bad."

I held her while she fought with her pain, and we went under a dozen times. When the pain subsided, she let out a wail, shook her head in surrender, as if she saw her future, saw the inevitable, then begged, "Let me go. Please, just let me drown. I've had enough of this life."

"No, no, there will be no drowning."

"I'm in so much pain. This is my fault; this is my fault. Let me die." I told her, "No."

She cried a moment. "I'm scared."

"I know. Just talk to me, if that helps."

"You're a nice man."

"My name is Ken Swift."

"You're a good man, Ken Swift."

"I'm just a man. Just a wounded man, with an ex-wife who never loved him, with a girlfriend too good for him, with a daughter who has no connection to him, in the deep end of a pool, treading in cold-ass water, ignoring my own pain, trying to keep you from drowning."

"He kicked me down the stairs. Motherfucker kicked me down the goddamn stairs."

"You can't be angry right now. Can't have your heartbeat get elevated."

"*He cut off my hair.* And as I lay dying, he *put his dick in* me. My husband raped me."

"Mask off. You have now seen him with his mask off."

"Someone needs to teach men *not to rape*. To respect women as their *equals*."

"I need you to focus. Right now, I need you to use less energy."

Garrett came closer. "Unfaithful bitch. Drown with the fucking nigger."

Sneezes, orgasms, and anger.

They stood around us, watching us go under, take on water, and come back up. They laughed, took bets on how long it would take us to drown.

They looked upon me with disdain. Black skin, different tribes. I was a pit bull, abused and raised on gunpowder. So were they. I saw prison tats, gang tats up to their eyeballs.

None were over twenty-five. Those gentlemen were from the Eastside.

I said, "He left your boy burning in the streets. He'll do the same to all y'all."

They looked at one another, contemplated what might've been on their minds.

I said, "I hope he paid y'all up front. He's not reliable when it comes to paying debts."

Garrett hated my words and fired at me. He came like he wanted to give me the John F. Kennedy special and send me to go hang with Biggie, Tupac, and Elvis. He stood at the edge of the pool, smiling at me without lowering his gun. Cagney with his finger on the trigger. He'd had enough of me. Enough of his wife. He hated her. And maybe he loved her. Maybe the latter was why she was still alive. This had gone too far to turn it back around. Roses, dinner, and a night of making love couldn't fix this. But Garrett didn't seem like the type to issue an apology. He chose a course and stuck to it. It was easier for some men to kill than it ever would be for them to apologize. I'd grown up in the South and I already knew that some men, educated or illiterati, would never apologize to a black man, educated or illiterati, but would demand an apology, even when the black man wasn't in the wrong. Men like Garrett would never apologize to a woman, but would demand an apology for her every complaint. Those were the most dangerous men on the face of the planet. Especially when they had a gun. That gun made Garrett think he was an alpha male's alpha male. Without a gun, Garrett was just an angry Pillsbury Doughboy. Men like him would nurture and feed a stray dog, would treat a dog with dignity and kindness, but would shoot me in my back, then go to Burger King, get two Whoppers for six dollars, and feed one to the dog.

If Garrett had known his armament was sleeping in the bottom of the pool, with his anger, he could have gone for a quick dive, recovered his toys, loaded up, and done the ultimate drive-by in Leimert Park just to show Jake Ellis who was the boss. With that cache of weapons and the league of bushwhackers he had employed as a well-armed militia, he could have driven from Crenshaw Boulevard down Stocker to Leimert Boulevard, taken that to MLK, shot up the area doing forty miles per hour, and killed innocents while he slaughtered gentrification, then been back on the 110 speeding north toward Pasadena before anyone in zip code 90008 had stopped screaming and had the nerve to rise from their floors or crawl from under their kitchen tables.

Garrett had come at us the way angered men like him had gone after Nat Turner. As if he had the right to do so. Suffering and dying in slave ships. Hanged from trees. Whipped to death. Beaten to death by slave catchers dressed in blue, shot dead in the streets, first to die in movies, or first to die in real life. Black death was normal, a nonevent. Because killing people who had never been completely humanized had never been a crime. History reinforced what savages were capable of doing today. History reassured savages of what they had the right to do, of things that had been labeled as okay to do by the savages that came before them. History lived in their minds, became the roadmap for continued manifest destiny.

Garrett said, "You came to the wrong house."

"We had the right address. GPS brought us to your gate."

"I was the wrong one to cook salmon for."

"It wasn't personal. I was just doing my job. You know how this business rolls."

"You break in my house, it's personal. Do you understand how violated I feel? And I don't care if my wife is an unthankful drama queen, that mammothrept is my goddamn wife."

"Tell San Bernardino you don't like the way things are done, not me."

"Touch my wife, it's personal."

"I never touched her."

"You ate my damn gelato."

"I didn't want to be rude."

"Keep that sense of humor. It will serve you well as a court jester in hell."

This pool had become my jail. And when he pulled the trigger, it would be my grave. As the freezing night air moved through a jungle of palm trees, as the American flag waved, I had no way out. I knew this was a wrap. I would be shot a few times, then die with lungs filled with water.

But an abrupt crash made us jump, made everyone turn toward the mansion. Glass broke, shattered, and a two-cell cinder block that weighed about thirty-five pounds flew like it weighed as much as a bottle of lotion. Garrett and his men shouted, ducked, then regained their composure, looked at the cinder block that had flown through the patio window. It had been slung with Hulk-like rage from the inside of the estate. It was the same cinder block Garrett had used to damage Jake Ellis's Mustang. Jake Ellis was here, fury his traveling companion. I couldn't see Jake Ellis from where I was in the pool, but they did. Mr. Garrett saw the African he'd called what white men, both rich and poor, had called black men, both rich and poor, for hundreds of years.

CHAPTER 23

MR. GARRETT RAN by palm trees in his private yard, ran by patio furniture unseen by anyone because of the high walls, ran with his well-fed belly jiggling as he bolted toward the broken door, gun aimed, ready to shoot, infuriated as he said, "He's here. The African is here."

Garrett had been waiting for Jake Ellis all along. He had kept me cold, tired, beaten, weakened. Three of his men stayed at the pool, tasked with watching us drown. Mr. Garrett took the rest running with him, each picking up a makeshift weapon on the way. Each confident.

Hours ago, Jake Ellis and I had broken into this nine-bedroom mansion, gone room to room and collected weapons; then we had stood out here, under palm trees, by fruit trees, in an enclosed backyard, secluded from the world, Garrett's gun collection sealed in plastic while magically moist salmon cooked in the oven, and we dropped it all in the bottom of this pool.

I whispered, "We're going underwater for a few seconds."

"No, no."

"Mrs. Garrett—"

"Elaine. My name is Elaine."

"Mrs. Garrett, I know you're scared as hell, but I'm gonna have to let you go, and I'll need you to hold your breath as long as you can. Have to go to the bottom. If you don't, we might die tonight."

"No, no. I can't go underwater and I can't hold my breath for a second."

"Take a deep breath. I'll be back for you in no time."

"Don't; please don't."

A moment ago, she wanted to die. Now she wanted to live. I had no other choice but to chance letting her drown. I pushed her away, let her go, watched her eyes widen as she freaked out and looked at me like I had betrayed her, watched her fight the water like she was fighting an ocean, then surrender to gravity, hold her breath, and go under. I took several deep, slow breaths, fought my pain, and tried to bend, had to get my legs in the air, had to get my head facing down, had to fight to swim downward while I exhaled slowly to equalize the pressure. I wasn't going to make it. I was going to drown in Pasa-fucking-dena. Couldn't turn back. Held my nose and blew, had to equalize the pressure a bit more in order to kick away discomfort in my ears. Wiggled my jaw. Bottom of the pool felt like it was deeper than the Y-40 Deep Joy in Italy, and that pool was 113 feet deep. They had beat me good. Everything hurt, even my thoughts. Had to use a lot of energy to go this short distance. Needed to go back up, but I touched the bottom, fought with the little air left in my lungs trying to make me float toward the top. If I went back up, I'd never make it back down. I ran my hands along the bottom of the pool, blew bubble rings, felt death begging me to exhale, then inhale one last time.

One deep breath could fix it all. No more taxes. No more problems.

Then I touched the edges of one of the black plastic garbage bags. It was hard to see the armament. The bag was too heavy to lift and carry to the surface. Ten rifles and a cache of automatic weapons were down at Davy Jones's locker too, but those were too heavy to lift. Garrett had more guns than a domestic terrorist. Severe gun ownership was part of his privilege. In my world, men who owned weapons like this were either paranoid or mental, usually both. I struggled with the bag, turned it over until I found the plastic drawstring, exhaled some oxygen as I tugged it open, and reached inside. Inside this bag were ten Ziploc bags that had been used to hermetically seal each handgun. The Ziploc bags were huge. Waterproof. Everything had been layered like Christmas presents. Rifles and assault guns had been wrapped in Saran Wrap, some put in giant Ziploc bags, then everything was dropped inside Hefty garbage bags. We had been careful, had used three layers of plastic to keep the weapons dry. Ten handguns were sleeping at the bottom of the deep end of the pool. Garrett had never found them. Or maybe he had never looked for them. He assumed we had stolen them. He saw two black men and saw two thieves. He'd been busy shoving his wife down stairs. He'd been busy recruiting warriors to come after me and Jake Ellis. After he'd squared up his tab with San Bernardino, we would've told San Bernardino where the guns were, and San Bernardino would have let him know where his armament was.

Lungs burning like a California wildfire, I struggled, grappled, grabbed the first gun I could, didn't care the caliber, but it felt like a Glock. It slipped from my hands and I had to fight with my lungs and the slipperiness of the plastic. I was underwater, trying to rush without panicking, knowing Mr. Garrett would reappear and start shooting down and offing me in this watery grave. He'd shoot until he saw red water rising and diluting to pinkness. I wasn't sure if I could shoot a Glock underwater without modification, but I knew if I shot upward, I'd be shooting blind. Water didn't compress and could bind in the firing pin chamber. And a shot from this deep underwater would be nonlethal. The shot wouldn't be accurate, and even if I got lucky, it wouldn't have the velocity it needed to kill a motherfucker who was standing over me trying to gun me down. The Glock had to stay in the Ziploc until I surfaced. Mind was in a frenzy. Was delirious from pain and the need to breathe. I couldn't carry two gats and swim to the top, not when one felt like it weighed a hundred pounds. I didn't have time to sort that out, so I tucked the first Glock in my waistband, hoped it was loaded, then got my feet under me, touched the bottom of the pool and pushed upward, pushed and felt the last of the air escape my body. As I glided upward, the gun moved down into the left pant leg of my joggers, became awkward weight, worked against me, tried to anchor me to the bottom. This wasn't working. Had to keep going. I looked up and saw nothing but darkness, didn't think I'd make it back to the top, and the surface looked like it was a mile away. I had taken my last breath. I wouldn't live long enough to inhale fresh air again. Dread owned me. I was in hell, pounds of water standing on my head. Garrett's pool was on Garrett's side. This water was his water. My body wanted oxygen and did its best to force me to breathe. I wanted to breathe. Holding my breath went against what my body needed. I felt the carbon dioxide level accumulating in my blood. I had to breathe. I was suffocating. It was a battle that no man could win. When I was about to black out, when it was too intense and my body tried to force me to gulp and try to drink an ocean of chlorine, I broke the surface, breathless, wheezing like I'd run two marathons uphill and back-to-back at top speed, came from a cold, watery womb into the world like a baby being born, right next to Mrs. Garrett's nude, bald, battered, lifeless body.

CHAPTER 24

STRUGGLING TO BREATHE, I turned Mrs. Garrett over on her back, tried to keep her head above water. She wasn't breathing. Struggling to stay afloat, Glock nestled in the leg of my joggers, I tried to kick, sidestroke, and pull Mrs. Garrett to the side, wanted to get to the edge of the pool, but the three homies Garrett had left behind came after us. I heard them talking. Couldn't understand a word they said. They thought I had drowned and were surprised when I had come back to the surface. My mind was fractured. A woman had drowned. One of Garrett's henchmen had been sent to follow Jimi Lee. And Jake Ellis was here. Garrett and his gun were after him. There was noise inside the mansion, a battle I could barely hear. My ears were waterlogged.

Another of the mansion's windows broke and a body flew out head-first, landed on top of the barbecue grill, a big number that had two propane tanks. They had Jake Ellis. They had trapped, shot, and killed Jake Ellis. The thugs hurried over to see the broken body. When they turned back toward me, I was out of the pool and had pulled Mrs. Garrett with me. She was on her side, still not moving. Still not breathing. I left her as she was. Jake Ellis was my priority. Limping across concrete, water dripping from my joggers like rain, wounded from head to toe, barely able to inhale, I hobbled toward the body. The thugs called out, hurried toward me. They expected me to try to escape. And they knew I was in no shape to run. They came at me until they saw the Glock. They were ten feet away when they realized I was armed, and their charge came to a sudden stop. Attitudes changed. The captors became the prisoners. Each had a shocked expression, wondering where the hell I had gotten a gun from, wishing Garrett had left them strapped. They had been overconfident. They didn't need to worry about the gun. Guns never killed anyone. Bullets were grave makers. And I had seventeen.

I expected at least one to jump bad, become badder than Jim Croce's legendary Leroy Brown. And one did think he was badder than a junk-yard dog and meaner than King Kong. One always did. He stepped forward, came toward me. "That motherfucker ain't gonna shoot nobody."

Before the baddest of the bad men could say another fucking word, I pulled the trigger, opened fire. I fired six times. The one who acted the baddest went down first; then the one who was the biggest charged at me. He contracted lead poisoning in the middle of his chest. He went down on a knee, then collapsed. I never shot at anything I didn't want dead.

But even now, with my life on the line, it was hard to put a man down.

The third man's skin was as dark as the night. The hue of a king. He stood in his spot, didn't run, and despite my gun and two men at my feet, he wasn't going to run. He wore a Denver Broncos skullcap, a Punisher T-shirt, and black sweatpants, his knuckles raw from beating me.

I said, "Black man."

He spoke like he was holding the gun. "Get back in that pool."

His accent told me he was Dominican. Black like me with roots of the same tree, only his ancestors' boat, one with hundreds of enslaved Africans, had stopped in the West Indies. African, West Indian, or born in America or the UK, to men like Garrett, we were all niggers. My lost brother challenged me. Sometimes the hardest thing to do was convince a black man he didn't have to yield a Pavlovian response and jump for men like Garrett, that he didn't have to answer to the bell that called out niggers. Gun in hand, I faced a black man who frowned at me like I was suffering from drapetomania, and I scowled at him like he was the one who had been brainwashed.

I nodded. "You know I'll die in that pool. If I couldn't swim, I'd already be dead."

"That's my job. To keep you in the pool. If you drown, that's on you."

"Walk away."

"Dead bodies. Burning buildings. And a dead woman. We gone too far to walk away."

I motioned toward the back door. "Walk away."

"I can't. He ain't paid me yet."

"I want you to just walk away."

"Shit, nigga, I can't walk away broke. I have three kids. I can't go home broke."

I said, "Well, I guess one of us won't be around for the *Black Panther* movie."

We had fallen into a civil war, Union against a fighter for the Confederacy.

He braced himself, made himself feel bulletproof, then ran at me screaming. My gat kicked, spat twice, put lead in his face and in the middle of the Punisher's skull. Dropped him between his second and third steps. He got the JFK special and a chest shot, then fell on his coworkers, became kindling on the pile. I wondered what the other men's stories were, how we ended up here at odds. Men who were sons, fathers, lovers, men who'd traveled the same pothole-filled road I had traveled since birth, a road that was designed for men like us and went only uphill, men I would have called my brothers in the streets or stood with or kneeled with at a rally for justice. Now they were unmoving, dying on damp concrete, in puddles of their own blood.

Those same men would have stood poolside and sipped a beer while I drowned.

In the back of my mind, I heard a voice whispering a rumor,

something some black folks claimed Harriet Tubman said, something not confirmed, yet I'd read it many times: "I freed a thousand slaves. I *could have freed* a thousand more if only they knew they were slaves."

A noise came from behind me and I turned, stumbled with pain, ready to shoot again. No man was there in the shadows; no one was hiding behind a palm tree.

It was Mrs. Garrett.

The bruised woman was on her side, coughing, puking, shivering, in agony, but alive.

Death had come to visit, had tea, but changed its heart, maybe left for bigger prey. That or the god that protected fools and babies had come to her side. That god hadn't rescued any black men tonight. Didn't matter if we were here or in Barbuda or Vieques, my designated people had to find the right god or learn to be our own gods. There hadn't been a deus ex machina for Flint or Saint Louis. We'd been living between two seas, praying for a deus ex machina since 1619.

Praying was wishing, and I knew there was no genie in the bottle. Mrs. Garrett vomited herself back to life while all of my thoughts went by in two blinks and a shuddering exhale, an exhale of relief. Now I had to get to Jake Ellis. My heart tried to beat out of my chest. I limped and in panic I gazed down on the broken body. My eyes burned. Focused. It wasn't Jake Ellis. I scowled upward, looked up at the back side of the mansion, heard a fight going on, one that sounded like Uganda's parliament was back in session. I stepped back, tried to figure what rooms were over my head. Either Jake Ellis had thrown one of Garrett's men out of the window during their fight or the street soldier saw what he was up against and decided to jump out and killed himself by landing on his head. I headed for the broken patio door, but before I made it ten steps, someone yelled for their life. A man screamed. Right away another window broke. Someone tried to escape, flew out of the mansion like he was trapped in the winds of a hurricane. Glass broke and he dropped fast and crashed on concrete. He crashed at a bad angle. Two legs snapped like twigs. The man was as broken as fuck, howled like there was no tomorrow. He had two knots on his head: One was the size of the Rock of Gibraltar, the other the size of Stawamus Chief. What mattered to me was that that gentleman wasn't Jake Ellis. I couldn't tell by his face, but I could tell by his body. His skin was the wrong shade of black. I held the Glock in my hand; water made my joggers feel like they weighed a ton. The night air made my heavy clothing turn cold against my skin. Pool water drained from my joggers like I needed a catheter, left a trail, dripped over dry concrete as I stumbled around broken glass, avoided getting my feet cut, then dripped across swank rugs and heated marble floors when I went inside the Garretts' mouth of luxury. I heard echoes from a battle upstairs and hurried that way, realizing the kitchen still smelled like magically moist salmon.

CHAPTER 25

ONE OF GARRETT'S bushwhackers stumble-ran down the stairs, bolted past all the amazing sculptures and art, tripped on his big feet, fell and got back up with panic, and again ran like his life depended on his escape. His face was jacked, a huge knot on his forehead, left eye bleeding a river. He'd suffered an absolute beatdown. His face had been pummeled by a pugilist. Probably was dealing with the effects of a concussion. The tall man in jeans and a North Face sweatshirt looked like something out of a Stephen King novel. He wobbled until he saw me. He saw me with the gun pointed at him, then cursed, took a breath and dropped down on one knee, then took another breath, eased down on both knees. He made pained sounds as he panted and raised his swollen hands. His right hand looked as broken as his spirits. The way he moved and groaned, I think his ribs were shattered too. He'd been too close to a real fighter.

The bushwhacker frowned. "You're not dead. Fuck. What are you made of?"

"Bad luck, hard times, and trouble."

He chuckled. Just to underscore how serious this was, I fired a shot near his head.

He trembled. "Hands up, don't shoot. Hands up. Please. Don't shoot."

"Don't scream."

"Just don't shoot me. I don't want to get shot again."

"You caught some hot lead tonight?"

"Three years ago. Right in the ass. Don't want to ever get shot again. That shit hurts."

"Where's my recalcitrant friend?"

"Your what?"

"Where is the pissed-off African?"

"Long as that crazy man ain't by me."

"He's alive?"

"I think so. Harder to kill than a goddamn Alabama cockroach."

"How bad is he hurt?"

"Might have been shot point-blank two or three times."

"Fuck. Then he could be dead."

"Fuck. I should've stayed my black ass at home and watched *Game of Thrones*."

"Garrett. The African. Upstairs?"

"They was."

"How many men on your side?"

"I don't know and I don't care. It's like every man for himself right now."

"But the African might be alive."

He panted. "How in the hell Africans end up slaves if Africans fight like that?"

"Read a book."

"Read a book?"

"Read a motherfuckin' book."

Then booms came from upstairs. It sounded like a bull charging into a wall over and over.

The brother on the floor heard the noise and wanted to rise.

I fired off another round, again near him, let him know I was his brother but I was not his friend, not in the middle of a stupid-ass war, and he stretched out, surrendered like a little boy playing cops and robbers. I would guess the boy was twenty. I was old enough to be his dad.

I said, "You better be here, just like that, when I come back."

At the foot of the staircase was blood. And blond hair. This was where Mrs. Garrett had landed when Mr. Prenuptial had come up behind her, foot first. Garrett had snapped and kicked his wife down the hard wooden stairs. This was where he had taken clippers or scissors and cut off his wife's hair. He had taken her vanity, de-beautified her, corrupted what many would see as a work of art. The way she now looked on the outside, how he had defiled her loveliness, that was the way he now felt about her in his heart. This was where he had assaulted the woman he'd promised to cherish before dragging her back up at least thirty wooden stairs. More blond hair on those stairs and drops of blood showed that she hadn't been lying; she hadn't exaggerated what had been done. No man could take back the scars put on a woman's body, on her soul. He knew that. She would never be the same. No woman is beaten and raped and returns to being the same. She was lucky to be alive. That had angered him; then he had thrown her in the pool to amuse his anger, was willing to watch her drown. He'd kicked her down the stairs and blamed her for falling. He would have drowned her in the pool, then blamed her for drowning. I understood why she had never confronted him since they had married. It had never been safe to do so. The devil was in that man. And the devil believed himself righteous. His rage had rained down on her because he felt slighted, and this level of madness had been incoherent and unjust. He had come after me, after Jake Ellis, wanted to kill us to alleviate his pain. Garrett was dangerous. Not when he was alone in a room filled with alpha males. He hadn't been dangerous when he was at his kitchen table. Irritating, but never dangerous. But gun in his hand, or when confronting softer women, when he had enlisted an army of warriors to do his dirty work, Garrett saw himself as being as powerful as a king. Upstairs it sounded like a new battle had broken out. Again it sounded like a raging bull charging into a solid wall. The noise was intense, terrifying. I raised my foot to hike the stairs, but I was in too much agony to climb.

There was a small elevator just off the kitchen. Those came standard with overpriced mansions. I hobbled that way and pushed the button to take me to the second of three levels. The level that had four of the nine bedrooms. When the elevator door closed, I leaned against the wall. Pain came at me in waves; the whitecaps made it hard to breathe. A shock of dizziness came hard and went fast. Felt like I was still underwater. I had to bend over for a second.

In between three blinks I thought about my daughter.

Rachel Redman.

Jimi Lee.

Jimi Lee. They had said someone was tracking Jimi Lee. So I had to go after Garrett. Death could have left here to go claim Jimi Lee. And now Death was back for more entertainment, back to enjoy the minstrel show, if not for prey. With each ragged inhale and exhale, I felt it walking behind me, sipping on tea. Yeah, Death was back, and still, as I closed my eyes, no genie in the bottle. I needed to leave this shit show. I had my own problems.

This had been the worst day of my life.

But this wasn't done.

I had no idea what the hell this fight was, why it was at this level, but it wasn't done. Dead or alive, I wasn't leaving without the African. If I had been killed and my body had been left in that pool and he was still alive, I knew he wouldn't leave without me. As soon as the elevator door opened, someone sprinted in like a linebacker, hit me hard before I could stand up, before I could raise the gun, charged and jammed me into the back of the carriage. He tackled me so hard everything went black, and again I saw stars. He came at me with so much force I thought the elevator was about to come apart and fall back to the ground floor. With a grunt, I felt the Glock loosen and drop from my hand. He started throwing blows. I had to bob and weave, had to move based on instinct, on years of being in the ring, had to become a moving target, but he had me cornered, stayed on me and made it hard to get my footing; still I had to find daylight, change this from defense to offense and do the same, hit him with bricks and bombs. I fell into another fight for my life, knew I had to kill another in order to stay alive. This was the way it had been in the Alligator State, when things had gotten out of control working for San Bernardino. Balthazar Wal-kowiak had been the only man I had killed before tonight. I'd been lucky in Florida, had made it out of that humid death trap traumatized but alive. It took two decades for shit to go wrong again. But this time, wet, damaged, beaten, unarmed, I wouldn't be the last man standing.

CHAPTER 26

I TOOK A punch, a solid shot that knocked me back to the wall, sent me backward like I had been shot out of a cannon. That blow buckled my knees, put me on my ass, and blurred the world. I looked up and saw a black boot raised high, about to stomp my face. I dodged the kick, caught his foot long enough to push him back, grunted, and did my best to throw him off-balance and make that murderer stumble and fall.

He was tired, bleeding, filled with anger, in a blind rage.

While he was scrambling to get up I snapped, "Jake Ellis . . . *Chale . . . Chale . . . Kwamena Gamel Nasser* . . . stop fighting me, motherfucker, before I hurt you. . . . It's me, fool."

We had traded blows at lightning speed, had almost taken each other's heads off before I realized I was battling Jake Ellis. His face was bloodied, and some of that blood was in his eyes.

He staggered back two steps, hands still in fists. "Ken Swift?"

"Bro, it's me."

"You called me by my real name."

"Kwamena Gamel Nasser, it's Ken Swift."

"Don't play with me. Black man, that you?"

"It's me. Your brother by another mother."

I made it to my feet. Then I helped my wounded compadre get back to his.

Jake Ellis was fucked up.

He asked, "How'd you know I was here after that Dumpster mayo?"

"I was here before you got here."

"You came after that cracker before I did?"

"His boys jumped me, kidnapped me, and tried to drown me in the cement pond."

"They bricked my Mustang and set it on fire. Then tried to set my building on fire. I was on the downstroke and my lady was just arriving in heaven when my car alarm went off. You know I had to finish. We get a lot of false alarms. I went out and Garrett and his gang came at me, then tried to shoot up Leimert Park." He coughed. "How many of Garrett's men left?"

"Shit, you tell me. His bushwhackers came out of an ice cream truck like clowns in a circus car. I saw about eight or nine. I left three with lead poisoning by the pool."

Jake Ellis spat on the wooden floor. "I threw a couple out the window. That's five."

"You ran one down the stairs. That's six. Could be two left."

There were at least ten bullet holes in the walls. Jake Ellis had almost been shot in the head, but it just broke the flesh. An inch to the left, he'd be pushing up daisies.

I asked, "Where's Garrett?"

"In that bedroom. Master bedroom. He ran in there when he ran out of bullets."

"What's he got up in there?"

"I don't know. Tried to ram and kick the bedroom door down. Door solid like a vault."

"I heard you when I was down by the pool."

Jake Ellis looked around, didn't spot a camera. "Tough like George Zimmerman. Take away the gun, he gets his sorry ass whooped by a kid every time. Stevie Wonder can see that."

I rubbed a knot. "He clocked the back of my head when his bushwhackers held me."

"He had his men hold you while he hit you from behind, like a coward?"

"Hit me with his gat. Pistol-whipped me while his goons stomped me."

"Fuck that. Let's set this bitch on fire. Get some gas. Pour it under that door. Light a match. Smoke him out. He'll either have to come out that door or jump out a window."

"Neighborhood of old money. Firemen would get here soon as we struck a match."

"A good fire will get on that ass and make him run out before the firemen and the cops."

"We don't want the cops here. He doesn't either."

"Cops come and he'll get lobster but we won't make it to the gate."

The elevator moved. It went back down to the first level.

I said, "I left a fool down there. He wasn't hurt. Didn't want to shoot him."

"He's coming with backup?"

"He probably has his boys. And this time, I bet those boys have toys."

"This shit is worse than Miami."

Jake Ellis took the gun, aimed it at the elevator door. I checked the stairs to see if the bushwhackers had regrouped, multiplied like Norway rats, and were storming us from two directions. No one was on the shiny stairs. Elevator came back up. When the lift opened again, it was Mrs. Garrett, alone, on the floor. Nude. Jake Ellis didn't recognize her. Mr. Garrett had done a Britney Spears on his wife's head and she looked like she was a cancer patient on her last legs. The cold water had shriveled her skin. Her complexion was beyond pale. Then Jake Ellis did recognize her. He hurried to her. She raised a hand, didn't want to be touched. I didn't have to say the damage he saw was done by Mr. Garrett, and Jake Ellis didn't have to ask.

I said, "He's a real tough guy."

"Some call Akufo-Addo the biggest coward in Ghana. Garrett is America's coward."

She tried to get up, couldn't. Needed assistance. Jake Ellis helped her to her feet, let her lean against the wall, then took off his bloodied hoodie, put it on her. It covered her like a miniskirt. She was ashamed and angry, wiped away tears, pulled the hood up and covered her head.

She asked, "Where is my loving husband? Where is my Dickie Bird? Doesn't he know his Apple Booty needs him now, for better or for worse? We have company and he's not entertaining or helping. I mean, there are dead men by the pool. A man outside crying over his broken legs."

Jake Ellis motioned toward the bedroom's double doors. Three-point locking system on each access. Even if we charged the entry at the same time, the doors wouldn't break open.

She wiped away tears and yelled, "Dickie Bird, want to come out for some more gelato?"

There was no response.

She turned to us. "No worries. I have a key. In my closet. I have a key because when he gets mad, he will lock me out. We can get in with my key. Bastard doesn't know I have a key."

Before I could ask, Jake pointed. "The bedroom across from that one is her closet."

She walked toward a bedroom that had the same style doors, told us, "Wait here."

While she dealt with shock and anger and wiped away more tears than were in her swimming pool, I asked what I really was concerned about. "Does he have more guns?"

She shrugged. "Don't know. I just know he had his toys everywhere. I know he bought guns like he was in the NRA's gun-of-the-month club. He was always going to Wyoming or someplace, always went to some gun show somewhere, then came back home with new toys. Once he brought back flowers and gave me chlamydia. Must've been a hell of a gun show."

Jake Ellis asked what was important: "Did we get all the guns in the house?"

Tears dropped as Mrs. Garrett touched her bald head. "You didn't get mine."

I asked, "You have a piece? San Bernardino didn't know that. We didn't know that."

"My husband doesn't know that. I hide it in the drawer that has my tampons and girlie stuff. That's the drawer men will never look in. Had a .380 for eight years and he has no idea."

"What happened eight years ago?"

"We had a black president. People were talking about race wars."

"Yeah. Well."

"I was going to buy a .22, but the man at the gun shop told me the bullet might not penetrate the brain. Said the bullets might follow the path of his skull. With a .380, no problem like that. That's why I hid out in my closet earlier. I love God with all my heart, and I prayed, but in case the Internet in Heaven was offline, or my prayers went to God's spam folder like they always seem to do, I had my loaded Pinkie Boo at my side just in case he went a bit too berserk."

"A marriage built on secrets is a marriage built on a foundation of sand."

"This one was built on quicksand in a tornado. I'm not stupid. I can guess the things he does. He associates with ruthless people. I knew that one day it was gonna get ugly around here. Bad people come and go, sit at our dinner table, swim in our pool. My closet would have been my hideout. And he gets mean. If he ever got crazy, didn't want him to know I had a gun too."

"Why didn't you peel a cap in his ass tonight? Justice would be on your side."

"I don't know. I ain't never shot anybody before. Should have shot him two years ago when he gave me chlamydia. Now he's thrown me down stairs. He cut off all of my hair. He made me ugly. He beat my face and made me ugly. What kind of monster would do this to a woman?"

"The kind that would slap you with a prenup on your wedding day."

"A man with no heart. A control freak with no soul. A goddamn wannabe gangster."

"But you jumped the broom. You married a man you didn't want to marry."

"For the money. I guess I mean, I couldn't *not* marry him and crawl back to Coco's and beg for my job back. Made me feel like I was a fuckin' moron. I would have had to give him back the BMW. I couldn't go back to driving my ugly bucket and being a two-bit waitress for minimum wage, not without people whispering. All the girls there were jealous. Real jealous. Those thots would have loved to have seen me fail. I would have been the laughingstock of Compton and Dominguez Hills. So, yeah. Yeah. To save face I sucked it up and married Richard Israel Garrett the Third. Dickie Bird. They called him that in Boston. He had a bad leg when he was growing up. A *dickey* leg. And he was puny until he went to Princeton. So, they called him Dickie Bird until he made it to university. Then he was Garrett."

"Macho, egotistical guy like him, seems like he'd want people to call him Butch."

"No, but he's mean and calls his sister Butch. She's the South End's biggest lesbian. She's a cop. I think she is the reason he left Boston. She hates him. He doesn't talk to her. Told her when she got off the clit and back on the dick, then maybe they could be family again."

"His nickname needs some Viagra. And you married Dickie Bird for the money."

"At first it was for love, would have been happy being the dutiful wife, would have lived to please my husband, but on my wedding day it changed, and I guess it became for money. I was angry, was going to marry him and try and take everything. Just never figured out how to do it."

I said, "The key. Mind getting the key?"

She moved like the walking dead, went to her closet, a closet the size of my apartment, a closet that had a bed and a full bathroom. When she came back she had pulled on funky leggings, had put on red Chucks, but still had on Jake Ellis's hoodie, her head and face covered.

"Let's open the door and go see how Dickie Bird's doing. Let me see if he's happy to see me after I didn't die. He beat me like I was a dog. He raped me. He locked me in a closet and let me suffer and bleed half to death. He paraded me around naked in front of all those strange men. And he threw me in the pool and tried to drown me. Like I wasn't shit."

I said, "We're both having bad days."

"So, since I've lasted through the in-sickness-and-in-health part of the contract, this little naïve girl from Compton is ready to see how this until-death-do-we-part is going to work out."

I stepped up. "Okay. But we can't just break up in there not knowing if he's armed."

Then she snapped, "And, yes, all of this art was stolen. Stolen from all over the world."

Jake Ellis said, "Some is from Africa. And it is authentic."

"He hates Africa, but he knows that's where the easy money is. The money that can't be traced when moved offshore. Him and all his rich friends are going to African countries trying to make bank. They want to chop up Libya. Or did he say Liberia? I know it started with an *L*."

"They come, take, never give. Rubber from our trees, diamonds from our mines, gold from our land. African leaders are complicit. They will sell our country to the highest bidder. They call it good business. I call it bullshit. Colonialism by another name is still colonialism. Nigeria could unite Africa and Africa could rule the world, if they allowed merit rule instead of mediocrity."

She sobbed. "He has had mistresses. Several. One was the house-keeper. I fired her."

Water dripping, making a puddle at my feet, I said, "Really?"

"That's what we were arguing about when we came home from shopping today."

Jake Ellis said, "Well, at least you came home to the magically moist salmon."

"He had hidden a bottle of Viagra and condoms in the glove box. A box of three. Two missing. We haven't used condoms. Ever. And the extra Viagra was a hundred milligrams. Bottle of twenty. Week-old prescription. Over half already used up. So he had a secret prescription. He knew I counted the pills in his cabinet. And we haven't used one in a very, very long time."

"Congratulations. You're definitely married."

"We've gone nine months. Wait, once we went a year. Best year of our marriage."

"Why get married and not have sex?"

"He knows I want a baby. *Wanted*. Even if I freeze eggs, they are no good without the secret sauce. And he has the damn sauce. He has to control everything. I wanted a baby so I would have someone to love and love me back. That's sad, huh? Makes me feel pathetic to admit that. I'm glad we don't have one. Who would want their child to ever see their mother looking like this? If he did this to me, just think of what he'd do to his child."

"He wouldn't touch the child. Men don't usually go Andrea Yates on the kids."

"I bet I wouldn't be the first woman he's done away with."

"They don't kill children. But rich men always do away with the mother."

"Right. Like OJ. Or Robert Blake. Lot of that kill-the-mother shit going around California."

"Sounds like he did everything but Phil Spector you and call it suicide."

"Dickie Bird *pushed* me downstairs, *bashed* my head, tried to *break* my neck, and then he tried to *drown* me like a roach. He did things that assholes do when they want to prove they own a woman. He's stronger, but I fought him back. People in my family hurt fast and bleed quick, but we don't die easily. He's got me mixed up with those weak girls from Altadena or Monrovia."

"No woman expects this to happen in her life."

"I'm not stupid. I knew what to expect when you marry a man like him, knew shit wasn't going to be a fairy tale when he had his lawyer hem me up with that damn prenup. I know rich men have their ways. He told me his ancestors used to rob banks, stagecoaches, and trains. Didn't bother me. Mine shot craps in the back rooms of bars and drank liquor out of brown bags in pissy alleys. I can take a lot of shit. I mean, I put up with a lot of shit, can put up with him being cheap, can turn a blind eye to lots of things he has done, to the women, but I can't take this."

"He went full Boston on you. He tried to kill you."

"Why do all that? Why torture me? Why didn't he just shoot me in my head?"

"Wanted you to suffer before you died. Wanted to humiliate you. Like you did him."

She groaned. "I think my arm is broken. It hurts. My legs hurt from falling too. He bumped my head over and over. Everything is kind of blurry, off and on, but I can hang on a little longer."

Jake Ellis said, "We will take care of this, then get you to a hospital, to Cedars-Sinai."

"If I go to the hospital, they'll call the police and I'll have to tell them what happened."

"He scares you."

"Men like him is why Clara Harris will always be my hero."

Neither Jake Ellis nor I had any idea who Clara Harris was. We didn't care.

Mrs. Garrett stepped to the side, arms folded across her chest, angry, shivering.

Jake Ellis motioned. "Go lock yourself in your closet. Stay safe in your panic room."

Her jaw tightened. "I'm done being a coward. I want him to see he didn't destroy me."

"Still, we need you to step back. Let this be between bad men."

She looked at us. "Don't kill him. If you kill him, things will get worse."

Jake Ellis said, "I'll try not to."

Apple Booty did take a step back, moved closer to the double doors leading to her closet.

Jake Ellis and I took deep breaths, evaluated wounds, readied ourselves to attack.

Thoughts came in dark flashes. Dead bodies were cooling by the pool. Injured and dying men decorated the patio and the first level of the house. Like I had offered those other black men, we could call it a push, lick our wounds, and hobble away. But like those institutionalized men, we weren't trained to back down; we didn't walk away. We hadn't walked away in two decades. We were institutionalized in our own way. Too many black lives lived behind invisible walls. America still had thousands of sundown towns, and this elite city might have been one. Garrett could be bold and call the slave catchers. He could break the code, then deal with San Bernardino later. He was in fight-or-flight, and he wasn't fighting, and no one was left to combat on his behalf. If I heard sirens, there would be dozens of cop cars, cars that had barking dogs, and cops who never used rubber bullets or Tasers. If black men weren't wearing football gear, even when wearing the same hoodies and hipster gear white men wore with Birkenstocks, to the biased eye we all looked like prison inmates. Guilty until proven innocent, and no one on this property was innocent. Even Mrs. Garrett was complicit. Mr. Garrett would point at us, and the protect-and-serve crew, men and women who respected his hue, would see my swarthy skin, would see Jake Ellis's dark skin, and right away think we were in league with other men scattered all over the property. Garrett could claim we all broke in to steal his precious art and rape his wife. He could say we attacked his wife. And maybe she'd think twice, clam up, let us take that charge. She had too much to lose. I'd saved her life, but I didn't trust her. I knew my history, knew her history, knew my bias, had to acknowledge my preconceived notions, but my gut instincts wouldn't let me trust her. But we were pissed off. We had the same adversary. We were all cold, sweating, furious. Tired. Bleeding. Half past dead. Mrs. Garrett looked like Rihanna after an evening with Chris Brown. Garrett had come after me and Jake Ellis. We had been disrespected on our own turf. Jake Ellis had been dodging bullets and I'd been gaffled, beat down, and could barely walk straight. We didn't start shit. But we ended it. Jake Ellis never backed down.

I wasn't no punk either. Never would be.

Jake Ellis handed me the Glock. He glanced at me and probably figured I needed it. I looked back at Mrs. Garrett, was going to leave the gun with her, but the battered housewife shook her head, wouldn't touch it. I assumed she wanted to keep her fingerprints off the neener. Again, that was the wrong answer to me. If she could get us all dead, she would win the grand prize. I'd seen that blockbuster movie before, where all the men were killed, and the femme fatale ended up on a Caribbean beach, sipping margaritas, rich, widowed, a dreadlocked lover for hire at her side.

I stood next to a man who didn't know how to lose. On the other side of that door was a man built from the same steel. An unstoppable force had met an immovable object.

I didn't want to be here, was as battered as Mrs. Garrett. I was ready to leave. Not out of fear. I was suffering, but I didn't know if Garrett's bushwhackers had hurt Jimi Lee. She could be dead. She could be in a car that had been bricked and set on fire. She had been my first love. The mother of my disrespectful child. I couldn't leave, couldn't pretend this shit didn't happen, sip brown liquor, use Kush to ease the pain, put Band-Aids on my wounds, and crawl back in bed with Rachel Redman, couldn't go on with my life without knowing whether Jimi Lee had been dragged into this. Even when it felt like I would drown, Jimi Lee's safety was on my mind. She'd never left my mind. Not a day for twenty goddamn years.

Jake Ellis said, "Bruv? You're shaking. You okay?"

I nodded. "I'm always ready. Especially when I'm not."

Ego was the anesthesia that deadened the pain of stupidity. And death killed egos; no anesthesia needed. Nothing killed stupidity. Stupidity had survived for millions of years. Like kudzu, it spread and spread and spread. It was a cockroach in the mind.

Jake Ellis took the key, twisted it in the keyhole, turned the door handle. Six locks clicked and disengaged. As soon as the door opened, bullets flew our way. Garrett screamed and fired.

I fired back. Eight bullets left. Seven. Six. Five. Then four.

Garrett's shots matched mine as his insults matched Jake Ellis's. And each time, Mrs. Garrett screeched and made her Apple Booty jiggle. Jake Ellis wanted to rush into the room, his rage the lie that made him feel bulletproof.

We were invading a master bedroom like it was a Middle Eastern country filled with oil, busy taking shots and being shot at, until the clip ran dry. We pushed the doors open and Garrett was alone, no bushwhackers, but he held his gun. A nice gun that had no bullets. He tried to fire again. The bitch was bone-dry. He casually put the gun in his waistband. It wasn't a sign of surrender. He had other weapons. He reached for two knives. Held one in each hand.

Swords, actually.

He had swords with short blades, the kind made for gutting a man.

Garrett was out of breath, stress-sweating, looking at us like he was a zombie killer.

He wasn't going to go down easily.

And he was still determined to take out Jake Ellis.

Garrett grinned that monkey grin. "I ain't scared of you mother-fuckers. Come taste this metal."

CHAPTER 27

JAKE ELLIS DIDN'T back away, so I pressed forward. Moving in opposite directions, we picked up lamps to use as weapons, something to block those blades, and we had one in each hand. Garrett huffed, puffed, then yelled, came at us swinging his blades, swinging his blades, swinging his blades.

Garrett charged at us, and we each threw a lamp. Jake Ellis's missed, but mine hit Garrett's right arm. That didn't stop the fat man who was once a boxer at Princeton from getting his balance and trying to cut our heads off. We were in an oversize bedroom that had a sitting area, king-size Italian bed, art, and pictures of him and his wife when they married.

The room was the size of the actual park in Leimert Park.

We tore up shit as we moved around his playground, pulled the big-screen off the wall, threw anything that wasn't nailed down, but he wouldn't let go of his blades.

An explosion came from behind us. A bullet hit a floor-to-ceiling mirror on the wall. Glass rained to the floor. Jake Ellis and I both jumped, looked back, and expected to see a well-armed league of bushwhackers here to protect their benefactor. I was ready to duck and dodge bullets.

It was Mrs. Garrett. She could barely stand but had her .380 in her right hand. It was a pretty gun, blushing pink with a handle made of pink swirling pearls, a sweet customized Ruger LCP made to look like a work of art. I wondered if it was loaded with pretty pink bullets too.

She used the doorframe to hold herself up. "Dickie Bird, put down the imported knives. Those are not toys. Those are stolen from Asia and you know those are very, very expensive."

"I bought these."

"I saw the invoice. From a man who stole them. Still stolen. Like everything else."

"Where did you get a gun from, Elaine?"

"Gun fairy."

"Doesn't look real."

The bald and wounded woman fired another shot, that one closer to her husband.

She repeated, "Sweetie, put the knives down. Next time I won't miss."

"You're going to shoot me?"

"No, but you're not going to cut up the man who saved me from drowning. I can't let you do that. So, put the knives down or I will shoot you in your nuts just to hear you scream."

He commanded, "Throw me that gun."

"No."

He snapped, "Give me the fucking gun."

"You raped me."

"Elaine."

"You raped me like I was some drunk bitch behind a Dumpster."

"A husband can't rape his wife."

"Your mantra."

"It's in the Bible."

"I hated you before, but I really, really hate you now."

"I love you. You just make me a little crazy. You drive me crazy, Apple Booty."

Her voice weakened, her soft spot. "Don't call me that."

"I love you."

She fired another shot into the bedroom's 105-inch curved 4K TV, and that was like throwing a hundred grand in C-notes on a bed of fire. But like Garrett had said, when you didn't make the money, its accoutrements had no value. Right now, Mrs. Garrett had lost her sweetness and was capable of burning this bitch down. I stepped to the side of her ire. And so did Jake Ellis.

Even a small woman, a demure woman, when enraged, terrified men like us.

The dam burst and she limped to and fro, waggling her gun, ranting.

"This house is nothing but a zoo, and you have been the zookeeper. I was your favorite pet animal. You kept me pretty, you fed me, just like I was an animal living in a cage. You bought me things like they were treats, gave me nice shoes like you were giving an animal an extra bone under the table. This is a zoo. A roadside zoo and not even a good zoo. Beautiful creatures caged in a roadside *zoo* made of marble and glass and bricks, where your possessions don't have basic rights to freedom and everything else that makes their lives meaningful. This is a zoo where you beat animals when they don't do what you want them to do or when they misbehave."

"What can I do to fix this, Elaine? Talk to me. Fuck, Elaine, lower the damn gun."

"I'm shaking. Can't stop shaking now. I have been filled with anxiety for too long."

"Elaine. I overreacted. I'm sorry. I overreacted."

She coughed like gallons of pool water were still in her lungs, coughed like she was rattling with pneumonia, then wiped her swollen lips, wiped her mouth, and spoke in a choppy, raspy, getting-sick voice. "You have . . . disappointed . . . me, Dickie Bird. Since our wedding day."

Garrett said, "I'll change the prenup. I will call and make it effective immediately."

She fired again, shot and almost hit him. "Zookeeper. You brutalized me, treated me like chattel, worse than a mutt, like one of your commodities, and kicked me down the stairs. You're the animal. You're the dog. You're the rabid two-legged dog. And you need to be put down."

"I'll change the goddamn prenup, Elaine."

"*I can change it myself.*" She took a breath, felt her physical pain, touched her bald head, coughed a few more times, then looked at Garrett, tears in her beet-red eyes. "Dickie Bird, I can change it myself. With one bullet. Zookeeper, I can change everything with one bullet."

Knives in hands, nowhere to go, the businessman tried to barter. "Elaine."

Bloodied lips trembled. Tears rained from bloodred eyes. "You tried to drown me."

Frustrated, Garrett clanged his blades together. "Elaine."

"Knives. Down. Now. I'm in charge now, Dickie Bird. This dumb *woman* is in charge."

"Bitch, give me the fuckin' gun."

She fired and hit him in the right shoulder. That surprised Garrett as much as it surprised me and Jake Ellis. Garrett exhaled, with the pain, the shock, and gradually dropped his weapons.

She said, "I wish I was a man for five minutes. I wish I was Suge Knight big so I could beat your ass the way I want to beat your ass, then throw you in that pool. But I'm not a big man. *And neither are you.* Having a dick doesn't make a boy a man. I still bet I could beat your ass."

"Can't believe you fuckin' shot me."

"Sorry, not sorry."

"Who taught you how to shoot a gun?"

"Compton, Dickie Bird. Surprise. Now, get ready to fight like a real man fights."

Garrett said, "You shoot me and now you want to fight?"

"If I wasn't hurting so bad, I'd fight you. I would drag you up and down those stairs."

"Elaine. Give. Me. That. Fuckin'. Gun."

"Shut up, Israel. Stop saying my name like I'm a child."

"Lower the gun, Elaine. Don't fucking shoot me again."

"Now you know how I feel. Now you feel the pain I feel."

"Shooting me is not called for. We argue. We fight. We don't shoot each other."

"You've done things to me before. But never like this. Never like this. You've slapped me. You've head-butted me before. I've made honest mistakes and you've thrown me against walls. I told myself it wasn't that bad. Told myself that I was being a bad wife. Learned to lie to you to keep the peace. Had to lie to keep from being hit. Convinced myself I deserved it when you did get angry and take it out on me, said I deserved to be locked in my closet, that it was all my fault."

"You get out of control. I only did what I had to do to get you to behave."

"Like an animal in a zoo."

"I never hit you out of anger, only to correct you."

"I'm not a child. Don't make it sound like I am a child, then sleep with me."

"I only discipline you. You act like a shrew and bring the punishment on yourself."

"Blame the victim. Everything you do is someone else's fault. Everything about this marriage is a lie. When that memory shit shows up on Facebook, when it forces me to look at our post-prenup marriage pictures from years ago, I want to call and curse out Mark Zuckerberg."

"Elaine."

"Let me see you hit a man the way you hit me. Let me see you correct a man."

"Elaine."

"You might be a zookeeper, but I'm not an animal in a zoo."

"*You fucking shot me*, with a gun my money paid for. You added insult to injury, and with me standing here bleeding to death, with your goons at your side, now you want me to fight?"

"Fight one of them, or catch some more lead."

"So, now you're the zookeeper."

"No, I'm your wife. I'm your wife, same as I've been since I was duped and married you."

"Elaine. You were never duped. How can you live like this and be duped?"

"I hear lead poisoning is bad for the health. As bad as the water in Flint, only quicker and with a lot less pain. I read that .380 bullets are very bad for the health. Even for animals like you."

"Elaine. You're better than this."

"No, I'm not."

"Don't point that gun at me while you're upset like that."

"Fight. Or get shot again. Be glad I'm giving you a choice. We're at a new altar. And I'm sorry, no attorney is going to magically appear so you can negotiate this postnuptial moment."

Garrett motioned at me.

His wife shook her head, stopped the match, still crying. "No, zoo-keeper, not him."

Garrett growled, "You gave me an option. . . . I choose to fight this one."

"You didn't give me an option on my wedding day. You gave me an ultimatum. You don't get to choose. You fight who I say you fight, or get shot again. I'm making the rules now."

He pointed at me like he was still in charge. "This one."

She coughed again. "No, Dickie Bird. Fight the African. After they left today you went on and on and on talking about how you could have kicked his *black* ass. Only you didn't use the word *black*. You called him the name of that Dick Gregory book a million times."

Garrett winced, held his wounded arm. "Don't do this, Elaine. For better or for worse."

"Dickie Bird, I think I'm covered by our contract. Not doing this is *not* in my prenup."

"Elaine. I'm shot. I need a damn doctor. *You shot me.*"

"*Fight.*"

"It won't be a fair fight."

"What's fair to a man like you? What's fair to a man who called his wife fat, old, ugly, and who was mean to her for fun? Unfair is the only kind of fight you know how to be in."

His wife was younger, but she was in charge. She was half past dead, rocking in PTSD, and in charge. The oppressed housewife had conquered, risen, and that had been Garrett's biggest fear. Garrett might as well have been trying to negotiate his bullshit with Judge Faith.

Mrs. Garrett held her side in agony. "I hope he kills you ten times."

"Elaine. How much? Just tell me how much you want. Two, three million?"

"What?"

"How much do you want a year? Just tell me how much. I will make it retroactive."

"I want nothing. I never wanted anything. But you hurt my feelings."

"I can have it wired to an account that no one will have access to but you."

"All I've ever wanted was to be happy. And children. You robbed me."

"Elaine."

"While I loved you, despite all of this, you have come up very short. I had faith. I was patient. Hoped you'd change. Hoped I wasn't a fool. I bet the whole town is laughing at me like I'm silly, poor, foolish white trash from Compton. You haven't put much love on the table, not like I did all these years. I did my best to be pretty enough, to be smart enough. I should have cheated on you a long time before, long before today, if a blow job is considered cheating."

"You and the kaffir."

"I have been depressed for so long. Sneaking to take pills. And ashamed to admit it."

"While I sat at my dinner table."

"You never should've talked down to me in front of them. I'd forgot what my momma'd taught me. Women'll always have more value than men. I forgot my worth. Eggs are expensive and sperm is cheap. You can have this house, the cars, and your boat, *Jesus of Lübeck*, but you'll never be worth more than me. Shit in a golden toilet still looks and smells like shit."

"*In my house.*"

"I know it goes against the original marriage vows, the legal document I regrettably signed after that prenuptial agreement was forced on me, but I enjoyed cheating on you. That made me a bad Christian, and I'll deal with that when I die and see Jesus, but I enjoyed it. About time I enjoyed something. Damn shame to live like this, to have all this, a life of silver and gold, and enjoy nothing in life." She was coming apart. "All this shit because you called a man a word that you should've kept on the other side of your capped teeth. Well, I'm not stupid, and I know it's more complicated than that, way more complicated, but even with you trying to rip off San Bernardino, I'll say that was the spark. You have called black people that since I have known you. I told you years ago you'd one day say that to the wrong black man. Well, we've had that day. This has been the most awful day of my goddamn life. The most awful. And I can't take another. I hope he kills you like you tried to kill me. I hope you feel like you've been kicked down stairs, raped, and get drowned in freezing water. Zookeeper, from this animal that you have kept in your magnificent cage, in this loveless marriage, I hope it takes a long time for you to see my Jesus."

"Elaine."

"Stop saying my name, Israel."

"Four million a year. For every year we've been married."

She fumed, offended and insulted as her words erupted: "I don't know how many times I've slept with you as your wife, Dickie Bird. But right now, I know that's over and done with. That bed. That bed right there. I hate that bed. I hated when you called me to come get in that bed with you. You might as well have had me upside down on a cross on Friday the thirteenth, because it felt like I was fucking Satan. All you ever did was sexualize me. You never saw me as an equal. I'm more than a sexual being. Women are more than sexual beings, Dickie Bird. I'm more than a cook and a maid. I was always scared. Afraid you'd get angry, that you'd do a few lines and have one Pabst Blue Ribbon too many and react to something I did, something you saw as wrong, and spend all night locked in my closet because I'd be afraid that you'd slap me again. You slapped me because I didn't fold your T-shirts as good as they do at the stores in the mall. You slapped me because I made the bed and the sheets didn't have hospital corners. *I was a good wife.* I'm intelligent, beautiful, brave, strong, supportive. And if you were wrong, if I corrected you, *you slapped me*. You hated that I was witty. *Optimistic*. Majestic. Loving. Nurturing. For that, you slapped me. *We're done.* I want a divorce. I don't know what life has for me next, but right now I know that I'm out of fucks. Zero fucks to give, you leathery piece of shit. *You destroyed my hair.* I put up with snoring, farting, cursing at children, burping, smoking, leaving the toilet seat up, had to put up with you watching the most disgusting porn, *and you have the nerve . . .* you cut off my hair. Why? How can one man be so evil?"

Wounded enforcers in the shadows, dead men by the pool, bullet holes in walls, furniture turned over, Garrett holding his arm, wincing, bleeding all over his beautiful beige carpet, and they fell into an argument. Jake Ellis was about to jump in. He had had enough, knew we were short on time, that this needed to be done, and Ghana was ready to put his paws on Garrett, but I didn't let him interrupt the woman. I had learned a long time ago to stop interrupting women when they talked. Especially an angry woman with a pretty pink gun. Now wasn't the time to shut down a woman who had just survived sexual assault, being beaten, kicked, slapped, humiliated, and almost drowned. If she wanted to curse him out until sunrise, I'd let her. If she shot that bastard in the head, I'd help her bury the body in Chino and do the same with the gun, then take bleach and scrub down this house top to bottom.

We were her sentries, our eyes on Garrett and those blades he would use as swinging guillotines, and that probably included using them on his wife, if he was given the chance.

"Elaine. I'm sorry. Let's . . . let's work on this marriage."

"I'm a fucking loser for marrying you."

"I am bleeding to death and I am trying to apologize for everything . . . for everything."

She let loose. "Zero fucks. Zero. Beyoncé got cheated on, and I got beat on. Men are trash and you are garbage made for the collector. I will never, never be in a relationship again. I'm done living this life. I am so fucking done. I'm tired. I am in so much pain, and I'm tired. Tired of . . . existing. I am out of this toxic relationship. Dickie Bird, I'm outta fucks. *All fucks gone.*"

A woman who had no fucks to give was beautiful and terrifying all at once.

She had had a lot to say, but now she signaled to us that she was finally done.

She'd unloaded years of rage.

Hands already in fists, Jake Ellis nodded. "This main event is about to be on."

I added, "And if you touched one hair on my ex-wife's head, if he doesn't kill you, I will."

My wounded compadre, Jake Ellis, regarded me. "Bruv, you mean the Eskimo?"

"Bro, it was Ethiopia, not the Eskimo."

"She came back? When did I miss that?"

"Long story. She left my spot and Garrett sent his boys after her."

"Why was she at your spot?"

"The blackmail problem."

"She's mixed up in this?"

"No. Just happened to be standing at the wrong place at the wrong time."

"You were with the Eskimo, then ended up with Ethiopia?"

"Let it go for now." I faced off with Garrett. "I need her to be safe. Untouched."

Garrett considered me. "If you want her to be safe, stop the African. I will make that call. And after you're done, the other offer stands. I'll raise it to two hundred thousand. You can cash in tonight."

Jake Ellis said, "Mayo, you're going to make that call anyway."

The wick of war had been lit. Jake Ellis shoved a bench out of the way, then went to the bed made for a king, grabbed two pillows, yanked the pillowcases off. He wrapped his hands with the pillowcases the best he could, like a champion wrapping his moneymakers before a title bout.

Mrs. Garrett coughed a handful of times, then fired another shot across the room.

While Jake Ellis had gotten ready, when Mrs. Garrett gagged again, Mr. Garrett had seen an opening and hurried, bent, and picked up one of his discarded blades with his left hand. That gunshot popped and he dropped the blade. Another shot from the .380 added an extra exclamation point to the conversation. Garrett stood, held his bloodied right arm.

Jake Ellis grinned. "Want to tell me all about Dick Gregory's book now?"

Garrett was defiant, wanted to call Jake Ellis a nigger again. It was in his eyes.

Jake Ellis stood tall. "Nigger, nigger, nigger. Well, this nigger has your Darwin Award."

I said, "This ain't about that slur."

Jake Ellis said, "Oh, bruv, we are way beyond fighting over European slurs. Way beyond that. This has nothing to do with San Bernardino. This man came to where I live, to where you live, bricked my car, set my town on fire, kidnapped you, and he has abused his wife?"

Monkey-faced Garrett barked, "You're still a nigger. You'll never be more than a nigger, and you know that. Being an African nigger hanging with an American nigger won't make you a better nigger, nigger."

I saw why Garrett had been a problem for San Bernardino. No one told a king what he could not do. He was still the fucking king of this fucking lawless piece-of-shit mansion.

Done pretending, Garrett attacked the weakest of the lot. "You cunt. You worthless cunt."

"Fake Christian. You haven't been to church once since we married in one."

"This is your last chance, Elaine. *Don't walk away from me.* Throw me that gun."

"This is my gun. I bought this with my money. You can't get mad and take this away from me like you will my allowance or clothes or my shoes or my car. This. Belongs. To. Me."

I moved and Jake Ellis looked at me. He saw me pulling pillowcases off pillows.

"What you think you doing?"

I said, "When you get tired of hitting the heavy bag, it's my turn to tenderize that fool."

Garrett snapped, "Motherfucker, I will rip your balls off."

"Nah, bruv, I got this." Jake Ellis held up his big mitts, hands of stone, and shooed me away, untracked me with his determination. "I'm the only unlawful detainer we need tonight."

"Serious?"

"You mad, bruv?"

"Not mad. You know I got mad love for ya."

I dropped the pillows at my feet. My joggers felt wetter, heavier, colder. My dark skin was ashen, pale, hands wrinkled from the water and looked like my flesh had aged a hundred years.

Mrs. Garrett said, "His eyes were supposed to be on the sparrow. I'm the sparrow. I am. He was supposed to watch over me." Then she made a hard face, wiped tears again. "Alexa. Play Biggie Smalls. I know I'm West Coast, should play some Tupac, because word to God, I've been ready to die since I was born. But this special moment calls for some Notorious B.I.G. Play 'Somebody's Gotta Die.'" Mrs. Garrett gave that command, then added, "And play that shit loud. Play it on the Apple Booty setting. Not the low setting for Dickie Bird. *Let's get turnt up.*"

Notorious B.I.G. came to life, took over ten thousand square feet from the grave.

She reiterated, "Alexa, Apple Booty setting. Song on repeat until I say otherwise."

Hard-core rap filled the room like deadly smoke that heralded the start of an out-of-control wildfire. So did the anger in Jake Ellis's eyes. His expression was that of a fighter at the opening bell, and he was ready to reduce a city block to ash. He was a fire that could be seen from outer space. Garrett raised his wounded arms the best he could, eyes wide, gunless, consumed with fear, and he backed up across the carpeted floor as Jake Ellis danced closer, backed around furniture that made this room look like the perfect showroom, stumbled over shoes, and when his back touched the wall, when he was cornered, when there was no room left for flight, his eyes widened more, and he knew he had to fight one-on-one. Garrett screamed like he was releasing all fear, like he was summoning some superpower, and went at Jake Ellis, raised his wounded arm and took the first swing at the Ghanaian who had trained on concrete in Africa's sun. He went after a man who had never been knocked down, a man who never lost a fight.

While that one-sided fight went on, I looked back, but no one was behind me.

Mrs. Garrett was gone. I caught her limping toward her closet, hoodie down as she ran her hands over her bald head, did that over and over, remembering her hair, her vanity, rubbed like she couldn't believe that this was where a promising life had taken her. She stopped limping, turned around in bits, slowed by agony, looked back, and she saw Jake Ellis handing her husband his ass ten times over. She nodded, content, then frowned at Mr. Garrett, gave daggers to a man who had said revealing things when she was drowning. He probably woke up each day boasting of his genetic superiority, and she knew he had considered her Compton relatives inferior people. White trash. He had probably told her they had better *genes* at Walmart than the gene pool in her lower-class family. Whatever she was thinking, while Biggie Smalls gave a beat that two fighters didn't follow, she nodded at me, then closed her double doors.

She hobbled away from her zookeeper and struggled to get back into her cage. Gun in hand, the wounded creature went where she felt safest from the architect of her pain.

Even angry, even after being abused, that woman wasn't capable of killing. She couldn't even watch her abuser, the man who didn't hesitate to do the same to her, being beaten.

He was still her husband. Maybe she punished herself for her choices.

I understood. Once upon a time, I had been the cuckold, and I understood. You loved them. From your soul, you loved them. Right or wrong, you loved them. Through the pain you loved them. And no matter how wrong they did you, you still couldn't kill 'em.

Each day was a new day and you hoped it would turn around.

Each day you hoped what was going south would self-correct and find true north.

You told yourself if you loved them hard enough, they would have to love you. You knew if you could make them love you all barriers would lift. You hoped that prenups, legal or metaphorical, would go away. You believed in the power of love. You believed in your love story.

But Time laughed. And eventually you realized nothing would change. What you felt was only what you felt. There was no love by osmosis. The one you loved would never feel what you felt.

They'd never love you. Two would never become one. You realized that where you were, ten degrees hotter than the basement of West Hell, was as good as it was going to get.

And in the end, all you could do was bow your goddamn head in defeat and walk away.

I was more worried about Mrs. Garrett than anything else.

Some of her last words had chilled me. "*. . . because word to God, I've been ready to die since I was born.*"

She had said that like it was her mission statement. Like this life was over.

While an incensed Ghanaian easily outboxed her husband, while a true pugilist from Africa outfought a silver spoon who had boxed behind the walls of Princeton, while a man who learned to fight under Africa's unrelenting sun knocked her husband to the ground, stomped him, then beat him with a lamp so hard he would earn cuts that needed a dozen staples, while a blow from the lamp broke Princeton's wrist, while solid face shots knocked half his teeth out, Mrs. Garrett was in that room, alone, wounded, humiliated, despondent, with a loaded gun.

"Somebody's gotta die."

Biggie Smalls rose from the dead and stressed that theme.

"Somebody's gotta die."

A hit dog was gonna holler, and with each hit, Garrett howled like a bitch in heat. But my heart drummed hard because I was afraid Mrs. Garrett was about to blow her brains out.

Many people walked to that door and pondered the abyss, but not all tried to enter.

I'd be lying if I said checking out never crossed my mind. I'd dealt with depression in my mid-twenties. I didn't even know I was depressed. Like other black men, I just called it the blues, then put on some music to match my mood; then it was me and Jack Daniel's working it out.

I stepped over everything that had been wrecked, took deep breaths, exhaled and shoved aside things that had been turned over, stepped and had to avoid broken glass. Garrett was begging for mercy as I held the wall and tried to get out of this boxing ring and hurry to that double door. I wanted to bang and make sure she wasn't in her closet about to buy an e-ticket to Jesus. One bullet could turn her closet into a mausoleum.

The moment I stepped out of the enormous bedroom and put my wet feet onto the wooden floors, the second I faced four more king-size bedrooms on this level, with Biggie masking any noise from downstairs, I saw movement. I jerked, paused, and as Biggie Smalls gave the beats to Garrett's beatdown, my heart thumped hard as I looked toward the front of the manor. I took a step, then froze and stared through a dimly lit home, squinted and tried to see beyond magnificent chandeliers, spied toward the circular driveway in front of the estate.

Two black SUVs were out there in the dark, bushwhackers creeping out of each one.

CHAPTER 28

JAKE ELLIS STOPPED standing over Garrett like Muhammad Ali had done when he taunted Sonny Liston, and ran to me when I roared his name. Both of his hands were covered in once virginal pillowcases that had been turned a bright revenge red, each Rorschached in blood.

I said, "We got company."

Jake Ellis asked, *"Koti?"*

"No sirens. No flashing lights. And they're just sitting there like they are waiting for us to finish up and come out so they can put us in a full set of restraints."

"Handcuffs, leg irons, and waist chain, and security boxes over the restraints' keyholes."

Jake removed the bloodied pillowcases, dropped them on the shiny wooden floor.

He asked, "Do you remember the layout? How many exits this maze have?"

"Too many to count."

"Each exit is an entrance. So they can hit us from a dozen entrances."

"Jumping that wall in the back might be the only out."

"I wish the other side of that wall was a part of Mexico that went into the heart of Ghana."

"Has to be a ladder around here. But we'd still have to drop to the other side."

"We'd have to skydive and run across the neighbor's sprawling estate. Floodlights might hit us the second our feet touched ground. Then we'd have to find a way out of that yard."

I said, "Two black faces jumping a white man's wall and running like Tubman."

"People at the mansion on the other side of the back wall are Chinese. Bruv, the Chinese have an entire museum equating blacks to animals in China. A lot of them hate blacks and despise Africans. The way we look right now, in this zip code, we jump that wall and they might shoot us down like we're two King Kongs on top of the Empire State Building."

I spoke louder than the bumping music. "What are our options?"

Jake Ellis responded in kind. "Your gun ran dry."

"Don't forget the cache of weapons we left sleeping at the bottom of the pool."

"We wrapped them good?"

"The Glock I managed to pull from Davy Jones's locker worked fine."

"Then I'm sure the other handguns and the assault rifles will be okay too."

I nodded. "We need to get to those. But we don't know what's out back."

Jake Ellis went back to the Garretts' bedroom. Sounded like he hit Garrett five or six more times, then came back with the two blades that Garrett had held when he faced us. Jake Ellis handed me one. We went down the stairs bit by bit, expecting trouble to be waiting, maybe with guns. At ground level, the brother I had left behind on my journey up was still there, on his belly, on the cold marble floor, hands over his head. Biggie's rant masked our descent. The traitor looked up, saw me and Jake Ellis, saw the blades, and cursed to God. He shook but kept his hands spread out like he was waiting on LAPD to take him away.

He'd been free to go a long time ago, but not all men knew how to be free.

Jake Ellis asked, "What's the plan, Mississippi?"

"Front door, Ghana."

"Like Butch Cassidy and the Sundance Kid."

"You know it."

"You've got balls almost as big as mine."

"Bro, I was just in freezing water."

"Bruv, steel balls don't shrivel. Who's going first?"

"Neither one of us."

I called back to the terrified young man on the floor.

I told him, "Get up, bushwhacker. Get on your feet, Stepin Fetchit, and come here."

THE MOMENT HE stepped out, it was like being surrounded by SWAT. Every man on that team was either white or could pass for white. The men threw the bushwhacker down, put him down hard enough to break bones, then had knees in his back and neck, practically suffocated the brother. Not until then did they call out to their boss. When we heard the name they called, blades in hand, Jake Ellis followed me out the front door. Four guns aimed at us. Red dots moving back and forth across our hearts. We stood where we were, blinded by bright light.

They came at us, ready to put us down, barking orders as we dropped the blades.

CHAPTER 29

THEIR LEADER WAS a bearcat, as lethal as LAPD, as no-nonsense as Olivia Pope, and moneyed like an A-list movie star. This crew didn't work for Garrett. They were here for Garrett on behalf of their superior. The back door to the second SUV was opened and their employer was let out. She was a drop-dead-gorgeous woman of a certain age who had slayed in her twenties and was still slaying now. She was timeless, ageless, and made being in her fifties look like she was barely in her thirties. Even at these moments before sunrise, she was style and grace, flawless in a hot white jumpsuit, iced up, and had a physique that'd send most women scrambling for the gym. Body, hair, skin, fashion, she lived in a state of consistent slayage. She was a doll. A real Sheba, with amazing gams. The word on the street was that her father had been a hard, shotgun-carrying blues man people called Big Slim. That one-legged, hard-drinking Mississippi gangster had been a rough, tough, mean son of a bitch who had run a pool hall in North Hollywood, a pool hall that had prison rules and housed a den of con men, thieves, murderers, double-crossers, and assassins. When boss lady was young the old man had sent her away to protect her. It had been better that no one knew he had a kid. Couldn't be exploited. He lived in that pool hall and didn't want her to pick up on the life in North Hollywood, so he had sent her to live in San Bernardino, an hour east of LA, near the military bases and the area formerly known as Sunnymead, where real estate was cheaper and the area was considered safer than the drive-by culture in LA. Far enough away, but close enough for him to drive and see her once or twice a month. When Big Slim's love child, a child some said he made with a Jamaican streetwalker one night, landed east in that place some people called West Hell, which was more about a part of hell itself than any geographical accuracy, she was barely a teen, but trouble was already in her blood. She ran things to the point that many gave her the city's name.

She was called San Bernardino. She was our boss.

She was here. She had left her throne.

I guessed we were in trouble.

She smelled like French wine and Italian perfume, both top-shelf.

Pasadena smelled like desert, lingering smog, and sudden death.

I asked, "Garrett paid his debt? Or you here to collect?"

San Bernardino said, "The transfer finally came through, ten seconds before midnight."

"Why are you here? You only show your face on Cadillac jobs."

"You didn't think I'd let Garrett talk to me that way and live to tell about it, did you? He messed with my cabbage, then called me talking out the side of his neck, popping off like he wants a Chicago overcoat. You think I was going to let him talk to me like that and call it a day?"

"No, ma'am. I didn't think you would."

"You have one minute. What happened here?"

Her security detail at our back, Garrett's sole bushwhacker still on the ground, I told San Bernardino as much as I could. She saw we had been through hell since the sun had set.

She asked, "Any bodies?"

"Some out back. Maybe three are ready to be fitted for a pine box. Some were injured pretty bad, because this was life or death, so could need four or five hearses by now."

She didn't react, nodded like she already knew. "Who did what to whom?"

"I shot a few. Jake gave two a back-door parole."

"Then this spot is already hotter than Death Valley."

"And like LA after the Rodney King verdict, it's the last place you need to be."

"I came to confront Garrett. No one talks to me that way. No one."

"Sleep on that anger."

"Are you telling me what to do, Ken Swift?"

"No, ma'am."

"Was there some promotion in my organization that I am unaware of?"

"Was only a suggestion."

"Did I ask for suggestions? Did I accidentally butt dial you for a consultation?"

"No, ma'am. No, you didn't. Was just trying to make you aware of the situation."

"Watch your tone. Don't get too familiar with me. And no mansplaining. I hate that shit."

"Sorry if I overstepped my bounds."

"You did overstep. Take your brake fluid and slow your roll."

"I apologize."

"Never let people walk over you. I came to collect my respect. That is one thing Big Slim taught me, if nothing else. My daddy said to never let anyone insult you and be able to walk away. He said everybody will talk down to a colored woman, talk to her any kinda way, but it was my job to never let them get away with it. That's my job and I'm showing up to work my shift."

"You waited on the money to transfer before you addressed this issue."

"Of course. Pussy and money: both make the world go around. If you have pussy, you can get money. And if you have money, you can get pussy. That's the law. I was born with the pussy. And you know I always get the money. Before anything else, I have to get the money. My daddy told me that a man has to keep his money pregnant. Money should give birth to more money. If you're not making sure your money is impregnated, you're the one being fucked."

I nodded. "And since your money gave birth to more money, you're ready to fight."

"We're safe from being ambushed? How many are inside?"

"None. His bushwhackers fled. The ones that could. Might be a couple severely injured moaning here and there. They weren't armed. They won't come after the team you brought."

"Good. I was waiting while my drone surveyed the property. My infrared told me there were four in the house. Three in one room and one in another. I watched every movement."

"Police?"

"We've monitored. No calls have gone out from here. Neighbors can't call out if they have Internet phones. I've disrupted that service for a half mile. You know me. I got that on lock."

"You came across all these freeways in the middle of the night to get your respect."

"I don't procrastinate and I don't play with other folk's children. You know that."

I looked up.

Over the whiteness of the stately mansion, I saw a fleet of Phantom drones, counted six of them, silent, hovering, feeding images back to her workers in the SUVs. I bet those had arrived and had been overhead before they compromised the code to the security gates.

San Bernardino said, "Take me to Mr. Richard Israel Garrett the Third. I need him to repeat all he said on the goddamn phone. Let's see the motherfucker talk that way to my face."

"Jake Ellis had some time with him. But you probably saw that on the infrared."

"Lead me to Garrett's ding wing and show me what's left of him."

"Yes, ma'am. Jake Ellis left Garrett contemplating life from his ghetto penthouse."

She asked, "Should I bring my daddy's double-barreled shotgun?"

"I don't think you'll need it."

"That disappoints me."

"He's been tenderized. I doubt if he can raise a hand to wipe his ass."

"I did not need that visual."

"Apologies."

"You're talking to a woman. Not one of your homies on the corner."

"Understood."

The boss regarded her team. I saw them up close. All were Caucasian men.

She told them, "Boys, stay alert. Watch my six."

Her men nodded.

She said, "Now. Jake Ellis."

"Yes, ma'am."

"Come with."

"Yes, ma'am."

San Bernardino said, "And turn that atrocious music off. I hate rap. It's maddening. Lyrics that promote violence and contempt for women . . . that misogyny . . . cut that crap off right away."

"Will see what we can do when we get inside."

"Cake-eater, take my left side. *My other left*. Ken Swift, put your Mississippi on my right."

"Yes, ma'am."

As soon as we started to walk, I pointed, said, "Shit. I see Mr. Garrett."

"Good. I want him to see me coming. I never hide. I want the motherfucker who had the unmitigated temerity to talk down to me to see that San Bernardino is here to make a house call."

CHAPTER 30

GARRETT HAD STAGGERED out of his bedroom, the well-appointed area that had been a squared circle for at least one good round of fisticuffs. Even if he couldn't fight, I guess the Pillsbury Doughboy could take a hard blow. Princeton looked like a refugee, like a wild beast that had barely survived a Middle Eastern war. I led the way, but Jake Ellis moved in front and opened the double doors to the palace. Ghana held one door and Mississippi held the other.

San Bernardino sashayed inside, moved her wrath and grace into the extravagance of her newest enemy, and we followed her until she stopped at the base of the stairs. She took a deep breath, nostrils flared when she inhaled the fading scent of salmon dancing with the stench of pool water that had permeated my clothing and body. With each step, I dripped. We looked up at the art, at the home that was an elegant museum, at images of Garrett and his wife. The queen from one kingdom had arrived riding on two black dragons, and she was here to handle this herself. The chandelier gave enough light and we could see King Garrett on high from where we were. He still smelled like arrogance. He had never learned to be afraid. He was too stupid to be afraid. He rested at the top of the spiraling staircase, bloodied, but still a man who looked like he was ready to beat his chest and proclaim he was the king of all of the goddamn Kongs.

Biggie Smalls was still on repeat. The rapper I loved as aggravating as a nagging wife.

Jake Ellis had given Garrett ten years of blood-pissing pain in less than two minutes. He struggled to stay upright, held the rails, then stood at the top of the stairs, breathing heavily. Curses rained down on us, most directed at San Bernardino. Biggie Smalls swallowed all words. I knew what Garrett was saying. He had only one note. He was beaten and threatened to have us all killed before the sun hit noon. He spat over the rail. While he stood there in his own agony, the double doors to Mrs. Garrett's closet opened. She hobbled out of her cage. Her husband didn't see her behind him. She hurried up and pushed him. She growled and shoved him, as he had shoved her. Mrs. Garrett shoved Mr. Garrett headfirst down the stairs. It happened fast. Dickie Bird tumbled head over heels, Jack without a Jill. Jack fell down and broke his crown, and Jill came hobbling after. Mrs. Garrett took one stair at a time, held the rail, made her way down. Mr. Garrett was broken but still twitching. I couldn't tell what damage was from Jake Ellis and what injuries had come from the fall. Mrs. Garrett stood over him and unloaded her .380 into his body.

Then, eyes wide, surprised by what she had finally done, she looked at us.

It took all of her energy to command, "Alexa, stop playing Biggie Smalls."

Mrs. Garrett smelled like pool water too. She smelled bad, and I knew I smelled worse. I could smell her pain, agony leaving her pores. San Bernardino took in Mrs. Garrett, took in her injuries, her black eyes and bald head, and she moved closer to the wounded woman. Mrs. Garrett looked so bad that, before she spoke, San Bernardino thought she was facing a man.

Mrs. Garrett wiped her nose. "He beat me. Cut off all of my hair. Raped me. Tried to drown me."

San Bernardino was unfazed. "Then that cowboy you married did a Dutch act."

"I don't know what that means."

"He committed suicide. If he did what you have claimed, this was a Dutch act. He had started a Dutch act when he talked down to me on the phone. All roads led to this moment."

"He beat me. Cut off all of my hair. Raped me. Tried to drown me."

Mrs. Garrett looked diminutive. Naïve. Body battered. Life shattered. Tears falling.

"He beat me. Cut off all of my hair. Raped me. Tried to drown me."

She softly, sweetly, innocently, and painfully said her mantra as if she were practicing it for the police. For attorneys. For the jury. For the judge. She practiced the words, sounded like a child, a child who hadn't done anyone wrong. She had the look. She had the pedigree. Killers didn't look like her. Even if she was a cold-blooded killer, she could put on a Casey Anthony routine at her trial. Her hair would grow back and it would be like seeing Taylor Swift being tried for manslaughter. She could become America's obsession. She could become every battered woman's hero. Jake Ellis moved forward to help, but I grabbed his arm. It would've been a tell that he had touched that woman. She might've thrown her arms around him like he was her hero.

I let the woman cry and shake and shiver and look down at the blood on the floor. Garrett smelled worse than rotten eggs cooked until they were burned using Vaseline as cooking oil. He had that new-death rank, the one that came when bowels loosened upon death. She cried, asked Garrett to get up. Begged him not to be dead. She asked her husband to please move. San Bernardino went to Mrs. Garrett, eased the smoking gun from the distraught woman's hand. San Bernardino was a hard woman, a thief, a con, a killer, but she was still a mother, and it didn't matter that the woman she faced looked like a refugee Caucasian from the mountains of Caucasia. Her dark hand held one that could have been the descendant of a Viking from Iceland.

"He beat me. Cut off all of my hair. Raped me. Tried to drown me."

Women could look at other women and recognize all the evil things that men had done.

Women had experiences that bonded them, had their own fears, same as blacks in America.

San Bernardino regarded me. "Is this contained?"

I nodded. "Garrett brought me here to make me swim with the fishes and probably to dispose of my body, so I'm sure he made sure it was contained."

San Bernardino told Mrs. Garrett, "I can fix this. I can make this nightmare go away."

Mouth bloodied, Mrs. Garrett babbled, "He cut my hair. He knew how much I loved my hair."

San Bernardino looked at the stunning pictures of Mrs. Garrett gracing the walls.

"What do I do now?" The widowed woman's voice splintered. "I don't know what to do."

"We do what we always do at times like this."

"Should I call the police?"

"Too much would have to be explained."

"I'm scared."

"Jake Ellis, I'm sure they have coffee in this barn."

"We have good coffee. The best coffee. Dickie Bird only drinks *kopi luwak* Indonesian coffee. Tastes good . . . like . . . like chocolate caramel. It's his coffee. It gives me gas really bad."

"Jake Ellis, make the coffee."

"Yes, ma'am."

San Bernardino handed me her phone. "Ken Swift, page my Honduran cleaners."

"Yes, ma'am."

"And the crematorium in Santa Monica. The one on Broadway I use from time to time."

"Yes, ma'am."

Mrs. Garrett was wide-eyed. "I shot Dickie Bird."

"While the men serve us, you and I will have a little talk."

"Why would we call the dry cleaners?"

"Sweetheart, you mean Richard is your husband and this is your first crime scene?"

"The worst day of my life."

"My cleaners are bioremediation specialists for the Mexican cartels. Do you understand?"

She sobbed, eyes on her fallen king. "What about my Dickie Bird?"

"You're having a meltdown."

"I shot my Dickie Bird."

"Mrs. Garrett, sit down in your kitchen."

"I did love him. Even when I cheated, I loved him."

"Sit and have a sip of water."

"Where did you come from? You just appeared like an angel. Who are you?"

"I am your savior."

"You're beautiful. I've never seen a black savior."

"We're everywhere, yet invisible to the world."

"Who do you work for?"

"I will help you fix this."

"Like a fairy godmother?"

"Better than a fairy godmother."

"You're pretty as the mayor of Compton."

"Prettier. When I look in my mirror, it says I'm the prettiest of them all."

"He tried to kill me."

"I just need you to take a few deep breaths so we can start."

"That monster cut off all of my hair."

"Men are trash."

"He tried to drown me. I think I died. I swear, I think I died."

"Dutch act. Whenever a man touches you in a bad way, make sure it's his Dutch act. Each time. My daddy told me to never let there be a person walking this earth who can claim they disrespected you. Women, all we have is our reputation. Your reputation always arrives before you do. So, we sit down. We talk. We take a lot of pictures. And we make an agreement."

"You can fix this?"

"You hire me to fix this, and in four hours, it will be like this never happened."

"He pushed me down the stairs. He tried to drown me."

"And he has paid the ultimate price."

When she said that, there was movement. And a groan. Garrett moved. Mrs. Garrett screamed. His hand moved back and forth. Moved his legs.

Jake Ellis stepped closer. "He's shot up, but he's not dead."

"I deleted him, and God undeleted him. God is rebooting Dickie Bird."

I asked the boss, "What do you want to do?"

San Bernardino said, "Good. He's alive. I'm happy he's not dead."

Mrs. Garrett said, "He will kill me for shooting him. He'll kill me."

"Probably. If someone shot me that way, Jesus knows I would."

San Bernardino reached in her purse, pulled out a pair of blue surgical gloves, eased them on, and went to the bloodied man. His eyes were open, but there were no words, just the look of a man who wanted help, a man who didn't want to die. He was made of something that most men weren't made of. And so was San Bernardino.

She said, "Glad you're alive. I needed to look in your eyes and dare you to talk down to me the way you did on the phone. That really rubbed me the wrong way. Because I was born with nothing, and because I was born a woman, doesn't mean I am nothing, Garrett. Speak up. You have no idea how much I have had to endure to get to where I am. At every turn, there is someone like you. Look in my eyes. Disrespect me. Talk down to me now, you swindling son of a bitch."

Garrett gurgled. It sounded ugly, grotesque, and still belligerent and challenging.

"Glad I didn't drive this far for nothing. Not with gas prices being ridiculously high."

San Bernardino held Garrett's nose and covered his mouth.

Mrs. Garrett screamed, "No, no, no."

San Bernardino looked at her, rage rising in her eyes.

Mrs. Garrett said, "He's my husband. *My husband.* I should do that."

The rage became a small smile. "Let me show you how."

"Can I drag him out back and throw him in the deep end of the swimming pool?"

"Let's keep it simple, shall we?"

"We can do it together?"

If there was another man inside every man, a stranger, a conniving man, that philosophy was the same for all women. San Bernardino covered Garrett's mouth, pressed down hard with her palm. His wife pulled back her hoodie, showed him what he had done to her face and hair, wanted him to see what he had done, and scowled in his panic-stricken eyes as she pinched his nose. He jumped. Filled with bullets, broken and battered, he bucked.

Mrs. Garrett snapped, then yelled, "Go to hell already, Dickie Bird. Just die, you moron. *'You worthless piece of shit from Compton. You're stupid. Without me you'd be nothing. Be glad you're pretty because that's all you have going for you.'* Tell me those things again before this Dutch act is over. You were horrible in bed, took too long to come, and you even die slow."

Seconds later, it was done. Once Death clocked in, it was efficient, never took long.

"You should have been nicer to me. Dickie Bird, you should've been a lot nicer."

San Bernardino removed her gloves, turned them inside out into a ball. Mrs. Garrett shuddered, wiped away tears, then washed her hands in the kitchen, put lotion in her left palm, creamed her hands, strawberry scent rising to meet death, and went back to San Bernardino.

San Bernardino sipped the decadent coffee Jake Ellis put in front of her, then smiled at Mrs. Garrett, patted the distraught woman on her leg twice, then asked, "Now, where were we?"

"You said you . . . you could . . . you can . . . you can make all of this go away."

"I can. Your black savior, your fairy godmother, can do just that."

"Will I get to keep his money?"

"Minus my fee."

"Even the fifty million he has hidden in a bank in Barbados?"

I went to the patio window that Jake Ellis had broken. Looked out back. Looked at the pool, imagined my body floating there, Mrs. Garrett's apple booty not far away. Saw the dead and the wounded. Jake Ellis followed me. We threw the wounded men in the pool. That was my idea. A man can't try to kill me and get to go home and eat Froot Loops.

The bushwhackers knew where I lived. They knew where Jake Ellis lived.

Jake Ellis said, "What about the one you sent out the door first?"

"San Bernardino will handle that."

"She scares me."

"Scares me too."

I looked up. San Bernardino's drones hovered over our heads.

Jake Ellis asked, "She know about Margaux and Balthazar Walkowiak?"

"Nah."

"Let's keep it that way. As long as we can."

"She's your goddaughter, Jake."

"I know. That's why San Bernardino hasn't been informed."

"I need to learn how to be that brat's daddy."

"Lite Brite."

I nodded. "Put on Billie Jean. Bet she *could* moonwalk. That was funny."

We went to our boss and Jake Ellis told all of us his part of the night, that Garrett had done a drive-by and tried to burn down Leimert Park like racists had done Black Wall Street.

Twenty minutes later, two vans arrived. Honduran cleaners.

CHAPTER 31

FIRE TRUCKS HAD come and gone, same for the police, an ambulance, and the crowd, but the stench lingered in Leimert Park. Nothing smelled like a car that had been burned until the fiberglass had melted into the concrete. Nothing smelled like a man who had caught fire and was unable to outrun the flames. We were people made of energy. And this morning, the energy was off. I felt the fear. People on Jake Ellis's block had been woken by gunshots, shouts, curses, a man on fire, and the screaming of sirens hours ago. Same level of noise had come from the slave-catcher-mobiles when they arrived in what had felt like Baghdad. Gunshots had hit four windows, had terrified everyone in the twelve-unit U-shaped building. More shots had hit the building, and the yellow police tape showed Jake Ellis's complex was marked as a crime scene, but no one was injured. His car had been set on fire. Scorned women did that all the time in the hood, the ones who had evolved beyond keying automobiles to make themselves feel better, but the slags knew this wasn't a lover's quarrel. The gunshots, the man on fire, the sounds of men screaming, put together, it had made it something else in the wild, wild west. Not even Crips and Bloods were rocking it that way, not on this side of town. We were too close to mansions and wealth.

A hundred windows faced Stocker from both sides of the pond. People young and old had seen Garrett's bushwhackers rush into an ice cream truck but hadn't seen their swarthy faces up close. Just saw strapping black men in dark clothes, men rocking Tims, the standard street attire of the Shaw since the nineties. On this side of town, if anyone had seen Richard Garrett on Stocker, in that darkness, on our dimly lit street just right of the midnight hour, they would have assumed Dickie Bird was either Creole or a light-skinned old-school Negro with processed hair. No one would believe that in California a white man had the balls to step into the 90008 and do to a neighborhood in flux what Klansmen had done in the Bible Belt. Good news was, the gunshots might slow down gentrification by at least one week. Bad news was, they would make prices drop. Lower prices would then accelerate gentrification.

"For all we know, they could've been white men in blackface."

"That's the kind of stuff they do. Saw it on the Internet."

"Me too. White boy in Ohio was robbing banks and drugstores and everyplace else wearing a mask to make him look just like a black man, and he almost got away with it."

"That's the kind of stuff they do to get police to shooting every black man they see."

Without race being factored in, with no way to tie last night to any gang, this was too big for the police to ignore but too small for the suntanned newspeople in LA to care about. There were no swastikas. No one this color had killed someone of that color. Couldn't blame Muslims. Jews lived in the area, but nothing anti-Semitic had been found. If this had happened six miles away in Beverly Hills, CNN would be out front with two trucks. But here, to America, this wasn't news. A police report would be done, for kicks, but there wouldn't be much of a follow-up.

I had missed it, but last night twenty cop cars had come and lit up the area with their rainbows of lights. Down where lower-income melanin-blessed Americans accused AT&T of redlining by giving them low-speed Internet access, it was being tweeted, retweeted, and repeated and liked and shared on Facebook. Video of the car fire and bullet holes was being circulated via the Nextdoor app's View Park section. The fire was out, but the cops would be back. They wanted to talk to the African called Jake Ellis. It was his car. It was registered to his true name, to his African name, not his adopted name. Jake Ellis's leased Mustang was unrecognizable. Had been set fire to, and with an accelerant, and it had burned from one end to the other. My .38 was inside, under the seat, probably surrounded by plastic from the stash box. The gun was clean, had no bodies on it, was registered to me, and I had no problem saying I had left it in my friend's car. The vehicles street-parked in front and in back of Jake Ellis's muscle car had caught some heat too, enough to melt plastic.

His Haitian lover had fled when Jake Ellis had gone after Garrett. The professor, the high-class, degreed, married woman couldn't be here when the cops came. She couldn't come running out of a burning building half-naked. People knew she had a younger lover here. But for appearances, Jake Ellis's landlord needed to be home with her husband when the call came. Then they rushed back to their damaged property as husband and wife. He was an intellectual.

She had her alibi. If her husband knew, it didn't show in public.

I asked Jake Ellis, "Bro, what you want to do?"

"Bruv, have them drop me around back. I'll hit the alley and go in my back door."

"You can come to my place until the crowd dies down."

"Nah. I'll go in my back door. I need a shower. And fresh clothes."

"Yeah, you stink."

"Bruv, smell yourself and fix your own stank before you talk about me."

From the back seat of one of San Bernardino's SUVs, while non-talking white men young enough to be our sons chauffeured us down Stocker, as we slowed by where Garrett's bushwhackers had attacked Jake Ellis, in front of his destroyed car, we saw more neighbors at once than we ever had. Black. White. Asian. Mexican. Puerto Rican.

Dominican. African. Windows were tinted limousine black. We could see the crowd. No one could see us.

Jake Ellis said, "*Them* here. Them all over. Standing and shaking heads."

"Them."

"Like Nathan McCall referred to the invaders. *Them.* The other people."

"Your car is the main attraction. Look at the faces. White people are suspicious of black folks and black folks are giving the white people the side-eye. Team Gentrification is fascinated."

"Sipping coffee, being nosy. Reminds me of how them all came this way after the LA riots. For entertainment. It was crowded like Crenshaw used to be on Sunday, bumper-to-bumper."

"Actually, it was much worse. But the police were nicer to the tourists than the locals."

"*Them* came to photograph destruction and see what animals looked like without cages."

Jake Ellis's Haitian lover was out front with her husband, inspecting the damage to their twelve-unit property. The husband was disgusted. His anger was strong enough to light up Crenshaw from one end to the other. So was she, but I bet she was worried about Jake Ellis at the same time. The older residents had come to see what had happened to the legacy of our African American neighborhood. People who had been here for decades cried when they saw the damage. Might have resurrected old memories, old fears. Watts. LA. Detroit. They remembered riots and fires. Outside of the bullet holes, the fire damaged the exterior, burned parts of the worn stucco. Even though it would have pleased Garrett to have burned Jake Ellis to the ground to get his revenge, the area didn't go up in flames like Black Wall Street. With the dry heat, with the dryness in the trees, with the way other parts of California were on fire, with what Garrett had done to the concrete jungle, we had been lucky.

I found out that one of Garrett's wounded men had been in contact with the thugs who had been sent after my ex-wife. One of the wounded men's tasks had been to maintain contact with that two-man crew in the middle of all this madness. One of the thugs going after my wife was a Jamaican, and the other was this fool's cockeyed, "fresh out of California Correctional Institution" cousin. The wounded man saw what we had done to his coworkers. From where he was, he had probably seen Garrett get pushed down the stairs, probably saw Mrs. Garrett feeding Mr. Garrett a clip of hot lead. Or he had seen her and San Bernardino get their revenge. The wounded man wanted to trade information for his life. He could have had the secret to curing cancer in his back pocket, I didn't care. I just wanted to know what had happened to my ex-wife. I needed to know what the Jamaican and this motherfucker's cockeyed cousin had done to the mother of my only child. What the wounded man told me helped ease my angst and slow my heartbeat. He said that Garrett's bushwhackers had followed Jimi Lee. Down Crenshaw near the entrance to the 10 eastbound, they ran into her car, ran her off the road. Six lanes of traffic. A million cars. Homeless people camped out or in the intersections asking for spare change. A half dozen people with phones tried to record the accident, hoping for a WorldStar moment.

Plus, the sirens.

There were always sirens screaming up and down the Shaw.

Sirens made bad men feel uneasy, made a bad boy wonder what they would do when they came for him. Garrett's boys had sped away, left Jimi Lee with a dent in the left rear quarter panel. They had bumped her car, that scam done to get people to stop before a carjacking.

Or a murder. Garrett's bushwhackers would have brought her to Pasadena and thrown her into his drowning pool with me and his wife. Jimi Lee had no idea what had almost happened. The wounded man assured me that Garrett's goons had failed, that his cousin and the Jamaican hadn't followed Jimi Lee after the roadside mash-up, and that my ex-wife was okay. He swore that on his mother's grave. He said he had his cousin's number. I made him call, put it on speaker, listened, heard his cousin say it himself. Heard the Jamaican confirm it too. They were frustrated she had gotten away. Luck had been on their side. Jimi Lee was safe. The wounded man told his cousin and the Jamaican to hurry back to Garrett's estate. His cousin said they were getting off the Pasadena freeway. The Jamaican said they were no more than ten minutes away. I killed the call. The wounded man begged me to let him go free. He didn't care what we did to his cousin and the Jamaican. The cousin was a relative by marriage, not by blood, and he'd sell the Jamaican up the river for a song. The wounded man saw it in my face. There was no way out. I beat him until Jake Ellis told me to quit, until San Bernardino said enough was enough, and while I was in that rage, I threw him into the deep end of the cement pond. Drowned him for even thinking about harming the mother of my child. A few minutes later, his cockeyed cousin and the Jamaican were back at what to me was no better than Simon Legree's mansion. They were tardy for the party, but I wasn't leaving until I saw them. We had business. Going to kill a woman, an innocent woman; in my mind, they were no better than the henchmen Quimbo and Sambo in *Uncle Tom's Cabin*. Five minutes after they arrived, they were blood-ied, battered, and broken, upside-down in the deep end of the pool, surrounded by the dead, on the road to a bad man's Valhalla.

I had killed at least three men. Three children of Africa. Black babies would be told they were fatherless. Black women would be told their lovers were dead, their husbands were killed. Black mothers would have to bury their children. That would be, if their bodies surfaced.

There were no alligators in Southern California, but there were cre-matoriums, so they might just turn to dust. They would go missing. And even if they were reported missing, nobody would ever look for missing black men, not even on Facebook.

That *Missing Black Men* special would never air on CNN.

Black man went MIA and the world assumed a brother was on lock-down visiting his best homies, maybe a few long-lost family members, at Club Fed taking advantage of three hots and a cot furnished by the kind, melanin-free people who brought us black folks mass incarcera-tion. Hard to find anyone from Goldman Sachs or JPMorgan Chase with the same accommodations.

I'd been beaten. Kicked. Shot at. And almost drowned. All since dinnertime.

Like a fairy godmother, San Bernardino would make everything vanish.

Bodies would burn, all except the carcass of Richard Garrett. San Bernardino had to be cleverer. Clever was in her conniving blood. A missing white man was not a missing black man.

A missing rich white man was a missing god worthy of weeks of news coverage.

San Bernardino's men had wrapped Garrett and loaded the man from Princeton in an SUV. He reeked like South Boston. Maybe all Southies smelled that way this time of day. Richard Garrett was cooling off in the same SUV that I was brought home in. He was in the back, rotting, the smell of death covering us. Jake Ellis did a dozen African finger snaps as he left the SUV.

He left without saying good-bye, but that didn't bother me. My mind was already in another place. Would have to face Rachel. I had been MIA all night long. And I still had other problems that had to be dealt with. I had them drop me off in the alley behind my home.

Then I eased up the rear stairs to my back door.

CHAPTER 32

WHEN I JERKED awake two hours later, the sun was screaming, but the curtains were closed; kept the bedroom as dark as midnight. I ached too much for a thousand milligrams of Tylenol to keep the pain at bay. My injuries were robust, couldn't be washed away when I'd showered and scrubbed blood from my hands. I was in my bed, buck naked. Garrett's death stench was in my nostrils. And I still smelled his wife's pain. I'd been asleep only off and on, for ten minutes at a time at the most, if that long. I kept jerking awake, expected to be back in the deep end trying not to drown.

Now, as I have for two decades, I expected to hear the cops knocking at my door.

Margaux would be with them, pointing, repeating the name Balthazar Walkowiak.

That recurring dream was why I woke up wanting to scream like the sun.

Jake Ellis had always been made for this shit more than I was.

I wondered about Mrs. Garrett. I saw her hobbling out of her cage, a creature in a Stephen King novel, then shoving her zookeeper down the stairs. Garrett took an ugly fall. Then I visualized his wife limping down the stairs, entranced, and popping her abuser until her pretty pink gun went dry. Her husband was dead, and the woman who had married up only to have a unilateral prenup was free, but now she was indebted, in bed with San Bernardino. I needed to break free. I'd been in that bed for two decades. I'd grown dependent, had become comfortable.

Rachel Redman rolled over on her belly, licked the inside of her mouth for a while, then groaned. She stretched and played with her braids. She reached for her phone and turned it back on, put in her password. Alerts came in rapid succession. Facebook. Twitter. Instagram.

In her morning voice, she said, "They want every black football player to boycott for one game. Solidarity for one week. To prove that patriotism isn't red, white, and blue, but green."

Hiding pain the best I could, I said, "You're going to sing the national anthem."

"Feels like they're setting me up to be on the FBI's Black Identity Extremist list."

"Good thing you speak Spanish. You might have to flee to Cuba."

"You're right. This could end my career. They will take my passport and black card."

After the last few hours, all of that felt irrelevant. I didn't care who kneeled or who stood up to take a shit. I didn't care about the Russian. I was glad Jimi Lee didn't end up like Garrett.

I'd never be able to speak that out loud. And I still had to deal with Margaux.

Rachel Redman started singing, loud and obnoxious, then said, "I need another shower."

She eased out of the bed, yawned her way to the bathroom scratching her ass. She started vocal warm-ups, always loud in the morning. I limped to the kitchen, came back with coffee from the Keurig and water. I hurt so bad that she had showered, changed the linen again, and was back under Downy-fresh sheets by the time I came back from the kitchen. She had nodded off again.

Rachel Redman barely opened her eyes. "You put honey in it?"

"Lots of honey in your coffee. Black and sweet like you."

"This is why I love you."

She handled the coffee. I sipped the water until I had flashbacks from the pool.

Alaska turned to me. "Did we have sex last night when we got back here?"

Feeling half past dead, I cleared my throat and asked, "What do you remember?"

"Being at the bar. Being in the Uber. The driver telling me to stop touching you."

"You showed your ass from the club back home."

"When you have a moneymaker that looks this nice, why not show it?"

"I'm sure it's online, all over social media, screaming for attention and likes."

"All over my Instagram page. I'm in the gym doing squats, motivating my sisters."

"You know men pull up your images and jack off to them, right?"

"Women do too. Just keeping it real. Well, look at me. I am pretty hot. Last night I was so hot the sun called to beg for its heat back."

"The bar. The Uber. That's all you remember?"

"Singing. Dancing. *Your finger.* The Uber driver telling us to stop kissing, then waking up."

"Did you hear the fire trucks last night?"

"What fire trucks?"

"There was a car fire up the street. Apartments too. On the next block toward Crenshaw."

"That alcohol and Kush had me. I was out like Dr. Conrad Murray had given me propofol. Or Pill Cosby had given me Jell-O shots. Tell me what you did to me while I was sleeping, you pervert."

"You remember decorating the hallway and making the paint peel off the bathroom walls?"

"I don't want to talk about that part of last night."

"You turned my bathroom into a bodacious chitlins factory."

"I hate you, Ken Swift." She sipped her coffee. "You forgot my birthday."

"You'll have another one."

"Lord willing and the creek don't rise."

"Make sure you remind me the day before."

"This has been the worst birthday I've ever had."

"Whatever."

"Wait. Fire trucks. What fire trucks? And an apartment caught on fire?"

"You're not awake yet. I think you've still got too much alcohol in your blood."

She squinted as she checked her messages, made faces, laughed, deleted messages she didn't want me to ever see, the ones scribbled in Russian. She made duck faces, took selfies. Moved her braids this way and that way. Made me get in and fake a smile, morning breath and all. She wanted to post them so her cyberworld would know she'd had the best birthday ever.

She started singing again. Not loud. Always singing. Pain rolled down my side. I rubbed my chest. Still smelled chlorine in my pores. Still smelled a rich man's death in my nostrils.

Rachel said, "You never told me where you were all day yesterday."

Knowing she would eventually find out, I told her about yesterday, about Margaux. My life, my past, I had told her a lot of it, but not all. I was up-front, didn't hide who I was. I gave her the option to be here or walk away. She had chosen to be here, with me, not with the Russian.

With a big smile she said, "Your daughter actually called you? I'm happy for you. I hope I can get to meet her one day. I can tell her how wonderful you are, counter the lies she's heard."

I told Rachel a bit more, revealed how the sit-down lunch had quickly gone south.

"Fifty thousand dollars? Did your child fall and bump her head on a crack pipe?"

I described the Mohawk, the tats, the piercings, the attitude.

Rachel asked, "Was her mother there? Did she come along for the fun?"

"Yesterday at lunch, it was just me and my daughter."

Then I told her a little more, about how I had been ambushed on Stocker.

"The idiot banging at your door was her bae, and you had to give stupid a beatdown in front of the building because he was mad that she was mad at you for putting her in her place?"

"Well, he'd better be glad Jake Ellis wasn't with me when I came home."

"That boy would've ended up on a meat hook being used as an African punching bag."

"I never should have told you about that."

"Everything you use to do your dirty work is sold at Home Depot?"

"Nail guns. Sledgehammers. Saws. Chains. Shovels. Plastic. One-stop shopping."

"I needed to know why you go away to places and I can't ever go with you."

"There is no other woman."

"I know that now. I've broken into your apartment and gone through all of your e-mails and personal belongings. It's disappointing for a sister to work so hard to bust her man, and then find nothing. I mean nothing. Nothing here that made me think you are anything like Jake Ellis."

"I'm not going to ask when you broke in my spot. Not going to ask how many times before yesterday."

"There is nothing for the po-po to find if they kicked down the door and tossed it like a jail cell. If there were, I made it vanish and end up in a neighbor's trash can. You can thank me later."

"I live the life of a poor man. That's all they'll see. I live like almost everybody else in this zip code, from paycheck to paycheck, always fifty dollars short for the month."

"What's on our agenda today?"

"Have to get away. Some business came up while you were sleeping. You can't go."

"Where are you going?"

"I have to go meet with San Bernardino."

Her tone turned serious. "You told me you were stopping with this lifestyle, Ken Swift."

"I did. You're right. I do need to stop. It's gone on too long."

"But you never stop."

"Like bills, I never stop. Being hungry keeps you in the game."

"You lied to me. You lied to me to my face."

"I did stop."

"You've had long breaks. A vacation is not the same as stopping."

"They needed a favor. You know I rise when the eagle flies."

She was restless. "I'm going to save you. I don't know how, but I'm going to save you. Get your passport. Leaving California, getting you out of America, that would be the first step."

"Geesh, Rachel. Don't do this to me."

"I don't want anything from you but your time and your love. Am I asking for too much?"

"I've never had a woman love me like that before. It's kinda scary. And beautiful."

"Stop talking. I might start crying. I'm ugly when I cry. I look like a chocolate gerbil."

I needed to get up, had things to deal with, but I collapsed in the bed with her. Rachel pulled me closer, offered me her breasts. I suckled one nipple and pinched the other. My hand found its way between her legs, and with two fingers, I made her dance like she was on the sun.

My mind tried to take me back to the house of corpses I had left behind.

Rachel asked, "You okay?"

"I'm fine."

I eased on top of her, and we kissed, dry fucked, warmed up. I sucked her nipples and made fire. She pulled her ankles back to the sides of her ears. I positioned her at the edge of the bed, dropped a pillow on the floor, and got on my knees. She made the sweetest honey. Her eyes rolled and she lost her breath. Rachel wrapped her feet around my calves and anchored herself to me. My body hurt, but I stayed like that, inside her, filling her up, kissing her while she drove me wild. I moved her braids from her face and sucked her lips. It hurt my lips to suck hers.

Bushwhackers had beaten me good. As good as Africans had once upon a time.

She asked, "Why did you stop moving?"

I had almost been murdered, had killed three men.

Pain rose; so did exhaustion. I told her, "I'm dead tired."

"Hangover?"

"Just tired."

"You're going soft."

"Rain check?"

"Nope. Let me fix that. We're not having a Deflategate this morning."

She pushed me off her, went down south, her oral fixation so intense and sloppy I called out like I was being tortured. She looked at me and smiled, stroked like Superhead, tea-bagged, gagged, did it all. When her jaw ached, she took to her belly, raised her bottom as she smiled.

I said, "Fuck. Damn. You know what I want to say, right?"

"I know. I give head like a white girl."

Then I was bareback, in Italy, on the wildest of wild horses, competing in the Palio di Siena. Mississippi rode Alaska hard, tried not to be thrown off at the treacherous turns in the piazza, stayed with her as we fell from the bed, took it to the floor, out of the bedroom, and down the hallway. Didn't want her to finish unmounted. My daddy was a jockey, and I knew how to ride.

Sex dulled the pain, made me feel better, became a much-needed analgesic.

I carried her back to the bed, put her facedown, ass up, grabbed her braids like reins.

Skin slapped and Rachel grabbed sheets. "You got me; damn, you got me."

I said her name like I did when I was close to coming. "Rachel."

"Come in me come in me I want to feel you come deep in me."

I didn't want to let loose a flood of baby making inside her, had flashes of my married life, flashes and thunder in my heart as I stroked like a madman, felt a wave that reminded me of trials and tribulations, thought about the freedom Jake Ellis had had all of his life, about all I had given up, didn't want to be enslaved again, didn't need any more responsibilities or obligations, told myself to invade Africa, to come in her ass, or on the sheets, or on her breasts, her face, or feed her every drop. But she worked it, and it felt too good to do anything but come inside her. She put her palms against the headboard, dominated me, had the bed rocking and rolling, the headboard banging like a drum, her moans saying she was ready for jazz. She booty-popped me to heaven, and as my toes curled, another evil arrived. Evil banged on my door like it was the cops or a herd of Citronella Nazis carrying tiki torches. That made me slow my roll, but Rachel reached back, put her nails in me, told me to not stop. Trouble and hard times banged the door and my headboard did the same to the wall. As the chocolate Alaskan with Eritrean roots worked me into a frenzy, as dark skin slapped dank skin and moans collided, I knew that this wasn't over.

CHAPTER 33

RACHEL REDMAN GRABBED one of my collared shirts, pulled it on like a robe, only buttoned one button, wanted whoever saw her to see her T and A and know that the man in this apartment was already taken. When she pulled the curtains back and let in a shock of sunlight, she finally saw my body, saw bruises the bushwhackers had left behind. My face was swollen. Bruises were on my torso and legs. The knot on the back of my head spoke to me in tongues.

"Dafuq?" Her face was in shock. "What the fuck? Dafuq happened to you?"

"Rough sex."

"You weren't bruised up like that when we came home."

"I know. I had to step out for a bit when you were sleeping."

"On my birthday?"

"You were sleeping."

"You got out of bed and went to work?"

"Work came to me."

"Fucking San Bernardino."

"It didn't start with San Bernardino, but it ended with San Bernardino."

"What the hell happened while I was sleeping?"

"Long story."

"You left me in your bed on my birthday?"

"Rachel."

"Is that who's at the door?"

"Could be cops. Could be trouble like it was last night."

"Are. You. Serious?"

"Take my gun."

"You. Are. Serious."

"If you're going to the door before I get dressed and ready, take my gun."

"What's the number to call bullshit?"

"Why the attitude?"

"I bet that's some thirsty thot thumping at your damn door."

She went to the living room, .38 in hand, before I was dressed. I changed my mind, yelled for her to wait for me to open the door. Her skin was still damp and she smelled like hot love and interrupted orgasm wrapped around sudden concern and profound anger. The swarthy Eskimo wanted any woman who had dared come to my door this early to know this was her goddamn territory. She had cheated on me with the Russian and was still convinced I had a chick on the side. Her guilt needed me to be as wrong as she was so she could validate herself, could have a reason to keep that expensive guitar her other lover had dropped in her lap for her birthday. I was away from Garrett, back to dealing with my personal life. She had searched, needed me to have another lover. Her wish had almost come true last night. I would have crossed the pond.

Because of that guitar. I would have crossed that pond to make myself feel better.

But instead, I almost ended up drowning in a pond in a former sundown town.

I looked out the window. Saw Bernice. She saw me and walked away. Then she came back, laughing, her company at her side, his arms around her. I walked away from my window.

Rachel Redman opened the front door and attitude filled up the apartment.

Negativity came in like a monsoon. There was chatter out front.

I had to wait for my erection to wane. Even after I came, it took a moment. I didn't want to run to the door fluffed. Especially if it was the cops. Slave catchers would yell I had a gun in my crotch and then I'd be the next resident of Hashtag City. Rachel took her temper to the door and I took my aches and pains to the bathroom, washed up, cooled down, wiped sweat from my brow. I pulled on a fresh pair of joggers and a Black Panther T-shirt. I could barely stay upright.

My house had gone silent.

Then Rachel Redman called, "Sweetheart, can you come here please?"

"What's wrong?"

"Come tell me who this thirsty thot is, the one who was thumping at your damn door."

When I stepped into the living room, I saw that my next problem was waiting, dressed in leggings and a red hoodie, her hair now four shades of green with blues and pinks, covered with a pink scarf, almost like a hijab. Margaux was here. Like her mother, she had a lot of nerve.

CHAPTER 34

I GUESS I felt the same way Garrett did when he came home and saw me and Jake Ellis in his kitchen. Margaux was seated on the big sofa. All tats and body piercings on skin pastier than the flesh of Mrs. Garrett. Rachel Redman was across from her on the love seat, my .38 on the small table next to her, the barrel pointed toward a wall. Anger danced with embarrassment.

Rachel Redman said, "She said she's here to see you."

"That's Margaux."

Swallowing disbelief, she said, "This is your daughter?"

"That's my daughter. All grown up."

"Oh. My God. I am so sorry I called you a thirsty thot."

Margaux adjusted her red Gap hoodie, said, "You know Rachel Redman?"

Rachel Redman was surprised. "You know me?"

"I recognize you."

I corrected Margaux's etiquette. "Good morning."

"Good morning."

"That's better. You don't just walk into people's homes and start talking."

She repeated, "Good morning."

"Good morning, Margaux."

"You know Rachel Redman?"

"I know her. She stops by to answer my door every now and then."

"With a gun?"

"In case a thot shows up thinking nasty thoughts."

"You're really Rachel Redman?"

"Yeah, I am. Nice to meet you. Wow. I've heard a lot about you."

"Have you?"

"You are all Ken ever talks about. Feels like I already know you."

"I know about you. Well, sort of. I have one African parent, another from Mississippi, grandparents from all over, but I was born in America. You talked about being the first generation of your family in America, being trapped between new ways and old traditions in one of your YouTube videos. I think you spoke and sang in Amharic, Spanish, French, and Russian."

"You watch my YouTube videos?"

"Well, yeah. I subscribe to your channel. You haven't posted anything in a while."

I let my fist hit the doorframe. "Margaux."

They looked at me and I stared at the child who had threatened me a day ago.

I cleared my throat. "Y'all running a good tag team on me. You here for money? Or you coming at me because I had to put my paws on the fool you say you're having a baby with?"

Rachel Redman said, "Kenneth Purnell Swift."

Margaux asked, "Did . . . my boyfriend beat you up like that?"

I asked Margaux, "Where is your pit bull?"

Rachel didn't like my tone and said, "Kenneth Purnell Swift."

Margaux answered me. "He's in the car. Kevin is in the car."

I asked, "Is your mother with you too?"

"No, she's not."

"Kenneth Purnell Swift."

"Stop saying my name."

"Answer me."

"Rachel, your phone is ringing over and over in Russian. Why don't you answer that?"

Rachel smiled at Margaux. "Nice to meet you, Margaux."

"Nice to meet you, Rachel Redman."

"Rachel."

"Nice to meet you, Rachel."

I asked, "So why are you at my door this early in the morning?"

Rachel stepped in. "Ken? A moment please?"

Rachel disappeared into the bedroom and I regarded Margaux, my child. She couldn't choose her father, and I couldn't choose my child. She looked at me like she knew I had just killed a league of bushwhackers and a misguided soldier to stay alive. She looked like she wanted her fifty thousand dollars. No, her look was *desperate*. Not malicious. She looked at me like she needed her fifty thousand dollars. I nodded, then turned and followed Rachel, her arms folded across her chest, her back to me. When I pushed open the door, Rachel Redman turned around and she had tears in her eyes. I knew why. My daughter. The bleached skin. The self-loathing, the self-hate.

She asked, "You're going to be a grandfather?"

"Go shower."

"Jesus. She saw me looking like this. Fresh off her daddy's penis."

"First impressions."

"And my breath smells like sex."

"Nobody told you to run your jealous ass to the door."

"With a .38 in my hand like I'm a hood rat and sex breath like a hooker."

Her phone vibrated.

"Why is the Russian calling you over and over?"

"Ken."

"He blew up your phone all evening, all night; now he's calling all morning."

"Ken."

"Is there something I need to know?"

"He's just jealous."

"Just don't Jimi Lee me, Rachel. I can't take being Jimi Lee'd all over again."

She swallowed, pulled at her braids. "What happened when you left here last night?"

"People died. I didn't. That's what happened."

"You had fun without me."

"Well, next time someone tries to kill me, I'll get you an invitation."

She took a breath. "Talk to your child. She is what's most important at this moment. I can see she's scared. Real scared. Be her dad. Be nice, even if she is mean. She's in pain."

"So am I, but no one seems to care. No one has ever cared."

"I care. I wouldn't have been here waiting when you came home if I didn't."

"With a gun in your hand."

"In case you had walked in with a thot."

"And if I had walked in with a thot?"

"Would have shot her without a second thought."

"Everyone is lying to me."

"What do I have to lie about?"

"You tell me."

She pulled her lips in. "Ken. Cruelty only breeds cruelty. Don't be cruel, not right now."

"Go answer the Russian."

I went back to the living room. Margaux stood up, nervous.

Still in awe, she said, "That was Rachel Redman."

"She stops by to wear my shirts every now and then."

"The first joke about her answering the door was better."

"What's going on? I guess you came to tell me off or collect money. Which is it?"

"I was angry."

"So was the guy who knocked you up."

"I've been angry with you a long time. He knows that. When you feel that way and tell someone who loves you, knows you, that you feel that way, when they have heard the negativity, nothing but the bad things, they tend to become overly empathetic, if not simpatico, and without having all the information in the matter, they take your side, adopt the same feelings."

"Why? What have I ever done to piss you off?"

"I felt abandoned by you. He's heard me talk about that for years."

"For years?"

"We met when I was in high school."

"He's been your boyfriend since then?"

"Not since then. But he's loved me since then."

"Since before the guy you went to meet at the Grove? Who was that guy?"

"He was . . . my first boyfriend."

"Your first love."

"Yeah. My first love."

"You know which one you're pregnant by?"

"I know."

"This money you need have anything to do with that?"

"Yes and no."

"Thanks for clearing this issue up."

"It's hard to talk about."

"Why?"

"I feel stupid. It's embarrassing."

"Who knows the truth?"

"Me. My boyfriend. And my ex."

"And the girl who was with your ex yesterday."

She looked surprised. "A girl was with him?"

I described her.

She said, "That was his new girlfriend."

"What does she have to do with this?"

"Nothing that I am aware of."

We sat in silence.

I said, "You see me as a stranger."

"You were never there."

"I was there, until your mother and her family took you away. A lot happened when I met your mother, a lot of ugly things. But to keep it short, I'll take the blame for everything bad."

"All I know is what my grandparents told me. They never said anything good about you."

"That's like listening to your president talk and expecting to hear the truth."

"My mother never defended you."

"What did she say about me?"

"Nothing. She never mentioned you. I asked her to tell me things, but she would get angry or walk away. She was angry because she never got a chance to go to Harvard."

"You grew up on lies. Grew up listening to a story about a fairy tale gone bad."

"I don't know what the truth is."

"You don't. No, you don't. And to be honest, maybe I don't either."

She put her hand on her belly. "I'm sorry that my boyfriend came here to fight."

"He said you're engaged."

"Sort of."

"I don't see a ring."

"Well, we had to sell my ring."

"Why?"

"Needed the money."

"No ring."

"Not at the moment."

"Then he's your boyfriend."

"Until we get another ring."

She rocked and I saw the fear loosening, but she still wouldn't say what was going on.

I didn't push the issue but didn't let it go. "Scared?"

"You're trying to add this up. I see you taking in everything I say, and you're trying to figure out what is going on. You want to know why I contacted you and asked for money."

"You're scared."

"A little."

"A little?"

"I'm scared to tell you what I'm mixed up in."

"But your boyfriend knows."

"He knows all about it. He's trying to help me any way he can."

"You love him?"

"Yeah. I think so. Yeah."

"Love when you're ready, not when you're lonely."

"I love him. I love Kevin."

"Not because you're pregnant."

"I loved him before I was pregnant."

"I hope he writes better than he fights."

"He's a great writer. He studied under screenwriter James Thicke."

I shrugged. Had no idea who that was. And didn't give a shit.

Silence. Awkwardness.

She said, "I'm pregnant. My hormones are out of whack."

"Your mother was the same way."

"Was she?"

"She was. After you were born, she was depressed a long time."

"She was? I didn't read that part of her journals. Not yet anyway."

Silence.

I said, "You have to stop delaying and tell me."

"First off, I came at you the wrong way yesterday." She swallowed. "I re-explained what happened and Kevin said I should apologize for being such a . . . brat."

"No need to. What's done is done and we can move on."

"We should apologize."

"I should too."

"My complexion surprised you."

"It did."

Silence.

"People treat me better."

"I believe you."

Silence.

Then I nodded. "I've been up all night. Running on fumes."

She motioned like she was getting up. "We can do this another time."

"No, stay."

"You sure?"

"Would hate for ten more years to go by before I saw you again."

"Sorry I threw my snot rag in your food yesterday."

"I'm sorry too. But it probably gave it more flavor."

"My mom came here?"

I nodded. "She went back and got her PhD."

"She did."

"Good for her."

"Did you ever go back to UCLA?"

"No. Not yet."

She nodded. "I told her I had gotten in contact with you."

I nodded. "She came to get in line with everyone else to tell me off."

"I'm sorry."

"So, you have a little brother."

She nodded. "Yohanes is his father."

I shook that off. "Tell me why you're scared. Anything to do with your stepfather?"

"No. He's never been very nice to me, but he's never been mean to me either."

"Stop procrastinating. Tell me what's going on."

"I didn't come here to talk about that. I really didn't."

"I know you ain't here to talk about the lack of recursion in sixteenth-century Germanic poetry."

Arms folded, body language closed like a petulant child, she said, "I came to apologize."

"This early?"

"I was up all night. Yesterday was the worst day of my life."

"You need a lot of money."

She looked at my apartment, at how I was living. "You don't have a lot of money."

"You said you're charging me seventy to keep your mouth shut."

"I just need the fifty. That's all I need."

"Tell me why you need it."

"Does it matter? If you don't have it, then it's pointless talking about it."

"You're my daughter."

"It's my problem."

"It matters."

"Not yours."

"You matter."

She shook and cried. "Can we start over?"

"After you tell me the truth about this money you need."

Saliva and angst glued her lips together. "I'm scared to say why."

"Why? You're not scared to ask for that much money."

"You'll see me differently."

"You have to say."

She pulled a tissue from the pocket of her hoodie, blew her nose. Then she went on, leg bounced as she picked at her cuticles. "Yesterday, you scared me because I guess I rambled, said too much, and you got part of it right."

"Which part?"

"The gambling. You picked up on that real quick. So fast it scared me."

"So, this is a gambling debt."

"Part of it. Money was spent betting on a long shot. I lost. I prayed on it. Googled it. Read about long-shot Super Bowl bets that could cost a Las Vegas sports bookie big money. And all I needed was one long shot to come through. I lost the USC bet. And me and my boyfriend took a chance. Kevin and I prayed on it. Last month we had put our last three thousand on another team that was going at a hundred-to-one. Three grand would have gotten me and my fiancé three hundred thousand."

"That was a foolish bet."

"It was a long shot, yes, but if I had won, then I would have been a genius."

"Your Hail Mary was yesterday when you gambled against USC and lost."

"I had to try one more long shot."

"Why?"

"Because the other part was true too."

"Which other part?"

"I'm being blackmailed. I had to gamble to try and pay the blackmailer."

"For the fifty grand."

"He's up to about that much now."

"Is this a group, an organization, or an individual you owe?"

"A person."

"Who is this person?"

Tears fell harder. The dam was loosening, soon to burst and flood the room with truth. She cried and cried and cried and I didn't reach out to her to comfort or coddle her. I couldn't be her father right now. I had to be that other guy, the one who worked for San Bernardino.

I said, "Talk. Did this blackmail thing just start?"

"No. It's been going on for a while."

"What's a while?"

"Almost a year now."

"And now they are asking for more money."

"One person. Just one. You saw him. At the Grove. He ran away when he saw you."

"What does that guy in the red BMW have on you?"

"You saw his car? How? You were with me. I didn't see his car."

"Don't talk to me like I'm dumb. Talk to me like you know I know the truth."

"I can't say."

"You will say. Or I will find out on my own."

"How did you find me yesterday?"

"Not your business. Just know I can find you if I need to find you."

"Then why haven't you looked for me all these years?"

"Maybe I did and just didn't recognize your new face."

She moved like she was insulted, wanted to stand up.

I said, "Sit down, Tsigereda. If you leave, I can find you. You can't hide from me."

She did as she was told. Crying. Pulled more tissues from her hoodie.

I asked, "Where is that boy from?"

"Kevin?"

"The one in the red car."

"He's from Morocco. Well, his parents are. He's first gen here, like me."

"What does he have on you?"

Again silence. My frustration mounted; I was exhausted, ready to throw her in the streets.

"Ken?" That was Rachel, coming back into the room. "Do you mind?"

She was fresh out of the shower. We had talked long enough for her to clean up and put on lotion that made her smell good. She wore leggings and a top, both by Nike, had her braids pulled back. That was how she usually dressed during the day, like she was about to hit the gym.

Rachel said, "Margaux?"

"Yeah?"

"Your daddy is trying to help you."

"I know."

"He just wants to help you. Forget what you've heard. He's a good man."

Margaux nodded. She trusted the kind words of a stranger more than she did me.

Rachel tenderly asked, "Have you had to pay more money each time?"

"It started off being about five hundred."

"Was he supposed to sell or give you something to make this end?"

"Something like that."

"Or delete it?"

She didn't answer, but her body language told us Rachel had touched a nerve.

Rachel asked, "Is it a video?"

It took a second. "I didn't know about it until after we broke up."

Rachel asked, "To be clear, is this an illegal activity, like a political scandal, a video of you stealing something? Did you run over someone in your car? Is it a Kardashian number?"

My daughter trembled. "I wish it was political. I wish it were a hit-and-run."

"It won't be the end of the world."

"It feels that way to me. I have disappointed so many people in so many ways."

Rachel said, "Margaux, you have to say. No need to be embarrassed."

"It's a Kardashian number. Please, don't make me say any more than that."

"That you didn't know about."

She nodded. Eyes on the floor, crying. "He secretly recorded us. I can't let my mother . . . can't let my grandfather and grandmother . . . my sibling . . . my stepfather . . . friends at my job . . . and he has threatened to tell them all. It would destroy me. He knows that would destroy my family."

Rachel said, "And now your first love wants fifty thousand dollars."

"We have paid him *month after month*. That's why we're broke. My fiancé has sold camera equipment. We've been late on rent. First month he wanted five hundred. But two weeks later he wanted twice that again. After that it's been between one and three thousand a month. I gave him over twenty thousand last year. I've used my savings. So now he's up to over forty thousand, and I need money to pay back rent and other bills. And I don't know what else to do."

"Does he want you back? Is that what this is all about?"

"I don't know. I don't love him."

"I need you to be sure."

"Who could love a man who would do such a thing to them?"

I said, "So you got to the end of the road, let him bleed you dry, tried to be a gambler, failed at gambling, let desperation take over, and you came after me."

"I read Mom's journals. There were hidden. I found them and I read them to know her better. And then I read things about you. I read things that I knew couldn't be true, but they were."

"You read about Florida in one of her journals."

"It was written in Amharic. She said you were a bad man and always had a lot of money."

"You said that man's name."

"And then you reacted. I knew what I had read in my momma's journal was true."

"Then, no games."

"No games."

"Do you have any idea who Balthazar Walkowiak was?"

"I just know he went missing. And my mother's notes said she thinks you killed him. She wrote about it in a different way. From the other stuff. When she wrote about that day, she was terrified. She cared about you but knew she couldn't stay with you, not even for my sake."

"Her notes. She wrote about what happened in Florida. In Amharic."

"And there was a newspaper clipping. Old and faded, about that businessman."

"What else her notes say?"

"The Postman. She called someone the Postman, but that part made no sense."

I had called myself that once or twice back in the day.

I asked, "How did you think it would go when you came at me with that?"

"I hoped you'd give me the money and go away."

"How long did you sit on that idea?"

"I came up with it ten minutes before I called you."

"Ten minutes? That's all?"

"Ten minutes before I called you, my ex called me with his new demand."

"For the fifty thousand."

That was when my phone chimed.

I nodded at Rachel. She nodded in return, then left us, let an estranged father have a moment with his wayward daughter, went to the bedroom to answer my phone.

I stood facing my daughter. She reached in her pocket, handed me a tissue.

I wiped my eyes.

She said, "All we need now is some soup."

"Soup can't fix everything."

"No, it can't."

"You saw this sex tape?"

"Parts of it. Saw enough of it. He showed it to me on his phone. It's on the cloud."

"Is it worth fifty thousand dollars?"

"It'd ruin my career at JPL. That one moment would follow me to my grave. It would follow me to grad school and beyond. My friends. My family. I can't have them see me like that. I can't have people just Google my name and see me in a way . . . like that. I can't allow that to happen."

"This ex, what is he worth to you?"

"Not a goddamn thing."

"And you're pregnant."

"Yes." She used the last of her tissues. "Between my money and my fiancé's money, I've given my ex over twenty thousand. I've gone days with no food over this. I've had to act like everything is fine. I had to pull away from my mother so she wouldn't be able to tell I was in trouble. I can't have my mother over and see I have no food. Can't let her see I've no furniture left and we're sleeping on the floor because I've sold piece after piece on Craigslist. I have this lease with my landlord that we're keeping up in order to save face, and I can't afford to keep that up. I gambled and won a little, won a thousand dollars, and that put food on the table, and I thought I could keep doing that. Then I lost three games in a row. I can't do shit right now. Nothing is right in my life. We have a movie we can't sell to make money. When will it end?"

I said, "Once started, blackmail never ends."

"I see that now."

"Do the tats and body piercings have anything to do with this?"

"Kevin does tats. He did all of mine. He does that part-time at Heavy Gold Tattoo on Eighth. I started tats after the blackmail. It was my idea, not Kevin's idea. If my ex released the video, I didn't want to look like the girl in the tape. I did a couple; then I guess I got addicted to the pain."

"The bleaching?"

"People treat light-skinned people better."

"On the video, you black or white or some hue in between?"

She asked, "Am I ugly to you?"

"No. You're beautiful."

"My skin?"

"I don't approve, but I don't have to. You're a grown woman."

Silence.

She said, "Rachel Redman is beautiful."

"She is."

"She looks like my mother."

"I don't think so."

"A more fun version of my mother."

"Your mother used to be fun."

"What happened?"

"Me. I changed her life before you were born. She will never let me live that down."

"Welcome to the club."

"I know how she felt. I only saw things my way. Never saw things her way. Was my fault."

"I read her journals. She was happy, then unhappy. I think she is happy now."

"Your skin?" I put us back on track. "What hue in the video?"

"I'm darker. My birth color. But my friends and family will know its me."

"You should have come to me with the truth. A year ago."

"I don't know you."

"Know me or not, you're my daughter. You need to understand that."

"I wanted to kill myself."

"Don't spread that into existence."

"Past tense. But I'm pregnant. I can't do that to my baby. Or my mother. Or my fiancé."

"Your ex put you in this position."

"Surprised me. I thought he loved me."

"He loves money. People who love money will hurt anyone to get it. They don't hesitate to screw people over. I bet when you were dating him, he cost too much to date."

"He did. I couldn't afford to be with him anymore."

Her body language matched her angst. Most of it. One part was off, a response she had given earlier, but not every truth was easy to confess. We were as close to the truth as Margaux was going to allow me to get. I think I had more of the story than she had given her boyfriend.

She knew she would have to tell me the truth. She was here because she knew she had no other option. She was here because her East African stepdaddy, Yohanes, couldn't help.

So she needed her true father. She needed the black man she had read about in her mother's journals. She needed the bad man to ignore his wounds and weariness and fix this.

I had wanted to put that part of me to sleep. Last night had been too much. If I had died, she would have had to face this alone. But I had lived, and maybe this was part of the reason.

I had enough of the truth and I didn't like this bitter pill. It was hard to hear that my daughter had a sex tape out there. It was hard for her to let me know what had happened.

It was hard to not be angry that some motherfucker was doing this to her.

Rachel Redman came back into the room, walked through our silence singing "The Star-Spangled Banner." She went to the kitchen, came back with cups of coffee for all of us.

In Amharic, Rachel asked my daughter, "Have you eaten?"

In Amharic my daughter replied, "I'm hungry."

Rachel smiled and in English said, "I can make you some breakfast, Margaux."

"Can I invite my boyfriend . . . fiancé, up from the car to eat?"

I nodded. "If you want Kevin up here, he's welcome in my home."

Rachel handed me my phone. I knew she had already read the text.

It was a message from my coworker Esmerelda.

I forwarded that message to Jake Ellis.

I had a feeling today was going to be like yesterday.

My daughter hugged Rachel Redman, then looked at me. "Our first breakfast."

"No, just the first one you remember. I made your breakfast all the time."

"I don't remember."

"I do."

"I don't want to eat and leave my boyfriend in the car."

"Go ahead. Tell your pit bull to come up here and eat too. I know you and he are short on money, so you're short on food, and I know if you're hungry, then he's hungry too."

"He's scared to come up here."

"He should be. He should turn and run like Usain Bolt when he sees me."

"Kevin thinks you're crazy."

"He attacked me and I'm crazy?"

"Said you might be a lunatic."

"He didn't give me a good first impression either."

"His nose is broken."

"Tell him to be happy his neck is okay."

"I didn't mean for this to jump the shark. I just didn't know what else to do."

"Tell Kevin I said to come up, or I'll go down there and pick up where we left off."

"You're going to let Rachel Redman cook for him too?"

I nodded. "One of you can bless the food."

"You sure this is okay?"

"Depends on how you feel about me."

"You divorced my mother and never came to look for me."

"Is that what you think?"

"Not anymore. I see your actions. And I believe in action." Tears fell and she wiped her eyes. "Action over words, Mr. Swift. I told you the worst part of me, and you didn't put me out."

I wiped mine too. "Just like your mother. Hard. Cold. Stubborn."

"And she says I'm just like you."

I said, "We don't know each other, that's true, but you are the blood of my blood."

"No, we don't know each other. But now you know my darkest secret."

"But I used to know you."

"I don't remember."

Silence.

I said, "That thing I did in Florida."

"What about it?"

"Never mention it again. Never say that man's name again."

"Why not?"

"The person I work for will kill you. Your boyfriend. Your mother. And the dog."

"We don't have a dog."

"I'm serious. You see how rough I look right now?"

"Yeah."

"Imagine this on your body ten times over. And imagine them making me do it to you, because if they come for you, you will end up buried in five locations in five different states."

Silence.

I said, "Since we're being honest. Know this. People tried to kill me last night."

"Is it safe here?"

"It's safer here than anyplace in the universe."

"What happened?"

"You'll never know. And you'll never meet people like that, unless you get cute and start talking. Get mad and snitch on me, fine, but I'm connected to other people, some bad people."

Silence, but she shivered where she stood.

She whispered, "There was a rumor Rachel Redman killed some-one in Alaska."

"Leave that in a box with the other rumors."

"Momma said you're a bad man."

"No matter who I am, I'm your father."

"Her journals."

"What did she say?"

"She needed to have space to grow without being attached to a man. She didn't want a serious relationship. You could have gone away and she didn't care. She would have felt freer if you did. She was too inde-pendent to be in a certain type of relationship. People have a hard time understanding an independent person. They take it personal. You took it personal. Your happiness was not her goal. Her happiness was her goal. She wanted Harvard. Leaving was a way of leaving everything behind. She wanted to push reset and move on."

Her words, that point of view, that realism, affected me. "Then I happened."

"No. I happened. I changed everything. I changed her life, not you."

Silence as she held a hand over her stomach, again being protective.

I asked, "We good?"

She nodded.

I asked, "Still hungry?"

"What?"

"Are you still hungry?"

"I'm still hungry. I'm pregnant. Now I'm always hungry."

"I have some things to give you later."

"What things?"

I didn't answer, left it at that, then told her, "You will tell me all about Dawit Wake."

Hearing that name shocked her. "How do you know my ex-boyfriend's name?"

"I know his name. I can find him. This is why you shouldn't lie to me."

That was enough for her to think that I was much smarter than I really was.

I said, "This is a hard question, but it has to be asked."

"Okay."

"And I'm not judging you if you did."

"Okay."

"Was part of the blackmail getting you back in his bed?"

"Why are you asking me that?"

"Because I need to know if there's a chance he's the father of your child."

Right then there was another knock at the door.

It was Kevin. Light-skinned boy who could pass for white. All tats and piercings and images of Buddha in his overstretched earlobes. Skinny jeans, Vans made for riding a skateboard, and a T-shirt with the number 7, same T-shirt Jay-Z had worn in his *Saturday Night Live* performance. The boy's eyes were blackened, his nose definitely broken.

I had hit him harder than I had realized.

He looked at me and was ready to take off running again.

I said, "Kevin."

He could barely inhale and exhale. "Is Margaux here?"

"You begin a conversation with a greeting when you're at a man's door."

"Good morning."

"Mr. Swift."

"Good morning, Mr. Twift."

"What can I do for you?"

"Is Margaux here?"

I nodded, extended my hand, offered him a handshake, shook his hand in a way that told him that when we were together, no matter how smart or rich, he would always be the lesser man.

He said, "I'm sowwy for yestewday. I was diswespectful and weally upset."

"You okay?"

"Face huwts. Hard to bweathe."

"You'll live."

"Don't hit me again."

"Come on in, boy. Come in and have a seat. We're about to eat."

"Hard to twallow."

"I'll have my girlfriend make you a smoothie."

He was going to be the father of my grandchild. We were family. Like it or not, we were family. His body language told me he loved my daughter. He would spend his last dime to make sure she was safe. He would do what he had to do to get this blackmail out of her life.

He was a fool in love for Margaux, as I had been a fool in love for Jimi Lee.

I said, "Let's eat and talk."

Margaux said, "Talk about what?"

"Tell me all you know about the motherfucking asshole blackmailing you."

She nodded. "After we bless the food."

Her boyfriend asked, "When was the last time you saw Tsigeweda?"

"Before yesterday? She was five years old. Her mother took her and left when she was five. She did what she felt was best for our daughter. And I can't say she didn't do the right thing."

My daughter said, "Don't say that."

"It's the truth. You know it's the truth."

"It's not my truth. I've needed you all of my life. I have. I really have."

"I've needed you too. All I did, all I gave up, I did for you. And I'd do it all over."

"Dad."

"That's not my title. You made that clear." I shook my head. "Don't call me that."

"You're my dad. My real dad. I'm the prodigal daughter who has finally come home."

With that she shivered like she had done an Ice Bucket Challenge, and when she let go of her tears, this time for a good two minutes, there was not a dry eye at the table. I had to get up and walk away, cry to myself, pull it together, feel my own deep hurt, then return to the table.

My daughter bowed her head, lifted her palms to the sky. "In the name of Allah . . ."

While we ate vegetarian omelets, toasted bread, and fruit, while we sipped juice and my future son-in-law sipped on his smoothie, there was a coded knock at my back door, followed by four wicked African finger snaps. Battered and bruised, barely able to stand, it was Jake Ellis.

Half past beaten and a quarter to dead or not, we had some nasty work to do.

CHAPTER 35

CRUNCH. CRUNCH. CRUNCH.

When I was a child, I went to a relative's funeral in Mississippi. The gravediggers had fascinated me. Some of the hardest work a man ever did was digging graves with a pickax and a shovel. I had relatives down in Mississippi who did that job for years, did it the old-fashioned way with a flat chopping blade. The sound of a shovel breaking hard dirt was an unforgettable sound. The sound it made when you dug to softer ground was just as memorable. That crunch, crunch, crunch had to be a horrifying onomatopoeia if you were blindfolded and hog-tied and knew that shallow grave was being dug on your behalf. If you knew that this was what you had earned, and the Postman had come to deliver the mail, each crunch, crunch, crunch was a terrifying sound.

DAWIT WAKE LIVED in Venice, two blocks from the beach in the area many people passed but never knew existed. There were actual man-made canals in one of the neighborhoods, a section that had been made to look like Italy, and that was why that beach was named Venice. Every home was pressed up against the next and each was unique, from a 1950s almost southern-style home to something that looked like it had come back from a thousand years in the future. The area was the Venice Canal Historic District and had been there since 1905, since the days when a lot of people who were black had felt like they had just been freed from the master's whip.

He had a thirty-year-old, two-bedroom, two-bath number on Linnie Canal. That 1,693 square feet was worth three million dollars. At least that was the asking price. It was on the market. The cheapest home in this community had to be over a million, the most expensive almost five million.

Most of the people didn't have curtains, and long after the sun had gone down, while people were out walking dogs, occupants lived with their one-, two-, and three-story homes lit up, like they wanted everyone passing to look inside and see how rich they were, to see them with lights on, lounging in white-walled homes, cuddling on their pure white sofas, some at the kitchen table eating, others with computers in one hand, some working on a tall cup of Starbucks.

It was like a zoo. I saw kids running up and down railless stairs playing. Small boats were at the back of most homes. Boats and ducks quacking away in dirty water.

This was my daughter's ex-boyfriend's lavish lifestyle, one that would cost a man like me almost eighteen hundred dollars a square foot. It was a lifestyle that was hard to maintain.

He parked in his garage and came into his home dressed in lime-green Nike gear head to toe, sweating but not winded. The house was chilled at seventy degrees. Outside was still fifteen degrees hotter, even at the beach. He had just left one of the local overpriced gyms. This wasn't like the Garrett job. There was no magically moist salmon waiting. There wasn't any conversation.

It was after eleven at night when the man with Moroccan blood came back home.

I had left at seven. I had been waiting since seven thirty.

He walked from the kitchen to the darkened living room and saw the windows he had left open to look out on the canals, saw all the curtains had been drawn. Then he saw Jake Ellis step out of the shadows. Jake Ellis was dressed in all black, African attire from the shop Lagos on Leimert Boulevard. He moved toward Jake Ellis until he saw Jake Ellis holding my second .38 in his gloved hand. Jake Ellis wore a mask from the movie *Scream*. That was enough to make a man yell like a bitch. He stepped backward and noticed the sound, heard the crinkle, crinkle, crinkle of the thick plastic that was on his floor. He heard the sound, probably saw the words from that onomatopoeia rise before his eyes. Plastic had been put out, and so had tools from Home Depot. He saw them and turned to run. I was behind him, dressed in black Adidas sweats, Chucks, a clown mask, and black gloves. He ran into my fist and dropped to the ground, down for the count, but not unconscious. I picked up a hammer, squatted, and scowled in his face. He couldn't see my expression through my mask, but he felt the harsh energy. It showed in his eyes.

"How much money did you blackmail her for?"

"Who?"

I brought the hammer down on his thumb and dared him to scream.

He struggled with the pain. "Which girl?"

"There is more than one?"

"Which girl?"

"Your ex-girlfriend."

"They all think they are my girlfriends."

"You have a nice little con going here."

"What girl are you tripping over?"

"Margaux."

"I don't know any girl named Margaux."

"Tsigereda."

Now we were on the same page.

Jake Ellis came in carrying the man's thirteen-inch MacBook Pro in his hand.

I said, "Pull up the video you're using to blackmail her. From the cloud. From all sources."

If Garrett had been as terrified as this motherfucker, my day would have been a lot better.

He pulled up the video. I didn't want to, but I had to look. I was going to make her boyfriend come on this trip, was going to make Kevin beat the shit out the motherfuckin' asshole who had caused them so much grief, but Kevin didn't need to see this. A man couldn't see this and stay with the woman he said he loved. If he saw this, it could not be unseen. I could've made Margaux come here, but that wouldn't be right either. I didn't want Rachel to stay. She had compromised the doors, had used her skills to bypass the locks, then skedaddled like she had been told. I refused to let Jake Ellis see my daughter in that way. So it was up to me.

It was little more than a glimpse, but I saw my daughter in a way a man should never see his child. The video was more than forty minutes long. For ten seconds, the hardest ten seconds of my life, as long as it took to verify that was indeed my child, as I was unable to breathe, as my anger took control of me, I saw why she would have paid fifty thousand dollars for no one to be able to see her the way she was, doing the intimate things she was doing, with a man she had once trusted.

Feeling hurt and nauseated, feeling like chopping a motherfucker up into a dozen pieces and feeding him to alligators, I shouted, "Delete that. Delete that shit now. Motherfucker, now."

As I looked, the blackmailer looked up at my mask, shook like he had a fear of clowns, like coulrophobia was his only phobia and my scary clown mask had reminded him of a multitude of childhood nightmares. He trembled, apologized, begged me to let him pay her back, as he deleted it from the cloud. That deleted it from everywhere. That was all I needed. He had videos of other women. African women. White women. East Indian women. And the girl Jake Ellis had seen him with was part of that playlist. I left those intact. Those weren't my daughter. Those weren't any of my business. That done, I got him in that LAPD chokehold. Tears in my eyes, I killed him.

I had to kill him. There was no clean way out, other than his death. He had picked the wrong daughter to fuck with.

Jake Ellis asked, "You didn't want to take any of that money back?"

"That car. This house. It's probably spent."

"Not all of it."

"Rich boys like this, I bet he's fifty thousand dollars behind in his bills."

"And I bet he has that much in a safe in this house."

"Not my concern."

"Not paying his bills don't mean he's cash-strapped. They stack chips and play the system. I bet he has rubber-banded wads of cash around here somewhere."

"He might have blackmailed a few, but this can't look like a robbery."

Jake Ellis asked what he didn't want to ask. "How bad was that video?"

I didn't answer. Not answering told him all he needed to know.

"Bruv, you did the right thing."

I remembered the last question I had asked Margaux, the one that had gone unanswered. If that blackmail had included sexual favors, I had no idea.

I told Jake Ellis, "I hope so. I hope this was the right thing."

I went to the counter, picked up notices from the IRS, opened one and saw a lien was being placed on this address. Just like in Leimert Park, the so-called rich were living paycheck to paycheck. They lived like this and were no better than the people they chastised and criticized.

Then I went back to his computer, back to his videos, back to the cloud.

I asked Jake Ellis, "Just to be clear, it will delete everywhere it's stored."

"It's deleted from everywhere in this and adjoining universes."

"Delete the rest. Delete the rest of the girls. Save other fathers the same angst."

"If she had told us this shit this morning, we would've fixed this in ten minutes."

"Delete every e-mail to my daughter. Take her name out of his system."

"I'll make her no longer exist in his world."

"Like he no longer exists in hers."

WE WRAPPED DAWIT Wake up in plastic. I pulled my BMW up to the empty side of the two-car garage and we loaded him in the trunk. I wanted to take him to Kenneth Hahn Park and bury him in a hole on the hiking trail, but that was too close to home. We took his body out to a plot of land in the Pomona area. Heat was still over one hundred out that way. We were well hidden. I dug a hole and put that boy five feet under. I wished he had still been alive to hear the sound of that crunch, crunch, crunch. We disposed of the gear from Home Depot on the way back, put it all in a Dumpster in Monrovia. Then I removed the bogus plates that had been on my car, tossed those and put my legal plates back on, opened a bottle of Gatorade, chugged it as we hit the freeway going west at three in the morning. We headed back to our box, went back to Leimert Park.

Jake Ellis yawned. "Bruv, why didn't you shake him down for money?"

"That would be too complicated."

"He got Margaux for a lot of money."

"Killing him was easier."

"She's still going to be broke."

"But she won't be hemorrhaging money because of one bad decision."

"What if there is blowback?"

"We covered everything."

"It was a rush job."

"He threatened to send that video out in the morning."

"I didn't know that."

"Margaux told me that. That's why she was breaking down like she was."

"That's why she came at you with an urgency."

"If there is blowback, now or ten years from now, this is on me.

She's free of this bullshit. She's free. I did what a good father would do, bro. I did what a good father would do."

Jake Ellis couldn't relate.

He asked, "Why the masks?"

"Kept us from being called niggers."

"Yeah. I guess they did."

"They might call a nigger a clown, but they never call a clown a nigger."

CHAPTER 36

MARGAUX AND KEVIN were at my front door the next morning, same time as the morning before. I let them in this time. Rachel Redman had taken over my life, got my child's digits, and invited them back over for another breakfast. They were broke, short on money, and the broke and hungry never turned down food. I did the cooking. I wanted to cook for my daughter, same as I used to do when she was a child. I hurried from the kitchen to answer the door, was shoeless, but had on jeans and a T-shirt that had MLK Jr. on the front, in speech mode, the message being NEVER FORGET THAT EVERYTHING HITLER DID IN GER- MANY WAS LEGAL. Rachel Redman came down the hall, appeared in the doorway, face and skin wet like she'd taken a fast shower and then put on a pair of my joggers and a UCLA T-shirt, my clothes swallow- ing her.

Rachel was excited, told my daughter to get comfortable on the sofa, then ran to my closet, the one where I had kept things for more than fifteen years. Under each arm she had photo albums, my hid- den pictures from two decades ago. I asked her to not do that, not right now.

She told me, "Ken, stop acting like you have a messiah complex."

"She's not interested in all of that. All of that would be corny to her right now. Margaux, honey, sit down. Let's take a look at the photos your daddy kept hidden."

Rachel Redman sat down with Margaux, with the photo albums, showed her pictures I had saved, images of her when she was a newborn, when she was ages one, two, three, four, and five, when I was in my early and mid-twenties, rocking clothes fashionable in the late 1990s and early 2000s. She stopped and stared at images of her with Santa at the mall.

She said, "I have these pictures. Well, similar ones. From different angles."

"I used up a lot of disposable Kodak cameras."

"Me and Santa."

"I took you to sit on Santa's lap at Fox Hills Mall every year."

"I have a lot of these pictures. Photos of me and my mother."

"None with me, I bet."

"None with you. You're not in them. I thought you were not there, never present."

"You don't see me because I was holding the camera."

"You have hundreds . . . thousands of pictures I've never seen."

"Look at these."

"Wow. Pictures of you holding me."

"And it looks like your mother isn't present."

"I guess it does."

"She was holding the camera. She had her own copies."

"If that is true, then I think she threw her copies away."

"Yohanes wouldn't want images of me in his home. Same would go for your grandparents. Those memories weren't allowed in your Ethiopian grandparents' household."

She asked, "And these are your parents? My paternal grandparents?"

I nodded at pictures of my mother and father, the one time they had met Margaux. Only six pictures of them were in my photo album. I cleared my throat. "They met you once."

"I heard they weren't nice."

"The day your mother met them, things were said, cruel things, and it was ugly."

"They still living?"

"Yeah. My parents are still living."

"Where?"

"View Park."

"Where is that?"

"Right up Stocker. They live five minutes from my apartment."

"You see them?"

"Not since you were a baby. Not since I defended my wife."

She clacked her tongue ring against her teeth. "There is a lot I don't know."

"Yeah. A lot happened back then."

"Why couldn't they just get along?"

"For us, metaphorically speaking, Africa and Mississippi were oil and water."

"I bet that's a long story."

"If you ever want to sit down some day, I can tell you the way I saw things."

"I just want to hear the good things for now. I can't handle negativity."

She looked at pictures of us at Disneyland, then at pictures of her as a child, playing in this very apartment. She saw pictures of her mother as well. She saw our past. My daughter became emotional, had to go to the bathroom a moment, had a cry.

Rachel told me to let her be. Let her sort out her feelings herself.

I went back to that same closet, told my daughter's boyfriend to come with me. Until he put another ring on her finger, he had been demoted back to being her boyfriend.

I told him, "Help me carry these boxes."

"These are Christmas presents?"

"And birthday presents. I had forgot how much stuff was crammed in this closet."

Those boxes were put out on the floor. Rachel stood next to me, and my daughter's boyfriend stood next to Rachel, all of us worried until the bathroom door opened again.

When Margaux came back, she asked, "What's going on?"

I said, "Happy birthday."

"It's not my birthday."

"And Merry Christmas."

"What is all this? You having a party over here today?"

"Party for you."

"What's going on?"

"All this is yours. These are things I bought you over the years. I wasn't with you, but I bought you a present for every Christmas, for every birthday, up until a couple of years ago."

"All this was for me?"

"Not was. *Is.* All of this is yours."

She eased down on her knees, looked at all the boxes, read her name on each one.

Then like a child she began ripping away the wrapping paper.

I had forgotten half the things I had bought her over the years.

There were Troll dolls, Cabbage Patch dolls, a Tickle Me Elmo, two brown Barbies, an Etch A Sketch, a Slinky, Bratz dolls. And for when I imagined her as a teen, there were perfumes.

Margaux sat on the floor smiling, laughing, ripping away Christmas wrapping and opening birthday presents while her boyfriend took the torn-away wrappings and stuffed them back in the boxes. As dead bodies cooled off, I gave my daughter Christmas in summertime. I gave her a birthday party for all the birthday parties I had not been invited to. I won't lie. I did it for me.

But I did it for her too.

I told her, "I know that stuff is outdated, so you don't have to keep it."

"Are you mad? All of this is mine. I'm keeping everything."

I turned on the news. KTLA channel 5 ran the story about the police investigating gunshots and a Molotov cocktail attack. They said two were thrown at apartments in the Leimert Park section of

South Los Angeles yesterday after midnight, and one landed on the roof, and the other hit the side of the building. Said fires were extinguished. They said the man who threw the Molotov cocktails accidently set himself on fire and died of his injuries. They assumed the gunman was his partner and had gotten away. It wouldn't be connected to Richard Garrett, not from what I could see. After a lame thirty-second report, the news moved on, said a soul-train line of hurricanes was coming, said wildfires were blazing on the other side of Burbank, then gave news reports on a president defending Nazis and supremacists, then more news on how the great nation was devolving into a reality TV show. My daughter and I had nothing in common, were strangers seated at the same table, but that corner of the news gave us a conversation starter.

We talked about a president who was attacking those protesting bigotry.

Rachel Redman said, "I know how I'm going to rock the national anthem."

My daughter said, "You're singing the national anthem?"

"At an NFL game."

"OMG. Are you kneeling?"

"Hashtag, I won't have to."

Her boyfriend pointed at the number 7 on his jersey and said, "Hashtag, you have to."

"I'd rather be original. I don't like doing what has already been done."

While San Bernardino's team of Hondurans loaded the bodies of dead men into a crematorium, while Richard Garrett's body was being driven out into a desert, while Jake Ellis dealt with drama at his crib a block away, I sat with my daughter, her boyfriend, and my girlfriend, eating Mickey Mouse–shaped pancakes, veggie sausages, and fruit, sipping juice and smoothies, having an awkward conversation, as if two days ago hadn't been the worst day of my life.

Rachel had turned her phone off. But I hadn't forgotten about the Russian.

—————

AFTER BREAKING BREAD, my daughter and her boyfriend followed me downstairs. I went out back to the alley, took them to my garage. I had a 2007 BMW 645Ci stored back there. I'd had it since it was new, and it had only forty thousand miles on the odometer. Mint condition. I wasn't big on driving. But when I did, I looked good on the road.

I took Margaux to the side and told her, "Your fifty-thousand-dollar problem is over."

She looked at me, took her a moment to repeat, "It's over?"

"It's over."

"What does that mean?"

"It means you no longer have debt to pay that boy."

She stood shocked, unsure, then started to cry as she exhaled. "It's over."

"You no longer have to borrow and gamble to pay a blackmailer."

"Should I ask what happened?"

"No. Never ask. And don't Google his name. Never. Not from your phone or computer."

"You found him."

"I found him and made him delete everything."

She pulled her lips in. "You saw the videos?"

"No. But he deleted them."

She swallowed, reading my body language as I had read hers, and my daughter knew I was lying.

She asked, "My ex?"

"He's deleted, Margaux. And that means what it means."

She swallowed again, this time knew my words were the truth.

She asked, "Are you mad at me?"

"Disappointed. But not mad."

She lowered her head, wanted to cry.

I didn't let grief or shock or tears have time to settle. "I know you're still in a bind."

"I don't know what to say right now."

"Focus."

"Okay."

"You paid a lot of money to keep your secret, but that account no longer exists. I want to help you get back on your feet, would love to drop that much cash in your hand, but I don't have money like that. I did when I was with your mother, and most of that was sent to take care of you."

"You've done enough."

"I haven't done enough. Not if you're still in trouble. If you had come to me at the start, this would have been fixed and money would have been saved. But this is where we are. Learn from that lesson, Tsigereda. Margaux, know that I am your father, no matter what. I can do this, and this is the best I can do for now. You can follow me over to CarMax on La Cienega, and I can sell this BMW right now, then give you what they give me, and that might be about fifteen grand."

"That's a nice car."

"Looks new, but it's not. I know that's a long way from the fifty. You can have it."

"You'd do that for me?"

"You're my daughter."

"I disappointed you."

"And I still love you. What belongs to me belongs to you."

She went to the side and talked to her boyfriend. I didn't like Kevin. He was a good boy, but he was weak. I didn't think he was good enough for her. I knew he wasn't. He'd never be able to defend her. And there was irony in that. But Kevin loved her and she adored him, so I'd never tell him that he wasn't good enough, and I'd never tell her she had made a bad choice, because I never knew what a good choice looked like. She had to figure that out, and I could always be wrong. I was good at being wrong. As long as Kevin treated her right, or just stepped away like a man if shit got too hot for him, I'd never show up on his doorstep and beat him half to death.

I didn't want to have to make another trip to Home Depot.

Margaux came back. "Your car is nice. It looks good and smells new."

"Low miles. I keep it clean and maintained."

She clacked her tongue, nervous to ask. "Can I just have your car?"

"Is that what Kevin told you to do?"

"It's my idea. I really, really like your car."

"You need money, right?"

"We're hurting. But we need a better car too. If we show up at a meeting and we're in a raggedy car, especially in Hollywood, people think you are a loser. Your car is your calling card out here. People see us rocking that car, top down, their perspectives will change about us."

"This Hollywood thing. That movie about slaves."

"Movie about the enslaved and the karma they bring."

"You're trying to do this together."

"We're a team."

I took a breath. "No problem."

"Is that a yes?"

I nodded. "I'll sign it over to you as soon as we get back upstairs."

"Serious?"

"Yeah. I can take my things out and you can drive it home. I will sign the pink slip over to you, but you have to take care of the insurance and have it in your name in forty-eight hours."

Her smile lessened, suddenly concerned. "How will you get around?"

"Overground railroad is coming. Between the train, Uber, and Lyft, I'm good."

"Thank you so much."

"And I repeat, you have to put the BMW in your name and on your insurance. I will fill it up with gas, but after that, I will not be responsible for one scratch, one dent, no accidents."

"Okay. I can do that tomorrow."

"Your insurance will go up?"

"We will figure that out. We have a dark cloud moved from over our heads."

I hesitated. "You in any other trouble, Margaux?"

"He's deleted."

"That's all you need to know."

"I made one bad decision."

"Is there anything else?"

"This was it. If I don't have to pay the fifty thousand dollars, if that is over, then I can manage to save again. Just needed money. Was too much at one time. Baby coming. Want to be married."

"And this is Kevin's baby."

"Kevin will be the only father my child knows."

"That wasn't the question."

"But please, Dad, for now, today, let that be the answer."

She called me Dad, softened me up with one word, so I nodded. "You need to move to a less expensive place."

"We know."

"Cheaper on this side of town. Eight miles from Hollywood. Parking for the metro is down Crenshaw at the lot next to West Angeles Church of God in Christ. You can get to work at JPL from there."

"How many trains?"

"It's a three-train ride. Maybe an hour one way on a good day."

"Faster than taking the freeway."

"Much."

"Lots of real nice apartments." She stared at my world. "Any vacancies around here?"

"Has to be. But I know one that might be happening pretty soon."

She fidgeted, thinking, but not committing. "Maybe I'll sell my car."

"You'll get less than a thousand dollars and a bag of curly fries for your bucket."

"I know."

"Why sell it? It's probably cheaper to keep it as a second car."

"We can get an inexpensive engagement ring."

As I had been all my life, I was being practical, logical. "Kevin doesn't have a car?"

"He sold his Jeep two months ago. That's part of the reason I want us to be able to keep yours. He had a Rubicon, but he was trying to save me. He used that money to pay Dawit—"

"Never say his name. *Never* again. We don't mention him. Ever."

"Or Florida."

"We don't mention that."

After seconds of silence she said, "We have secrets."

"We float together, or we drown together."

"We have secrets that bind us."

"Every relationship, every family, has secrets."

"No journaling about this."

"No journaling."

She nodded, clacking that metal against her teeth.

I inhaled. "Your boyfriend's car?"

"Kevin sold his car and paid . . . my blackmailer. That week we needed food really bad. We needed the money so we could pretend we had money. Most of that money was gone in a day."

"Your ex took you for a lot of money. More than folks make in a year."

"He bankrupted me, more or less."

"He made you his slave."

"What do you mean?"

"You were his financial slave."

"And I'm still enslaved to the system."

"We all are."

"Debt makes us slaves. Does this ever end?"

"No, it never ends. You have to pay to be born, and you pay an exit fee to the mortuary and IRS at the end. Death and taxes."

She clacked that tongue ring again. "I need money, but I also need a dependable car."

"With Bluetooth. And a navigation system."

"Well, yeah."

I said, "You drive my car and you let him drive yours."

"Why not the other way?"

"You're the girl. I'm your father."

"You're my dad."

"In that case, end of discussion."

She ran her hand over her colorful Mohawk, clacked that tongue ring, thinking as she rocked from side to side, still stressed, but not as much. "We will work the money part out."

"I can give you about five thousand in cash."

"You've done enough."

"I can give you that."

"What about you?"

I took a breath. I had money, cash from the Garrett job, plus about ten more. I'd never be broke. I'd never be rich, but I'd never be broke. That was the money I had been trying to save up to eventually buy a house. Maybe next year. Or the year after. But not anytime soon.

I told her, "I can manage."

"I don't know what to say."

"Come see me even if you don't need help. When you have time. Up to you."

"Okay."

"And if you're in trouble with people, I'm the guy you need to talk to. If your guy is in trouble, he needs to sit down with me and come clean and see what I can do to make it right."

"People owe him money over a movie deal."

"He signed a contract?"

"Yeah. Some guy made all these promises, got him to sign, and now he's screwed."

"Then it's legal. Unless I did like people say Suge Knight did Vanilla Ice, unless I dangled whoever ripped your boy off like Death Row dangled Vanilla Ice over a balcony, unless I threatened to drop him and was ready to make good on that threat, you have to suck it up."

"It's a bad deal."

"How bad?"

"They paid him next to nothing and he will get no residuals for replays."

"Then he's fucked. That's the long line to the left in Hollywood, that one that leads to that midnight train to Georgia."

"It's not fair. He's artistic, talented, just not good with the legal part of Hollywood."

"He will have to learn from that and do better next time."

"Did Suge Knight really do that?"

"So goes the legend."

"Urban legend."

"Scares Vanilla Ice whenever it's mentioned. Say *Suge Knight*, and Ice shits his pants."

"Have you done stuff like that?"

"This is where this conversation ends."

She smiled a nervous smile. "You're easy to talk to. I can't talk to my stepfather about any of this. I messed up in a big way, and you talk to me like . . . like . . . this too shall pass."

"You're a grown woman. I will respect that. I have to respect your choices."

"Why are you so nice to me?"

"We're related."

"I am related to other people; none are nice to me, not like this."

"This is who I am with the people I care about."

"Were you like this with my mother?"

"Tried to be. In my mind, I was."

"Did you love her?"

"I loved her. But I was twenty-one then. I was twenty-one and a man in a world where we still expected women, no matter how smart, no matter how black, African, intelligent, or freethinking, to pat their Afros three times when we walked in a room and be our subordinates, to do what we said. I don't think I was that kind of a man, but I was raised around those types of men. Being unintentionally misogynistic is still being misogynistic, same as being unintentionally racist is still being racist. So, based on what you said your mother wrote in her journals, based on her feelings, maybe to her I was nothing more than her zookeeper. I was just her zookeeper."

"She wrote other stuff, most of it over ten, maybe fifteen years ago."

"Probably made me sound like a monster."

"There was some romantic stuff. Said your kisses were like nourishment. She was poetic at times. Corny too. Real corny. But some of it was cute. Said she was famished for you the night after she had met you. She loved you. The best she could. She loved you. Just not enough."

"She came back to see me."

"I know. You told me."

"I mean two days ago. She came back here. To this apartment. To talk."

"Wow. What did she have to say?"

"I guess she told me the truth."

"That she still cared about you."

"More or less. In Amharic. But her primary concern was you."

My daughter said, "Yesterday was horrible, and so was the day before, but today has been a good day. One of the best. I feel that things will be much better for me now."

"For me too."

"You're a good cook. You're not as bad a person as I thought you were."

I nodded. "Now walk up the street with me."

"What's up there?"

"Gentrification."

"Besides that?"

"Good people. Hardworking people of all nationalities. And your godfather."

"I have a godfather?"

"The guy who came over when we were having breakfast yesterday."

"I have a Nigerian godfather?"

"Ghanaian."

"Wow, that's so . . . cool."

My daughter's boyfriend saw our chat had ended, then came over to where we were. He was scared of me. He would always be scared of me. But he respected me too.

We started the walk toward Audubon Middle School. Dozens were heading that way. Big meeting to protest gentrification was about to pop off. My neighbor Bernice Nesbitt was half a block in front of us, walking hand in hand with her new guy, another fireman.

As we strolled, I asked my daughter's boyfriend, "Where are your folks?"

"My mom lives in Encino."

"Your dad?"

"I didn't grow up with a dad. He died in . . . he was incarcerated. Was killed in jail."

"Sorry to hear that."

"Truth came out years later that he didn't commit the crime. They put him in the system and made him a modern-day slave when I was six. He never saw freedom again."

I nodded, understood his passion, and understood his movie. It was personal. Incarceration was enslavement. He needed to pen away his anger, give his father revenge, if only just on the big screen. We'd have a long talk, man-to-man, about his pain, some other day.

I said, "I like your idea for that movie."

He smiled a little, maybe sensing I felt the connection. "Yeah?"

"Yeah. But you might have to add in the Holocaust, have them come back for the Germans. Hollywood would probably be more open to Jews killing Germans than blacks doing all the killing of the whites, but you can work it, make them happy, have a good movie, and get paid."

He nodded. "Will give that some thought. That would change the movie to a miniseries."

"But you can still have your Harriet Tubmans, your Bussas, your Nat Turners, could have the enslaved Africans come back and have a Haitian-style victory on part of North American soil."

"And at the same time, the Holocaust victims, even Native Americans, do their thing."

I shrugged. "It's a thought."

"Yeah. It's a very good thought. Third act would be like Spartacus and the Third Servile War meets Nat Turner's Rebellion meets the Zanj Rebellion meets the Haitian Revolution meets the 1733 St. John Insurrection meets the Baptist War meets Gaspar Yanga's Rebellion."

My daughter countered, "Maybe we should go back to the original idea and work on the script about Empress Taytu of Ethiopia."

I said, "I read about her. She ran Ethiopia awhile. I think the emperor died, had a stroke or something, and she took over. I read about her when I was married to your mother."

Margaux said, "Yes, Taytu was the one running it all. She was a boss. She needs a Hollywood film."

They argued. That was the most Kevin had said since I had met him.

He had a lot of Spike Lee in his blood. She was stubborn, like her mother.

I showed my daughter where she had lived as a baby, walked the streets where I had carried her in my arms or her mother had pushed her in a stroller; then as we browsed books at Eso Won, I gave her the history, told her about what used to be here; the twins who had run Lucy Florence, 5th Street Dick's coffee shop playing jazz until four in the morning, slamming poetry at World Stage, the African drummers in the park on Sundays, the African American Museum.

Then with them at my side, I joined the looky-loos, saw Jake Ellis's car being towed away on a flatbed. Heard rumors that this was definitely the work of neo-Nazis or the KKK from Simi Valley.

Jake Ellis had gone into the scorched car and pried the box with my .38 out of the damage. The gun was no good, but that was off the table, so all was good in the land of Oz.

A blackmailer was dead.

So was the man who had tried to kill me and Jake Ellis.

My daughter said, "I want to find my godmother one day."

"Why?"

"I've found my godfather. It only makes sense."

"She's Ethiopian."

"Barely remember her. But her name is in my mother's journals a lot."

I nodded. "You said you remembered her name?"

"Gelila. Everyone called her Lila."

"Yeah, they did."

"I know Auntie Lila drove a red Corvette."

"She did."

"And lived in Malibu."

"She did."

"She sounds awesome."

I inhaled, exhaled my own memories. "She was your mom's best friend. They would have started university around the same time."

"I want to know why she and my mother stopped being friends."

"Life does that. Your mother was busy trying to figure out how to be a wife and mother at eighteen. Lila went to university. Pepperdine."

"Any idea where Auntie Lila is now?"

"Years have gone by." I shrugged, shook my head. "She might be married with three or four kids and living in another land by now."

"I don't get it. My mother and Auntie Lila were best friends."

"Then they went down different roads, had separate lives."

"I still want to meet her."

"Why?"

"To know my mother. Only way I learn about her is by reading her hidden thoughts. I want to know what she was like before me."

"Your mother has always been closed off like that."

"It's the African in her blood."

"She's from a family of proud people."

"Strict people."

"Probably no stricter than mine. Mississippians don't spare the rod."

"Mom writes her feelings in so much detail. Heartbreaking and poetic at the same time. I didn't read them all. But it sounds like she used to party in Hollywood like she was out of her mind."

"Oh yeah."

"She was pretty wild."

"Oh yeah."

"So were you."

"I still know how to throw down a mean Cabbage Patch."

"Dad. Don't. Don't ever. Never."

We laughed.

It was a hot summer day, half of Southern California was in a brush fire, but my daughter was at my side. No amount of smog or smoke could make me think this wasn't the freshest air I'd inhaled in more than ten years. My beautiful daughter, who was now white, covered in colorful tats, and violated by body piercings. No matter what mask she wore, no matter the hue, she was my child.

Before she left she kissed me on my cheek.

Later on, as I smiled to myself, with love in my heart and blood on my hands, I cried.

CHAPTER 37

RACHEL REDMAN'S VERSION of "The Star-Spangled Banner" started off smooth and sexy like Marvin Gaye's classic version of the song. But then she sang like Whitney Houston, hit notes and garnered applause as her pro-black Afro bobbed. Rachel was draped in patriotism, dressed in red, white, and blue. And then she sang the third verse, the one where slave owner Francis Scott Key wrote about killing hirelings and slaves who had freed themselves. That song's third verse threatened to kill all blacks who had the audacity to want to be free. I guess my fellow Americans knew our national anthem as well as they knew their Bible, and most didn't know their Bible, only a few verses used out of context as sound bites and weapons. Football fans and team owners were perplexed, and the cameras panned across multicultural faces that had identical perplexed expressions. Some football fans had hands over mouths; some were flabbergasted. Bent-knee football players looked up, confused, then whispered to one another, raised a fist, and smiled.

Rachel Redman finished, then unzipped her white hoodie, eased it off. The message in red and blue letters on her white T-shirt was better than kneeling and a raised fist combined.

WE MARCH. Y'ALL MAD.

WE SIT DOWN. Y'ALL MAD.

WE SPEAK UP. Y'ALL MAD.

WE DIE. Y'ALL SILENT.

That red, white, and blue message was larger than life on the jumbotron. That scorching-hot day, I was in the stands, my daughter at my side. My skin-bleached daughter with colorful hair, body piercings, and her hair in a bright yellow hijab. Margaux had wanted to see this.

Over the roars, boos, and cheers, as Rachel left the field, Margaux said, "Wow."

"Yeah."

"That's original."

"I'm surprised no one has done that before. Sang that verse out loud."

"I'm sure they did. Around trees decorated with strange fruit."

"Yeah. And I bet they sang that verse as loud as they could."

AT THE SAME time Rachel Redman was being applauded, booed, glorified, and jeered, there was breaking news on KTLA, news that would bleed over to CNN. Two weeks ago, philanthropist Richard Garrett had been reported kidnapped. He and his wife had been attacked, and she had been found beaten in their Pasadena estate. The attackers had knocked her unconscious and cut away her hair, abused her, then thrown her down the stairs. She had been in Cedars-Sinai for a week. She knew nothing. She didn't see who broke into their home and attacked them. Security footage had been stolen. When Mrs. Elaine Garrett had come to at the base of her stairs, her husband and the vicious men were gone, but blood had been left behind. San Bernardino had left just enough blood and hair on the stairs, cleaned up the pool area, and crafted a wonderful story. Some of Garrett's blood had been left at the base of the stairs for dramatic effect. It looked like he had been beaten, kicked down his flawless stairs with his wife. The only fingerprints found in the home belonged to Mr. and Mrs. Garrett.

Margaux asked, "We're staying? People behind us are talking about lynching folks."

"Rachel Redman has earned that Jennifer Hudson paycheck. So, we're done here."

"I like the Rams. This is my first time at an NFL game in years."

I asked, "You like football?"

"Yeah. All day, every day. But my boyfriend isn't big on sports."

"Me too, but I need to get Rachel out of the building and off the grounds."

"Black Twitter is blowing up. She's already trending."

"This game is broadcast live. Millions just saw that."

Transients had found Garrett's decomposing body inside a stolen SUV near Zuma Beach. That was fifty-two miles away from Pasadena. When they opened the vehicle, it was a bona fide fly-and-maggot festival. He had been beaten like a piñata and filled with bullet holes from a .380, then left in a car during the hottest season on record in California. Inside a closed SUV, in direct sunlight, the temperature could quickly climb to 172 degrees. He'd had at least four days tanning in the blistering desert sun.

Nothing had been said about Dawit Wake, not by local news or the mainstream media. I Googled his name from a computer at the Culver City Library every couple of days.

A male. Black. African. Missing. Even if they found his body it wouldn't be news, but the real estate people in that area would be happy to step in and sell that three-million-dollar property for his grieving family, turnkey, all amenities included, even the boat and ducks at the back door.

Phone in hand, Margaux said, "POTUS just tweeted a nasty tweet from his golf cart."

"What?"

"Trumplethinskin tweeted."

"What?"

"Pussy grabber of the United States' last tweet is trending at number one on Twitter."

"What?"

"Trumpty-Dumpty. Look. He stopped golfing long enough to tweet."

I heard her that time. "Who is the Twitterdent attacking this time?"

"Watch out. Someone just threw a soda down this way like we're at a political rally."

I pulled her closer to me, ready to strike out at any offender. "We have to get out of here."

Margaux reached into her purse and took out her mace.

Worried about Rachel, I led the way, moved my daughter toward the exit.

The local media had made Garrett sound like a saint's saint. They skipped the part about him having ties to Boston, to Southie, didn't mention his dealings with bad men and wicked women, didn't mention he was the son of a man who robbed banks, a man once on the FBI's most wanted, never said he was a dedicated friend to gangsters. They only said the Princeton graduate had left Boston and had gone west to start over. That was code meaning he had been run out of Boston. He had met a girl named Rebecca Elaine Cookenboo-Yochelson at a Coco's in Compton, fell in love the moment he saw her, then married. They were happily married and had been working on having a child. They wrote about his grieving widow like she was the next Mother Teresa. The picture of her with flowing blond hair, looking like the ultimate American woman, was all over the news, trended on social media. Fox News loved her as much as they did on CNN.

I stood in a safer spot with Margaux, the stadium still roaring.

Margaux asked, "You're really going to move away to London?"

"Maybe. With Rachel. We might get run out of town with torches after today."

"You and her getting married?"

"Not sure. We have issues."

"Everyone has issues. No relationships are perfect. Marry her."

I grinned. "You're giving me relationship advice?"

"I like what I see. She's definitely into you. She sings. She dances. She's awesome."

"I should get married again and move to London."

"I said marry her. No one said anything about moving to the land of beans and toast."

"She's moving. And she wants me to go with her. Would have to if I married her."

"Then don't marry her. I just found you again."

"You don't want me to go?"

"It hurts knowing you'll go and it'll be years before I see you again, if ever."

"I didn't know you cared one way or the other."

She hugged me. "Don't be happy without me. That would make me sad."

For the first time since she was five, I hugged my daughter.

I hugged my daughter and the unborn child in her belly.

I asked Margaux, "Want a back ride?"

"Are you for real?"

"I used to give you back rides all the time. Until you were about five. Until you left."

"I'm no longer five, have gained a little weight, and might be too big for a back ride."

"Never. And I think I might owe you a back ride or a hundred."

"In that case, yeah. I want a back ride."

We laughed, and that sound was lost in the animosity around us.

She acted like she liked me. All I had to do was kill a man and give her a few Barbie and Cabbage Patch dolls to get her to act like she liked me. If only her mother had been so pliable.

Margaux said, "Dad, we have to go save Rachel Redman from this racial madness."

She told me to hurry, did African finger snaps.

I had no idea she could do that shit.

It made me proud that she could.

CHAPTER 38

AN HOUR LATER, I was with Rachel. Margaux and Kevin were with us.
We were in Inglewood's Hyde Park Plaza, at Zula Ethiopian and
Eritrean Restaurant, eating *kitfo*, sharing a dozen amazing dishes,
talking, laughing, getting to know one another. I still didn't like my
daughter's boyfriend. Kevin was from this generation, the soft generation dependent on Bitcoins. He should've been the one who had wrapped
my child's problem in plastic and buried it in the ground. But he wasn't
like me. What I had done had nothing to do with San Bernardino. It
was a father thing. No man would be good enough for her. Same as with
Jimi Lee's self-righteous dad; no man was good enough for his daughter.
Least not I. Still, I had learned from the way he had treated Jimi Lee,
had learned from how my wife was treated by her own father, so I guess
I owed that motherfucker something for that lesson. Unlike him, I
respected my child's choices. All of her choices. I couldn't unsee what I
had seen on her blackmailer's computer. It hurt. It hurt me bad. I'd
never understand how she ended up in such a place. I'd never be able to
see life through my daughter's eyes.

Just like Margaux would never be able to see life through mine.

But I did respect her.

She was special to me, unique, an Ethiopian child with the blood of Mississippi in her veins, a social experiment come to life. She was a grown-ass woman some called Tsigereda.

She had lived in Africa. Her mother had taken her home. She had touched the soil.

All roads led back to Africa. A man just had to get off his ass and get on that road.

Jake Ellis was on a plane to Ghana. His Mustang had been torched, a bushwhacker had accidently set himself on fire and died running from the scene, and there had been gunshots in the midnight hour. Slave catchers were asking too many questions and his landlord had become uncomfortable with the sudden drama. For a man like Jake Ellis, it had gotten too hot and he was going back home to kick it in the motherland, to lay low a few months and enjoy good Jollof.

He'd made enough money living rent-free and working for San Bernardino to get by.

When he was ready, he'd be back. He'd be right back in Leimert Park.

And I was sure his landlord would keep his apartment vacant.

She'd be waiting for her lover to come back.

While we rode in an Uber, I asked him if Mrs. Garrett was going to meet him in Africa.

Jake Ellis answered with a wink, a laugh, and ten hearty African finger snaps.

It wasn't my business.

I still envied him, his choices, his freedom. But my complicated life was mine, and his was his. He was Ghanaian, African, going home. I was American, a born Mississippian, still dreaming about a better home than the one I had. I wanted to live where I felt like I belonged, wanted to sink my feet in the soils and swim in the waters from which my people were stolen, if only for a while.

Somewhere out there, San Bernardino was sipping champagne.

I imagined Mrs. Garrett was in her mansion, eating gelato, music blasting, in high heels, dancing to African music as she counted to fifty million.

———

AT LAX, JAKE Ellis had told me, "If you come over, that Senegalese girl is still waiting to meet you. She believes that you are the love of her life. She believes that you are her soul mate."

"I'm happy with Rachel."

"I'll check back in a few months."

"You might have to call me in London."

"Even better. You'll be closer to Africa."

"Bro, why are you always instigating some shit?"

"Bruv, because it's fun. Because that is what I do."

"And you do it so goddamn well."

He did African finger snaps and we laughed, hugged, and parted ways. I went and caught an Uber back home, rode alone, half-smiling, half-thinking about what my life had been so far.

I HAD UNTIL Rachel decided what she was going to do with that guitar to decide about London. Until I decided if I was going to stop by Home Depot and pay the Russian a midnight visit. If not, if her heart somehow took her back to Russia, even for a night, like Jake Ellis had told me over and over, there was always a Senegalese woman waiting for me to arrive over in Africa.

But for now, I was cool.

Late at night, Bernice Nesbitt stood in her window every once in a while.

But I didn't have the urge to cross the pond.

For now, I had Rachel.

I had my daughter.

I had a grandchild on the way.

I had love coming at me like never before, from all directions.

For now, I had enough love to hold me here.

ACKNOWLEDGMENTS

HELLO, O YE FAITHFUL READER!

As AOL used to say when I logged on, "Welcome!"

My friend, my reader, thanks for stepping inside of a good old-fashioned bookstore, or downloading, or stopping by the library to check out my latest offering. I hope you enjoyed reading about Ken Swift and his crew from start to finish. Again, we have come to the end of a new adventure and the introduction of a few new characters.

From the bottom of my heart, whether you've been on this train since back in '96 or just copped your e-ticket and climbed on board with the rest, thanks for the support. I hope you enjoyed the wild ride.

I'm getting over the flu, so I'll cut to the chase.

Time for the shout-outs! Drumroll, please.

I have to thank my agent, Sara Camilli, for all the support, especially over the past couple of years. I'm still trying to get up to novel number one hundred. Thanks for being in my corner since the '90s—time flies!—and thanks for always being available no matter what time of day or night.

Stephanie J. Kelly, my amazing editor, thanks for the wonderful feedback, notes, and magnificent editing. You are the best of the best.

Much love to Emily Canders (congratulations!) and everyone working hard in the publicity department and in every other department at Penguin Random House. I'm glad to be a part of an amazing family.

Kayode Disu, my Nigerian brother running the yard across the pond in the UK, thanks for reading bits and pieces of this novel along the way. Loved your feedback! Keep holding it down for Gideon.

And you, special person, invaluable one, of course I'm not going to forget you. I would *nevah* forget about you. The best for last.

I also want to thank _____ for their assistance and support while working on this novel.

Pop by **www.ericjeromedickey.com**, and from there you can find me on social media. Follow or add a brother!

Now, everybody come in closer so we can do a group hug and take a quick selfie. Closer. Little bit closer. Smile, everybody!

☺

Ken Swift and his crew can now let their wounds heal, pull up a barstool next to Gideon, Driver, Destiny, Inda, Tommie, and Nia, grab a drink, and join the rest of the characters chilling out in the Dickey-verse.

January 3, 2018. 3:19 P.M.

73 degrees, mostly cloudy, 20% chance of rain

Faded Old Navy jeans, Wolverine T-shirt, Chucks, NYPD cap

33.9930° N, 118.3491° W

Carolyn's son. Miss Virginia's grandson.
Mrs. Gauses's godchild.

That dude from Kansas Street in Memphis, Eric Jerome Dickey

ERIC JEROME DICKEY is the *New York Times* bestselling author of twenty-four novels and is also the author of a six-issue miniseries of graphic novels for Marvel Entertainment, featuring Storm (*X-Men*) and the Black Panther. He also penned the original story for the film *Cappuccino*, directed by Craig Ross Jr. Originally from Memphis, Tennessee, Dickey is a graduate of the University of Memphis, where he pledged Alpha Phi Alpha, and also attended UCLA. Dickey now lives on the road and rests in whatever hotel will have him.